Amish Friends Knitting Circle: Smicksburg Tales Two

Karen Anna Vogel

Lamb Books

He restores my soul

Amish Friends Knitting Circle: Smicksburg Tales Two

© 2012 by Karen Anna Vogel

Second Edition 2013 by Lamb Books

This book is a work of fiction. The names, characters, places, and incidents are products of the writer's imagination or have been used fictitiously and are not to be construed as real. Any resemblance to persons, living or dead, actual events, locales or organizations is entirely coincidental. Contact the author on Facebook at: www.facebook.com/VogelReaders Learn more the author at: www.karenannavogel.com Visit her blog, Amish Crossings, at www.karenannavogel.blogspot.com

ISBN-13: 978-0615916811 (Lamb Books)

ISBN-10: 0615916813

:

Books by Karen Anna Vogel

Amish Knitting Circle: Smicksburg Tales 1

Amish Knitting Circle: Smicksburg Tales 2

Amish Knit Lit Circle: Smicksburg Tales 3

Knit Together: An Amish Knitting Novel

The Amish Doll: An Amish Knitting Novel

Amish Knitting Circle Christmas: Granny & Jeb's Love Story

Amish Pen Pals: Rachael's Confession

Christmas Union: Quaker Abolitionist of Chester County, PA

Coming soon:

Amish Knit & Stitch Circle: Smicksburg Tales 4

The Herbalist Daughter: Amish Knitting Novel

CONTENTS

INTRODUCTION

Pickwick Papers (Charles Dickens), *Adventures of Sherlock Holmes* (Conan Coyle),and *Anne of Green Gables* (Lucy Maud Montgomery), have two things in common; they started as continuing short stories and became classics. I've always felt we should learn from the best, and to me, a continuing short story invited readers to participate in the storyline, helping the author see their blind sides.

Amish Knitting Circle, Granny Weaver's first circle, hit a nerve with women. Women who felt like she was their very own grandma. So, Amish Friends Knitting Circle was fueled by readers enthusiasm. Amish Friends Knitting Circle runs through summer and autumn, and the Amish are usually very busy, working most of the time. But readers like Helen Hevener and Sue Laitinan, made me think. Barn raisings, plowing by horse, summer gardens, putting up preserves....I guess I'm so familiar with the Amish these things wouldn't interest anyone. Basically, I live a rural existence canning, gardening, feed chickens...I'm not a city dweller, but 80 percent of people are. So, again, readers saw my blind side, and this series wouldn't have been written without their insight.

I also didn't want Granny to 'die' after one book. I too started to call myself 'One of Granny's girls' like many readers. Like many readers who don't have a granny they could talk to, we were prompted to go to other older woman for advice. This is the Amish way of thinking, and I hope our culture shifts to make it an American way again. Respect for the elderly and the sage advice they give needs to be restored.

Granny also taught us all how to pray. Her "casting off prayers" became popular as each episode ended with Granny Weaver casting her cares on the Lord. This became a mainstay, since so many told me they learned to pray; Granny is frank and talks to God like she would a friend.

I'm so encouraged because other readers are reaching out to women they see hurting, like Granny Weaver, believing women are stronger spun together. Oh women, we do need each other. We are more beautiful spun together; we are the nurturers of the world, and are needed.

AMISH-ENGLISH DICTIONARY

Ach – oh

Boppli – baby

Brieder - brothers

Daed - dad

Danki – thank you

Dawdyhaus – grandparent's house

Dochder – daughter

Gmay - community

Goot – good

Guder mariyer – Good morning

Jah - yes

Kapp- cap; Amish women's head covering

Kinner – children

Loblied - The second song sung in a church service, sometimes twenty-five minutes long.

Nee- no

Mamm – mom

Oma – grandma

Opa –grandfather

Ordnung – order; set of unwritten rules

Rumspringa – running around years, starting at sixteen, when Amish youth experience the outsiders' way of life before joining the church.

Wunderbar – wonderful

Yinz – plural for you, common among Western Pennsylvania Amish and English. A Pittsburghese word, meaning 'you ones' or 'you two'

Dedication

To faithful readers worldwide who feel that the fictitious Granny Weaver in my Amish Knitting Circle: Smicksburg Tales One was their very own grandmother, giving them sage advice. Your encouragement fueled me to continue writing about her, keeping Granny alive. A special thank you to Helen Hevener and Sue Laitinan for helping me see how interesting an Amish summer and autumn could be..

To Tim, my husband of thirty-three years. You're the best!

To Jesus Christ, who keeps me spun together in His love.

Psalm 139:13

EPISODE 1

Planting Time

Granny loosened a rock with her hand spade to make a deeper hole. Memories of planting sweet peas with her *mamm* flooded her heart and made it warm as the spring day. She brushed dirt from her black apron and stood up, shielding her eyes from the sun, and looked back toward the fishing hole. Jeb had fallen asleep again, fishing pole in hand. She sighed. *We're both getting as old as dirt.* She rubbed her left knee, sore from kneeling down planting since twilight.

A door slammed and she turned to look over at her son's house. Soon Jenny was walking as fast as her seven year old feet could take her. When she got to Granny, she stomped one foot. "*Oma*, I just don't like it."

Granny opened her arms and Jenny hugged her middle. She patted her blond hair, parted neatly down the middle to form two braids. "Give it some time, Jenny. Every day will be easier."

"With Lizzie as my new *mamm*, I keep thinking of my *real mamm*. But *Daed* doesn't."

Granny swallowed hard. This was Roman's biggest fear. That if he remarried, his three girls would think he didn't care for their deceased *mamm*. "Jenny, your *daed's* been so lonely since your *mamm* went home to glory. He loved her dearly, and there was a big hole in his heart. Lizzie's helping to fill it again. Understand?"

"But he has me….and Millie and Tillie…."

"And he wanted you to have a *goot mamm*."

Jenny snuggled in closer to Granny. "We have you. You're like a *mamm*."

Granny kissed her granddaughter's head and then pulled her away. "What are we doing? I have dirt all over me, and now look at your apron."

"I can wash it myself. I know how to use the scrub board."

"Well, now, why don't you let your new *mamm* do that for you? Lizzie, I mean your *mamm*, will be glad to do it. Beautiful day to hang out laundry."

"Are you going to do washing today?"

Granny nodded, knowing how much Jenny loved to hang clothes on the clothesline. Jeb had made one with a low rope just for her. "Do you want to help me?"

"*Jah*, but just with hanging…not with scrubbing…"

Granny grinned. "Then we'll hang clothes after lunch."

Jenny gave her another hug and ran back to the chicken coop to collect eggs. The sound of chirping came closer and closer and Granny pretended to look for birds. Soon Tillie and

Millie came out from behind her rhododendron bush, laughing. "We tricked you again," Millie yelled.

The twins came skipping toward her, their chestnut brown hair in braids, looking more reddish in the sun. She warned them not to hug her, not wanting them to get dirty, but Tillie was soon in her arms, not paying attention.

Tillie squeezed her tight. "*Oma*, I just love you....*and* my new *mamm*. I love you both."

Granny took a deep breath, relieved that the five year old twins had taken so kindly to Lizzie. It had been only three weeks since the wedding and the twins followed their new *mamm* around like baby ducks. "I love you too, Tillie." Granny looked over at Millie. "So what are you girls doing this morning?"

"We're going to help *Mamm* and Daed in the garden all day. I'm so excited, because I love to plant seeds." Millie, the twin who chattered endlessly, said, "Lizzie, I mean, *Mamm*, said we could have our own pumpkin patch."

Tillie, the timid one, nodded her head in excitement. "Even little white pumpkins, *Oma*."

"Can I help in your patch?" Granny asked.

"*Jah*," Millie said. "I like to plant but not weed so much."

Granny pursed her lips to hide a grin. The girls were learning the art of gardening at a young age. More memories of her *mamm* letting her have her own sunflower garden blew through her mind. Was this the aging process, to have vivid memories of childhood? She shook her head to clear it. "How about *yinz* go down to the fishing hole for me, and wake up your *Opa*. He fell asleep again."

Millie and Tillie nodded and skipped away. *To be a kinner again, and have all that energy!* Granny thought of all she and Jeb talked about at breakfast. He didn't want her in a knitting circle since summer demanded so much work. And he knew how much she loved to garden. *Give it a break, Deborah. Don't even be in a knitting circle this summer,* he'd said.

But she knew the demands of life would take over, and she'd only see her circle friends at church every other week. Knitting for charity was something she took pleasure in, too. But Jeb was right about one thing. Knitting shawls in the summer wasn't appealing. Too hot and muggy to knit something so large. She knew the shawls made for the tornado victims in Missouri were appreciated, but in the summer, she imagined knitting something small. Nothing that would lie on the lap, like a blanket.

Well, it was Wednesday and the girls would all be coming over tonight. So much to talk about with the double wedding that took place right where she was standing.

"*Guder mariye, Mamm,*" she heard Lizzie call from her back porch.

Granny waved at her fondly. Lizzie was officially her daughter-in-law and it was a good dream come true. Sometimes she patted herself on the shoulder, giving herself some credit, having started the knitting circle last November so Lizzie would be at her house a lot, and would bump into Roman. But she knew God was the great matchmaker, not her. Lizzie walked toward her with bare feet. "Aren't you cold, Lizzie?"

"*Nee.* I won't be wearing shoes until October again. I like being close to nature."

Granny hadn't seen Lizzie beam like the sun above for years. She'd overcome a lot and now her face held no trace of her former pain. Pure joy poured out of her like water from a hand pump. "How are you today, *Dochder?*"

Lizzie hugged her. "I am your *dochder*, now. It's nice to have a *mamm* again. And I love living here, away from the store."

"How's your *daed* doing?"

"He likes having Fannie and Melvin live with him, but he can't stay with them forever. We'll need to build that *dawdyhaus* this summer for sure."

"I'd give it time. That store means a lot to him."

"*Jah*, it does. Lots of exercise too, which is *goot* for MS and arthritis. But surely Fannie won't want him there forever."

"You know my favorite saying, 'Give each short hour to God and the years will take care of themselves.' I don't look too far down the road…"

~*~

Fannie pushed on the spade to cut through the grass. She pushed the handle down to turn over the sod. This was what her life was like, turned upside down, but she'd never been happier. To think of how ugly and fat she thought she was last November, before the knitting circle started. She thought of Granny catching her looking at glossy glamour magazines at Punxsy -Mart. How she used to compare herself to those perfect women. The knitting circle helped her recondition her mind, along with Melvin, who was now her husband. When his big green eyes looked at her, she felt just as beautiful as the women in the magazine, maybe even prettier.

She sighed. It was inner beauty that counted the most, though. Was she being vain now, thinking she was so pretty because Melvin always told her she was? Fannie knew beauty faded, but when she looked at Granny she found it hard to believe. The woman was seventy and her gray hair only accented her light blue eyes. And she was still so petite…

Fanny wondered if she'd be pretty, like Granny, as she aged. What if Melvin found her unattractive as the years rolled by? She put up one hand. "I am fearfully and wonderfully made," Fannie said out loud, shaking off her old self and

6

putting on the new. Over the past three weeks since her marriage, she'd had to take the compliment box Melvin made her and pull out all the little things he wrote…little compliments. Why did she feel secure one minute and insecure the next? Granny told her that when so many emotions happened at once, they bring up the old. She looked over at the flapping laundry; how her emotions swayed.

Well, she was so happy and overwhelmed at the same time. Helping to run the store with Jonas was more work than imagined. His MS slowed him down and it pained her to see him fumble and drop so many items. She jumped every time she heard a can hit the floor. And then there were Amish men, friends of Melvin's, always at the house, digging the foundation for the store addition and a new workshop. Melvin's clocks were temporarily being shown to customers from her living room. The only constant was the seasons, and planting time was her favorite.

Melvin had suggested raised beds, since it required less weeding. How thoughtful of him to make the frames and help her dig up the soil. Men usually didn't tend to the garden, but he seemed to want to do everything with her. Her heart fluttered with love…would it always be like this, or was love as fickle as roses? Blooming in abundance one year, the next looking dead? But she knew Granny put banana peels on the grounds around her many red rose bushes to nourish them;

love needed to be nurtured. She'd tend the love she and Melvin shared, because he was certainly a gift from God.

~*~

Ruth watched in amazement as Luke worked alongside her in the garden. He'd never helped before and now here he was, digging up an area around her bird feeders so he could plant *Backyard Birds,* the kit he got at Punxsy-Mart. Her dark brown eyes misted. *It was a miracle he was doing this.* Last November when Granny invited her to the knitting circle, she didn't go at first. Shame of being in an abusive marriage had turned her into a hermit, and somehow Granny saw that. Once she opened her mouth, the bishop and elders descended on Luke like eagles on their prey. With firmness and love, they'd helped restore her marriage.

She walked over to Luke. "*Danki* for doing that for me."

Luke looked up at her, his dark blue eyes filled with love. "I know how much you care for those feathered friends of yours." He took off his straw hat, revealing his blond hair. "Do you know some people take wounded birds and restore them back to health? I'd like to do it."

Ruth felt joy bubble up from within. Luke wanted to add one more thing to the list of things they did together. "I'd like to do it, too. But it's lots of work. Baby birds need fed every two hours."

"Do you think your folks would like to help? They live right there." He pointed to the house behind them.

"They might. I don't want to do it unless we do it as a family." She looked down and enveloped the grass with her toes. "I'm hoping Mica will have a brother or sister soon…"

Luke ran over to her and grabbed her shoulders. "What are you saying? Are you pregnant?"

"I'm not sure yet. I mean, I might be, but I might not." She put her arms around his neck. "I love you so much."

He kissed her and pulled her close. "I can see that. *Danki*. I don't deserve it."

"Don't look back, Luke. We have spring all around us, dead bulbs in the ground budding with new life. Our relationship was dead, but is as beautiful as the irises around the side of the shed."

~*~

Ella sat on the grass to take a break. Starting a garden and watching twins was just too much. If only Zach didn't work with the English and could be home like other Amish men, he could watch Moses and Vina while she tended the garden.

Dust blew in from the field behind their house. Hezekiah had offered to plow it up for them again this year. The roadside stand gave them much needed extra income and sweet corn would be added this year. Expenses were mounting up. Vaccinations, check-ups, disposable diapers; *kinner* were expensive, but worth every penny.

She walked over to the playpen. Vina and Moses were sound asleep. Her heart filled with love and gratitude. Being barren had been so painful. Ella remembered getting the letter from Granny to come to her knitting circle last fall. She knew Amish women talked about their *kinner* and didn't want to go, but went to knit for charity, and try to be content having such a *wunderbar goot* husband.

But once she shared her pain with the circle, the wheels were set in motion. First, Ella felt encouraged to take in foster *kinner*, but she soon received the greatest Christmas present of all: twins from a woman in Troutville. The fact that Lavina, *mamm* of the twins, lived in Smicksburg didn't upset her anymore. Lavina didn't marry her old boyfriend, knowing he'd be a harsh *daed*, having endured a rough *daed* herself.

Ella closed her eyes and took in the smell of lilacs that were in full bloom. Bowing her head, she prayed God would redeem Lavina's life, that He'd restore what was taken away. And a long prayer of gratitude was said again for the twins.

She went back to her kitchen garden and with bare feet, pushed the shovel into the ground. Fatigue ran through her. She needed help, but who could she ask? And how could they pay for it? Again, Ella bowed her head and said a casting off prayer. Granny had used the knitting term, "casting off", as the name of her prayers when she started to fret. *Cast your care upon the Lord for He cares for you.1 Peter 5:7*

~*~

By six that night, Granny was plumb worn out. Planting time was busy, but she had to catch up on laundry today. Jenny's help was greatly appreciated. *Should she cancel knitting circle for the summer? Was Jeb right?* Granny massaged the back of her neck. She'd let her girls decide tonight.

Did Jenny need more attention, feeling so left out of her *daed*'s life? So much change going on a stone's throw away and maybe she needed to focus her energy on her *kinner*. She was used to mothering the twins, and even though Roman looked at his daughters as the apple of his eye, his eye was always on his new bride.

Granny quickly said a casting off prayer and put the egg salad, pickled beets and bread on the table. Jeb yawned and stretched his arms over his head before he plunked down in his chair. "*Danki*. Need something cool for supper. Mighty hot day for the end of May."

Granny sat down and took his hand to say a silent grace.

"I should have let you fish *all* day, Love. You've been working too hard. But the girls needed help in their garden."

Jeb pulled his long gray beard. "*Jah*, it was easier to just sit and fish, but those girls are growing up mighty fast." He spread egg salad on a slice of homemade bread. "They need our help to adjust."

"I was thinking the opposite. Maybe get out of the way so Lizzie can be their *mamm*…"

Jeb eyed her. "You planning on having that knitting circle?"

"Socks. I'm going to bring up socks at the circle tonight. The Baptist church said there's lots of homeless people right here in America. In the winter they'll need warm socks…"

Jeb's head darted up. "Homeless? Where do they live?"

"Janice Jackson said her church goes down to Pittsburgh to feed them. Some live under bridges. Some in cardboard boxes."

"Jack has it better than them, and he's a dog. Don't these people have any family?"

Granny sighed. "Janice said whole families are without a home. I was thinking about scripture. 'When I was naked you clothed me'…"

Jeb bowed his head. "You've done it unto Me."

"*Jah.* We don't know these people, but if the Lord came to us in the form of a homeless person, would we feed him? Clothe him?"

"Deborah, you're not thinking of going to Pittsburgh and feeding them, are you?"

Granny raised her eyebrows. "Never thought of it, but *goot* idea. We could have a baking frolic and take the food to the city."

Jeb groaned loudly.

"Now what's wrong with that?"

"Why not just have the knitting circle? Isn't that enough?"

"But you don't want me to have it. Think I'm too busy."

Jeb reached for her hand. "If you don't have the knitting circle, you'll do something else, and that's what I love about you. Such a big heart."

Granny squeezed his hand. "So you don't mind? Me having the circle?"

"Not at all. I didn't know there were people living worse off than a dog…I just didn't know."

Granny bowed her head. "Jeb, I have a confession to make…"

"This sounds serious…What is it?"

"Well, I would have brought it up over the winter, but you were against my Jane Austen books then, and was afraid."

"Of what?"

"Well, you know how I always went visiting on Thursday afternoons? Suzy picked me up in bad weather?"

"*Jah*, and it's a *goot* thing to visit…"

"Well, I was visiting, along with Sarah Mast, and Millie and Katie Byler."

"What's wrong with that?"

"Well, it was always at Suzy's…"

Jeb scratched his head and slouched. "Deborah, what you women folk do is none of my business."

"But I feel deceitful…"

"Why?"

"I learned to dye yarn colors and we always knit. Mittens for *kinner* in Romania…with needles. Not a loom."

Jeb pursed his lips. The ticking of the pendulum clock was like the pounding of a drum in Granny's head. She got up and started to clear the table. Then she heard that familiar chuckle of her husband. She turned to see tears in his eyes.

"What's so funny?"

"You are. Honestly, don't you know Jacob Mast and I knew our wives were always in that yarn shop? Remember, we live in Smicksburg. Everybody knows each other's business."

Granny felt the plate in her one hand wobble, so she quickly put it in the sink. "How long have you known?"

"Well, when Jacob didn't want Sarah to be around Ginny Rowland, he came here and asked me to do the same."

"But you didn't?"

"No. I knew Jacob was in the wrong. Anyhow, I trust your judgment. You know when to step back from the English."

Granny ran over to Jeb and hugged him from the back. "Thank you...Old Man." She kissed his cheek.

He patted her hands. "*Jah*, Deborah, I trust you to have that knitting circle with the English here. With old age comes wisdom and you'll know how to handle the differences."

She kissed his cheek again. "And you're wiser than me, being older, *jah*?"

~*~

Granny heard Jack bark and knew a buggy was making its way down her long driveway. She pulled back the white curtain to see Ella and Ruth in one buggy and Fannie and Melvin in another. Melvin would most likely be spending time visiting with Roman or Jeb. Granny stepped out on the porch. "You girls want to knit out here on the porch until it gets dark?"

"*Jah*, sure. And admire your roses climbing up the trellises," Ella said.

Granny embraced each girl before they took a seat on one of the cedar benches. "Hope my roses do well this year."

Fannie sighed as she collapsed onto a bench. "I am worn out. Gardened all day."

"Me too," Ruth said, blushing. "But Luke helped me this year."

"So *goot* to hear," Granny said. "How about you Ella? Did you get your kitchen garden in?"

Ella shook her head. "The twins kept waking up and needed my attention." She put her knitting loom on her lap

15

and started to knit. "Sure wish Zach didn't work such long hours for the English. Now he's being pressured to work Saturdays…maybe even Sundays."

"Sunday?" Fannie nearly screamed. "He can't work on Sunday."

"He spoke up yesterday and his boss got mad. Said he was tired of the Amish saying they can't work on Sundays and our other holy days."

Granny grimaced. "But there's laws in place to protect us."

"Zach said he'd use them, if it came down to it. He also kept talking about Marathon…"

Fannie gasped. "Move to New York? You won't, will you?"

"I think Zach was just talking out loud. Sure hope so."

Jack barked, announcing another buggy had arrived. Maryann and Lavina were soon waving. When Maryann nimbly got out of the buggy and led her horse to the hitching post, Granny's eyes filled with tears. Maryann had beaten cancer and had more of her energy back, despite radiation therapy. *Praise be.* And to think Lavina was living with Maryann, who was once her harshest critic. *Maryann treats me like Mary Magdalene,* Lavina used to say, crying on Granny's shoulder. Cancer and possible death had made Maryann realize she was also sinning, being so harsh and judgmental toward Lavina. *God works in mysterious ways, His wonders to behold.*

~*~

Lizzie leaned forward to welcome another kiss. Roman's lips still tasted like the peppermint tea they'd just shared. Did she *need* to go to knitting circle? She wanted to live in Roman's tender embrace. For the past three weeks since the wedding, she feared she'd wake up from the sweetest dream. But the Good Book was true: God could do above and beyond what we hoped or imagined. "I need to go…all the women have arrived."

"I know," Roman said, pulling her tight. "I need to spend some time with *my* 'Little Women' tonight, *jah?*"

Lizzie cupped his cheeks. "I love that book. I read Granny's, I mean, *Mamm's*." She kissed his cheek. "I'm thinking Jenny needs a *goot* book like that, but one for her age."

"She reads as *goot* as me," Roman said. "Suzy finds *Mamm's* books on the internet, or at Punxsy -Mart. Maybe ask her?"

"I will. A story that has a *step-mamm* in it. A nice one who's concerned."

Roman drew her to himself and cradled her head against his shoulder. "Give her time. She remembers Abigail; the twins don't."

"I know, but I just wish she could open my heart and see that she's in it. I love all the girls, as if they were mine."

"They are yours."

"You know what I mean. Their *real mamm.*"

A knock shook the side door. Soon Melvin's voice was heard talking to the girls. "You best go over to *Mamm's.*" Roman kissed her again. "You know how much knitting circle means to her."

"*Jah,* I do." Lizzie gave him one last hug before turning to get her knitting loom that now sat in the corner of the living room. She thought back to the first circle meeting and how she avoided Roman. Granny had given her *Pride and Prejudice* for a wedding present, saying she was indeed a Lizzie, but Lizzie Bennett, and Roman was Mr. Darcy. She'd gobbled up the book over the past weeks and realized how she'd misjudged Roman's cool way with her. He was so hurt but had hidden it behind a wall of pride.

She looked up to the pendulum clock. It was seven and she needed to get going and quit being so daydream-like. But then again, she was living in a *wunderbar goot* dream.

Lizzie greeted Melvin before she ran over to Granny's. She waved at the women on the porch, but they seemed a little on edge. What was wrong? As she approached, and the rounds of greetings ceased, she quickly caught on to the conversation.

"But why don't we just keep knitting on looms?" Maryann asked. "Becca has one handed down from her *oma*."

Granny wiped the sweat beads forming on her forehead. "Suzy wants us to have knitting circle here because her store's being remodeled and she wants me to invite folks from the Baptist church. Lots of them…"

"*Ach*, Janice is lots of fun. Will she come?" Ella asked.

"*Jah*, and that new home they have, Forget Me Not Manor, the Rowland's old house, is now a place for homeless *mamms*. We should invite the girls who come to live there."

"They need our support," Lavina said. "I could have been one of them." She turned to Ella. "So *goot* to know the twins have a nice cozy home, with you…"

"*Danki*, Lavina. And I really mean that," Ella said, her voice breaking from emotion.

"But can we knit shawls with needles? It looks hard," Ruth said.

"Well, to be honest, I already learned. Suzy taught me…"

"How come you never mentioned it?" Fannie asked.

"Didn't think it was important. Jeb knew…Suzy dyes her own wool and was willing to teach me. I do love color."

"And Jeb was fine with it?" Maryann asked.

"*Jah*," Granny said. "God made color. Look at all the flowers popping up."

Ella looked up from her loom and cleared her throat. "Suzy's a *goot* friend to us all. I'm willing to learn. Emma Miller makes crocheted rag rugs in her store. She said it's similar to knitting with needles."

Lizzie's mind kept wandering to Jenny. Would she like to learn to knit? Could this be something special they did together? Her stomach did a turn. Jenny seemed to challenge every word she'd said all day. This was part of married life she gave little thought to, being a *mamm* to the girls. Jenny had always been so excited to see her, and when she was going through counseling, it was Roman and the girls who made dinners for her, trying to show her they could be trusted. *Where was the once happy Jenny?*

"Lizzie, what do you think?" Fannie asked.

"About what?"

"Daydreaming of your new husband?" Lavina teased.

"*Nee*, something else." She turned to Fannie. "What do I think about what?"

"Making socks and hats for the homeless."

Lizzie nodded. "Sounds like a *goot* cause. As long as I'm knitting something…so *goot* for the nerves."

Granny stood up and motioned Lizzie to come into the kitchen with her. "Can you help me bring out the angel food cake and ice tea?"

Lizzie put her arm through her new *mamm*'s as they went inside the house.

"Lizzie, don't let Jenny get you down. She'll come around, in time."

"I hope so. I do worry she'll never accept me…"

"You call me *Mamm*, *jah*? What did you think of the first time you called me that?"

Lizzie looked down at the spotless oak floors and the image of her *mamm*, taken too soon, appeared. "My own *mamm*…*Ach*, I see."

"Just don't fret about it. You'll never be only three weeks married again…"

Lizzie picked up the tray with paper plates, each having a large piece of angel food on it. "So much cake!"

Granny snickered. "Jeb loves it so much, I made three. He likes it with fresh strawberries from the patch."

Lizzie went back outside and served each woman a piece of cake. When she handed Fannie a plate, they both grinned at each other. "I still think about our wedding, a lot."

"If Suzy hadn't let us use her tent, there'd be no wedding." Fannie turned to the women in the circle. "Suzy is truly a trusted friend. She wouldn't ask us to take in Outsiders that would drag us away from our faith. I say we do it."

"Me too," Ruth said. "I'd like to see Marge come. She'll be living down the road shortly."

Granny came out with the iced tea and smiled. "I'm glad some of us are seeing eye to eye." She looked over at Maryann. "Is it too much contact with the English, or is there something else?"

Maryann shrugged her shoulders. "I don't know. Could be that now that school's out, I want to spend more time with the *kinner*..."

"But you see them all day," Lizzie said. "I've been a *mamm* for three weeks, and know I need to be with grown women all the more."

Maryann looked intently at her cake. "Life is short. Cancer taught me that. What if it comes back? This could be my last summer with my *kinner*."

Granny leaned forward. "Maryann, did you get some bad news?"

"*Nee*, no trace of cancer. But it'll be a five year wait to be truly cancer free."

All was quiet, except for the peeper frogs and katydids. A barn swallow swooped down into the porch and darted back out. Granny shifted in her chair. "Well, I'm sure you'll be fine, Maryann. But I understand if you want to take the summer off. Will you join us again when school resumes?"

"*Jah*, I'd like that." Maryann looked around the circle. "And I'll pop in once in a while during the summer."

"Well, you'll need to come on Thursday nights," Granny said. "Baptist have church on Wednesday nights."

"How come?" Fannie asked. "I see cars there at the church *every* Sunday. Isn't that enough?"

"Well, the Baptist church service is shorter than ours, so maybe they have special meetings on Wednesday." Granny took a bite of cake and looked up at the nesting birds in the porch rafters. "Is everyone, besides Maryann, in agreement? We'll meet Thursday nights and invite the Baptists?"

More silence. Lizzie knew Granny was more friendly to Outsiders than the rest of the group. But she was older and wise, so it must be a *goot* thing, she supposed. "I'm all for it. If you want to knit on Thursday with the Baptists, and other *Englishers*, raise your hand," Lizzie said.

All hands went up except Maryann and Ella's.

"Ella, what's wrong?" Granny asked.

"With Zach working so much, I don't know if it's fair to ask him to watch the twins."

Lizzie's mind raced. Jenny could help keep an eye on the twins. Make her feel needed. She'd played *mamm* to the twins for years, and maybe she missed it. "Ella, maybe Jenny could come over and help with the twins."

"But she's only seven."

"Almost eight…"

Granny clasped her hands. "I don't think Jenny could care for twins so young. Ella, you talk to Zach about it. Maybe get a sitter?"

Nathan came around from the side of the house and walked up on the porch. He looked at Lavina and smiled, then turned to Granny. "*Oma*, the garden's been planted."

Granny's eyes were filled with relief. "So *goot* to have you with us this planting time. There's egg salad and bread in the icebox. Open a can of chowchow, Jeb and I cleaned off a whole jar of beets."

"I will. I'm famished." He looked over at Lavina again before entering the house.

Lavina tucked a runaway strand of auburn hair under her prayer *kapp*, nodded and grinned.

Granny's eyes darted from Nathan and then Lavina and then down to her cake. "Nathan is staying here in Smicksburg for *goot*." She looked up slowly at Lavina.

Lavina cleared her throat. "That's *wunderbar*."

"So many changes here since the last circle began," Fannie said. "And all *goot, jah*?"

"*Jah*," the women said in unison.

~*~

Lavina hugged the dear women in the circle before leaving. How much healing she'd experienced by just being accepted by another human being for who she was. Suddenly, anger stirred within. Why didn't she ever feel loved growing up? *Why was her daed such a harsh man and her mamm so quiet?* If she only had parents like Granny and Jeb, she'd never had looked for love in another man's arms at such a young age.

An image of her with Christian, in bed, made nausea wash over her. She was only fifteen and he was nineteen. Christian had started seducing her at fourteen, and controlled her in a year. How he'd withhold any affection, even an embrace, if she stepped outside his well-defined "terms" in the relationship.

She watched as Ella left, and thanked God her twins were being raised in a loving home. In an odd turn of events, the twins were her salvation. Maternal love woke her up to all the lack in her life. When Christian and her *daed* threatened her to confess before the congregation that she didn't know who the father was, she knew the twins had to be raised elsewhere. But sometimes, she longed for them...to be their *mamm*. A sharp pain stabbed her stomach and she reached for her middle.

Lavina felt an arm around her shoulder and recoiled. But it was Nathan, the one man who treated her so differently. "*Ach,* you scared me."

"I scared you? By touching your shoulder?"

"*Jah.* A little nervous today."

"Hop in the buggy and we'll take a stroll and loosen you up."

Lavina took Nathan's hand and got into the buggy. *What did he mean, loosen me up? Were all men like Christian?* She wiped her sweaty palms on her black apron. *Surely not…*

Nathan hopped into his side of the buggy and urged the horse forward. Lavina waved at Granny and Jeb standing on the porch, barely making them out in the twilight. Was it concern on their faces? She looked ahead, trying to relax.

Nathan took her hand. "So you heard I'm staying in Smicksburg, *jah*?"

"*Jah.*"

"Can you guess why?"

Lavina looked into Nathan's penetrating blue eyes. "*Nee…*"

He leaned over and kissed her cheek. "Found someone I want to know better."

Lavina felt like embracing this man, who'd been only pure kindness the day they met at Granny's seventieth birthday in February. Over the past three months, they'd gone out in groups, but now he said he wanted to be alone…to *know* her. What did that mean?

Nathan put his arm around her. "Lavina. You don't seem happy I'm staying. Did I do something wrong?"

She pursed her lips, and looked down. "I'm afraid, is all."

"Of what?" Nathan turned the buggy right onto the main street and then a sharp turn left on to a deserted dirt road.

Lavina smelt the pungent aroma of apple blossoms, but the sickening image of Christian taking her down dirt roads overcame her. She put her trembling hands over her face. *No, this can't be happening again!* When Nathan pulled the buggy over to the side of the road, she turned to him, fury rising within her. "Nathan, I won't do it."

Nathan took off his straw hat and raked his fingers through his brown hair. "Lavina. This is our first buggy ride alone and I wanted to make it special." He reached to the back seat and put a little white box in her hand. "I got you some fudge at the Sampler."

Lavina looked at Nathan again. He had not one trace of lust in his voice or eyes. Could it be that there were men like Jeb her age?

He took her by the shoulders. "Lavina, look at me. I know about the twins. About Christian. I am not him. Understand?"

The scent of the blossoms filled her and peace settled over her soul. He did know her whole story, yet cared for her. He was so much like the Jesus she loved; the merciful God who said, *"He who is without sin, cast the first stone...."* She let Nathan embrace her and years of shame and pain seemed to fall off. She whispered in his ear. *"Danki."*

He gently took her chin and kissed her lips. "For what?"

"For the healing...you know."

He kissed her cheek and then her nose. "It's God who heals, *jah*?"

"But it's nice to see Him in a man. Didn't know it really existed until I met Jeb."

Nathan sighed. "My *opa* is a *goot* man, but most men are like him. You just came from…"

"The pit of he--?" Lavina clasped her hands over her mouth. "*Ach*, I didn't mean to say such a thing."

Nathan grinned. "Well, it is a word in the Bible." He put his hand on her cheek. "Was it that bad?"

A tear slipped down her cheek. "*Jah*, it was. And I get so angry sometimes."

"Have you sought advice from an older woman in our *Gmay*?"

"*Jah*. Maryann. And she helped a lot. I also talked to Marge."

"Marge? She's not Amish."

"I know, but she came to the house all the time when Maryann was getting radiation. We talked a lot, and she has strong views about what happened to me. Called it abuse."

He took her hand. "My *oma* and *opa* love their dog, Jack. They rescued him from an abusive home. I remember Jack used to be skittish, but love cured him." He kissed her hand. "The more you're loved, you'll be as mellow as Jack, too."

More tears fell down her cheeks but she didn't care. She let Nathan brush them aside. This was what a normal relationship was like. What Maryann and Michael had…Granny and Jeb, too. It's what she'd longed for her whole life. She thanked God for Nathan as he drew near to kiss her, tenderly.

~*~

The next morning, after chores, Jeb hitched up the buggy for Granny and she kissed his cheek. "*Danki*, Love."

"Want me to come?"

"*Nee*, I'll be fine."

"Spending too much time with the English lately…"

"Jebediah, I am going to a home for single *mamms*. Helping those in need, Amish *or* English."

Jeb winked. "Don't get your dander up, Deborah. I'm actually proud of you."

"Not *goot* to be proud."

Jeb scratched his head. "Okay, you're like everything an elder's wife should be…like the Good Book says. Given to hospitality and helping the needy."

Granny felt a rush of emotions, as if she were a teenager again and Jeb her steady boyfriend. "Jeb, you'll make me blush." She cleared her throat. "Want something special for dinner or something…"

Jeb chuckled. "You cook so *goot*, I can't pick a favorite."

29

"Jebediah, what are you getting at?"

He rolled his eyes. "Can't a man give a compliment? I don't want anything. You women folk are always looking for some hidden meaning."

She kissed his cheek again. "Sorry, Love. Now make sure to pay attention to Jenny. She told me she hardly ever catches a fish."

Jeb grinned. "I'll make sure she 'catches' a whopper."

Granny spryly hopped into the buggy, smiled at Jeb, and then clucked her tongue to make the horse move forward. When passing her large lilac bushes on the side of her house, she inhaled and closed her eyes for a second. How she relished the month of May; the scent of lilacs along with the blossoms from their many fruit trees filled the air, but nothing could compare to the scent of her roses. Her beloved roses were a testament to the daughter she never had, the daughter that was still born.

She looked back at the house before it went out of view. The roses were climbing up the trellis again, as usual, a reminder of new life: eternal life. Jeb had gotten her a rose bush to cheer her up after the tragic death, but back then, she didn't want to be cheered up. She was mourning the loss of a daughter. *She* would have been her youngest, not Roman, and a friend and companion in the kitchen. But now, thirty years later, Granny was glad Jeb planted that one climbing rose bush.

He divided them every year and now they engulfed her wrap-around porch.

Granny led the horse left onto Sunrise Road and listened to the steady clip-clop of the horse's hooves. Almost as comforting as the clicking of Suzy's knitting needles. Truth be told, she wanted to learn to knit with needles, just to hear that sound. She'd never tell anyone, they'd think she was batty. But when Suzy visited, the steady rhythm of the needles calmed her, and Suzy said it raised chemical levels in the brain to calm a body down. Granny needed that the more she aged, and just couldn't wait to learn.

She soon saw a red sports car and knew Marge and Joe were at their new place. How easy the English thought they could live off the grid. She chuckled, remembering when she met Marge in the hospital waiting room. The animated woman, who ran around the farm for sale, saying it reminded her of *Little House on the Prairie*, had confused her to no end, until Marge lent her the book to read. Marge and Joe wanted to live like Ma and Pa Ingalls; she hoped they knew the work involved and didn't get discouraged.

Granny waved when she met Marge as she came to the mailbox. "*Guder mariye*, Marge. Did you get the turkeys ordered?"

Marge clasped her pudgy hands and jumped up and down. "I am so excited. We're getting seventy to start. And I did consent to raising rabbits, thanks to Luke."

"Luke? You mean Ruth's Luke?"

"Yes. He is one sweet man. Offered to help us move in and learn how to live off the grid. Gave us a catalog to order oil lamps with hangers to put on the walls. Do you think they're safe?"

"I've used them all my life."

"We might order a cook stove from the catalog, but really need your opinion. Ruth's getting a bigger stove and I just might order the same kind. What do you think?"

Granny thought of the knitting circle. Learning how to live off the grid after years of conveniences would take more than a few conversations. "Marge, would you like to come to my knitting circle? You'd learn so much from all the Amish women who come. It'll be on Thursday nights."

Marge put her hand to her full face. "I can't believe you're asking me. I'm not Amish."

"Well, neither are some of the others I'm inviting."

"Oh, I love to knit. Learned to do it from my grandma years ago." Her eyes misted. "Deborah, I'm so glad to be your neighbor."

"Me too, but call me Granny. All my girls do."

"Your girls?"

"My knitting circle girls. I'd like you to be one…"

"*Danki*, I mean, thank you. Being around all the Amish has made me pick up some of their slang."

"What slang?" Granny asked.

~*~

Granny pulled into Forget-Me-Not Manor and admired the sign. It read:

Forget-Me-Not Manor ~ All girls are princesses, ever in the heart of their King.

Granny had always admired how the Rowland's had sold their home below its value to help homeless *mamm*s. Janice had told her all the details and she had to admit, some of the English really inspired her.

There was no hitching post and she didn't know where to tie the horses' reigns. The split-rail fence would have to do, but her buggy might still be too close to the road. A young woman came out onto the front porch and asked if she needed help. She ran back inside and soon Janice appeared. Janice wore a white blouse and her smooth black skin looked lovely. When she flashed her broad smile, revealing straight white teeth, Granny thought she needed to be in one of those glamour magazines, but quickly dismissed the idea, knowing those magazines had brainwashed Fannie into thinking she was ugly.

"Mornin' Deborah. Suzy said you'd be stopping by."

"*Guder mariye*, Janice. I came to talk to you about knitting."

"Suzy told me all about it. I'm all for it. These girls need mentored by some godly women. And knitting is good for the nerves." She motioned for Granny to come inside.

"Where can I hitch my horse?"

Janice put a slender finger up to her cheek. "We don't really have anything, like they do in town. Could you hitch it across the street at Rueben Byler's?

"*Ach, jah*, I could. Will be back in a minute."

~*~

Janice turned to the women around the breakfast table. "Not one of you wants to learn to knit? And knit for charity? I'm sorry, but *yinz* know you have to do some type of charity work in order to live here. Remember, charity has been given to you, and you need to give back."

All eyes looked down, except for a girl with honey-amber colored hair that matched her honey-hazel eyes. "I can knit. Not good at it, but I can do a knit and purl." She looked down at her oatmeal and then back up at Janice. "And you say it's Amish women?"

"Yes, Colleen, and they're ever so kind. All the pies you eat here are made by Amish women."

"Do they give baking lessons, too?" Colleen asked.

Granny came around the corner, out of breath. "I can teach *yinz* how to make a decent pie. Learned when I was five."

All eyes at the table turned to Granny. They eyed her mauve dress and black apron. "See, I'm ready to bake all the time, always having an apron on." Granny smiled at the girls, but they all turned away, except the pretty girl with a heart-shaped face and dark, golden hair. Granny saw something in this girl. A longing to learn Amish ways? Or was this her imagination?

"Colleen's the only one who wants to knit." Janice pointed to the girl with shoulder-length hair.

Granny just couldn't pinpoint what it was about this girl that made her like her immediately, but she did. "So, Colleen, you'd like to come next Thursday?"

"Can I bring my daughter?"

"Well, it depends on the age. My *kinner* are there but the youngest are almost six."

"My daughter, Aurora, is four, almost five, though."

Granny narrowed her eyes to take in Colleen more. She didn't look a day over twenty. "Can we talk private-like?" Granny asked Colleen. She nodded and eagerly made her way over to Granny. "How about we talk on the front porch?" Granny asked. "Just beautiful outside."

"I agree."

Colleen followed Granny out on the porch and they sat on the white wicker porch swing. Janice followed and sat in the wicker chair opposite them.

Granny patted Colleen's knee. "You have a daughter almost five? How old are you?"

"Twenty-one."

"And how long have you been here in Smicksburg?"

"Well, not long." Colleen looked over at Janice fondly. "Sure glad they had room, though. Living on the streets with a child was rough, to say the least."

"But don't you have family?" Granny blurted. For the life of her, she didn't understand why there were homeless Americans.

"My parents are on drugs." Colleen bowed her head.

Granny took her hand. "But, if they're sick, why not go home and help them?"

Colleen looked up at Granny, and then over towards Janice, baffled, then back at Granny. "They're on cocaine."

Granny slapped her forehead. "*Ach*, I'm sorry. *Those* kind of drugs. Not the *goot* kind." She thought of several teens who had gotten involved with illegal drugs during their *rumspringa*, but the Amish community helped them turn from such a temptation. Who was helping Colleen's parents?

Granny was speechless; she'd never heard of parents being on drugs. She pointed to the sign in front of the house.

"I like that saying… *All girls are princesses, ever in the heart of their King.*

Colleen grinned at Janice. "I even believe it now. Actually, I even changed my daughter's name to Aurora because of that sign."

"Why?" Granny asked.

"Aurora's the name of Sleeping Beauty. That's my favorite fairytale."

"Never heard of it. My English friends have given me many books, though, and I'd like to hear this princess's story." Granny smiled at Colleen broadly; something about this girl was just loveable. "I brought a few pies over for the girls. Colleen, would you like to walk across the street and help me bring them in?"

~*~

Granny pulled out of Forget-Me-Not Manor, shoulders sunk. Was Jeb right? Did she need the summer off from having a knitting circle? Colleen's story only underlined the fact that there were people in dire straits, right here in America. *Parents on illegal drugs*? Who raised Colleen to be such a fine young lady? Now a homeless girl with a child….

She'd read every word from Christian Aid Ministries newsletter, and they did care for the needy in her own country, but she never deep down could grasp it. The tornado ripping through Missouri she understood; of course people were displaced after a natural disaster. The earthquake in Haiti was an ongoing effort of this dear ministry she loved, but why were there people who had no family? She'd only seen it a few times in cases of a shunning, but the People were still available to the one who strayed if in need.

Granny took a deep breath as she headed toward Suzy's knitting shop. She needed some colorful yarn to match the season…maybe some pinks, the color of the flowering crabapple trees on her land. Such vivid colors weren't allowed to be worn by the People, but it was a small price to pay to live in unity. But she could make colorful things for Outsiders, and that's what she planned to do.

Pink ribbons adorned the hospital when Maryann went in for radiation therapy; the nurse had said it was the color of breast cancer awareness. Yes, she'd buy shades of pink for hats and mittens, even socks. And she'd make the first set of mittens for Aurora, a little princess who Colleen treasured.

Colleen refused to give up her child for adoption. Was it wise? She'd lived on the streets in dangerous places with a little one. Once again, Lavina's bravery in giving up her twins to a loving home struck a chord in her heart.

How Nathan adored Lavina, even though he knew everything about her past. Somehow, when she looked at her twenty year old grandson, she felt proud to be his *oma*. But if they got married, would he feel differently? When they shared the marriage bed?

Granny looked up at the puffy clouds that dotted the blue sky; *Cast your cares on the Lord, because He cares for you,* she admonished herself. With every casting off prayer, she was reconditioning her mind, to think God's thoughts. He cared and was in control. He didn't need her help in being a matchmaker.

She needed to cross over Route 954 and she white knuckled the leather reins. When would she ever get over this fear of crossing this road? The busy road that took Abigail's life, leaving the girls without a *mamm.* She was so thankful Roman found love again, being so lonely for three years, but sometimes Granny looked at Jenny only to see Abigail, a spitting image of her *mamm,* and still missed her. *No winter lasts forever. No spring skips it's turn,* she remembered her *mamm* always saying. She needed to see the spring all around her, and not dwell on past winters.

Granny looked both ways and nudged the buggy quickly across the road. All the little shops that continued to spring up were a blessing since cars slowed down, seeing so many pedestrians. A car came close behind her and she slowed the horse to a walk and pulled over to the side of the road. But this car didn't. *How odd.* When she pulled up Clarion Street, the car followed, and when she turned into Suzy's driveway to hitch her horse, it pulled up to a parking spot. Must be a knitter getting yarn or taking classes.

"Ma'am, can I take your picture?" a man, not much older than a teenager, asked.

Granny put her head down. "We don't want our pictures taken."

"Why not?"

"It makes a graven image of our face, and it breaks the second commandment."

"Can I take one from behind?"

"I can't stop you," Granny tried to say as politely as possible. She quickly got out of the buggy and shielded her face from the man with one hand. How violated she'd always felt when the English did this. She thought of Marge and other English friends. They would never do something like this.

Granny opened the door to SuzyB Knits and heard the familiar little bell ring and the yapping of Suzy's beloved dogs. But when she saw Suzy, she knew she'd been crying. "What's wrong?"

"Molly...." Suzy sat at her desk in the corner, hands over her face. "She's not good."

Granny went over and put her hand on Suzy's shoulder. Her little terrier had been a constant comfort to Suzy when her *mamm* died a long, painful death. Now the little black and white dog lay in a cushioned basket. Granny leaned forward to see if

Molly was breathing, and the blind dog looked her way. "You precious little thing."

"Granny, I can't do the knitting circle at your place. Not with Molly like this…"

Was this the sign from God she needed to not have the circle? Did she need such handwriting on the wall to hear the gentle nudging of God?

Granny nodded. When Jack passes on, it will be a day of mourning…a month of mourning. "I understand, dear friend. I'll just cancel for the summer."

"You can't. What about knitting for charity?"

"We can do it in the winter…"

Suzy put her hand up in protest. "I'll do it for the homeless. Seeing those girls at Forget-Me-Not has put a face on them." She swiped away a runaway tear. "I'll do it, but if I start to cry…everyone will understand, right? I mean, I've hardly ever seen an Amish person cry."

Granny's mouth gaped. "Really? I see it all the time….all the time…"

~*~

When Granny left the shop, a bag full of pink yarn in various hues in tow, the *Englisher* was waiting on the porch, camera angled right at her as he snapped a picture.

"I'm sorry. I need the money…" he said.

Granny's eyes narrowed. "Money for what?"

The man looked down, his long hair hanging onto his camera. "Amish pictures are hard to get. I try to sell them on the internet. Lost my job and…"

Granny sat on one of the chairs of Suzy's vast front porch. "Are you homeless?"

His jet black eyes mellowed as they met hers. "No, not yet."

"What does that mean? Have you lost your job and living with a friend?"

"Yes, a good friend. But I feel like I'm interfering. He has a wife…"

"How old are you?"

"Twenty-seven. Pretty pathetic, huh?"

Granny didn't know what he really meant. Amish took in friends and family of all ages. "I don't see anything wrong with it. Living with a friend. Count your blessings that you have a *goot* friend."

He sat in the chair next to her. "Thank you, Lady. My name's Clark. What's yours?"

"Deborah Weaver."

Clark clasped his hands and glared at his fiddling thumbs. "You know of any work? I don't like sneaking around taking Amish pictures."

"Well, I'm glad to hear it. What work can you do?"

"Construction, plumbing, welding. Good with my hands."

"Well, Amish are *goot* at building things, too. If you give me your phone number, I'll check and see if anyone needs an extra hand, and call you."

"But the Amish don't have phones, right?"

"We have phone shanties, and trusted friends who let us use theirs."

Clark got up to enter Suzy's store. "Where are you going?" Granny asked.

"The lady in here, well, she knows me. My situation. I live at her pastor's old house...lost the phone number."

Granny's eyes grew as round as buttons. "Jerry and Janice?"

"Moved in a few weeks ago. Came up from Pittsburgh, but I'm not a girl, so *I* can't live at Forget-Me-Not."

Granny hugged her bag of yarn and looked up at the birds nesting in the porch rafters. "I was just there, and saw Janice. She didn't say anything."

"Well, it's just temporary. I hope."

Granny gazed again at the sparrows in their nest. She'd prayed for clear direction about her knitting circle, wondering if homelessness in America was really true. The Lord put proof right in her path. She looked over at Clark. "I have Janice's number. If I find work, I'll call her."

"Thank you so much."

~*~

Granny pulled into Miller's Variety to get her list of dry goods on the way home. The whole place was buzzing with construction workers, some digging on the side of the store, others at the sight of the new workshop. She opened the store door and saw a very weary Jonas leaning behind the counter. Fannie was measuring out spices beside him. Was it her imagination, or was there tension in the air?

"Hello, Jonas. Fannie. Needed to pick up a few things." She took one of the bentwood baskets Jonas provided for his customers, and walked towards the baked goods aisle.

Granny jumped when she heard a bang. Soon Fannie came over to her, green eyes ablaze. "He treats me like I'm five. I *do* know how to use a scale to measure," Fannie blurted in a loud whisper. "Don't know if I can handle this much longer."

Granny drew nearer to Fannie. "You have to. Until he no longer feels he needs the store."

"But Melvin and I own this place now, and we're never alone."

Granny wagged a finger at Fannie. "Remember, you don't own this place until you've paid for it, every penny. Until then, Jonas still owns it, just like a bank."

"I'm thinking this whole land contract deal was a mistake. We shouldn't have let Jonas stay…"

Granny reached up to cup Fannie's red face. "Patience. With patience, possess your soul." Fannie stomped one foot and crossed her arms. "Fannie, you're acting just like my little Jenny. Now stop this nonsense."

She heard shuffling and turned to see Jonas coming toward them with the aid of his hand crutches. His MS seemed to be actually improving on the experimental drug.

"Fannie, can you bring a sack of oats from out back? We're low and need to bag some up."

"It's huge. I mean, it must weigh a hundred pounds."

"It weighs fifty, and Lizzie carried that amount all the time."

"But I'm not Lizzie, and I'm tired. It's planting time." She held out her hand. "I barely have time to clean my nails and it's embarrassing."

Jonas rolled his eyes. "Lizzie never complained like you do," he said with a huff, then spun around and headed toward the counter.

"Can I help?" Granny asked.

"You?" Fannie gasped. "*Nee*. We need a man to carry that sack, and that's exactly who will do it. Melvin will carry it out next time he comes in."

Granny walked over to Jonas, who was visibly shaken. "Can you afford to pay help?"

Jonas looked up at her and shrugged his shoulders. "Never had to when Lizzie was here."

"Jonas, we have to live in the present, *jah*? Lizzie is now my *dochder,* too, and she has new responsibilities. Being a wife and a *mamm*."

Fannie marched past them and went into the attached house, slamming the door.

"She's a moody creature," Jonas mumbled. "Lizzie was even-tempered."

"Jonas Miller, it is not *goot* to compare Fannie to Lizzie. Fannie's only been helping in this store for three weeks. Have some mercy."

"I do, but I never knew she was so moody. Hard to live with a yoyo."

Granny put an index finger over her lips, and tapped her foot. *A yoyo? Surely not!* "Jonas, do you want us to start that little *dawdyhaus* down by Jeb's fishing hole? You'd be *goot* company, and Lizzie misses you."

"I don't know. I love this store…when Fannie isn't here." He groaned. "Maybe she's just not cut out to work as hard as Lizzie. Maybe I do need to hire some help."

"Can you afford it?"

"Maybe one day a week. For heavy work."

Granny leaned forward. "I met a man in town who's awfully sweet. Living at Jerry and Janice Jackson's old place until he finds decent work. I know he could use the cash."

"Deborah, you amaze me. I'll look for an Amish worker first."

"And the Lord be with you because it's planting time. Every man is out plowing, planting, or working construction. Do you have someone in mind?"

"*Jah*. Nathan. Your grandson."

"He's working with Roman and they're mighty busy, expanding into cedar lawn furniture. No, Nathan can't be spared."

Jonas stared at the ceiling. "Can I trust this Englisher you hardly know?"

"The Jackson's know him. He'd be homeless if it wasn't for the Christian charity of the *Baptist*."

The little bell over the door jingled and Jonas nodded to customers. "I need to really think this over. Everything's changed since I now live with Fannie. I always thought her the most pleasant girl, but you never know someone until you live with them."

"Maybe Fannie's thinking the same thing," Granny said, a little too defensively. But Fannie was one of her girls, and when it came to her girls, she was a hen among her chicks: protective.

~*~

Granny put the roast beef on one of her good China platters, and then told Jeb to open his eyes. "For you, Love, meat and potatoes. Eat to your heart's content."

Jeb got up and kissed her cheek. "*Danki*. I really appreciate it. You could have pan fried the fish 'Jenny' caught, but went to all this bother."

"It's your favorite, and I said I'd make it."

Granny sat with Jeb, hands clasped, and they bowed their heads for a silent blessing.

"Met a girl today that is so different. She's Baptist, but I think she yearns to be Amish."

"Why?"

"Well, she wants to knit and learn to make pies."

Jeb grinned. "Let me guess. You offered to teach her."

Granny nodded. "I did. Want to get to know her better..."

Jeb put a slice of meat on Granny's plate and then his. "Don't spread yourself too thin. I was hoping you'd spend more time with Lavina. Seems like you avoid her."

Granny's head shot up. "I do not. Do I?"

"Well, Nathan lives here and when she comes over, you're off to Roman's."

"So they can have privacy...."

"Deborah. I know you better."

Granny put a hand on her heart. "Afraid Nathan will get hurt. He's so innocent…"

"And Lavina's not? She repented and the Good Book says she's as white as snow."

Granny clasped her hand tighter around her fork. "Love, I know it's in my head, but it's going to take some time to get it in the heart. Nathan and I have always been so close…"

Jeb snapped his fingers. "Maybe that's it. Are you jealous that Lavina takes up all his time? Feel left out?"

Granny swatted at the air. "He lives here. How can I miss him?"

"He's always at Roman's working or out planting. Any free time goes to his sweetheart."

"She's not his sweetheart, I don't think. He's just so tenderhearted; he's helping to build up Lavina. He knows the story."

Jeb hit his knee and laughed. "We see what we want to see. He's in love, Deborah."

"Did he tell you that?"

Jeb leaned forward. "Trying to 'read between the lines' like you and Roman can do. Remember last fall when you said you knew Roman still loved Lizzie, and I thought you were daft? Well, you were right, and now I'm watching people more close-like. Nathan loves Lavina."

Granny pursed her lips. Nathan had that special gift of compassion, and if the Lord intended it to be used on a hurting young girl, she'd have to accept it. She closed her eyes and quickly cast her concerns for Nathan on the Lord. "The Lord's will be done... not mine."

~*~

Granny couldn't sleep. Why did she take an immediate liking to Colleen but not Lavina? It was Old Christmas when Lavina showed up at her place last year, and it was all a shock. The day of fasting and reflection turned into another church counsel day with Jeb called out to intervene. Then he'd brought her into their home to stay for a few weeks.

Was she jealous that her husband took such care for a hurting girl? Surely not. And as for Nathan, Jeb was wrong. She and Nathan had a special bond no one could break. Her grandson confided in her about matters of the heart.

She turned over on her side and stared out the bedroom window, still open as spring aired out the house. The melody of a lone nightingale might bring much needed sleep if she only closed her eyes and listened. Granny breathed in deeply the sweet scent of freshly plowed earth, an aroma that always took her back to her childhood.

After a few minutes, sleep still eluded her, so she looked out the window, into the stars and prayed:

Lord,

You know me through and through. Is there something in my heart not right? Why does fear grip me when I think of Nathan being with Lavina? I know you're in control, but I just feel sometimes like I'd do things differently, and I'm sorry. You're God and I'm a little human who doesn't know anything compared to your vast wisdom. I cast Nathan's heart onto you...turn it the way you want it to go.

And Lord, Jenny's sad little face breaks my heart. I couldn't be happier having Lizzie for a daughter, but to see Jenny this way took me by surprise. Bless her little heart and help her see the love her new mamm has for her. Maybe they'll bond over knitting...I don't know, but I cast her on you, for you care so much.

In Jesus name,

Amen

Dear Readers,

I hope you enjoyed the first episode of *Amish Friends Knitting Circle.*

I leave you once again with a recipe in every episode, just like *Amish Knitting Circle,* the prequel. When May rolls around the hills of Western Pennsylvania, strawberries are in abundance. There's nothing like fresh strawberries sliced over angel food cake.

Amish Angel Food Cake

½ c. egg whites (11-12 eggs)

1 ½ c. sugar, divided

1 ½ tsp. cream of tartar

1 c. cake of pastry flour

½ tsp. salt

1 tsp. almond extract (or vanilla)

Sift together ¾ c. sugar and flour at least 3 times. Set aside.

Beat eggs until frothy, and then add salt and cream of tartar. Beat this liquid mixture until thick peaks can be formed. Add ¾ c. slowly, 3 Tbsp. at a time, each time beating well with egg mixture.

Slowly fold in the sugar and flour mixture you set aside, adding ½ c. at a time.

Add almond or vanilla flavoring.

Pour into ungreased angel food cake pan.

Bake at 375 degrees for 35-40 minutes or until done.

Enjoy!

EPISODE 2

Tea Kettles Sing

Granny gasped as the girls ran in barefoot, tracking dirt across her freshly polished hardwood floors. "*Ach*, you girls need to wash your feet in the basin on the porch. *Oma*'s told you before."

Millie jumped up and down. "Sorry *Oma*. But we couldn't wait. Our pumpkins are coming up."

Tillie gave Granny her usual hug around the middle, and then took her hand. "Come see, *Oma*."

"I'm having someone over for tea, Honey. She'll be here any minute."

Jenny crossed her arms. "Who's coming? Fannie? She's fun."

"*Nee*, Janice Jackson. Remember her? She's the pastor's wife of the Baptist Church in town."

Millie pointed to her arm. "The sun turned my skin brown, but Janice's is black."

Granny scrunched her lips to one side, wanting to laugh, but knowing it was these times, these coming and going times, that the girls were learning important lessons. "Millie, Janice was born with black skin. It's the way God made her. My sheep are all colors, *jah*?"

"No," Jenny said. "There's no blue sheep, or pink sheep…."

"*Ach*, Jenny, you know what I mean. Animal colors. Some sheep are white, some brown, black, cream color….the way the *Goot* Lord intended. My yarn isn't one color, *jah*? Would be boring to look at? God made people different colors too."

"I think Janice is pretty. Her black skin makes her teeth look whiter," Tillie said.

"Now you girls need to call her Mrs. Jackson. The English don't go by their first names. They use Mr. and Mrs. to show respect."

"How come we don't?" Jenny asked, her arms still crossed.

Granny didn't want to admit it, but Jenny's constant challenge to everyone's words was getting on her nerves. How many times over the past few weeks had Lizzie come over in tears, feeling she was a bad *mamm*? Roman wanted his new bride happy, and chided Jenny too. Jenny didn't need to hear it from her.

Jack's bark sounded the usual sign; someone was coming down the driveway. "You girls make sure Jack has enough water. *Ach*, all the animals need to be checked. It's noon and mighty hot today."

"Jack has plenty of water and –"

"Go check the animals again, Jenny," Granny said, forcing a smile.

Jenny rolled her eyes.

"Jenny, we need to talk soon, *jah*? And you know what about…"

Jenny's now steady eyes penetrated Granny's soul. *Such hurt.* Why wasn't she as happy as Millie and Tillie to have a new *mamm*? What could be done to make Jenny see she was loved…needed?

A knock at the door sounded and Janice opened the screen door. When she flashed her brilliant smile, Millie pointed at her. "See, her teeth are whiter."

Granny gasped, but Janice let out a laugh.

"Sorry, Janice," Granny said.

"No need to apologize." She took off her flip-flops and walked over to the girls. "I hear you girls are gardeners. Growing a big pumpkin patch." She put her finger to her cheek, as she looked over at Jenny. "You're almost seven. I bet you could teach some of the little girls who live with me how to weed."

Jenny put back her shoulders and grinned. "*Jah*, I can show them."

"How about we come over sometime and you teach gardening? I know I'd learn a lot, too."

Granny's heart felt warmer than this hot June day. Her English friend had been praying for Jenny and now encouraged her. Praise be. "You girls go check on the animals, like *Oma* told you to do."

All three girls nodded and skipped out of the house. Granny hugged Janice. "*Danki*, for that."

"What?"

"Making Jenny feel needed."

"Deborah, I need help. Wish I had a green thumb, but…it's black."

Granny chuckled. "Do you want your tea hot or cold?"

"Cold. It has to be eighty degrees out there. How do you live without air conditioning?"

"Never had it, so don't know what I'm missing, I suppose. But we Amish don't fight nature, but go along with it. The Lord made the heat, *jah*?"

"No electricity. Don't know how you manage." She took the glass of iced tea from Granny. "Can we sit on your porch? Your flowers are gorgeous."

"*Jah*, let's do that." Granny led the way out to the porch swing on the far side of the wraparound porch, where the trellises with climbing roses were, for more privacy. "What's on your mind, Janice?"

"Well, I know your husband's in the ministry, being an elder. I thought you could relate." She took a sip of tea and looked down. "Do you ever feel jealous? Feel like your husband loves the ministry more than you?"

Granny remembered last Old Christmas, when Jeb was

called away for church duties. "*Jah*, I suppose. At times."

"I haven't felt this way before. Ever since Jerry started his doctorate, he's just too busy. Not there for the girls at Forget-Me-Not."

"But I see other men there, trying to be *goot* role models for the girls. Men like James Rowland…"

Janice's chin quivered. "I know. The church volunteers and all but…"

"You're lonely?" Granny asked.

A tear slid down Janice's cheek. "Not lonely. I have lots of friends. Just miss Jerry, but he doesn't seem to miss me."

Granny tilted her head. "Don't *yinz* go out every Friday night? Call it your date night?"

"Yes, but the conversation always turns to theology. What Jerry's learning in school."

Granny didn't know why the English went to school for the Bible, when they could just read it. It wasn't too hard to understand, but kept her thoughts to herself. She eyed Janice and noticed crow's feet around her eyes. "How old are you?"

"What?"

"How old are you? I never asked, but I am now."

"Why?"

"Well, women go through the change. I went through it young, in my mid-forties. I remember feeling sad over nothing."

"I'm over fifty, but that's all I'm saying," Janice said, as if embarrassed.

"With age comes wisdom, *jah*? No shame in it. But as we age we need to take *goot* care of ourselves. Have you told your doctor about this? Maybe get a hormone level test done."

Janice wiped a stray tear. "This was the last thing I thought I'd hear. I thought the Amish didn't go to the doctors, only herbalists."

Granny choked on the tea she'd just sipped. "Doctors? They saved Maryann's life. Of course we go."

Janice sighed. "I'm sorry. I thought you grew herbs and made tonics for everything."

"Well, we use herbs and medicine. But you need to see a doctor and take care of yourself. Let me see your fingernails."

"Why?"

Granny reached for her hand. "Brittle fingernails are a sign of the change. Do your nails chip?"

Janice's chin started to quiver again. "Yes, all the time. I used to have gorgeous nails, real healthy-like. I thought it was low iron."

"Do you have that, too?"

"Yes, but I'm taking supplements."

Granny squeezed Janice's hand. "I think you're going through menopause. Hot flashes at night?"

"It's hot out. It's June!"

"Sudden burst of tears when you are usually a pillar of strength?"

Janice bowed her head and wept. Granny got up and sat in the swing next to her. "It's natural. God's plan. Don't fight it, Janice."

"I feel like I'm going crazy, too."

"Mood swings. Jeb almost built a house near his fishing hole when I went through the change, saying he couldn't take it."

Janice looked up at Granny. "Seriously?"

"*Jah*. He's the one who made me see a doctor. Now you go for Jerry's sake, or else he may want to live in your church building."

Janice let out a sigh of relief. "I feel a little better, just knowing this has a name. Menopause. I hardly ever think I'm fifty-one. Still feel like I'm in my thirties."

"I'm seventy and some days I still feel like a kid." Granny patted Janice's hand. "You coming to knitting tonight?"

"Yes, along with Colleen and her little one. Maybe Jenny could read to her. I know Jenny loves to read."

"*Wunderbar goot* idea. *Wunderbar.*"

~*~

Ella heard the screen door open and turned to see Zach. "Home for lunch?"

Zach took off his work boots and threw them on the black

rug by the door. "Ella, we need to talk."

Ella cringed. She'd been up half the night with Moses, and snapped at Zach this morning. But did he need to come home? They could make peace at dinner time.

Zach collapsed in a rocker in the living room and she followed him in, sitting on the bench. "I'm sorry, Zach. Moses is one colicky little baby. I didn't mean to talk so harsh to you this morning."

Zach shook his head. "What?"

"Our quarrel this morning. I was exhausted."

Zach got up and sat on the bench next to her. He took her hand. "Ella, it's not that. I was let go today."

"Let go? You got fired? Because you wouldn't work Sundays?"

"*Nee*, the boss said it was a layoff. Cutting back workers and giving more hours to the ones who stay…who can work longer hours…Sundays.

"But there *are* laws, Zach."

He put both hands up, as if in surrender. "I'm not fighting his decision. This is the sign we've been looking for. Maybe God wants us to move."

Ella shot up and walked over to the window. "Leave Smicksburg? We just plowed up the fields. We can grow twice as many pumpkins. The English pay *goot* money for a pumpkin. And we can grow more sweet corn."

"Ella, we don't have enough land to farm. We can't live off of sweet corn."

"Your brother's helping Marge and Joe start a turkey farm. Why can't we do something like that? And I could bake pies. Start a bakery."

Zach got up and scooped Ella into his arms. "You're a *mamm* of twins and barely have time to make one pie." He kissed her cheek. "Would it be that hard on you to move? The settlement in Marathon is doing *goot*. I got a letter today from the Coblenz's. There's real money in organic milk." He pulled Ella to himself. "You know I've always dreamed of being a farmer…"

"I know. And working for the English is hard on you. Almost ruined Luke."

Zach held her tighter. "So you'll visit Marathon? Give it a chance?"

Ella thought being barren was the deepest pain she'd experienced, but now she knew differently. Leaving the people she'd known her whole life, for twenty-seven years, was deeper. She tried to agree and be the help mate Zach deserved, but couldn't open her mouth, knowing once she said yes, she was giving her word.

Zach tilted her head towards him. "Ella, is it that hard?"

She nodded and looked away, but Zach's eyes met hers. "I won't force you to move."

Shame seeped into Ella's soul. Zach cherished her and always thought of her happiness before his own, but did she do the same? "Zach, it won't hurt to visit New York."

~*~

Fannie grabbed the edge of the kitchen counter. Fatigue washed over her. She'd never needed a nap in the afternoon, but Melvin was a hard worker, and hard to keep up with. She walked into her living room, glad that the past two weeks of building a shop and addition were over. All the clocks were now displayed in the store addition, not her living room. The crew of Amish men had worked fast, but no one faster than Melvin. Seemed like all he did was work.

She sat in a rocker and picked up the needles Suzy had told them to practice with: casting on. It was easier on a loom, but she did want to learn to knit with needles. Fannie took the yarn in one hand and made the triangle shape Suzy had shown them. It looked so easy when Suzy did it. She couldn't remember anything at all. She just knew she should have two loops on the other needle.

Fannie leaned her head back, and closed her eyes. Why was she so exhausted all the time? Melvin was nine years older, but had more energy. Jonas was almost sixty and had MS, and even he didn't tucker out like she did.

The screen door opened in the kitchen, and the bird in the cuckoo clock came out one time. *It was one, already?* She didn't have anything on the table prepared for Melvin, but she just couldn't move.

Soon Melvin came in the room, hands on hips, concern etched on his face. "Fannie, are you alright?"

"I'm so exhausted. I'm sorry. "

He put his hand on her forehead. "No fever. Maybe it's allergies. Lots of pollen out there."

"I'm not allergic to anything."

"You should see the doctor. This has been going on for too long."

Fannie's eyes met Melvin's green ones. Was he irritated with her? Think she was a lazy wife? "It's probably just the heat. Sorry Melvin."

Melvin sat in a rocker near her. "Nothing to be sorry about, but we're going over to see the new doc in town, after lunch."

"We don't even know him. Let's wait and go to Indiana, like we always do."

"We never had a doc in town and he's only here on Thursdays. I say we welcome him and give him a try." He took her hand. "To be honest, I'm worried."

"About what?"

Melvin chuckled. "You make me laugh at the oddest times. Your health. *You*. I'm worried."

Fannie still felt like she was living in a dream, just like Lizzie. They both married the men of their dreams and were afraid they'd wake up. "Melvin, you are so patient with me. I'm not only tired; I'm always being crabby."

"I know. Jonas tells me all the time."

Fannie closed her eyes. Jonas. The man she adored until she had to live with him. Always comparing her to Lizzie made all her feelings of inferiority come back like a rushing river. "When is that man going to go and live with Roman and Lizzie?"

"When he feels ready to let go of the store. You know his fears of being useless."

"I know. I'm sorry. He has MS and can't live without his store, but something needs to change. He's wearing me out."

Melvin got up. "Let's eat and then go to see the new doc. Let him decide what's really wrong."

Fannie leaned forward and slowly got up, but the room started to spin. She stepped forward but couldn't seem to find her equilibrium. Soon Melvin's arms were around her and she rested her head on his shoulder. This man God gave her was her rock, but she was failing as a wife. Something was causing extreme fatigue. *Cancer?* Maryann had it. It could happen to her. She clung to Melvin until the room came into clear view. *Such a terrible dizzy spell. Maryann had fatigue and dizzy spells!*

~*~

Ruth waved at Marge as Luke led the buggy behind the large farmhouse and up to the little *dawdyhaus* in the back. Why

Marge wanted to live in the small house and not the farmhouse, she would never understand. Since she and Luke had been helping them learn how to live off the grid, Marge knew her cook stove and wood burning stove would heat the bigger house.

Luke gave her a hand as she stepped out of the buggy. "*Danki.*" She turned to Marge who was standing on the front porch. "Are you sure you want to learn baking on such a hot day?"

"Joe's sick of cold cuts. Wants a real meal."

Joe came out onto the porch. Ruth noticed his blond hair looked lighter as his tan got darker. *Such a handsome man.* Blond hair and blue eyes, just like her Luke

"How are you, Joe?" Luke asked.

"Tired to the bone. Starting this turkey farm and taking care of animals is work!"

"That's why I'm here," Luke said. "To help you out."

"How do you find the time?" Marge asked.

"We make the time," Luke said, looking over at Ruth smiling. "And I get to take my pretty wife on a buggy ride."

Ruth felt heat on her cheeks. *Pretty? Luke was saying this in public?*

"We're still going to have a car, but do want to do things more local-like. You know, go to the auction in Dayton, get involved with a food co-op *and* the Baptist church," Marge said, looking over at Joe.

Joe put a hand up in protest. "I don't believe in God."

Ruth noticed Joe's eyes suddenly grew cold. What could blind someone to not be able to see that there was a God?

Marge persisted. "I think we should go as a couple, but if not, I'm going by myself. It says in my off-the-grid magazines to get involved with a local church to know your neighbors. Country people go to church, Joe." She huffed. "And I was raised Baptist…"

"But you stopped when we got married…"

"Only because you wore me out every Sunday, harping on me for going." She glared at Joe. "We're in God's Country now…at least I think that's what they call it up here."

"Do what you want," Joe swatted at the air. "Luke, can you take a look at our cow? I'm not sure I'm milking her enough."

Ruth felt Luke's hand squeeze her shoulder. She looked up to see that he was grinning.

"I know exactly how to help him," he whispered in her ear.

Ruth put her head on his shoulder. Their marriage used to be divided and they'd had flair-ups over the littlest things. But religious beliefs were not a little thing. *And if a house be divided against itself, that house cannot stand.* The bishop and Jeb had many talks with Luke about the importance of unity in the home. Could Luke help Joe, or would Joe be a bad influence?

She wrapped her arms her middle, where the new life inside

her was growing. *Surely not. Luke would influence Joe…*

~*~

Lavina poured the blueberries she'd just picked into the largest pan Maryann had in her kitchen. Feeling like she was earning her keep was important to her, even though Maryann said she was like part of the family. *Families help each other out of love,* Becca had said.

Lavina poured white sugar into the pot and set the gas stove on low. She'd always made jam with her *mamm.* Did she need to go up to Troutville to visit? See how she was? Why couldn't she have come from a family filled with love, like Maryann's? Becca, her oldest, almost sixteen, was appreciated. Michael never screamed or slapped her, and the more she lived with this kind family, the more she realized the lack in her life.

Nathan had told her forgiveness was freeing, but he came from a loving home, too. Who could she talk to about this pain she carried? Who would understand?

Lavina looked out the window at one of Maryann's many *kinner.* Two were in the tire swing while an older one pushed. Her twins had a tire swing, and for that, she was thankful. Yes, she'd made the right decision in letting Ella adopt her babies.

A wagon pulled up to the hitching post in the back of the house. *Her daed and Christian? What were they doing here?* Relief washed over her when another buggy came into view; Jeb was driving and the bishop sat next to him. She wanted to run and hide, but knew eventually she'd have to deal with issues back home. But she turned eighteen next week, and according to her English friend, Marge, she had rights.

Maryann came up to her and put a hand on her shoulder. "Maybe I should have told you. We were worried you'd run away."

"Not from here, Maryann. I have nothing to fear here."

"I'm here to stand beside you, understand?

Lavina wanted to be cradled in Maryann's arms, and pretend she was her real *mamm*, but she was too old for such things. The back door opened and the four men entered. The bishop nodded to Maryann and Jeb came and stood beside Lavina. *What was going on? Were they going to make her go back home?* She willed away the knots forming in her stomach.

"Lavina, will you sit down at the table?" Jeb asked, tenderly.

She nodded, feeling numb. Maryann stayed close beside her, sitting next to her on the bench. Her *daed* and Christian sat across from her, but she refused to make eye contact. The bishop and Jeb sat at both ends of the table.

Bishop Mast took a handkerchief from his pocket and wiped his forehead. "Lavina, your *daed* and Christian have something to say."

She looked over at Jeb, gaining strength from this man who had become like an *opa* to her. A real example of what a *daed* should be. Then she met her *daed's* eyes. "I'm listening."

"Lavina, your *mamm* misses you. She wants you to come home. Cries all the time."

Bishop Mast let out a gasp. "This is not what we talked about. I agreed to let you see Lavina for you to ask forgiveness."

"I'm getting to it. Just saying her *mamm* misses her."

Lavina started to tremble. She knew he wasn't here to apologize. He'd never respected any bishop in the past, but would only uproot the family every time he got a warning. She forced herself to look at Christian, her old boyfriend. Why was he here? To her horror, he winked at her and looked at her lustfully.

"Lavina, we came to say we're sorry," her *daed* continued. "We never should have forced you to say you didn't know who the *daed* of the twin was. But Christian wanted to marry you, and still does." He patted Christian's back. "Wants to be a *daed* to the twins."

Lavina shot up. "Never. And I agreed to give the twins to another couple. "

"But I didn't," Christian snapped.

The bishop pounded the table and turned to Lavina's *daed*. "You gave your word. So did your wife. Your bishop knows this and is in agreement that the twins stay here, in their adoptive home."

"You're a cruel man," Jeb said. "Cruel. " He eyed Christian.

"And you. You're a man in need of growing up, and repentance." He looked across the table at the bishop. "Don't you realize our bishop and your bishop agreed to this meeting, only to extend forgiveness, not threats?"

"We're not threatening!" Christian shouted. "Those twins are mine."

Jeb reached for Lavina's hand. "Where were you the first four months of their life? Before Lavina gave them up for adoption?"

Christian's sly eyes looked at Lavina, again filled with desire, like a hungry wolf. "Waiting on her to marry me."

Lavina shot up. "I won't and you can't make me. You don't love me, you lust me."

To her surprise, Maryann stood up beside her. "Lavina. I see how Nathan looks at you, and –"

"Who's Nathan?" Christian face turned as red as beets.

"My grandson," Jeb boomed. "Now I've had enough of this if you have, Bishop. They have no intention of reconciling or asking forgiveness."

"*Jah*, go back to Troutville where your bishop will know of this behavior," Bishop Mast said evenly.

"But I already have a warning, and so does Christian."

"We're well aware of that," Jeb said. "Next you'll be put out."

Lavina's *daed* pointed a finger at her. "This is your fault.

70

You never listened to me, and now you're breaking your *mamm's* heart."

Maryann put both arms around Lavina. "A *goot* husband can always heal his wife's heart. It's not Lavina's job. Now please leave my house."

Lavina's *daed* looked at her spitefully, as did Christian, but they both got up and walked out the back door. Lavina smelt something burning and tore herself from Maryann and ran to the jam. She lifted the lid, only to see a pot full of bubbling jam, burnt around the edges of the pan. "I ruin everything. Everything…" She could hold it in no longer, but bowed her head and wept.

Jeb went over and put an arm around her. "That's not true, Lavina. Not true at all."

Lavina turned and hugged Jeb around the middle. "I wish I had a *daed* like you."

She felt Jeb patting her back. "You gave your twins up for adoption, and from what I know about your *daed*, he never deserved to have such a daughter. How about I adopt you?"

Shame filled Lavina. She was eighteen now and too old to be adopted. "I'm not a baby to be adopted."

"God adopted us as his *kinner* at baptism," Bishop Mast said. "Why can't you be adopted by Jeb?"

Jeb grinned. "*Ach*, I know why. She'd be Nathan's aunt."

Lavina looked up at Jeb and tried to smile. "That's not

why."

Jeb put his hand on her cheek. "*Goot* to see you smile again. Those two had me fit to be tied. I wouldn't have been as kind as you."

"Kind? I wasn't kind."

Maryann came over and slipped an arm through Lavina's. "Yes you were."

"But I shouted…"

"You sat at the table hoping to reconcile, and sang," Maryann said.

"I did? I don't remember that…"

"I tell my *kinner* all the time, 'Be like the tea kettle; when it's up to its neck in hot water, it sings.'"

Jeb grinned. "I heard you sing, too."

~*~

Lizzie took Jenny's hand and led her out to the front porch. Rhododendrons were in full bloom, the large flowers in shades of purple, dripping off the brush. How she wished Jenny would open up. She took her floral padded journal and pen and asked Jenny to sit on the glider next to her. "Your hair gets lighter every day. You have the same color hair and eyes as your *mamm*."

Jenny gave a faint smile. "*Daed* told me that, too."

"I remember my *mamm*. I get my brown hair from her. Sometimes I really miss her. Especially when I pick wildflowers."

"Why?"

"Because my *mamm* and I used to pick them together when I was a little girl."

Jenny peered up at her. "You can remember that? You're old."

"Like it was yesterday."

Jenny swung her feet nervously under the glider. "Can I go now?"

"I thought we'd take some time before dinner to write a poem. Maybe submit it to *Family Life Magazine.* You seem to really like the children's section; you can write something for it."

"But I'm only seven."

"Almost eight. In a few months…" Lizzie opened her journal. "Let's write this poem together. You've been saying how spring is your favorite time of year."

"But it's summer not spring, right?"

"No, according to the almanac it's still spring. In a few days summer begins, so let's write our spring poem *now.*" Lizzie tapped the pen on the journal. Would Jenny ever stop challenging every word she said? "'Spring is my favorite time of year'. How does that sound for the first line?"

Jenny shrugged her shoulders and Lizzie's heart sank deeper. "Jenny, why do you like spring so much?"

"The flowers. And the robins come back home."

"So the next line will be?"

"I like robins and flowers."

Lizzie wrote what Jenny said. "Now, my turn. Let me see… 'Animals come out of hibernation,'".

"What does hibernation mean?" Jenny asked.

"*Ach*, I thought you knew. Some animals, like black bears, don't like the winter, so they sleep through it."

"Why?"

"It's the way God made them. They sleep in the winter."

"But they miss the snow. Why would they do that?"

Lizzie took a deep breath, and closed her eyes. *Lord, help!*

Roman opened the porch screen door. "How are my girls doing?"

"*Daed*, why do animals sleep all winter?"

"Because there's no food for them to eat." He sat down on a cedar chair across from them and Jenny ran over to sit in his lap. "So, the animals eat like hogs all summer and sleep all winter."

Jenny giggled. "Like we do after *Oma* makes a big supper?"

Roman squeezed Jenny. "*Jah*, something like that." He looked over at Lizzie. "I'm feeling like a bear in summer: mighty hungry."

"Well, let's eat then," Lizzie said, trying to be cheerful.

"Jenny, you go help the twins wash up. I want to talk to

your *mamm.*"

Jenny spun around and skipped into the house. Roman came and sat next to Lizzie. "No progress?"

Lizzie found Roman's arm around her a great comfort. "Every word I say, she challenges. Sometimes I think she needs disciplined."

"You think she's doing it intentional... spiteful –like?"

"Sometimes I do." She leaned her head on his shoulder. "I need peace in my home...I'm not used to this."

"It's a season, I think. Your *daed's* not happy living with Fannie, either. We're all just adjusting."

Lizzie looked over at Roman as he bent down to kiss her. She reached for the back of his neck and pulled him closer. Such sweet kisses were stolen throughout the day, and she treasured every one. When she was in Roman's arms, all fears that Jenny would never accept her seemed to fall off like the blossoms on the trees. He pressed her closer to himself and she found herself lost in this loving moment, until the screen door opened and Jenny ran over to them, gawking...again.

~*~

Jeb, Granny, and Nathan bowed their heads in silent prayer, and then Granny passed the fish to Nathan. "You caught a big one this morning."

Nathan grinned, light blue eyes twinkling. "*Jah*, but there's so many fish, hard not to catch one."

"It's a *wunderbar goot* hole," Jeb said. "And puts food on the table." He cleared his throat. "Be praying for Lavina. She had an awful run-in with her *daed* and old boyfriend."

"She went up to Troutville?" Nathan asked, concern etched on his face.

"Nee, they came here, for a reconciliation meeting, but they had no intention of reconciling."

"What happened?" Granny asked.

"Her *daed* said he wanted her to go home and marry Christian, of all things. And take the twins back...be a family."

Nathan pushed his chair out and ran to the peg to retrieve his hat. "I need to see Lavina."

Jeb motioned for him to sit down. "Nathan, she'll be here tonight for knitting circle."

Nathan slowly put his hat back on the peg. "Is she okay?"

"She's a strong one. That old boyfriend of hers is a poor excuse for an Amish man. They'll be getting another warning. Most likely be put out."

"Shunned?" Granny asked. "For wanting to have Lavina go home?"

Jeb swatted at the air. "Nee, they aren't listening to their bishop or ours. And her *daed* isn't protecting her from a man who..."

"I know," Nathan said. "Doesn't deserve such a girl."

Granny patted the table and told Nathan to sit down. "I

know her *daed* was abusive, but are *yinz* saying her boyfriend was too?"

"*Jah*. Started to seduce her when she was fourteen and he was eighteen, and her *daed* knew. The English have laws against that."

Granny shoved her fork into the fish. "That's two years younger than Becca. That's despicable."

Jeb took some bread from the basket. "Pray for Lavina, and sing like a coffeepot."

"Sing like a coffeepot? What's your meaning?" Nathan asked.

Jeb's eyes softened. "Maryann has changed. She's so tender now. Lavina was so upset after they left, and Maryann came over and said, when troubles come, sing like a coffeepot."

Granny furrowed her brows. "Like a tea kettle, Love. When you're up to your neck in hot water, sing like a tea kettle. Coffeepots don't sing."

"*Jah*, you know the meaning."

Granny looked over at Nathan, and shrugged her shoulders. Jeb knew that Amish proverb well and could quote hundreds by heart. She feared the weight on Jeb's heart was dragging him down. He'd been gone most of the day doing some type of ministry. She'd spent many days alone due to his calling. Maybe Janice wasn't going through the change. Maybe being an elder's wife was getting to be too much for her.

"Have another meeting with the elders tonight," Jeb sighed. "Folks having lots of problems of late."

"But you've been gone most of the day," Granny protested.

Jeb cocked his head. "Deborah, this has happened before. What's wrong?"

"*Opa*, maybe she's afraid you're wearing yourself out." Nathan put his hand up. "Not saying you're old, but just worn out. Working in the rocker shop and farming…"

"We don't farm. Only have a few animals and sheep…and a big garden."

"The English call that a hobby farm. Saw it in a magazine at Punsxy-Mart." Nathan snickered. "Farming's not a hobby though."

"It is to me," Jeb said. "And I love it. Quit treating me like I'm as old as dirt."

Granny gasped. "We're not. I'm only two years younger." She patted his hand. "Just think you spend too much time in the ministry."

Jeb withdrew his hand and glared. "I chose the lot, Deborah. What's come over you? In all our years of marriage, for the first time, you seem resentful of me being an elder."

"Am not. Just concerned."

"*Nee*, I know you." He looked over at Nathan. "We'll talk about this later."

She nodded, and tried to smile at Nathan.

~*~

Granny grabbed a basket to house her freshly baked blueberry muffins. She looked at the bottom of the basket to see *Nathan Weaver, Age 10* written in black marker on the bottom. She held the basket tight. Nathan was so undone after hearing Lavina had such a bad day, that he reacted by wanting to comfort her. How he reacted told her everything. She held the basket out and looked at the natural colors of bent wood with the wood dyed blue. Nathan was so good with his hands, but she worried about his heart. He was too compassionate. Too caring. Did he not realize the extra weight Lavina would bring into a marriage, if he pursued this girl? *Cast your cares upon the Lord for He cares for you. First Peter 5:7,* Granny forced her racing mind to shout. She would not worry about Nathan. God was in control.

She heard the screen door open and Granny could tell she'd been crying. "Lizzie, is it Jenny again?"

Lizzie took a deep breath and slowly let it out. "Patience. Roman said to have patience. Jenny remembers her *mamm*."

Granny admired Lizzie's respect for Roman. She didn't know if she could be so patient with Jenny. It was six weeks since the wedding and Jenny seemed to be getting more contrary. Maybe she needed disciplined, given a talking to, but Roman didn't want anything said.

"Any more ideas? The poem isn't working out." Lizzie

helped take the blueberry muffins they'd made together and put them in the basket.

"You remember how Abigail pressed flowers. Why not do that? Jenny might warm up to something her *mamm* did."

"*Goot* idea. I'll try that. The girls made me cards of some of Abigail's pressed flowers, remember?"

"*Jah*, that was sweet."

Jack barked out on the front porch and Granny peeked through the window. It was Janice with a packed church van. *What on earth?* Only Colleen and her *kinner* had decided to join, not all the girls at Forget-Me-Not Manor. She wouldn't have enough muffins. She watched as Colleen got out of the front seat and slid the door open. Ruth, Ella, Suzy and Lavina got out. Granny sighed with relief. Janice had picked up the girls.

Nathan ran from the side of the house and grabbed Lavina's hand. They quickly walked off, back down the driveway. Granny ran to the other window to get a better view as the dirt road turned a little to the side of the house. Nathan had his arm around her and she had her head tilted on his shoulder.

"*Mamm*, what are you looking at?" Lizzie asked. "You look worried."

Granny spun around. "Nothing. Nothing at all." She made her way over to the screen door and welcomed her guests.

Colleen's eyes moved rapidly around the room. "It's so cute

in here. So simple."

Granny patted Aurora's shiny brown hair. "Looks like you've brought some books. Can I see them?"

Aurora lifted the little books up to Granny. "Let's see. We have *Sleeping Beauty* and *Snow White.*"

"Maybe Jenny could read them to her," Lizzie said, walking over to Aurora. "Would you like that?"

The little girl nodded, and Lizzie took her by the hand, leading her outside to meet Jenny.

"Sorry I'm a little late," Janice said, "but I didn't realize it would take so long to pick everyone up."

"Everyone? Where's Fannie?"

"Sick," Ella said. "Melvin took her to the new doctor in town."

"What's her symptoms?" Granny asked.

"Dizzy spells and fatigue."

Granny held on to the side of the counter. *The same symptoms Maryann had before being diagnosed with cancer.* She took the glass pitcher of iced peppermint tea and poured herself a glass, but her hand started to shake, so she sat down.

"Deborah, what is it?" Suzy asked.

"Nothing…"

Ella sat next to Granny. "She'll be fine. Dizzy spells and fatigue are common. She does *not* have cancer."

"*Jah*, I've been having dizzy spells and fatigue too," Ruth chimed in. "But I know why." She patted the front of her black apron. "I'm pregnant."

Ella squealed and ran to Ruth. "I knew it! You have that glow about you."

Everyone made their way to Ruth to give her a hug. Granny looked up with misty eyes. God was blessing this dear woman with another *kinner*, another life really. Her marriage seemed as right as rain now, all because Ruth decided to forgive, and Luke accepted church discipline. And Jeb had a big part in helping them reconcile.

Suzy cleared her throat. "I only have two hours and this is only our second lesson." She looked around at all the women. "Sorry I had to cancel last week, but I didn't think Mollie would make it…"

Janice put an arm around Suzy. "We understand. When our kids are grown, pets can become like children."

Granny nodded. "Let's sit outside. All new cedar furniture made by Nathan and Roman." She grabbed the basket of muffins and asked Janice to get the iced tea and paper cups. Then she ran back inside to retrieve her knitting supplies.

Suzy told the women to go into their groups according to skill level. "Where's Marge?"

"I figured she'd drive her own car, since she lives down the road," Janice said.

"I'll have to go check on her tomorrow. She was awful

excited about coming." Granny took a long strand of pink yarn to cast on her needles. "Actually, she's been looking mighty tuckered out."

"Luke and I stopped in today. I'm teaching her how to bake in her new stove," Ruth said. "Janice, she said she'd like to go to your church."

"She's more than welcome," Janice said.

"But her husband's an atheist…"

"That would make him a fool then," Janice said with a grin.

"What do you mean?" Ella asked.

"Only a fool says in his heart, there is no God. That's in the Bible."

"Where?" Ruth asked.

Janice opened her large *Vera Bradley* purse and held up a small silver item. "I can find anything on my electronic Bible."

"Oh, I'd love to have one," Suzy sighed.

Granny felt like shaking her head, but didn't. Her well-worn Bible had real pages, underlined in special places. She still read her *mamm's* Bible and often read her notes. Why did the English have to do everything so fast? If you can't find a Bible verse, you could look it up in a concordance.

Janice slapped her knee and chuckled. "I found it. Psalm 14:1. David wrote it, but listen to it in the Message Bible:

Bilious and bloated, they gas, "God is gone." Their words are poison gas, fouling the air; they poison rivers and skies; thistles are their cash crop.

"Now that sounds *serious*," Janice said, slowly, as if deep in thought.

"That's not in the Bible," Ruth said. "Doesn't even make sense..."

Janice was silent as she read it again, and then looked up. "What's bilious mean?"

"Sickly," Granny quipped.

"Okay, so sickly and bloated with gas?" Janice asked. "Now I'm more confused."

"Maybe it means they're empty. Gas doesn't take up space?" Suzy said as she showed Ella how to cast on again. "I'd feel totally empty without God."

Ruth nodded in agreement. "*Jah,* empty."

Granny noticed Ella was being too quiet. Ever the Bible reader, she could have quoted the King James Version of this verse easily. "Ella, something on your mind?"

Ella's eyes locked with Granny's but she didn't speak.

"What is it, Ella?"

"Zach lost his job."

Granny gasped. "Over working on Sunday? There's laws against that."

"Zach told me he wants to farm..."

"But you don't have more than twenty acres," Ruth said. "How will you do that?"

"He wants to visit Marathon…New York…"

"*Ach, nee!*" Granny blurted. "You'd be so far from us."

"I know," Ella said, a tear making its way down her cheek.

"Is Marathon far?" Colleen asked sympathetically. "I mean, New York isn't far…"

"It's far in a horse and buggy," Suzy said. "They'll have to hire drivers just to visit."

"Oh," Colleen said, turning toward Ella. "I'll pray for you."

Granny's throat was starting to ache, trying to swallow this grievous news, but Colleen's gentle way warmed her heart.

"Is there anything I can do?" Colleen continued.

Ella looked aimlessly ahead. "Come and help me with my twins so I can put up a lot so we can make it for a long while."

"What's 'put up' mean?"

"*Ach*, canning and preserving. Tending the garden and getting things to the root cellar –"

"You have a root cellar?" Colleen beamed. "I'd love to see one."

Janice smiled. "Colleen, you know all the girls have to volunteer at Forget-Me-Not. I think helping Ella counts."

"Really? Oh, I'd love that!"

Ella leaned toward Colleen. "I think the Lord may have sent me an angel. *Danki*. Now all Zach and I need is a way to make twenty acres produce enough for a family…"

Granny jumped when she heard Jenny yelling. She and

Lizzie quickly got up and went to the other side of the porch. "What's wrong?" Lizzie asked.

Granny saw Jenny's eyes, round with fear. "What on earth?"

"*Oma*, Aurora said this book is true and wouldn't stop. So I shouted."

"But you know the story isn't true, *jah*?" Lizzie asked. "And Aurora's only four, not knowing the difference between make-believe and what's real."

Jenny stomped her foot and glared at Lizzie. "But part of it is true..." Jenny turned to Aurora and then tore past them, out of sight.

Granny shook her head and asked Aurora if she could see the book. *Snow White*. She took Aurora's hand and brought her to her *mamm*. "Colleen, this book really upset Jenny. Do you know why?"

Colleen set down her needles and stared at the book. "Well, there is a wicked stepmother in it. She tries to kill her stepdaughter."

Granny felt the blood drain from her as quick as a flash flood.

Lizzie gasped. "Why would anyone make up such a story? And why would Jenny say part of it was true?"

Granny touched Lizzie's knee. "Jenny's only used to farm stories. She'll be fine." Granny took her needles and counted three knit stiches, and then three purl. She'd thought she'd learn to make socks and caps easily, but Suzy had insisted on making scarves first. Well, homeless people needed scarves, too.

She counted three knits again and her mind started to wander back to Jenny. How fiercely she looked at Lizzie. Maybe she did need disciplined. It wasn't fair to Lizzie to be treated so, and this behavior wasn't tolerated among the Amish. Granny looked up over at Lizzie, and could tell she was grinding her teeth again. *Ach, Lord, help her. She's concerned about her daed, too.*

~*~

Lavina put her nose into the bouquet of wildflowers Nathan had picked for her as they walked. Summer was a time she'd always relished. Christian and her *daed* were too busy out in the fields to see them much, and she spent many long days with her *mamm*. Her dear *mamm*....

Nathan led her to a large tree stump. "Sit down, Lavina." He sat next to her. "I feel a wall between us. Tell me what's wrong."

"I told you about my *daed* and Christian coming down...."

"It's something else, though." He took off his straw hat and fidgeted with the rim. "Do you miss Christian?"

Lavina wanted to laugh at such a preposterous thing, but felt like she couldn't move. She'd never thought about

87

Christian in a long while. "*Nee*, I don't miss him."

"How come I'm not convinced?" Nathan said, softly.

Lavina turned to see hurt in Nathan's eyes. "I feel...guilty."

"About what?"

"Not seeing my *mamm*. Leaving her alone to care for the younger ones. Summer's such a busy time."

"Why not go up and visit? Just because you live here doesn't mean you can't have a work frolic with your *mamm*, *jah*?"

Lavina felt her throat constrict. "I'm...I'm afraid to go home..."

Nathan leaned down to kiss her cheek. "Don't go alone. Take my *oma* with you. She loves to put up most anything from the garden. Makes the best jelly."

Lavina rested her head on Nathan's shoulder, needing strength. "Sometimes I think your *oma* doesn't approve of me. Would like to see you court someone else."

"What makes you say that?"

"I don't know."

Nathan kissed the top of her head and leaned his head against hers. "*Oma* just wants God's will. She may have a time warming up to it, but her soul kneels before God."

Lavina remembered kneeling in prayer as a *kinner*. It was a resting time; something she hadn't done in a while, just trying to survive living in such turmoil. "I need to kneel, too."

"Look at all the lightning bugs out tonight. As it gets darker we can see them better. Makes me think of dark days in my life, when God's love seemed to shine brighter."

"You've had dark days?" Lavina thought it hard to believe. She almost envied Nathan for having such a normal family.

"*Jah*, I've had dark days..."

They sat in silence, listening to hush that night brought. The only sound was the *clip-clop* of horse hooves in the distance. Then a dog's barking. Both sounds came nearer and nearer, and Lavina hoped the dog was friendly. She squinted her eyes and soon saw Jack. "What are you doing out here?" She could barely make out the black dog, but could tell he was agitated.

Then the buggy came closer and to a halt. Roman jumped out. "Have you seen Jenny?"

"*Nee*," Nathans said. "What happened?"

"*Ach*, she ran away. Left a note saying she's going to live with the dwarves."

"But we don't have any dwarfs here in Smicksburg," Nathan said. "Wonder where she went."

Lizzie came around from the other side of the buggy, a hanky up to her nose. "Can *yinz* search the woods?"

Lavina nodded. She remembered running away as a *kinner* and she always went to her secret spot. "Is there a place Jenny goes, just to be alone?"

Roman looked down and pulled at his beard. "My minds racing so fast, I can't think."

"Her pumpkin patch," Lizzie gasped. "She said the other day the corn was high around it. A *goot* place for hide and seek."

Roman and Lizzie raced back to the buggy and soon the wheels kicked up dust, Jack racing close behind them.

~*~

Lizzie's throat ached as she called Jenny's name over and over again, but she was nowhere to be found. Roman took her home in case Jenny came home, being afraid of the dark. She looked up into the star-studded night, and then over to the full moon which gave everyone a better view to see Jenny. Millie and Tillie had been watched by Granny and Jeb, but the anxious grandparents had gone out to look for their granddaughter now, too. All was quiet; much too quiet.

"Why can't Jenny love me Lord?" Lizzie said as a tear slid down her cheek. "Lord, protect her. The rivers are so high after last week's rain."

She reached over to her knitting and began to cast on, just like Suzy had taught her. After casting on thirty stitches she attempted to knit a stitch. But which way did the needle go, in the front or back? Her mind a muddle, she placed the needles in her lap and let out pain she'd been carrying since her wedding day, both sorrow and anger. She had to confess that she was indeed angry with Jenny. Her constant *contradictions* had been robbing her of a peaceful home.

When her mind started to think ill of Jenny, she always read *Rules of a Godly Life*. She got up and went inside to get her little brown book that contained the forty-seven proverbs used by the People. Lizzie took the book and sat in her rocker. When she opened it, she read until she got to Part 1: Rule 10:

In tribulation be patient and humble yourself under the mighty hand of God, with these thoughts foremost in your mind: first, that it is God who chasteneth; second, it is for your good; third, God will ease the burden; fourth, He will give you strength to endure; fifth, He will deliver from affliction at an expedient time.

She read it over a few times, and *He will give you strength* warmed her heart. She was no stranger to affliction, and God was faithful, over time, to always bring comfort or answer to her troubles. She cast her anxiety on God and went back out on the porch to knit. With a clear mind, she was able to make the knit stitch. The feel of the yarn against her fingers and the tapping of the wooden needles soon made the knot in her neck work its way out. After a few rows, she soon dozed off….

~*~

Marge clung on to Joe as they made their way down the steps. She knew Joe's views on guns, and she vehemently disagreed, being a pacifist in her heart. But Joe felt if someone intruded into their house, they'd be the one getting hurt, and not them.

The noise was on the porch. Marge closed her eyes and hoped it was just a raccoon or other critter, and they could soon shoo it away. They tip-toed to the front window and saw movement; lots of movement. Their rabbits they bought at the auction last night were jumping all over the porch; someone had let them out of their crate. She felt Joe's arm tense, and to her horror, he cocked his gun and made his way over to the door.

"You can't shoot someone for letting the rabbits out!" she snapped. "Joe, get a grip."

He ignored her completely, but opened the door and yelled, "Put your hands up!"

A squeal came from the side of the porch and soon Marge saw Jenny with both hands up in the air. "Oh, my Lord. Joe put the gun down!"

"Already did." He walked outside, startled. "What are you doing here?"

"I-I came to talk to the bunnies," Jenny said, eyes wide.

Marge ran out to the porch to comfort the little girl. "Why would you do that? And you're here alone, so late at night."

"Bunnies know where the dwarves live…"

Marge leaned closer. "Say that again…"

"You know. Snow White was taken by birds and bunnies to

the dwarves. The dwarves love little girls."

Marge knelt down and embraced Jenny. "Oh, Honey. I know you've been having a tough time. Your Grandma told me. But your new mom really loves you."

"My dad loves her more than me, and he forgot about *my mamm.*"

Marge took Jenny's shoulders. "Do you think your dad has a heart problem or something?"

"*Nee*, he's fine."

"I'm glad to hear that, because the way you talked, it seemed like he did. A person with a healthy heart has enough room in it to love lots of people."

"Really?"

Joe stepped forward. "I felt left out as a kid, too. My parents lived at church…."

Marge glared at Joe. "Now's not the time."

"Sure is. We can feel left out for lots of reasons."

Marge's eyes softened. "You're right. Jenny, I felt left out when my little sister was born. All the attention went to the baby, and all of a sudden I was expected to act older." Marge patted a bench on the front porch while Joe started to collect the baby rabbits. "Sit here, Jenny. "

Jenny snuggled up next to Marge.

"I know your Grandma put you in charge of the pumpkin patch, right?"

"*Jah*,"

"And how does that make you feel?"

"Like not a kid anymore. And Lizzie, I mean, *Mamm*, makes me in charge of more!"

Marge grinned. "It really stinks being the oldest, huh?"

Jenny burst into tears. "I was a little girl until *daed* got married. He made me in charge of things, though."

Marge couldn't help but embrace the girl. "Growing pains, Honey. You're going through growing pains."

"But nothing hurts."

She pointed to Jenny's heart. "Inside you're hurting. You're *gonna* be eight, and that's a hard age. You're not little or big."

"Marge, we best get her back home. They must be worried."

She nodded. "You're right," she said, and hugged Jenny again. "Things will work out over time. But for now, you need to promise me you'll never run away again."

Jenny's hug around her neck made Marge yearn for a daughter of her own. Hopefully, one day God would give her this secret dream.

~*~

"Growing pains?" Jeb huffed. "Are these growing pains contagious because my legs are aching. Been walking the land for ours." He looked sternly at Jenny. "Do you know how upset your *daed* is?"

"You don't have to be so strict," Joe blurted. "She's only seven."

"I'm just being direct. She needs to learn to obey."

When Granny heard the commotion, she ran from behind her house. When she saw Jenny she opened her arms and Jenny flew into them. "There, there. Everything will be alright." She walked over to Marge and Joe. "What's all the hollering about, Jeb?"

"I think Jenny needs to be grounded. Learn a lesson. Joe thinks I'm being too stern."

Granny knew from talking to Marge the extremely strict religious rules Joe's parents imposed on him, and it made him resent God, and his family. Did he think the Amish were all rules and not love? "Jeb, you know love covers a multitude of sins…"

"She didn't sin!" Joe belted.

Granny reached up to pat Jeb on the cheek before he could speak. She knew he was a man of rules, but full of mercy. She'd have to share with him about Joe's past later. "*Nee*, she didn't sin, only being a *kinner*." Before Jeb could argue, she asked Marge and Joe to walk over to talk to Lizzie.

"I don't want any more pains," Jenny said. She hugged Marge's middle. "Can I live with Marge and Joe for a while and help with their bunnies? They don't have kids."

Granny gawked. "Pains? What on earth?"

"Growing pains," Marge said. "She's not little or big and they call this awkward stage growing pains."

"*Ach,* I see. I can't remember being seven going on eight, but I think Lizzie remembers. How about we ask her about it?"

Jenny looked down, but marched over to her house. Lizzie greeted her behind the screen door. Granny asked Marge and Joe in for tea and blueberry muffins, knowing Lizzie needed time alone with Jenny.

~*~

In tribulation be patient. In tribulation be patient, Lizzie said over and over in her mind as Jenny stomped up the steps. Jenny didn't come in the door, but instead plopped herself down on a hickory bent rocker on the porch. Lizzie sighed, not knowing whether to pamper the girl or discipline her. How she wished Roman was home. She retrieved her knitting and when she touched the yarn, a thought came to her; a parable Granny had made up.

She went outside and sat in the rocker opposite Jenny. "Jenny, come here."

Jenny slowly got up and, with hunched shoulders, moseyed over to Lizzie.

"Do you see this scarf I'm trying to make?"

"Not too *goot.* It's dark out here."

Lizzie took the matches in her apron pocket and lit the oil lamp on the table. "Now can you see it?"

"*Jah…*"

"What colors do you see?"

"Blue, green, white, and pink…"

"Do you like the design the colored yarn is making?"

Jenny looked down and shuffled her feet. "*Jah.*"

"Now come here and put your nose up against the scarf."

"What?"

"Put your nose up to the scarf. I want to show you something."

Jenny obeyed.

"What do you see?" Lizzie asked.

"Nothing. Black."

Lizzie tried to embrace Jenny but she recoiled. *In tribulation be patient. In tribulation be patient.* "Jenny, your *Oma* helped me a lot when my *mamm* died. She told me to put my nose up against one of her quilts and asked me what I saw. Nothing, I said. She had me slowly move back, and then asked what I saw. And I said a beautiful quilt. Well, your *Oma* corrected me. She said I saw the pattern and design only when I moved back."

"I don't understand," Jenny said, slowly sitting in her rocker.

"Well, sometimes we don't see the beautiful pattern God is making in our life until later. When my *mamm* died, all I saw was black, understand? I was very sad. But that was years ago and I've been able to step back and see the pretty pattern of my life."

"It still doesn't make sense. I'm only seven…"

In tribulation be patient. In tribulation be patient. "Jenny, I'm trying to tell you that it's okay to have 'black' days. Give it time, and step back, soon you'll see God works everything together for the *goot*."

Jenny's chin started to quiver. Lizzie got up and to her surprise, Jenny met her midway, hugging her middle. "You saw black, too?"

Lizzie kissed her head. "*Jah*, for many days. But now I'm happy because I have a new *mamm*, too. Your *Oma*."

Jenny sobbed in Lizzie's arms. Her attempt to tell Granny's parable had failed, but Jenny understood that she cared. She led her to her rocker and sat her on her lap. Lizzie stroked her blond hair and rocked her, and Jenny soaked her black apron. She heard foot-steps. "*Ach*, Roman, I'm glad you're home."

"It's Joe, Lizzie. Checking on Jenny."

"*Ach*, I didn't see you. I think she'll be fine."

"Just don't want her getting in trouble…"

"Why would she get in trouble?"

"I was whopped a lot as a kid. Don't want to see that happening…"

Lizzie heard pain in Joe's voice. This was a man who said he was an atheist. What had tainted him to believe there was no God? Did he not have a loving father? Did he think God was the same way? "Joe, I really appreciate your concern, but we make allowances for others weaknesses."

"But Jeb's awful mad."

"He's awful tired. He's been searching for Jenny for hours. Just needs a *goot* night sleep."

Jenny wiped her eyes and looked over at Joe. "Can I play with your bunnies sometime?"

Joe beamed. "Anytime you come *with* your mom."

Jenny's head spun around to look at Lizzie. "*Mamm,* can we go tomorrow to see the bunnies?"

Jenny called her *mamm* naturally. Lizzie feared it was her turn to cry, so she bit her lip and willed self-control. "*Jah, dochder,* I'd like that." She looked over at Joe through blurry eyes. "Is that *goot* with you?"

"I'll be home all day. Making a rabbit hutch. Could use some company."

~*~

The next morning, Jeb was still on edge. "Deborah, no. We don't read any other Bible but the German or King James Version."

"But the translation Janice has flows so *goot*. It's called *The Message Bible*. Don't see the harm if it helps me understand the scriptures better."

Jeb stuck his spoon in his oatmeal. "*Nee.*"

Granny went over and picked up her Bible. "I love this

Bible with all my heart. It's my rock in life, you know that. But words have changed. Do you know that when it was written, the bowels were considered the seat of the emotions?"

"Deborah, what on earth? You aren't talking like yourself."

"It's something Janice said that's stuck in my mind and I can't explain it any other way. The emotions in Bible times were believed to come from the bowels, not the heart. So when it says to love each other with bowels of mercy, it means a heart full of mercy. It makes more sense."

Jeb got up to pour himself another cup of coffee. "Deborah, you are scaring me enough to make me want to forbid you to have that knitting circle with the Baptist. "

"But you read Max Lucado, and there's other Bible translations in his books."

Jeb pulled at his beard. "There is?"

Granny ran into the living room to get the book Jeb was reading and flipped through a few pages. "It says here in the front, 'Unless otherwise indicated, all Scripture references are from the *Holy Bible, New International Version*'."

Jeb's eyes grew round. "Let me see." Granny handed him the book.

Though the birds were singing in the morning, for some reason, they were giving Granny a headache. Why was Jeb so upset? He even scared Joe last night.

"You're right, it isn't in *King James*. Maybe I should get rid of it."

"You got it from the bishop, *jah*?" Granny reached over to take Jeb's hand. "What's really troubling you, Love?"

Jeb put his head down. "Change, as usual. The older I get, it just gets harder."

"Well, being set in right ways is *goot*. I'd never stray from the Amish, if that's what you're fearing."

"It's the little foxes that spoil the vine…"

Granny knew what he meant. It's the little ways we slip from the faith that cause a real backslide. "I'm Amish to the core, but I'll take your advice to heart, Love."

He opened his arms and she sat in his lap. "I love you, Deborah."

"I love you too…old man."

~*~

When Jeb went out to feed the chickens and collect eggs, she knew she'd fret if she didn't do a casting off prayer. Something was eating at Jeb, but what could it possibly be? How gruff he was with Joe last night wasn't typical of his *goot* nature. And he looked pale. *Dear, Lord, no!*

She sat in her rocker, bowed her head and prayed:

Lord,

I can't live without Jeb and he doesn't look goot. He looks ill or old age is making his personality change. Lord, Jeb is my rock, and I just couldn't go on without him. But you have carried me through deep valleys and will continue to lift me by your grace, until you carry me into eternity. But Lord, please help Jeb. Something isn't right. Does he know something I don't? Is he upset he'll have to share a fishing hole with Jonas since he'll be moving here, most likely? Lord, I give my dear husband to you. Shower him with your love and strength.

In Jesus name,

Amen

~*~

Thank you for reading *Amish Friends Knitting Circle: Tea Kettles Sing*. I leave you with this recipe for blueberry muffins. Enjoy!

Blueberry Muffins
1 ½ c. flour
¾ c. sugar
½ tsp. salt
2 tsp. baking powder
1/3 c. vegetable oil
1 egg
1/3 c. milk
1 c. blueberries

Mix ingredients and put in muffin cups 2/3rd full. Add Crumb Topping (below). Bake at 400 degrees for20 minutes. Cool.

Crumb Topping
½ c. sugar
1/3 c. flour
¼ c. butter

EPISODE 3

Berry Picking Time

Ella handed little Moses to Colleen. "*Danki* ever so much for helping me pick berries and watch the twins." She kissed her daughter's head. "Looks like Vina needs a nap. I'll take her upstairs."

Sitting on the back porch, Colleen's heart was pricked. How she longed to have peace like Ella. The woman exuded tranquility while managing so much stress, laboring extra hard in her garden, hoping their vegetable stand at the end of the driveway could make ends meet until Zach found another job. The frugal recipes Ella had shared made Colleen yearn to live off the land…off of little.

"Mommy, what's wrong?"

Colleen turned to her daughter, Aurora. "Nothing. Why?"

"You look sad. Your mouth is going down at the ends."

"Do I need to turn my frown upside down?"

Aurora snuggled up on the glider next to her. "Mommy, why are we here? And when will we go home? I want to play with Maria and Kim."

Colleen sighed. Good question. When would they ever be home? A real home and not Forget-Me-Not Manor, as thankful as she was for the place? "Soon, Aurora. Mommy's helping take care of the twins."

"The man in the barn is really nice. He said my hair's as black as a row."

"What man?"

"Like a crow, not a row," Colleen heard a mellow voice from behind say.

She turned to see a man who held her gaze. Was this the Hezekiah Fannie had a crush on before she met her husband? If so, she could see why. His sandy blonde hair and green eyes would make any girl swoon. But she'd learned her lesson; a handsome man could have an ugly heart.

"Hi there. I'm Hezekiah. You must be Colleen."

"Yes, I'm Colleen."

He took off his straw hat and sat in the cedar chair across from her. "How do you like helping on a farm?"

"I've only been doing it for a week, but seems like I was born for it, somehow. Can't really explain it."

"Have any relatives that farmed?" he asked. "People tell me it's in the blood."

"I never met my grandparents, so I don't know."

Hezekiah cracked a knuckle. "Do they live in another country? You have an accent."

"What?"

"You talk more like us than *Englishers* . Where are you from?"

Colleen grinned. "I'm from Pittsburgh. We do have an accent that sounds a little Dutch. There's even a book called *How to Speak Pittsburghese*." She rolled up her sleeves, the heat of the sun making it unbearable.

Hezekiah's smile matched the noonday sun, and kindness poured from his eyes. "So how'd you like berry picking with Ella?"

"It was fun. But I was afraid of bears."

"Bears?"

"Yes, they eat berries. Saw it on a nature show on TV. So I thought we'd see one and was a bit nervous."

Hezekiah began fanning his face with his hat. "Haven't seen a bear in years. And black bears won't hurt you."

"Like *The Three Bears*?" Aurora asked, her feet dangling under the glider. "Mama Bear, Papa Bear, and Baby Bear are all nice..."

Hezekiah cocked an eyebrow. "Well, not if you get in between a mama bear and her baby. She won't be too nice."

"It's a story she knows. About talking bears," Colleen explained.

Hezekiah smiled at Aurora and then Colleen. But his eyes slowly went down to her bare arms. "You're all cut up. What happened?"

Colleen gripped Moses tightly. "I, ah, must have scratched myself berry picking."

The concern in Hezekiah's eyes made her heart jump into her throat. Very few men ever showed concern. Ella opened the screen door with a bowl of berries for Colleen and Aurora. "Here you go. Hezekiah, you want some?"

Hezekiah put up a hand in protest. "*Danki*, but no. Ella, Colleen is new to the country. Did you tell her to keep her sleeves down when picking berries? Look at her arms."

Ella took her arm and looked at the scars. "These aren't from thorns. How'd you get them?"

"I had a run in with a cat. A nasty one."

"Did Janice report the animal?" Hezekiah asked.

"No, I didn't tell her. The cat was just hungry. When I fed it, it went off...."

Hezekiah's eyes rested upon her, as if he knew she was lying...

~*~

Granny saw a black and white sheep and asked Janice to stop the car. "Well, I never! It's spotted like Holsteins. Wonder if they sell them."

"Well, they're obviously Amish. Do you know people up here in Troutville?" Janice asked.

"I know them," Lavina said from the back seat. "Won't be talking to me, though."

Granny's head spun around to meet Lavina's eyes. "Why not? You're not under the ban."

Granny saw Lavina blush; a deep redness started on her neck and slowly rose to cover her face.

"People talk…" Lavina sighed. "It's why I stay in Smicksburg."

Seeing how odd Lavina acted since they'd come to Troutville grabbed Granny's heart. A girl only eighteen seemed too young to be so full of pain. She thought of her nephew, Nathan, and how she feared his attachment to Lavina. Was she adding to Lavina's pain? Was Nathan a healing balm?

Janice interrupted her thoughts. "Let them think what they want. It's a sin to be looking down on others. Let me tell you. I know. I'm a black spot on an otherwise white Holstein cow." She looked at Granny and burst into laughter. "Sorry, couldn't pass it up."

"There's no shame in being Black," Granny said.

"Oh, Deborah, I know that. I'm proud of my heritage. But I do live in a mostly white community and know what it feels like to be looked down on. Not like back home in the Deep South."

"Are you sad living here?" Lavina asked.

"Some days I want to pack it all up and move back home, I won't deny it. But then Jerry cautions me about the lie, 'The grass is greener on the other side'. No I've learned to be content, no matter what state I'm in." She grinned. "That's a Bible verse….Be content in whatsoever state you are in."

"In the King James, too," Granny said. "That's *goot*." She turned back to Lavina. "I'd like to see if these here people can sell me a lamb or know where I can get sheep like these ones. Will you walk to the door with me?"

Lavina shrugged her shoulders. "I suppose so."

Granny silently prayed for Lavina. If the people knew her, and shamed her, she'd have to teach her how to recondition her mind. See herself as God saw her…forgiven….pure. But Granny knew her own mind had to be reconditioned concerning Lavina, too. She feared Lavina's past immorality would make for an unhappy marriage to her Nathan.

As they approached the front door, Lavina reached for Granny's hand. "I remember this place. I need to go back…"

"You need to go forward. Remember Lot's wife. She looked back and turned to salt. Couldn't move." Granny gripped Lavina hand tightly. "You're too young to get stuck in life."

Lavina didn't resist, but instead teared-up. "Granny, *danki* ever so much. I *am* stuck."

Granny embraced her. "You have me and a circle of friends now, *jah*? Some say our knitting circle's full of knit picks, I know that." She pat Lavina's back. "But we do. We pick each other up, *jah*?" Lavina started to shake. "*Ach*, I didn't mean to make you cry."

Lavina pulled back. "You made me laugh. *Danki*. I like that. Knit picks."

"You're picking up Maryann, *jah*?" Granny asked.

"*Jah*, and love it. Hope to have a family as big as hers someday."

"*Yinz* lost?" a man's voice called from behind the screen door.

Granny walked up the three steps, yanking at Lavina all the way. "I'm curious about your sheep. I've never seen one like it."

"*Ach*, we breed them," he said. "Do you want one?"

"*Jah*. I spin wool and what nice yarn the wool would make."

The man looked over at Lavina, and groaned. "I know you. You're from around here."

Lavina put her head down, not meeting his gaze.

Granny silently prayed.

"You're the girl who gave up her twins, *jah*?"

Granny prayed all the more, as she noticed Lavina blush again.

"'Tis a shame…"

Granny put her hands on her hips. "She's not in shame anymore…"

"*Ach,* I didn't mean that. It's a shame the way you were raised. Didn't want to say it."

"Do you know my *daed*?" Lavina asked, almost in a whisper.

"*Jah*, I do. We had words. Not being in the same church district, I stopped visiting and all."

"Why?" Granny asked.

The man opened the screen door and wiped the sweat off his forehead with a hanky. "I don't want to say in front of the girl."

"My *daed* threatened you, *jah*? If you told anyone…."

"*Jah*. But a group of us told your bishop, and that's what started the whole thing…"

"Started what?" Granny asked.

"You don't know?" he asked, surprise coloring his voice.

"*Nee*, we're on our way to the farm to check on my *mamm*."

"They're gone. Been put out."

"Where did they go?" Lavina blurted. "Does anyone know where my *mamm* is? My brothers and sisters?"

The man pulled at his long gray beard. "No word, yet. But if you give me your address, I'll send it to you when we find out."

"You'll never find out because my *daed* never let anyone know where we were going."

"You're not from around here, I know that. Moved here a while back, *jah*?"

"Six years ago. My *daed* never got along with the bishops. My *mamm* said she moved several times…"

Granny put her hand to her mouth to hide her quivering chin. Lavina had told her about her *daed* beating on her *mamm*. Sometimes Lavina tried to stop him, and she paid the price, being beaten instead of her *mamm*. How could she have missed the selflessness of this dear child? Her mind seemed to be in a tunnel, only seeing immorality. But Lavina had qualities she lacked at seventy. Granny couldn't help herself. She embraced Lavina, and wept.

~*~

Lizzie looked over at Roman and then her *daed* again. "Well, now you have to move in with us. Fannie's pregnant?" She took a copy of the *Penny Saver* from the counter and fanned her face. "Why's it a secret?"

111

"Well, she's afraid of having a miscarriage. A bundle of nerves she is." Jonas wiped sweat from his brow.

Roman pulled a stool up to the store counter. "Lizzie, you look worn out. Take a seat."

"*Danki.*"

Roman leaned on the counter with an elbow. "Jonas, we're your family now. You're the *Opa* to my girls, *jah*? You're needed at my place."

"*Daed.* It's time…the season to move on," Lizzie said. "Understand?"

Jonas' eyes scanned the store from behind the counter. "Lots of memories in this store, and it's something I can do. I do have limits." He held up an arm attached to a brace. "Can't do woodworking with Jeb. And my chickens are here. Make a *goot* profit."

"I thought you were getting sick of the chickens," Lizzie moaned.

"Now that I have to go, I realize how little I can do with this MS." He looked down and stared at the floor.

Roman gazed at Lizzie and shrugged his shoulders. "Why can't we move the chicken farm to our place?"

"It's too much," Jonas said. "You'll be adding on a *dawdyhaus*. No, I won't have it."

Lizzie beamed. "*Daed*, you make money from your chickens." She snapped her fingers. "*Ach*, you'd be living down the road from our new English neighbors, Marge and Joe. You could show them how to feed and water their turkeys the way you do, by just pressing buttons."

"*Jah*, you could teach others how to live off the grind," Roman said.

"*Grid.* Live off the grid," Lizzie corrected. "It means no electricity." She pursed her lips. "I have another idea. Got it from Janice Jackson, the pastor's wife at the Baptist church."

Jonas didn't say anything, but he leaned forward.

"She said we should have an Amish day camp. Let English kids get a chance to milk a cow, collect eggs, shovel manure, ride in a buggy." She shifted. "But most of all, the English would like to talk to a real Amish person. Ask questions about our heritage and what-not. *Daed*, you'd be ever so perfect."

Jonas' eyes got wide. "You mean the English are interested in how we live? Why?"

"I don't know. It's a mystery. Maybe they've never been to a real farm."

Roman took off his straw hat. "What do you say, Jonas? We'll move the chicken building over to our place, build a *dawdyhaus*, and maybe have an Amish camp."

Jonas chuckled. "Sounds kind of interesting, that Amish camp. I've always liked to tell stories...."

"So *Daed*, can we start making plans? Tell Fannie she has the store to herself and will need to hire someone?"

"*Jah*, I suppose so...."

~*~

Marge took a deep breath, but didn't get out of the car yet. She hadn't been in a church for ages and the fight she and Joe just had sapped her strength. But her model marriage was Granny and Jeb's. They both had strong opinions, but they yielded to each other, within reason. Granny didn't start the summer knitting circle until Jeb was fine with it, but she'd stood her ground while Jeb was thinking it over. Maybe Joe was thinking tonight he needed to be in a local church since her off-the-grid magazine said you should. Living so far from neighbors, it was a good place to see them regularly.

She looked at the church that Janice had said was once a dairy barn; was even in *Country Magazine*. Marge had to admit it pulled on her *Little House on the Prairie* yearnings. To live in an era of simplicity, like Ma Ingalls and have your life rooted in a local church was so appealing. And the church was white clapboard, too. Her stomach flipped; if this is like *Little House*, is this where gossipers come too? Like Mrs. Olson? Surely not.

A knock on her window brought her out of her daydream. She rolled down the window.

"You going to come in?" asked a chipper lady with short brown hair, carrying a guitar case. "I'm Ginny. And you are?"

"Marge. I think we've met somewhere."

"In my bookstore, Serenity Book Nook?"

Marge popped out of the car and clasped her hands. "I love that place*!* So cozy and the coffee's good. But I've never seen you there."

"Most likely working in the back room. So, where are you from?"

"Indiana. Moved up to live off the grid. Live down the road from Granny Weaver."

The church bells rang and Ginny gasped. "I have to lead worship! Running late. Are you coming in?"

"Yes, I am," Marge said, feeling more confident. Country folk were friendly, and she need not fear nasty gossip. She followed Ginny as she ran into the church. Ginny went to the front, but Marge sat in the last pew. *So quaint*, she thought. *But is God mad I haven't visited Him in years?*

Ginny fidgeted with sheet music, and then put a piece on the music stand. Janice ran the overhead projector, and Marge looked at the title. *You Saw Me.* She didn't know this song. She looked down at the bottom of the song and it read, *Hillsong.* Her friend in Indiana had given her one of their CD's but Joe wasn't too happy, so she'd returned it. *How silly.*

Ginny strummed her guitar with eyes closed and then everyone in the church stood up and sang the song, some hands raised. Marge felt like running out, being near the back door. But she looked over and saw Colleen, that single mom that was a part of the knitting circle. She looked like she was ready to cry, tears brimming in her amber eyes. Should she go over and sit next to her. What on earth was wrong?

Marge looked ahead at the words everyone was singing, so heartfelt:

And You saw me
When You took a crown of thorns
And Your blood washed over me
And You loved me
Through the nails that You bore
And Your blood washes over me

Marge thought of her father making fun of the new music in some churches. But as she watched Ginny with her head up and eyes closed, strumming the guitar as if she believed every word, it made her feel like crying. Her face tensed up when she sang about the crown of thorns. Marge looked down at her hands and stared at the bruises the thorns made while picking berries.

More childhood memories flooded her mind as she looked at the words. *And you loved me...Jesus loves me this I know, for the Bible tells me so.* She felt warmth in her heart. How she'd missed church. Agreeing not to go after marrying Joe was a mistake. A big one. But would he understand if she became a regular attender?

~*~

Luke stepped back, shocked at what Joe so easily said. *There is no God and I hope Marge realizes it soon.* But Luke knew there was a God, ever since his wife forgave him of abuse. Her changed heart was a miracle, no doubt, and the Bible they shared daily had melded them together, just like Jeb and the church leaders had said. He crossed his arms and leaned against the barn. "How do you think you got here if there's no God?"

Joe took a swig of the homemade root beer Ruth made. "I don't know, and I don't care. All I know is if, and I mean *if*, there is a God, he screwed up, big time."

"How?"

"Suffering. Children starving around the world. . Sickness and death. I could go on..."

"He didn't make that stuff." Luke did a quick casting off prayer, like Ruth so often did under pressure. Casting her cares on God.

"If he didn't, then who did?" Joe asked.

Luke felt hope rise in him. Joe asking questions was good. He wanted answers. "You do know the story in Genesis, when God made the earth, *jah*?"

"Since I was a kid, in church, Sunday morning, Sunday night and Wednesdays, too. I know, God created the world, so to speak, then a devil with a pitch fork came and tempted Eve to do something really bad...eat an apple." Joe laughed. "That's as silly as Jenny thinking she could find the Seven Dwarfs by following rabbits, only she's really cute."

Luke pointed to the magenta and blue swirls in the sunset. "Can't you see, only God could make something like *that*? And soon the stars will be out, held up by God's hand."

"Gravity," Joe snarled. "It's all science. You did learn science in school, right?"

"Only went to eighth grade in the Amish school, but Ruth has me reading all kinds of books about nature and I'm hooked like a fish. Seeing nature was what made me believe in God...less than a year ago..."

A slight wind blew across the meadow, and Joe threw a few more handfuls of cracked corn to the baby turkeys. He stared at them as they pecked at the food. "You say only a year ago? Weren't you born Amish, though?"

"*Jah*, I was, but I never knew Christ in here." Luke put his hand on his heart. "I didn't like God, really. Blamed him for a lot, and then took it out on Ruth. She left me for a while."

"Wow, that's a shock. *Yinz* look happy…"

"We are now. The Amish bishop and elders, Jeb Weaver being one, helped me in many ways. They said how I treated Ruth was…abuse."

Joe raked his fingers through his hair. "Man, what on earth did you do? Hit her?"

"*Nee*, never. But my words did. Like I said, I was mad about something else. But Ruth forgave me, and if that isn't a miracle, I don't know what is." He willed back tears. "Only God can do a miracle."

Joe gently closed the door to the turkey coop, and shoved both hands in his pockets. "I can relate, in a way. I get fuming mad about how religion was shoved down my throat all my life, by a dad who's a complete hypocrite."

"Is your dad alive?"

"Ya, lives in Indiana. Most likely will be up to tell me what a nut I am for following another one of Marge's whims…living off the grid…"

"Forgive your *daed*, Joe. Unforgiveness can cause problems. Believe me."

Joe's eyes softened. "I appreciate you sharing what you did about your marriage. That took guts." He attempted to fist bump but Luke gave him a puzzled look. "You're supposed to make a fist and punch mine."

"*Nee*, I'm a pacifist."

Joe burst into laughter and hit his knee. "It's like a handshake. The way we English do it. Well, some of the men."

Luke made a fist and quickly met Joe's in mid-air. "Like that?"

Joe shook his fist and winced. "Not so hard. Just a tap."

~*~

Ruth looked over at her knitting loom that leaned against the corner in the living room. *Knitting on a loom is so much easier.* But she was determined to knit one, then purl one, without confusing the two. As she looked at the pink yarn, her mind turned to Luke. Why was she so afraid for him? Like he'd have some kind of relapse and return to his former self; the mean Luke. Images of him screaming in her face jolted her, and she placed a hand on the baby she carried inside. *I need to be calm for the boppli's sake.*

She thought of Fannie's news, and how they'd both be holding their new *kinner* in mid-winter, when the snow could blow a soul away, and was a perfect time to stay home with a new young one. Her mind again went toward Luke. Was something wrong? Was she supposed to pray? Did Joe have girlie magazines in his barn, just like his uncle when Luke was only a boy?

Her fingers gripped the yarn, and she bowed her head to pray a casting off prayer, when she heard the side door open. It was her *mamm*.

"Forgot to bring over your mail for two days."

"*Ach, Mamm*, I could have gotten it."

"There's a letter marked Ohio. Maybe a pen pal wrote." She smiled at Ruth and placed the mail on the table near her, next to her birding magazine. "Putting up enough blackberry jam for the two of us, and need to get back."

"*Mamm*, just because I'm pregnant doesn't mean I can't help."

Again her *mamm* beamed at her, her dark eyes twinkling. "You're adding on to this little house soon, *jah*? Lumber will arrive in a few days and you'll be cooking for the workers?"

"*Jah*. But I'll have help."

"Well, just the same, you rest. Anyhow, you know how much I love putting up jam." She winked and went out the side screen door.

Ruth looked at her *mamm*, love filling her heart. If her parents hadn't been so kind as to give them the little *dawdyhaus* to live in while Luke was under church discipline, which way would her wildly meandering marriage be drifting? Now it was calm waters, thanks to the community that surrounded her.

She picked up the mail and soon saw the letter from Ohio. No return address? How odd. And the handwriting didn't look very feminine. But it was addressed to Luke and her, so she opened it. She scanned the paper to see the sender. *Uncle Otis?* Ruth put a hand on her throat, as if that could help it from constricting.

> *Dear Luke and Ruth,*
>
> *I haven't written in ages, but through the grapevine I hear Zach lost his job and may be selling his little patch of earth. Since I lost his address, tell him I may be interested in purchasing. I'm a lonely old man since your aunt passed on, and I want to be around my family, not hers.*
>
> *Otis*

Without thinking, Ruth crumbled the letter in her hands. Uncle Otis, moving to Smicksburg? Having no *kinner*, were Luke and Zach, the ever dutiful nephews, supposed to care for the very man who led her husband down the dark, filthy hole of pornography? Holding back tears, she bowed her head.

Lord, are you testing me? I know you don't tempt, but test. Uncle Otis would be one big test, that's for sure. Ach, Lord, I'm sorry. Maybe I have unforgiveness in my heart. Or bitterness toward Uncle Otis. Help me! I cast this all on you, because you care for me. 1 Peter 5:7. I've memorized that verse, Lord. Maybe need to memorize other similar ones.

She picked up the pink yarn and couldn't think, for the life of her, how to purl, or knit.

~*~

Fannie lay on her bed knitting, but her eyes slowly moved to her swollen feet. *Fat feet. Her mamm's feet. Feet of an old woman.* She looked up at the robin egg color she'd painted the ceiling. *I am fearfully and wonderfully made...*even though her feelings needed to catch up with the verse she so often quoted.

Melvin said she glowed, but all she felt was blown. Blown all over by emotions she hadn't felt since her school days. She knew it was hormones, like the new doctor in town said, but could she last another seven months?

Fannie looked down at the mint green yarn and tears blurred her vision. She loved Melvin with all her heart and was so happy she conceived on their wedding night. But he deserved a wife who didn't cry all the time. Fannie heard footsteps coming up the stairs and soon saw her handsome husband entered their little sanctuary. She was pleased he washed up and the scent of Ivory soap was upon him.

"I have news," he grinned as he lay on the bed next to her.

She put her knitting on the nightstand. "Go on. Must be *goot.*"

"Jonas is moving in with Lizzie. They're going to build –"

"*Danki,* God!" Fannie blurted, and then covered her mouth. "*Ach,* I'm so sorry. I do love Jonas."

Melvin chuckled. "Just don't like living with him, *jah?*"

Fannie burst into laughter. "*Jah*. Not to live with. I know I'm more emotional and all, but he always compared me to Lizzie."

Melvin pulled at his newly forming beard. Fannie reached over to stroke his face. "You look so handsome in a beard. And it tells everyone that you're mine."

Melvin scooped her into his arms and lay on the bed holding her. "Are you okay? I mean, you're having a *boppli*."

Fannie tilted her head up to kiss him. "I won't break."

"Just afraid of a miscarriage, *jah*?"

"My *mamm* had several…"

"Doesn't mean you will." Melvin kissed her hand. "Remember what the doctor said. Rest, don't fret, and *eat when you're hungry*."

She clasped his hand and drew it to her heart. "What if I get fat?"

"You never were, Fannie. Remember, it was all in your head. Now, eat *goot* for the *boppli*."

Fannie didn't know if Melvin knew she weighed herself on their scale obsessively. And she was gaining weight, in her thighs! To have a handsome husband stuck with a fat wife gripped her heart with fear. But the doctor said weight gain around the thighs was normal, and she'd soon shed it once the *boppli* was born. "Pray for me, Melvin. I'm afraid."

He pulled the ribbons of her prayer *kapp* and gently took it off. He turned her on her side so he could unpin her hair, kissing her neck as he did. "What are you afraid of?" he whispered in her ear.

"That you'll think I'm fat and ugly."

"Never," he said, as he let down her hair, kissing it now. "Fannie, you're the most beautiful woman I know."

She turned to him and their lips met, and for a while, all her fears vanished in perfect love.

~*~

Granny snatched the lid off the Mason Jar, and Tillie quickly put in another lightning bug. "We'll have a lantern, soon," Granny said, beaming at Tillie.

Soon she heard panting, and saw Jenny. "*Oma*, I have six in my hands. Open the jar. One's getting away."

Granny didn't take orders from her *kinner*, but knew Jenny was just excited. When she deposited her bugs in the jar, they all stared at the warm glow of the bugs.

"Why do they light up?" Tillie asked in a whisper, as if speaking loud would disturb such an enchanted moment.

"God made them that way," Granny said, observing the bugs. She felt a large hand on her shoulder: Jeb's.

"Deborah, can we take a walk? Have something on my mind…"

Deborah? He usually called her by nicknames, mostly "Love," but "Deborah" meant he wanted to correct her on something. She cringed. Jeb's odd behavior over the past week was wearing on her nerves.

He took her hand, telling the girls to go over to the bonfire with their parents. "Marshmallows needed to be roasted," he told them with a grin. Granny watched the two skip away and she put her other hand on Jeb's. "What's wrong? Something's not right."

He started to walk down the path to his fishing hole. Granny was ever so thankful for the white gourd purple martin house Jeb made her for Christmas. Those birds feasted on mosquitos, so now sitting by the pond, on Jeb's bench, was a joy. Her stomach clenched even more as Jeb's grip on her hand tightened. His nerves were so easily frayed over the past months, and she feared dementia with all her being. To see a man as active as Jeb, and who had as quick a mind, would be such a contrast if his behavior became permanent. *Lord, I cast Jeb on you!*

When they got to the bench, Jeb sat with his head down, hand shaking as he wiped sweat from the top of his upper lip. "Deborah, you know how Noah Mast is dressing fancy, thinking of marrying the Rowland girl?"

"*Jah*, but he's not baptized, so he hasn't broken a vow."

"Remember when his brother had that wild *rumspringa?*"

"Who could forget, but it was long ago." She put her hand on Jeb's sullen face. "Love, what does this have to do with anything?"

"The People are thinking the church district is too large for Jacob to handle, being over two hundred. Some feel that we need to divide into two church districts."

"You mean *Jacob* wants it to be turned into two districts."

"*Jah*, he does. Needs to tend to things at home, he feels. And his nerves have gotten bad. How he treated Ginny Rowland was harsh and we feared back then he was over worked. So, he asked the ministers to draw the lot for a new bishop for the new district."

Granny saw the ashen color on Jeb's face, even at twilight. She closed her eyes and said, "You're the new bishop?"

"*Jah*. All the church meetings I've been attending have been about his matter. All the bishops agreed on the district, and so the ministers drew the lot." His voice caught in his throat. "I don't feel worthy, Love. And I'm old."

Granny wanted to hitch up the wagon and visit Bishop Mast; tell him that Jeb was too old, and how could he put such a burden on him, but she softly said, "God won't lead you where His grace won't keep you, *jah*?"

To her shock, Jeb started to sob. Did he want her to protest him being the new bishop? But it wasn't their place to question God. If God didn't want him bishop, he wouldn't have picked the Bible with a piece of paper stuck in it.

Jeb put his arms around her as if needing strength. "I don't feel worthy."

Granny willed back tears. She looked up over the hill to the bonfire. Lavina was sitting on a log next to Nathan. "Jeb, you are so worthy. Where would Lavina be today if you hadn't been so capable and loving? Since Old Christmas, you gave that girl hope. Isn't that what a bishop does?"

Jeb's tears fell on her and all he could say was, *I'm not worthy.*

Granny heard a fish come to the surface of the pond. Dragonflies skimmed its surface. "Jeb, Love, you're the finest man I know. But truth be told, I'm glad you feel unworthy. Doesn't God use those who feel inadequate? Seems to me it's somewhere in the Bible."

"'*My grace is sufficient for you: for my strength is made perfect in weakness...*' Paul said that in Corinthians. I've memorized it, under the circumstances."

Jeb straightened as if he found new strength. Granny leaned her head on his shoulder. "And I'm here to help you, too. I don't have to have the knitting circle. Things change."

Jeb patted her cheek. "*Nee,* Deborah... at least for now... at least for now..."

~*~

Nathan slid a marshmallow onto the pointed stick and handed it to Lavina. "Now, don't burn another one."

Lavina looked at him, his eyes glistening as the flicker of the flames danced on his face. She didn't deserve such a man. But then again, Nathan hadn't made his intentions totally known. Not a word about marriage. "*Danki*, Nathan. But I like my marshmallows black." Black as coal, just like her sin.

Nathan sat next to her and was silent, again. She stared into the fire, and put her stick in, turning it to brown the marshmallow evenly. Her mind turned to her family being put out, shunned. How her *mamm* must be suffering, and her brothers and sisters as well. Had she done the right thing, not marrying the *daed* of her twins? Giving them to Ella and Zach? As she watched the white blob on her stick turn brown, she thought of sin. How slowly it took hold of her, slowly turning her from what she knew was right and moral. Eventually, her sin was as black as the moonless night around them.

"What are you thinking about?" a little girl's voice asked.

Lavina turned to see Tillie, whose sensitive heart saw into her own. "*Ach*, nothing." She gripped the stick firmer. "Have you made a s'more?"

"She's had two," Roman said from across the fire.

"Three," Lizzie corrected. "And I think it's time you girls went to bed."

Jenny sprang from the log she sat on, next to Lizzie. "Tomorrow, I get to go see Joe and Marge's bunnies." She beamed at Lizzie. "So let's go to bed so tomorrow comes sooner."

Lizzie hugged Jenny, and then led the three girls to the path leading to their house.

"I think I best turn in, too. Lots of orders to fulfill tomorrow." He grinned at Nathan. "*Yinz* young ones have fun out here, *jah?*"

Lavina couldn't help but notice that Nathan was nervous. That he seemed to not want to be near her. She took the now black marshmallow off the stick, and blew on it to cool. A barn owl hooted and a gentle breeze made the corn rustle, but Nathan was silent. *Stop being so self-absorbed*, she admonished herself. Thinking about others took her mind off herself.

"Granny and Jeb are still down at the fishing hole. Do you think they're alright?" she asked Nathan.

"My *opa* could live there. Took me fishing as a *kinner*, and once we fell asleep, with our fishing poles in our hands."

"Wasn't Granny worried?"

"*Nee,* not at all."

Something *was* wrong. She could talk for hours with Nathan, but he kept holding back. Again, she stared at the fire, and the silence seemed to underline the fact that she was an immoral woman, making life hard for her *mamm*. Why would

Nathan want a woman like her? As much as he told her 'Though her sin be as scarlet, she was now as white as snow', shame still filled her.

She inhaled deeply, and turned to Nathan. "I understand."

"What?"

Her stomach flipped. "You don't seem interested in me anymore...."

Nathan set his face like flint, looking intently into the fire. "I'm confused..."

Lavina felt nausea wash over her and wished she had knitting in her hands to calm down. Just the feel of the yarn on her hands made it feel like someone was holding them. "Is there someone else you like better?"

Nathan sighed. "*Nee.*"

"Then what is it? Nathan, talk to me."

He didn't turn to look at her, still staring at the fire. "I'm needed on the farm back home in Montana. Got a letter from my *daed.*"

Lavina knew he came to meet a woman to be his wife in Smicksburg. Did he think she'd say no to marriage? Or was there someone back home she didn't know about? "But you said your *daed* sent you here to meet more...people."

"His letter was confusing. He knows I'm working with Roman and expanding a business, and he could get help on the farm, unless there's something in the letter he's not saying..."

"Like what?"

"Maybe my *mamm* isn't well, or one of my *bruder*. Or it could be my *mamm's daed*. My other *opa*. Must be ailing."

He groaned and the sound echoed in Lavina's ears. "What about us?" she asked, feeling too forward, but desperate for an answer.

He took her hand. "Maybe some time apart will be *goot*. Our relationship started hasty-like. And we need to be in pace with nature, *jah*? Not rush things?"

"Marriage? Is that what you mean?"

Nathan squeezed her hand. "*Jah*. Time apart will show us how strong our love is."

"How?" Lavina blurted, tears forming in her eyes.

"Well, I can make plans and direct my own steps, but I want to make sure I'm in step with my Maker."

"But you said you loved me…"

"I do. But I'm scared, too. Marriage is a big step. One I need to be sure of…"

Lavina could hold back the tears no longer, her heart feeling pierced. She sprang up, tossing her stick into the fire, and ran to Lizzie's house.

Nathan did not follow.

~*~

Granny was glad that the girls from Forget-Me-Not Manor were warming up to her. Was it the pies she'd just delivered, or was Colleen spreading the word that the Amish weren't some backwards people, their austere clothing making them appear unfriendly? If only the English really knew why they dressed as they did; their plain material was always cheap, and the patterns reusable. It was a symbol of their unity, too.

Her mind wandered to Lavina as she coaxed the horse away from Forget-Me-Not, and headed towards Suzy's.

How could her son ask Nathan to come back to Montana without a *goot* reason? In their regular letters, she had expressed to her son that she thought Nathan was being too impulsive, falling for the first girl he met...and that she was worried about Lavina's past. But now that she knew the girl, and her unhappy circumstances, she wouldn't have thought Nathan hasty at all, only compassionate and a *goot* judge of character. Had she caused this whole ruckus? Roman was also taken back, expanding the business, only to find Nathan would be leaving, at least for a spell. Who could help him? Granny prayed out loud:

"Oh, Lord, I cast this on you. We do make a muddle of things, and it's a miracle you can make everything turn out for the goot. For that I am so thankful."

She wasn't going to let the weight on her heart ruin such a gorgeous day. Blue skies dotted with white chunks of wool.

She saw yarn waiting to be spun everywhere, but today she needed to treat herself to a yarn order from Suzy's. The news of the church district being divided and Jeb being the new bishop was a secret until it was announced at church on Sunday. Some of her girls would not be attending her *gmay*, and this caused more pain than Granny thought imaginable.

She didn't have any favorites, really, but Fannie came to her the most to talk. The girl had come so far and with being pregnant, her fears of being fat gnawing at her heart, it wouldn't be as easy to check on her.

Granny looked both ways, and then crossed over Route 954 in a hurry. Summer tourists walked up and down the streets, easily crossing over this route on foot, but she was still nervous crossing it in a buggy. She made her way to the intersection of Clarion Street, then turned right, and a few houses up, turned into SuzyB Knits. Clark, the young homeless man living at Janice's old house, was pounding nails on the side of Suzy's house. Granny waved, glad to see Suzy hired him to put up the new white siding she'd talked about.

When she opened the door to the yarn shop, the familiar bell that jangled was a comfort, as was the brightly colored yarns that filled the shelves on three walls, from floor to ceiling. There was no one in the store, but soon Suzy came in from her back room, eyes red and swollen.

"What's wrong?" Granny asked.

Suzy put a tissue to her eyes and bowed her head. Granny could easily see her body jerking as she sobbed. "Suzy…is Molly gone?"

Suzy shook her head. "She's just so ill."

"Can anything be done?"

"Dave made an appointment with the vet, but we can't get her in until tonight." Another sob escaped. "If the vet wants to put her down, I need to be there. I'm sorry."

Granny went over to embrace Suzy, and then stepped back, puzzled. "What are you sorry for?"

"I can't make it to knitting circle. I gave all the girls assignments, but –"

"Don't worry yourself. Marge is coming and can knit. She can help us."

Suzy stiffened. "Well, Deborah, there's knitters, and then there's *knitters*."

Granny thought she understood Suzy's meaning. Some women were real quilters, and others not, just doing it out of necessity, and it showed in their work. "I think Marge is the *goot* kind of knitter. But if not, we have next week, *jah*?"

Suzy's eyes softened. "Thank you, Deborah. I've been missing so many classes, but my Molly is like a child."

Granny patted her on the shoulder. "I feel the same way about Jack. That dog is a comfort. When I'm down or sick, he won't leave my side." She jumped when she heard a loud knock.

"Looks like Clark is back to work. Must have taken a break," Suzy said. "He's such a good worker."

Granny looked out the side window to see Clark up on a ladder. He looked much better than when she met him. He seemed more settled in Smicksburg. "You say he's a goot worker, *jah*?"

"*Jah*, I mean, yes, " Suzy said.

"Does he have a full-time job yet?"

"No, still looking, but with all kinds of odd jobs, he's paying his bills. Why?"

Granny inhaled and pursed her lips. "Nathan's going back to Montana for a while, and Roman needs help."

Suzy's eyes widened. "We prayed at church last night for Clark to have more work! This could be the answer. Roman could teach him how to make those hickory Amish rockers."

Granny nodded, deep in thought. She'd have to talk to Roman. *So much change…*but yarn was always available to knit and calm her nerves. She surveyed all the yarn on the shelves, but her eyes always rested on the various shades of pink. How she loved that color. She went over and fingered the yarn. "So soft."

"It's alpaca and it's warm."

"I'll take some." Granny tilted her head. "Can't a scarf be used as a hat, too?"

"I suppose so. If you're homeless and cold, I see no reason why not. But Deborah, you're advancing so much, you could learn to make a hat."

Granny looked down at the pink yarn in her hand again. "I need to knit and not think hard. I can make a knit and purl now without thinking. Best I just be knitting it across and back. Would it look right?"

"Of course it would." Suzy stepped near Granny. "What's wrong. You're always eager to learn."

"Nothing… 'this too shall pass', *jah*?"

Suzy tilted her head. "I needed to hear that. Molly can't live forever. If she has to be put down…this too shall pass. And God is close to the brokenhearted." Suzy put a Kleenex up to her eyes again. "So He'll be *real* close to me."

~*~

Luke plunked a blackberry into the metal bucket, and then stared at a berry-laden bush. "Glad you found this spot. Never been here before."

Ruth had known of this old abandoned *dawdydaus* for years, but kept it to herself. It was her place for reflection. But today, she wanted a heart-to-heart with Luke, away from her family that lived next door. She took a berry and bit into it.

"They're so ripe. Sweet. Need to make jam over the next few days."

"Well, you know how much we go through. So *goot* spread on oatmeal."

Ruth lowered her head, said a silent prayer, and then looked over at Luke. "So, how was your visit with Joe?"

His head spun to face her. "You sound awful anxious about me spending time with him. What's wrong?"

"Bad company corrupts morals. I hear Joe's an atheist."

"Doesn't make him a bad man. He's just confused from what I can tell."

A male and female pair of cardinals swooped down into the brush around them, thinking they weren't seen. How vibrant the male was, bright red; the female had dull colors of brown and muted red, for camouflage. Were women supposed to be like birds? Blending in and not being noticed? She thought of Granny and how happily she was married; she always spoke her heart to Jeb.

She ate another berry. "Luke, I am worried. The English can pull us away from our roots."

Luke took off his straw hat and swatted at the growing number of gnats. "You don't trust me, do you?"

"It's not about trust at all. It's being careful. We all have feet of clay, able to fall, like the Bible says."

"But you think my feet are weaker, *jah*?" Luke snapped.

Ruth felt the old fear coming in to choke her. Her worst nightmare would be for Luke to become the *old* Luke; the man who was abusive. She thought of what Granny told her. *Talk from your heart…*

"Luke, I'm afraid."

"Of what?"

"Of losing the love we share…"

Luke's eyes softened. "Why?"

"I don't know. Could be I'm pregnant and more emotional. Or, could be Joe and Uncle Otis coming combined. I just don't know."

Luke walked over and drew her to himself. "*Danki* for sharing that. You've been looking at me curious-like, and I thought you were judging me."

"Judging you for what?"

Luke grinned. "I don't know. Maybe I'm afraid too, of us getting stuck in old ruts, like the buggy wheels."

Ruth hugged him around the middle. "We have others to help pull us out, if we get stuck."

"*Jah.*" He held her head to his chest. "Uncle Otis coming out has me as nervous as a deer in an open field. Should I tell him how much he messed me up, with his girlie magazines?"

Ruth sighed. "Maybe have Jeb do it. You should never have to talk about it again."

Ruth could hear Luke's heart beating out of his chest. "My big concern is Uncle Otis doesn't have any family but Zach and me. We are responsible for him."

"I know. That's been on my mind too. I couldn't have that man live near us….Unless…"

"Unless what?"

"He's changed. Or is willing to change."

~*~

Granny got up on her tip-toes and kissed Jeb's cheek. "Like I said, I don't need to have the circle, you being bishop soon."

"And I said I'd let you know when I need you." He encircled Granny in his arms and patted her back. "I smell smoke…"

Granny ripped herself away and ran to her stove and quickly opened the black door. Smoke billowed out. "*Ach*, I burnt all the cookies. Now what will I give the girls?"

Jeb grinned. "You think I don't know, do you?"

"About what?"

"The cookies you have hid around the house."

"Old Man, what are you talking about?"

Jeb took a chair and placed it next to the pantry. Getting up on it, he opened the door and reached for the top shelf. "I'm talking about this, Deborah. You hide cookies from me…"

Granny gasped. "Those are from Christmas. I hid them from the *kinner. Ach*, too high for me to see up there. I forgot."

"They're still *goot.*" Jeb tapped the side of the plastic container. "These storage things you got at Punxsy-Mart really work."

"How do you know?"

"I tested the cookies."

Granny tried to hide laughter, but couldn't. "Jeb, you and your sweet tooth."

"You have two more containers. Why not give them to the girls tonight?"

Granny moaned. "They've got to be stale."

"They're not. Taste one."

Jeb leaned down and Granny took a round cookie and bit into it. "Amazing." She took another bite. "These are thumb print cookies without the jam." She looked up at Jeb and winked. "Just made berry jam. Can you help me fill them real quick?"

"*Jah*, sure, Love…"

~*~

Granny walked out onto her porch with a tray of jam filled cookies. Lizzie followed with Meadow Tea. "So glad to have this porch to catch a breeze. Awfully hot," Granny said. She looked over at Marge. "And so glad to have Marge as our teacher."

The girls nodded in agreement.

"I think we should pray for little Molly," Janice said. "Such a sweet little dog."

Ella gasped. "Pray for a dog? Doesn't sound…normal."

"God cares for a sparrow that falls," Janice said. "Why not a dog?"

Ella shrugged her shoulders. "Doesn't seem sacred, or something."

"Well, I pray about everything," Janice said. "God knows my heart."

Marge got up and took a cookie from the tray. "You really believe that, don't you?"

Janice nodded. "Yes I do." She got out her knitting needles. "How'd you like church?"

"Well, it did bring back lots of memories. But the funniest thing was when I got home. Joe wasn't upset about me going anymore."

Jenny looked up at Lizzie. "*Mamm* and I fixed his heart yesterday."

"What?" Marge asked as she walked from one woman to another, looking over their knitting.

"*Mamm* and I talked to Joe about God. He thought God was mean, but we told him He wasn't. Didn't we *Mamm*?"

Lizzie beamed. "Well, Joe brought it up. He was scared that you went to the Baptist church. Said he was afraid you'd get legal."

"Legal?" Marge asked. "What do you mean?"

Lizzie looked down at Jenny to let her speak first, but she was trying to cast on. "He said when he went to church it was too legal."

Marge stared at Lizzie for a few seconds. "Legalistic. Oh, I understand that."

"What does it mean?" Ruth asked.

"Rules, rules, and more rules," Janice said. "Some churches have a rule for everything."

"We have rules." Granny shifted, wishing they didn't have to talk about religion.

"Seems like Joe only saw rules and nothing else. He said he always feared he'd go to hell," Lizzie said.

"His father was a strict man and preached fire and brimstone. Nothing about the love of God at all. Once Joe was caught writing a note to a friend in church and his dad beat the tar out of him."

Granny leaned forward. "That's sad. So he thinks God's mad all the time. But I thought he didn't believe in God."

Marge looked down at Fannie's knitting. "You did the purl backwards." She took up the yarn and showed Fannie her mistake. "That's the odd part. Joe says there's no God, but get so upset that God's mad at him."

"He knows there's a God," Jenny said. "I told him to look at the cute bunnies. God is good and makes good things."

All the women stared at Jenny. Granny felt pride swell within her soul. "Jenny, what did Joe say to that?"

"Well, when *mamm* went in to see the turkeys, he told me a secret."

"A secret?" Marge asked.

"*Jah.* He believes in God, but doesn't want to ever go to church again."

Marge put a hand on her heart. "He said that?" Tears welled in her eyes. "Thank you, Honey. It's just like I thought. He does believe…."

"And we'll just have to show him our church isn't legalistic," Janice said as she pulled more pink yarn from the skein.

"How are the cookies?" Granny asked, hoping to lighten the conversation.

"*Goot,*" Fannie said. "But I better not eat too many. Getting as big as a cow."

Ruth sighed. "Fannie, you're pregnant and need to feed your baby. I'm gaining weight, too."

"But you're skinny."

"So are you," Ella chided. "And you should be grateful you can get pregnant. Stop worrying about your weight."

"*Jah*," Granny said. "Need to recondition your mind again?"

Fannie looked across the circle at Granny. "I'm trying. Have scriptures memorized and all, but I feel like I'm so huge. My fingers even feel fat as I knit."

"Water retention," Janice said. "Comes with hormone imbalance. I have the same thing, only it's because I'm going through menopause." Janice looked over at Granny. "Thanks for going to the doctor with me. I was so nervous."

"But he said it was more than menopause, *jah*?"

All eyes went on Janice. She slouched. "*Ya*, Dr. Pal said I have a problem with anxiety. So embarrassing as a Christian..."

"Why?" Ruth asked. "Luke gets anxious. Takes medicine for it."

"I just feel like I don't have faith..."

"Well, Luke's doctor told him it's no different than a diabetic taking insulin. Did the doctor give you medicine to help?"

Janice was not beet red. "No. Not yet. Wants me to walk...and knit."

Granny patted Janice's hand. "Knitting releases natural hormones that help calm a body down."

Janice slipped a smile to Granny. "So, I'll be knitting a lot."

Everyone got quiet as they concentrated on their knitting. A hummingbird whizzed in to drink the sweet water Granny put in a feeder hung from the porch rafter. Granny couldn't help but stare at her knitting after making a short row. The hues of pink mesmerized her. Marge came over and checked her work and marveled at her even stitches. After a few minutes, Granny got up to get a glass of Meadow Tea. She looked over at Lavina, who hadn't said a word. So she went to sit next to her.

"Lavina, you alright?"

Silence. Lavina pursed her lips and didn't say a word. Respecting your elders was the Amish way, and Granny felt irritated. If Lavina blamed her for Nathan leaving, why not come out and say it? Confronting problems head-on was also their way. "Let's take a walk, *jah*?"

"*Nee*, I'm tired."

Granny stiffened. "Later on tonight then?"

"I'm going home early. Need to help Maryann."

Granny said a quick casting off prayer. It wasn't her fault Nathan was leaving, and God was in control. She looked over at Colleen who sat on her other side. "So *goot* to have you here."

"I'm glad to be here." Colleen smiled warmly at Granny, and she had to admit, she did feel attached to this *wunderbar* girl. She watched Colleen knit, as she was more advanced than her. But as she did, she noticed cut marks on her arms. "Did you go berry picking in short sleeves?"

"No," Colleen said. "I wore long sleeves, like Ella told me."

"Then how'd you get so cut up?"

To Granny's horror, Colleen burst into tears. Granny put her arm around her. "Want to talk about it?"

Colleen nodded, and they both got up and went into Granny's kitchen. Jeb was sitting in his rocker reading *Pennsylvania Fish and Game*, but his eyes widened as they entered the kitchen.

"What's wrong?" Jeb asked.

"Colleen's upset. Wants to talk, private like."

"I can go..."

"No, that's alright," Colleen said as she brushed away a tear, attempting a smile. "This is your home."

Granny put her hand on Jeb's shoulder. "Maybe you can help, *jah?*"

Jeb looked warmly at Colleen. "What ails you?"

Colleen sniffed and put a Kleenex to her nose. "I was embarrassed. Granny saw my scars." She held out her arms, wrists up. "I'm a cutter, but getting help."

"A cutter?" Jeb asked, softly. "What's that?"

"People who cut themselves on purpose. For me, it's a way of crying. When I feel numb and can't cry, I cut myself and for some odd reason, I feel better."

Jeb took her hands. "But doesn't it hurt?"

"Yes. That's the point. When I feel numb, it's scary. I don't feel human, but when I feel pain, I do."

Granny went over and embraced Colleen. "Child, if you feel numb, why not talk to someone? I do…"

"You feel numb sometimes, too?"

"We all do," Jeb said. "And you're right, it is scary. Especially if you're old and you fear your mind's going."

Colleen kissed Granny on the cheek. "You are so easy to open up to. I've talked to Jerry and Janice about these numb spells, but it took a while. It's when the healing started…"

"So Jerry's helping you?" Jeb asked.

"Yes. And a girlfriend at Forget-Me-Not. She knows about it. When I feel the urge to cut, I tell someone."

"And they make you stop?" Granny asked.

"They talk to me until I don't feel numb and can cry…I can cry now. I've come a long way."

Jeb squeezed her hands. "Well, now you have two other people to talk to. Do you think if we met once a week, and you shared all the pain bottled up, it would help?"

"And we could make pies," Granny offered, embracing Colleen again.

Colleen started to laugh and cry at the same time. "If I spend too much time at Ella's and with you, maybe I'll turn Amish…"

Granny looked at Jeb, eyes aglow.

~*~

That night, Granny took her pink yarn and needles out on the porch, along with an oil lamp. A full moon made it easier to see, but she needed the added light. The scent of roses filled the air and the nightingale sang. She closed her eyes and listened to all the melodies this bird sang. She thought of her girls. They all sang a different song too. Ella a sad and tired song. Though she worked hard to make ends meet, it seemed inevitable that Zach would want to buy land in New York when they visited next week. A sob got caught in her throat, and Granny swallowed it down. How she loved Ella…

And her Nathan moving back to Montana temporarily? Sometimes temporary meant permanent. Granny groaned. Just when she began to accept Lavina and feel she'd be a *goot* match for Nathan. Why Lord? Was there trouble in Montana her son wasn't telling her about?

She took up her needles and began to knit. Doing all knit stitches without trying to figure out how to do a purl made the scarf grow faster. Some little girl, homeless in the USA, could certainly use it as a hat too. Colleen's little one would be homeless if it wasn't for the Baptists opening up a house of refuge. Colleen's scars on her arms ran through her mind and pierced her heart. Hopefully, the more she talked about her feelings as they baked pies and whatnot, she'd never cut herself again.

This Sunday church would be at Roman's, and the announcement of the church district splitting would be announced. Most likely the women would come on her porch and shed tears, and the men would solemnly encourage Jeb with the heavy burden of being a bishop. Granny thought of Fannie as usual. She was like a *mamm* to this dear girl. When Fannie stayed after knitting circle to talk to her, she admitted to trying to diet. Lord, why is Fannie relapsing into her old way of thinking?

Feeling overwhelmed, she bowed her head to say more casting off prayers:

Lord,

Thank you that you hear me when I pray. It's a comfort to know you never change. Jesus Christ, the same yesterday, today, and tomorrow, like the Good Book says.

I'm afraid, Lord, and I give my fear to you. You make me strong in my weak areas. I don't want to be the bishop's wife, but Jeb has drawn the lot. Truth be told, I don't feel worthy. Jeb, he's worthy, but who am I? An old woman who sits out in her rocker at 2:00 a.m. fretting and not trusting you. I'm sorry Lord. Why can't I see you have everything in control? Jeb seems to have a keen understanding of it. Help me see as Jeb sees.

And Lord, as more women come to knitting circle, more problems come too. Was this your higher purpose? Not so much the knitting as helping each other? I did think women would be stronger spun together, but Lord I need more wisdom to help the girls. Lord, I've never heard of anyone intentionally cutting themselves and I don't know what to say. Could just listening make that much of a difference? And what do I say to Fannie? Lord, she needs to listen to her body and eat.

Maybe it's You who needs to speak in the gentle whisper. Lord, please whisper to all my girls how much you care. Give them direction. Lead them by still waters and feed your sheep green grass. You know I love them so…

I cast them all on You in Jesus' name,
Amen

Dear Readers,

Thank you for joining Granny as her knitting circle increases. I leave you with a recipe for Thumbprint Cookies, in case you get company and have nothing to serve, just like Granny. These cookies can be stored in airtight containers or frozen with no jam filling. Simply add jam to imprint and heat in oven for a few minutes.

Karen Anna Vogel

Thumbprint Cookies

1/2 c. butter
1/2 c. shortening
1/2 c. brown sugar
2 egg yolks
1 t. vanilla
2 c. flour
1/2 t. salt

Mix shortening, sugar, egg yolks, and vanilla in bowl. Slowly add flour and salt and mix well. Roll into 1 tablespoon sized ball. Press thumb gently into center. Fill well with jam. Bake at 350 degrees for 15-18 minutes. Cool on cookie rack.

Episode 4

Peaches & Cream

Granny scooped hot peaches out of her blue enamel pot, slid them into a jar, and turned to Colleen. "Now, you need to make sure the top of the jar is clean and dry, so it will seal right." Granny handed the ladle to Lavina. "Can you show Colleen how it's done?"

Granny hoped Lavina would enjoy the company since she hadn't heard from Nathan in three weeks. To her surprise, Lavina was doing well, her nose always in her Bible. But she did need fellowship too, and canning bees held a special place in her heart.

Granny thought of her *mamm,* who only asked her closest friends to bees. They were all gone to glory, but the picture was clear in her mind. They always took a noon meal break and chatted about their *kinner,* and Granny's eyes misted when she thought of how her *mamm* talked so fondly of her. She used to hear through the screen door as a young one, no older than Millie and Tillie.

Did Colleen or Lavina ever hear words of praise from their *mamms*? Well, if they didn't, they'd hear it from her. "You girls are making your Granny mighty proud, in a *goot* way."

Lavina turned and smiled. "I never knew my granny. *Danki.*"

Colleen stared straight ahead, as if in a trance. "I've done this before…"

"What?" Lavina asked. "You've canned?"

Colleen put her hands to her cheeks. "I don't know. I just thought of something as a preschooler."

Granny went over to her breadbox. "It's hot and we all need a break. Come sit down."

Colleen and Lavina obeyed. Granny sliced the bread and put a plateful on the table. "Now, this is the fun part. Hot peaches on homemade bread." She went over to the large stock pot full of peaches, scooped them into a bowl, and sat it on the table. Lavina got up to get plates, but Colleen still seemed to be daydreaming.

"Colleen, are you okay?" Lavina asked.

Granny fetched some Meadow Tea from the icebox. "Drink this." Colleen reached for the tall glass with shaking hands and quickly drank it. Granny wondered if she needed to talk. Talk until the tears came… "What ails you, Colleen?"

Colleen took a deep breath. "You'll think I'm crazy…"

"Never. Now tell Lavina and me what's wrong. Remember, you have friends, *jah*?"

Colleen nodded. "It was probably nothing. I should get back to Forget-Me-Not. Aurora might be missing me."

Granny reached across the table for Colleen's hand. "Aurora's playing with her friends. Janice is watching them. And you wanted to make peach pies later on."

Colleen gave Granny a hollow look. "The more I live here, among the Amish, I keep remembering things, or imagining them. I can't tell."

"What kinds of things?" Lavina asked. "Good or bad?"

Colleen's chin quivered and Granny prayed that this dear girl would learn to cry and open up, never cutting herself again.

"Happy thoughts, but I'm in an Amish home. But there are lots of quilts. So silly."

"How many of these thoughts do you have?" Granny coaxed.

"They just keep coming. When I saw Ella's root cellar, I thought I'd been there before. But with an older Amish woman. Again, I'm a little girl." Colleen put her hands to her cheeks as a tear escaped. "Sometimes I think I'm going mad."

Granny got up and sat on the bench next to Colleen. "Maybe you're remembering a place you visited as a child. Did your *mamm* ever take you to visit an Amish settlement? Popular among the English."

"My mom wasn't there. And she'd never take me to an Amish house."

"Why?" Lavina asked.

"She doesn't like the Amish. Used to ridicule them, but she was either drunk or on drugs."

"What did she say?" Granny prodded.

Another tear slid down her cheek. "She'd tell my dad…" Colleen's eyes grew round and she remained silent.

"She told your dad what?" Lavina asked softly.

Colleen reached for her middle and sobbed. Granny embraced her and pat her back. "Let it out, even if it doesn't make sense. We won't be offended."

Colleen clung to Granny and in between sobs, said, "The Amish ruined my life…."

Her mamm thinks the Amish ruined her life? How could they? Unless… Granny put her hand over her heart. Could her instincts be true about Colleen?

~*~

Lavina listened to the even rhythm of the horse hoofs against the road, and it calmed her heart. Had she been too hard on her *mamm*? Colleen's *mamm* was a drug addict, but hers was always strong. Emotionless, but a constant anchor during her *daed*'s rages. Three weeks and no news through the Amish grapevine was unusual. If they went back to Ohio, surely she would have heard something.

No letter from Nathan either. But for some reason, Lavina didn't panic. Everything she was learning from Maryann about the Good Shepherd seemed to be blotting out the guilt she'd carried. If a sheep strayed from the flock, God would leave the ninety-nine to find the one in danger. He did that for her in the form of Granny and Jeb Weaver. How she blamed Granny for Nathan having to leave, thinking her immoral past had made his parents demand he come home. *Love covers a multitude of sins*, she'd read this morning. If Nathan loved her, he'd only see her as pure.

She pulled the buggy into Maryann's driveway and once again, thanked God for this *wunderbar* family that took her in. Becca ran out the side door in bare feet, a letter in hand. "You got a letter from Montana!"

Nathan. Just the sound of his name made her heart warm and cold at the same time. She took the letter from Becca and got out of the buggy.

"I'll take the horse back to its stall," Becca said. "You enjoy your letter."

Now that Becca was sixteen, she seemed closer in age to Lavina's eighteen years. Nineteen soon. "*Danki* Becca. I won't be long."

Becca had concern etched on her face. "Ever hear the English call the summer 'lazy days'? 'The lazy days of summer'? Why not take a lazy day? You help *mamm* and Granny enough."

"*Ach*, canning bees are fun. Not work at all." She managed a smile. "But *danki*, again."

Becca nodded and then led the horse toward its stall behind the house. Lavina looked down at the letter. It was Nathan's handwriting. He'd learned from Roman how to leave her little messages in woodpecker holes…usually words of love and encouragement. But what would this letter hold?

Lavina walked to the front porch since no one was on it, sat on the cedar rocker Nathan made for her before he left, and opened the letter:

Lavina,

When I think of you, I imagine you at a canning bee, and I hope you're having fun.

I need to tell you something. My daed did need me on the farm, but he had other reasons to want me home. I never told you, but I was engaged two years ago. I was so young, but I courted Sarah since I can remember. But she refused to be baptized, and instead, left the Amish. She wanted me to leave with her, but I refused. Well, she came back, fully repentant, and will be baptized this fall.

I came to Smicksburg to find a wife, saying there was no one in Montana for me. But it was a half-truth. I just couldn't get over Sarah, so I left. But I found love again with you. And I do love you, Lavina, but I feel torn. Part of me still loves Sarah.

I'm so sorry you have to hear this, but I need time. My daed said my heart will keep turning to the woman I really love over a period of time. Right now, like I said, it's divided.

I'll write again soon.

Nathan

Lavina couldn't understand why Colleen had a hard time crying, because tears freely came and blotted the letter. She ran into the house to look for Maryann.

~*~

Ruth wiped the rim of the Mason Jar and placed the lid and ring on top. Janice said if you turned jars upside down they would seal without a water bath, and she decided to try this method. She placed the jar on the tea towels that lined the kitchen counter. While most women were enjoying canning bees, she liked the solitude canning brought, although many hands did make work light. But peaches she relished, for the whole kitchen smelled like an orchard.

She heard a knock on the side door. Ella peaked in. "Need some help?"

"You're home!" Ruth exclaimed, running to her friend. "I've missed you so." Ruth quickly took off her apron and went to embrace her dear friend, but was surprised that Zach stood behind her. "Zach, welcome back. Luke's in the workshop with my *daed*."

"I'll get him. Important news." Zach turned and ran toward the shop.

"News?" Ruth asked. "About New York?"

Ella took Ruth's hands. "*Jah*. I have to admit, I loved it."

Ruth wanted to hold on to Ella's hands forever. How would she manage without her best friend living nearby? Letters would be sent regularly, but it wouldn't be the same. "Did Zach like New York, too?"

Before Ella could speak, Zach popped into the kitchen, Luke following. "I love it up there, and land is cheap."

Ruth went over to the peaches she'd canned. As she opened a can up, she shot up a casting off prayer. *Lord, I can't bear this. Help me.* She went to her icebox and took out fresh cream. "Who wants peaches and cream?"

"I do," they all said in unison, laughter following.

Ruth placed four bowls on the table, scooping hot peaches into them and drizzling cream on top.

"Where'd you get your peaches?" Ella asked.

"*Ach*, the fruit auction. *Mamm* and I bought too many bushels. Do you want one?"

Zach cleared his throat. "Will be hard to move all the canned goods to New York."

Luke leaned forward, arms crossed. "So you're moving?"

Zach looked at Ella with a grin. "We found land. Five-hundred acres."

"In Marathon?" Luke asked.

"*Nee*, in a new settlement outside Cherry Creek. Thirty families moved to a town called East Otto, and the land's so rich, it's black. In a big valley, so the land is rich in silt."

Ruth feared tears would come, so she got up and took a pitcher of Meadow Tea out of the icebox. *Lord, help me! I should be happy for them…* She placed four glasses on the table, along with the pitcher, and then sat on the bench next to Luke, needing him near.

Ella's eyebrows shot up. "Ruth, you don't look *goot*."

Luke squeezed Ruth's hand. "I'm sure Ruth's feeling the same way I am. We'll miss *yinz*."

Zach's blue eyes twinkled. "Not if you come with us." He clapped his hands and laughed. "Remember how we dreamed of having a dairy farm as kids? It could happen."

Luke froze, peaches halfway to his mouth. "What?"

"The land is *dirt* cheap," Zach said, laughing. "And the *kinner* will have plenty of room to play…"

"They have room now," Ruth said, thinking of the new slide and swing set her *daed* just finished making for Micah.

"I know, but this way, they'll have an inheritance, too. Luke and I can pass land on to our *kinner*. What greater gift?"

"Can't you find land in Smicksburg?" Ruth blurted. "Maybe up toward Troutville or over in Volant?"

"Not as cheap as New York," Zach said. "And the state will give us a generous amount for organic milk. We'd all do well."

Ruth glanced at Luke. His eyes were bright, just like his brothers. "Luke, we're building on to this house, *jah*? The shell is up for the addition."

Zach put his hand up. "Don't give us an answer now. No pressure. But we would like to go over the numbers and see if you'd be interested. Then you'd have to see the land for yourself."

Luke yanked at his blond beard. "How about your place? Will you sell it to Uncle Otis?"

"Selling it to Hezekiah. Already shook hands." Zach took off his straw hat and fanned his face. "He deserves to have it. Helps me so much."

Ruth felt nauseated. Moving to New York *and* not knowing what to do with Uncle Otis. The man had been a handful on his brief visit, and her *daed* and Jeb had to have words with him. She had to admit, she was relieved when he went back to Ohio, for the time being. But it was their responsibility to care for him in his old age. She stared at her peaches. How could she leave Smicksburg? How could Ella do it so cheerfully? Was New York that *wunderbar*?

~*~

Jenny rubbed her fingers over the rabbit's velvety ears. "*Danki* Joe."

"*Jah*, Joe, so nice of you," Roman added. "Want some peaches?"

"Nope, just wanted to bring over the rabbit for my favorite seven year old." He winked at Jenny. "And, get out of the house…"

He sighed as he sat on the porch step next to Jenny. "Marge is going to church again?"

Joe chuckled. "You don't miss a beat, kiddo." He nudged Jenny. "Ya, getting all religious on me."

"And you don't like Baptist?" Roman looked up as he leaned against the porch rail.

"Well, I don't mean any disrespect to you, but I think religion is a crutch for weak people."

"*Jah*, you're right. My father-in-law, Jonas, has crutches and needs them. No shame in it."

Joe wiped his brow. "I mean God is a psychological crutch. You know. For weak-minded people."

Jenny giggled. "If God's a crutch, He must be a big one."

"I don't mean a real crutch, honey." Joe looked down at Roman. "I don't want to put doubts in her mind, since you're all religious."

Roman smirked. "Jenny can hold her own. She knows God in here." He pointed to his heart. "I think the religion you're talking about is the one Jesus hated."

"Jesus…hated?"

"*Jah*, he called the Pharisees hypocrites and sons of the devil."

"Who were the Pharisees?"

"Religious leaders in Jesus' time."

Jenny sat up straight "*Daed*, Joe said his dad is a hypocrite. Is he a son of the devil?"

"It's not for us to judge a person's heart. Most likely we'd be too harsh. God's longsuffering."

Joe slouched. "What's longsuffering?"

Jenny put up two fingers. "It's two words put together. A compound word. Long and suffering. So, it's someone who suffers for a long time."

Roman pat Jenny's head. "The closer to eight you get, the smarter, *jah*?" He pulled on her braid playfully. "You're right. It's what your new *mamm* was with you. She was patient."

Jenny slipped a smile. "*Jah*, she was, and I made her suffer for a long time...."

"*Nee*, only a few months."

Joe rolled his eyes. "Jenny's easy to like. My dad, well, he's a hypocrite...."

~*~

Fannie sliced peaches and tried to turn her mind from the fact that she was no longer in the same church district as Granny. She understood the *Gmay* got too big and needed to keep under two-hundred, but to not see Granny and her knitting friends every other Sunday jabbed at her heart more than she thought possible. She remembered sitting on

Granny's knee when a *kinner*, as she attempted to stop her fidgeting. Fannie smiled through blurry eyes; she'd acted up in church just to sit on the dear woman's lap.

And the Amish grapevine was faster than the internet, as Janice always joked. Word had it that Zach and Ella loved New York. How could Ella love a place so far from Smicksburg? Wouldn't she miss the knitting circle? Ella was someone who she looked to as a role model too, being a little older, and someone who lived-out her faith. How many times had Ella helped her with her weight obsession? And now being pregnant, and her mind plagued with old fears that resurrected themselves...she needed Ella. She needed all the girls in the circle.

Fannie tapped her fingers on the counter. Being fidgety never ended....She took off her apron and went into her living room, propped her feet up, and picked up her knitting basket. The new alpaca yarn she got was soft and as she knit one, purl one, she let the yarn calm her. The rhythm of the needles along with the scent of peonies wafting in from the open window took the tension out of her neck, but the pain in her lower back continued. Most likely from over exerting herself canning peaches.

As she knit, she struggled to keep her eyes open. She almost drifted off, but a sharp pain in her abdomen made her yelp. Fannie grabbed her middle and screamed, and then the room began to swirl.

~*~

Later that night, Marge ran from her front porch to meet Granny. "Oh, Deborah, we heard. You don't even have to ask. Janice and I will drive the knitting circle down to the hospital."

Granny dabbed her eyes with her handkerchief. "I met you there."

"What?"

"Remember? I met you in the hospital. So glad I did."

Marge's eyes softened. "Me too. Changed my whole life…"

"I'll tell the girls you can pick us up at seven. Is that okay?"

"Sure. See you then." Marge charged back into her house and headed right to her woodstove. She stirred the peaches furiously so they wouldn't burn along the edges. It was times like this she wanted a gas stove. She'd come to Smicksburg with visions of *Little House on the Prairie* dancing in her head, but reality was setting in.

Joe came in the back door. "Something burning?"

"No, I caught it in time but I'm sick of this woodstove. It heats up the whole kitchen. We need a gas one."

To her shock, Joe started to laugh. Being upset, hot and in a hurry was not a good combination. She spun around and eyed her husband. "What's so funny?" she snapped.

"You are, Mrs. Ingalls. Never thought it would be this hard, huh?"

"Joseph, I am not in the mood. Fannie's in the hospital and I need to drive my Amish friends to the Indiana Hospital." She went over to her icebox, took out some cheese, and tossed it to Joe. "Have this for dinner. I didn't cook anything."

Joe stood as still as a statue.

"Oh, don't be in shock. I cook every night..." Marge wondered how much more she could take today.

"So, you're not going to church?" Joe asked in a monotone voice.

"No, and neither is Janice. We have to haul half of Smicksburg to the hospital."

Joe sat down slowly. "But Janice is the pastor's wife. Won't he be mad?"

"Why would he?"

"Because she missed a service...."

Marge tried to understand Joe's meaning, but was stumped. "Joe, what's running around in that mind of yours?"

"Being whooped, that's what. If I missed a Wednesday night service, my rear-end would ache for a week."

Marge went over and sat at the table next to Joe. "I've been trying to tell you that these people aren't like that. It's love God first, not rules and religion. Don't you understand?"

Joe took a deep breath. "Kind of hard to forget how much church messed me up."

Marge snapped her fingers. "There, you said it. The church your dad pastored messed you up, not God."

"I didn't say that."

"No, but I know you. You're comparing everything you see from the Smicksburg Baptist Church to your dad's and seeing that you were raised in a dead church."

"A dead church?" He looked out the window. "May be on to something. Not much life in it, that's for sure." He met her gaze. "Have to admit, I've never met Christians who seemed free."

Marge reached for his hand. "Free from what?"

"Rules. I mean, Janice is missing church when the doors are open. My mom would have heard about it for a year."

"Seems to me like people are more important than church. The Amish help me see the church is simply a group of people gathered to worship. They don't even have churches."

"I know. It's given me a lot to think about. Not saying I'm a believer, but if Jenny has her way…"

"Jenny? What's she got to do with your faith?"

Joe snickered. "She's a female preacher, so the Amish can't say they don't have them. That little girl thinks it's a pity I don't believe in God. She gave me some of her books about Jesus. Really touched my heart, have to admit."

Marge grinned. "So those little books you read, all solid colored, are Jenny's?"

Joe pointed at her. "They're schoolbooks. *Pathway Readers.* Do not tell a soul, understand?"

Marge felt like laughing, just the thought of it. Joe had been sitting up reading by the oil lamp, but when she asked what he was reading, he's just say, 'nothing'. Hopefully the books Jenny gave him would help him see the church he grew up in tainted his view of God: destroyed it.

~*~

Fannie clenched Melvin's hand as they waited for the doctor. *How could I be so vain? So stupid?* To think she was fat, not eating when hungry; God's way of telling a pregnant woman the baby needs food. Is this what her body image problem had come down to? And how would Melvin forgive her if he knew?

She heard a faint knock on the hospital room door, and thinking it was the doctor, the room started to swirl. But she managed to make out a group of women. She laid her head back on the pillow and closed her eyes to stop the dizziness.

"How are you feeling?"

Fannie felt warmth in her heart. "Granny," she whispered. "Glad you're here."

"We're all here. The whole knitting circle was concerned and needed to come."

"*Jah*, we're here to help carry your burden," Ella said.

Fannie opened her eyes and looked over at Ella. "Wish you wouldn't go…"

Ella kissed her cheek. "You're tired. Rest now."

Janice leaned forward. "You want me to elevate this bed so you can sit up?"

"I keep getting dizzy, so do it slowly." Fannie concentrated on the lights above her and held her queasy stomach. When she was elevated enough to see everyone, she put her hands over her face and wept. How could she face these women, having starved her baby to death?

Colleen came closer. "It's good to cry, Fannie, instead of bottling it up. Believe me."

Granny gave a forced smile at Colleen. "*Jah*, get it out. Cleansing tears."

Fannie gripped the sheets on the bed. "No tears will cleanse me!" she blurted.

"What needs cleansed?" asked a burly nurse who sauntered into the room. "Something wrong?"

Melvin got up. "Please, can we see the doctor?"

"He's in the next room. Will be over in a jiffy." She took Fannie's temperature and pulse. When she took her blood pressure, she asked, "Do Amish always bring this many visitors?"

"*Jah*," Granny said. "Took three cars to get us all up here." Granny looked over at Joe. "Really appreciate all the help."

"It was nothing," Joe said.

"Absolutely," Marge added. "We're not Amish...yet." She looked at Joe, then burst into laughter. "Just kidding."

"Never know," Colleen said. "The more I'm in Smicksburg, the more I like the Amish ways."

Fannie heard the doctor's voice and fear gripped her like never before. The doctor asked her if she minded the visitors hearing what he had to say. She nodded. "We're all like family. Go ahead."

"Well, I have good news. You're still pregnant."

Melvin shot up. "What?"

The tall, lanky doctor put a hand on Melvin's shoulder. "Your wife expelled old blood. Lots of it. But the baby's fine. Strong heartbeat."

Fannie couldn't contain the good news. Melvin bent down to hug her and she rested in his embrace, letting the tears flow freely.

"You are a little anemic, though. Eat lots of leafy greens, but I'm putting you on prescription iron."

"Doctor," Fannie said between sobs. "I'll eat everything and anything for my *boppli*."

The doctor's eyebrows shot up. "Well, don't eat just *anything*. Some things aren't good for the baby, or *boppli* as you Amish call them."

Fannie nodded. "That's what I meant. I'll be eating plenty and *goot*." She met Granny's eyes. The light, blue eyes that could see her pain without her even saying a word. The woman who helped her overcome her body image problems, and when they came back to haunt her, overpowering her at times; Granny was still right there to help her get through…along with her knitting circle.

~*~

Granny awoke to someone pounding on the side door. She shot up, looked at her wind-up clock on the nightstand, and panicked. Nine o'clock? How could she have slept through half the day? And where was Jeb? Did he get his breakfast?

She heard talking and quickly changed into her dress and apron. She combed her long gray hair and gathered it at the nape of her neck, and then took her long barrettes and pinned it into a swirl. This way, her massive amount of hair would stay in place under her *kapp*.

Taking some water from the basin she filled last night, Granny splashed her face, helping her wake up. Then, as usual, she took her Tea Tree Oil soap to cleanse, and made her way quickly out to her company.

When she walked into the kitchen, she didn't like the look of Jeb's face. What was wrong? Ella, Zach, Ruth, and Luke all sat at the table, drinking coffee.

"Morning," Jeb said.

"*Ach*, why didn't you get me up?" She put her hands on her warm cheeks, embarrassed.

"Deborah, you were up late with Fannie. You're no spring chicken anymore…"

Granny ignored his comment, went to the blue speckle ware coffeepot and poured a cup. "So *goot* of *yinz* to visit." She turned to see that Ruth had tears in her eyes. "What happened?"

Jeb pat the bench next to him, and she took a seat. "Ella and Zach found land in New York. They want to split it with Luke and Ruth."

Granny immediately started to remind herself to breathe. Deep breaths had helped her through harder times, and calmed a body down. It also gave her time to think of what to say. But she couldn't find words. Just like when she was speechless when her sons moved away. She'd heard Ella and Zach found land, but didn't think they'd move. *Now Ruth and Luke, too?*

The pendulum clock ticking and the coffee pot percolating were the only sounds in the room. Jack breathed heavily through the side screen door. "I need to feed the dog," Granny said. Before anyone could stop her, she quickly made her way outside to see her dog. How this black lab was able to calm her body down was a mystery. No wonder Suzy was so upset seeing her little Mollie decline. She went to the old metal milk churn where Jack's food was stored, and taking the scoop, she filled his bowl. Granny stoked his shiny back, as he chomped on his food. "My comforting friend," she whispered.

"Granny, are you alright?" Ella asked as she joined her on the porch.

Ruth followed, a hanky held up to her eyes. "Luke and I aren't sure we're leaving. We came for Jeb's advice, since he's our bishop now."

Granny sat on a cedar chair, still not able to speak. How could she tell them she'd miss them, since they were like daughters? Amish folk moved all the time, mostly for land. Always land. The People were being scattered for lack of farmland. It was a cross the Amish were learning to carry.

Ruth and Ella sat on the bench across from Granny. The fear in their eyes made her wonder if she was scaring them, making them think she was ill. "So, you found land at a *goot* price?"

"*Jah*, and it's in a large valley, so it's rich," Ella said. "It's always been Zach's dream…mine, too."

Granny met Ruth's gaze. She knew Ruth was planning on building on to the *dawdyhaus* next to her parents. And she was expecting. As another tear slid down Ruth's cheek, Granny couldn't help but join her in shedding a tear. Tears cleansed a body…

Ruth got up, bent down and hugged Granny.

"We don't have to move," Luke said, as he came on to the porch. "We're just talking about it, Ruth." He put his hand on her shoulder. "God won't lead you where His grace can't keep you."

Ruth turned to embrace Luke. Granny took in the words Luke just spoke. It was a saying among the People she'd heard often, but it took on new meaning when you had to believe it. Would God give her the grace to carry her through yet another valley? And would her girls be carried, too, since they've never moved from Smicksburg and didn't know the loneliness that came with a new settlement?

Zach soon appeared and sat next to Ella. "We didn't mean to upset you, Granny."

Again, Granny put her hands over her warm cheeks, most likely beet red. "Zach, as long as you get lots of advice before making such a change, you have my blessing. But remember, the grass always looks greener on the other side."

"But it is greener in New York," Zach said with a grin.

"In the summer," Jeb blurted. "But the winters are brutal. Best be talking to folks in New York when *yinz* go up."

Granny's mouth dropped. "So you've already decided to all go up and visit?"

They all nodded, and Granny lowered her head and said a long casting off prayer.

~*~

Ruth clung to Granny before she got into the buggy. "We'll think about all you said. Zeal without knowledge isn't *goot*." She looked over at Jeb. "*Danki* for the advice, Bishop."

Jeb grinned. "You best be calling me just 'Jeb.'"

"I'll see you tonight, at knitting circle," Ruth said to Granny. "Knitting really calms me down, and I need it."

"And the homeless need hats and scarves." Granny grinned. "Will we ever advance from making scarves?"

"I don't know. Glad Suzy doesn't give grades out like in school."

Ruth made her way to the waiting buggy and waved good-bye, along with Luke, Ella, and Zach. Granny attempted a broad smile, but could only produce a forced one, at best. "Change. Does it ever stop knocking at my door?"

Jeb put his hand on Granny's shoulder. "Would you want it to? Life could get boring."

"I like it boring. Nice and steady, like how the plants grow. We need to keep in pace with nature. Zach's being impulsive."

"He's a man who wants a farm."

"Well, we're not apt to agree on this, Old Man."

"*Oma*! *Opa*! He grew some last night," Jenny nearly sang as she skipped through the yard, holding her rabbit. "Look!"

Granny looked at the black and white rabbit. The baby rabbit did look bigger than yesterday. She pet its head. "Could spin some nice angora yarn from its fur."

Jenny pulled the rabbit back. "Would it hurt?"

"*Nee*, does it hurt when you get a haircut?" Jeb asked.

Jenny narrowed her eyes. "I don't know. Never had my hair cut."

"Well, I can tell you it doesn't hurt." He pat Jenny on the head. "So, Jonas tells me you'll have a surprise today. Can you guess what it is?"

Jenny held her bunny to her cheek. "*Nee*, but I'm afraid."

"Of what, honey?" Granny asked. "The surprise is *goot*."

"Jonas doesn't want to come live here. I heard *Daed* and *Mamm* talking. And when he comes over, he seems mean."

"Sad, not mad," Granny said. "Sometimes when people are sad, they look mad. Understand?"

"I'll try to. Going to be eight in the fall, and need to grow up…"

Jeb put both hands on her shoulders. "Even when you're grown up, change is hard. Scary." He looked over at Granny.

"*Jah*, we don't know what's going to happen around the next corner. Can only trust God to hold our hand tight. Things work out in the end."

Lizzie ran barefoot down her porch steps and over to them. "Jenny, I need some help with breakfast dishes." She turned to Granny. "The girls will be over around eleven. Will only be gone an hour."

Granny put a hand up. "You and Roman go out and have a nice long picnic." She winked. "You deserve time alone."

~*~

Roman spread out the blanket under the oak tree in Old Smicksburg Park. "This spot will always be ours."

Lizzie put the basket down and sat next to Roman. "You saved me. When you read the note, you didn't reject me."

Roman drew her close. "Just wish I'd found it ten years earlier. *Mamm* is right in calling me Mr. Darcy. I was so proud."

"I should have told you, but couldn't, is all." She leaned her head on Roman's strong shoulder. How she wished she could turn back time. After the attempted assault, she'd felt so unclean, she couldn't speak. Not even to Roman, her fiancé. So she'd put a note in the woodpecker hole in their tree, thinking he'd find it, like all the other letters. But he didn't, and when she broke the engagement off, he soon met Abigail.

"Lizzie, you know you can tell me anything now, *jah*?"

She squeezed his arm. "Of course."

"Then what's ailing you?"

"Nothing. I'm fit as a fiddle."

He tilted her head up and she looked into his unflinching brown eyes. "Lizzie, in your heart. What ailing that sweet heart of yours?"

She held his gaze. "You'll think I'm selfish."

"Never. You can tell me if you don't want your *daed* to build next to us."

Lizzie's eyebrows shot up. "I love *Daed*. I want him near."

"Then what is it?" Roman took off his hat and ran his fingers through his chestnut brown hair. "Remember, no secrets."

"I know. I kept one for too long. But I've learned to speak up if I'm upset. To talk about things…."

"Then why aren't you?"

Lizzie was touched that Roman had prepared a basket full of her favorite cheeses and homemade bread, fresh from Granny's oven. This dear man could see her heart. They were becoming one, more each day. If she held back, hiding her feelings, their hearts couldn't be melded together. "Roman…I'm so afraid."

She felt his hand on her cheek. "Of what?"

"That I'm barren. When I see Ruth and Fannie pregnant, well, I worry."

He drew her near and kissed her gently. "We've only been married since May."

"Fannie got pregnant on her wedding night. Lots of girls do, but I'm an old woman…thirty-three now. And maybe that's the reason."

Lizzie looked up at him and saw Roman purse his lips. He always did that when he tried to hide a smile. "You think I'm being silly, *jah*?"

He nodded. "And impatient." Roman reached for the basket and cut her a slice of tomato-basil cheese. "But *danki* for sharing that with me. We can pray about a *boppli* together."

She took the cheese and bread Roman handed her. How she loved this man. She could share anything with him now. If only she'd opened her mouth ten years ago. How God worked everything out for the good was a miracle in itself. She loved her step-daughters in a way that surprised her. It came so naturally. And when she won Jenny's approval, Lizzie felt such fulfillment. Being a *mamm* was always her dream, and she hoped Roman was right. She was just being impatient…

~*~

Colleen walked behind Janice as they made their way up a long, steep sidewalk. "Seriously, I'm learning plenty about the Amish from Granny and Ella."

Janice kept on climbing. "But you said you like to crochet, too. Emma crochets rugs, and you could help."

"But I'm helping Ella," Colleen said, trying to understand why Janice was in such a hurry to steer her toward this Emma Miller. "And Hezekiah…"

Janice spun around, almost losing her footing. "Hezekiah?" She put her hands on her hips. "Colleen, what's going on?"

"Nothing. Just making lots of friends."

"You are *not* Amish. Of all the girls at the house, why do I have to keep reminding you of that?"

Colleen knew Janice meant well, but she was an adult. Janice hovered too much. "I'm fascinated with the Amish. Is that so bad?"

Janice narrowed her eyes. "Fascinated with the Amish or Hezekiah?"

Colleen stopped in her tracks. "Janice. I'm twenty-one. Almost twenty-two…"

"And I have eyes," Janice said. "Hezekiah is a very handsome young man. I've seen Englishers fall for an Amish person before. It rarely works out. Be careful." Janice turned and made her way up the side steps to the white store, attached to the huge farmhouse.

Colleen followed and tried to put any notions of Hezekiah out of her mind. Until Janice mentioned how handsome he was, she'd never really thought of him as more than a friend…but now that she thought of him, he listened so well…

Janice walked in without knocking, and soon two women came from a door that led to the main house. There was also a window, most likely left there from when the store was attached. A large oak table like Granny's was in the kitchen. And a black cook stove, icebox. If it wasn't for the light blue walls, it would be Granny's kitchen. Colleen nodded to both women as she turned to eye all the items for sale: baskets, Amish dolls, aprons, rag rugs…purses. She took one of the purses off its hook. It looked like a Vera Bradley but when she opened it there were no tags.

One of the Amish women came over to her. "Do you like that?"

Colleen always tried not to stare when she met another Amish person, but she couldn't help it, especially with the women. She always wondered if they needed make-up or not. But this woman's eyes were a warm brown with thick lashed. She didn't need mascara. She could use foundation to smooth her complexion, and some hair dye, since the small portion of hair that showed was graying. When she realized she was staring, she quickly asked, "How much is the purse?"

"All the items have a price tag pinned to them. I think the purses are eighteen."

Colleen found the white paper pinned to the purse. It read, "$18.00 / Iva Miller."

"I made that one myself. I'm Iva Miller." The Amish woman beside her beamed. "Do you want it?"

Colleen looked over at Janice. One other thing about Forget-Me-Not was the Dave Ramsey course, required by anyone who was a resident. Living debt free was something Jerry was adamant about, but sometimes she felt he went too far, keeping her checkbook. Again, she felt like a child, but then scolded herself for not being grateful. She looked at Iva. "I'm sorry. Can't afford it right now."

"Well, maybe you can learn to make one. I hear you want to help make crocheted rag rugs. I can easily show you how to make a purse while you're here."

Janice walked over along with the other woman. "Colleen, this is Marie. She makes the crocheted rugs, along with her mother."

Colleen looked at Marie, who looked so similar to Iva. But if Marie was Emma's daughter, how old was Emma?

The confusion on her face must have registered. Marie grinned. "You came to meet my *mamm, jah*? Since it's Emma's

Quilt Shop?" Without waiting for a response she continued. "Iva and I are sisters. Emma's our *mamm*."

"Emma needs to sell those herbs she takes." Janice said. "Must have powerful anti-aging powers because she looks your age."

Iva, the jovial one, put up her hand as if in protest. "So, Marie, we look as old as *mamm*. Must be raising so many *kinner*."

"I didn't mean it like that," Janice laughed..

Iva chuckled, making her belly under her black apron jiggle. "I know. We come from a big family, and make big families." She patted her stomach. "This is number thirteen. Will make a baker's dozen."

Colleen openly gawked. "You're having your thirteenth child? Any twins?"

"No. I've given birth twelve times. This will be thirteen. *Mamm* gave birth fourteen times, but had fifteen *kinner*."

"I have only eight," Marie meekly added.

Janice turned to look at quilted wall-hangings, leaving Colleen time to chat to the two women. "Marie, eight is a lot of kids."

"Well, we're hoping for more."

Colleen knew if she was a cat, she'd be dead, because she was so curious. "So, how many grandchildren does Emma Miller have?"

The two women looked at each other, faces serious. Marie put up one hand and started to raise fingers, mentally counting. Iva threw her hands in the air. "I lose track. Over a hundred, last count. But we don't know all the *kinner* because some of our siblings left the Amish…"

The look of pain on both women's faces was undeniable. Janice walked back over, a basket in her hand. "Didn't one of your siblings marry an Outsider?"

"*Jah*, she did. In a bad state, she is," Iva said. "How we loved her, but she and another sister left us for the outside world."

Colleen frowned, uncomprehending. If you loved each other, it would be unconditional. She loved Aurora on good and bad days. "I don't understand shunning," she blurted out, immediately regretting it. "I mean, my mom talked about it, for some reason. Thought it was cruel."

"Did she have an Amish friend who was shunned?" Marie asked.

Colleen never could understand her mom's ranting behavior towards the Amish. "I don't know. She always said they ruined her life. But my mom's on drugs. Not the good kind, though. So maybe she was high."

Marie folded their hands and looked down. Iva put a hand on her sister's shoulder.

"I'm sorry. I didn't mean to shock you," Colleen said.

Marie slowly looked up. "Never mind me. Memories of my sisters who left still sting at times, even after all these years. Shunning is something that hurts us all."

~*~

Granny heard the sound of flying stones and the rumble of a diesel engine. She put down her knitting needles and sighed. Her little break was over. These little knitting vacations, as she named them, brought peace and took the tension out of her neck. Only twenty minutes a day of knitting was supposed to be good for your health, according to Suzy. So, sitting and knitting after the noon meal was something she started as a daily ritual.

But now Joe was here to deliver lumber for Jonas' new place. Change again. Would it be easy having Jonas as a neighbor? Would it be hard on Lizzie and Roman? Jonas had been cantankerous since Lizzie got married in May. Fannie found him hard to live with….Would they?

Joe came from around his large Silverado truck and opened the door to let Jonas out. Jonas soon made his way over to Granny. "Hi Deborah. Where's Roman?"

"He and Lizzie haven't come back from their picnic yet."

"But I said I'd be here with the lumber at one…."

Joe shielded his eyes from the sun. "Can't unload the lumber myself. Is Jeb around?"

"Went to visit someone. Bishop's duties."

Jenny ran from Granny's house. "Hi Joe."

"Hi Sweet Pea. How's my favorite Amish little girl?" Tillie and Millie came out on the porch and stood beside Jenny. Joe quickly added. "And here's the rest of my favorite Amish girls." He winked at Jenny. "Jonas has something to tell you."

"Is it our surprise?" Jenny scratched the side of her head, attempting a smile. "Lumber?"

Jonas leaned on his arm braces and made his way closer to the porch. "Well, lumber can be made into many things, *jah*?"

Jenny nodded.

"Can you guess what some of this lumber is for?" Jonas asked, eyes aglow.

Jenny shook her head.

"Guess," Jonas said.

The girls looked at Granny, but she'd already gone back to knitting. "*Oma*, we need a hint," Millie begged.

Granny put down the pink yarn. "It's something you've wanted for a long time. Jonas found out about it."

Tillie's eyes grew round. She jumped up and down. "A tree house!"

Jonas laughed. "You're right. I got extra lumber and workers will make you a tree house. But we need pictures of what kind of tree house you want."

Tillie ran down the steps and hugged Jonas' middle, almost tipping him over. "*Danki!*"

Jenny and Millie took each other's hands and jumped up and down. "A tree house! A real tree house," they chirped in unison. "*Danki* Jonas. *Danki.*"

"Now, where do you girls want it built? Which tree?"

"Our tree," Jenny said. "The one on the side of the house.

Granny grimaced. If Jonas built onto the house, that tree would have to be chopped down. The girls all pointed to their beloved maple tree that stood on the right side of the house. Jonas's expression fell.

"What's wrong?" Jenny asked. "Don't you like our tree? It's strong enough for our tire swing…"

He looked over at Joe and then Granny. "Well, if that's the tree you've picked, then we best be unloading the lumber by it. As soon as Roman shows up."

The girls all joined hands and jumped up and down, chanting, "We're gonna have a tree house" over and over. Granny's heart swelled with love and hope. Jonas had his heart set on building onto the right side of Roman's house, nearer to the fishing hole. But he just gave his word, and she knew he'd keep it. How Roman would feel about it was another matter, but for now, she hadn't seen the girls so animated in a long while, and she put her knitting down and watched the girls.

~*~

Joe dug his hands in his blue jean pockets. Jonas showed him the blue print for the new addition. Well, it was handwritten, not done by an architect, but plans were in motion. This man who had lots of upper body strength due to using arm crutches would certainly get more of a workout going to Jeb's fishing hole. How could he make such a rash decision?

He went over to Jonas and asked again where he needed to park the truck to unload the wood. Jonas pointed to the maple tree, and Joe wondered if he should wait for Roman to show up, but there was something going on here he didn't understand. Jonas' word was like a done deal. He asked Jonas to speak with him privately, and they took a short walk across the yard.

"Jonas, I don't get it," Joe admitted. "Kids are spoiled in America, but I thought the Amish were different."

Jonas cocked his head to one side. "Say that again?"

"Everything's revolving around the girls and their special tree. Isn't that being spoiled?"

"Well, I look at it like this. These girls have had lots of change, and it's hard for them. Just want to help carry that burden a little."

Joe gawked. "But you're going through more change, and it's a burden for you to walk to the fishing hole. Sorry, don't mean to bring that up, but you are a, ah…"

"Cripple. Say it. It's the truth." He shifted his weight. "I keep reading *My Utmost for His Highest,* the book I told you about. Chambers says, 'If you do wrestle with God, you will be crippled all the rest of your life'." Jonas attempted to put a hand on his heart. "I'm not a cripple in here. Are you?"

"What do you mean?"

"Well, all kinds of things can just cripple or keep us from walking on the inside. I struggle with bitterness and self-pity, but I struggle until I win. You say you don't believe in God, so you struggle with that disbelief of yours. You're more of a cripple than me."

Joe let out a nervous laugh. "That's ridiculous. Lots of atheists are happy."

"I don't believe it," Jonas said. "Bad things happen all the time. I lost my wife and have MS. My house burnt down after my wife died. Don't see how anyone can get through trials without God."

Joe shrugged his shoulders. "We're all entitled to our own beliefs."

"And some are wrong…Only one way to God, and that's through Jesus."

Joe wished he wasn't talking to an Amish man who was also a cripple, or he'd deck Jonas at this point. The gall to say Christianity was the only way to God. "So, you think only Christians are going to so-called heaven?"

"What are you going to do about Jesus?" Jonas asked.

"What?"

"Oh, people make lots of excuses for not believing in him. Some say he was a good teacher, but would a good teacher lie? And some of the things Jesus said made people think he was a lunatic. So what do you think about Jesus? Was he a liar, lunatic…or the Lord?"

Joe snickered. "Did your buddy Chambers say all that? Sounds pretty profound."

Jonas' eyes twinkled. "C.S. Lewis. Have his book, *Mere Christianity* over at my place. Want to read it?"

Joe nodded. "If it makes you happy. But don't tell anyone. I am an atheist."

"So was Lewis…"

~*~

Granny slowly scooped Peach Pocket Pie into bowls, Lizzie beside her topping each with cream and sugar. Feeling like she needed to crawl in bed, she arched her back and took in a deep breath. "So, Lizzie, Roman eased your mind some?"

"Well, I'm still worried. But it feels better that Roman knows."

Granny stopped and looked over at her beautiful daughter-in-law. "He loves you, Lizzie. Whether you can have *kinner* or not."

Lizzie fumbled with the metal milk pitcher and spilled some on the oak table. "*Ach*, so clumsy."

Granny took a clean towel and mopped up the liquid. "You didn't spill much, and there's more from where that came from." She bit her lower lip and observed Lizzie. "I'm sorry. What I said upset you. I'm not saying your barren, just that Roman loves you unconditionally."

Lizzie's eyes brimmed with tears. "I love him too, and want to have a little Roman running around. I know he wants a son."

"Cast your cares upon the Lord…"

Lizzie grinned. "I know. Because He cares for us. 1 Peter 5:7."

Granny continued to fill bowls. "I'm having to cast lots of things on God. I see Jeb casting for fish out there over and over again, but I think I cast more than him, if you know what I mean."

Lizzie nodded. "I sure do."

Jenny ran in from the side door. "*Mamm*, Janice feels light-headed."

"Pour her a cup of Meadow Tea. *Oma* has some in the icebox," Lizzie said. "Must be her low blood sugar."

"Menopause, but Janice won't face it. She comes over and gets hot flashes so bad she has to run outside to get fresh air. When your hormones are unbalanced, you can experience lots of things."

"Like what?" Lizzie asked. "I mean, I have dizzy spells and hot flashes, too."

Granny shooed a fly. "Lizzie, you're thirty-three. You're not going through menopause."

"Remember how Sarah Yoder went through it at thirty? She was glad she got married and had her *kinner*..."

Granny walked over to Lizzie and put her hand on her shoulders. "Lizzie, you are fine. You hear me? You're young and healthy." She stroked her face. "Nice rosy cheeks."

Lizzie embraced her. "*Danki.*"

Ruth came in the side door. "Need some help?"

Granny smiled. "You're hungry, *jah*? Eating for two?"

Ruth pat her growing middle. "Can't wait to see this *boppli*. And, yes, I am hungry..." She took the tray from Granny and headed out to the porch.

Lizzie grabbed paper cups and iced tea. "*Danki* for listening. It means a lot, not having a *mamm* to talk to about these things."

Granny put a hand up. "You have a *mamm*, remember? And you're looking at her. I love you like my own."

Lizzie beamed and made her way out to the porch, putting the pitcher and cups on the table. "Help yourselves."

Silence. All the women had already dived into Peach Spoon Cake. Granny took a bowl and sat in her rocker. She let the pudding-like cake melt in her mouth and looked around the circle. Suzy didn't seem like her usual chipper self. "How's Mollie, Suzy?"

"She's declining but is fifteen years old," she said in a low, monotone voice.

"She's distancing herself," Janice said. "She's come to realize Mollie was a gift and she may be taken soon."

"Sounds like Pastor Jerry's counseling her," Colleen said. "He really is good."

Suzy got up quickly. "Okay, we didn't come here to eat, but knit, and some of you are behind."

All eyes in the circle were on Suzy.

She looked around and burst into tears. "I'm sorry. I try to hold it in, and then it gushes out."

Janice got up and embraced her friend. "It's okay to cry. Grief is starting now, like we said. Even though Mollie's here, you're grieving the loss of the old Mollie...the active, healthy Mollie." Suzy continued to sob in Janice's arms.

"I can teach," offered Marge. "Want me to?"

Suzy shook her head. "I need to do this. You women take my mind off Mollie, and this circle is a blessing."

Marge sighed. "Well, I'm glad you can teach. I'm plumb tired. Homesteading is harder than those books and magazines make it out to be."

"If you were raised Amish, you'd be used to it," Ruth said. "But you and Joe are doing *goot*. Just keep working and then you'll be all snug in your house come winter. Firewood chopped, enough put up to eat. Winter is my favorite time of year, I must admit."

"And you and Fannie will have babies in the winter," Colleen said. "I had Aurora in the winter and there's nothing like holding a baby all snuggly when it's cold out."

"I thought you were homeless," Marge said.

"Not when Aurora was born. I stayed with an aunt for a while. Three years."

"So why'd you leave?" Lizzie asked.

"My parents would come over high on drugs, begging for money. Drug money. When they threatened me, I went to a friend's, but they found me there, so I went to the Baptist shelter."

"Does your aunt know where you are?" Granny asked.

"Aunt Miriam knows I'm in a half-way house and safe. Funny thing, but Iva looks like her. Met her today at the quilt shop."

"What did you think of Emma's?" Marge asked. "I'm making some crafts to sell there. Real nice lady."

"Oh, I didn't meet Emma. She was out, but her daughters, Iva and Marie, were there. Iva's so animated. She made me laugh."

Granny looked up and Janice's eyes met hers. She knew Janice was thinking the same thing, and she was so thankful that the Baptist had a dutiful pastor's wife who would take care of the situation. Maybe Janice wasn't going through the change, just stressed out, like she said.

Suzy walked around the circle checking everyone's knitting. "Well, we'll definitely have lots of scarves that's for sure," she said, curtly. "When are we going to advance to hats?"

"It looks so hard," Lizzie said. "Four little needles." She pointed to the hat Marge was making. "Don't think I can do it."

Marge looked up. "Well, crocheting a hat is easier."

Suzy held her heart. "I don't like crocheting. I've knitted for thirty years."

"Crocheting looks lacier." Marge continued to knit. "And you only use one needle."

"I'd love to learn to crochet a baby hat," Ruth said. "Can you teach me, Marge?"

"If I get a spare moment to myself," Marge huffed. "You'll need lots of hats up there in New York."

"New York!" half the circle screamed.

To Granny's amazement, Ruth beamed. "Luke and I are going to visit East Otto, New York. Zach and Ella found five hundred acres at a *goot* price." She looked over at Granny. "But Jeb, our new bishop, advised us to not move in haste. So, I'm looking at the trip as a vacation." Again, she smiled at Granny.

Granny was grateful Jeb gave such wise counsel. Her heart swelled with pride for the man she loved…too much at times. "So, when will you visit?"

"In a few weeks. Not real sure with Ella trying to get a good crop in this fall. She's most likely working the fields now, weeding her pumpkins and gourds, along with Zach and Hezekiah."

"I can help, too," Colleen said. "I'll just be volunteering at the quilt shop one day a week."

"But you need to start visiting schools," Janice said. "All the girls at Forget-Me-Not have to learn skills to make a living."

"I know, but I just love being over at Ella's…"

Granny saw a buggy come down the driveway and soon saw Lavina's face. The girl was holding up rather well, considering Nathan left. Maybe she didn't really care for him.

After Lavina hitched her horse to the post, she greeted everyone with a smile. "Sorry, I'm late. Took some peaches over to Ella and we started talking about New York. Then I started talking to Hezekiah. How wunderbar it is that he's buying the farm, although Ella will be sorely missed. And the twins…"

Granny held her breath, hoping Lavina wouldn't mention anything more about the twins.

"I fed the twins some peaches and they smacked their lips. I'll miss them."

"We'll all miss *Ella* and *Zach's* twins, *jah*?" Granny asked.

Lavina nodded. "Moses and Vina, although adopted, have a bond with their parents I never even had with mine. Well, maybe with my *mamm*…"

"Still missing her?" Janice asked. "Any word?"

"No. Nothing. But I'm learning to trust God with that and with Nathan. Maryann's a good Bible teacher. We sit at night and read it, along with other *goot* books, and I'm learning that God really cares about me. So I'm not worried."

Ruth looked up from her knitting. "Really? Even after Nathan hurt you so much?"

"Nathan didn't plan to hurt anyone," Granny quipped, defending her favorite grandson. "He just needed to go back to Montana to help on the farm."

"And see if he's over Sarah. His former fiancé who left the Amish, but came back," Lavina added.

Granny felt her stomach tighten and then flip. *Sarah*? The most fickle Amish girl she'd heard of? "My son encouraged this?"

"*Jah*, he did. He wants Nathan to be sure where his heart is…" Lavina took the yellow scarf she was working on out of her basket.

Suzy inspected the stitches. "Nice and even." She held the scarf close to her eyes. "But seed stitch is knit one, purl one. You have a few purls together here." She held the scarf down for Lavina to see.

"*Ach*, I see. Do I need to rip everything out? It took me an hour today…I knit after receiving Nathan's letter, and it does calm the nerves."

"Half-hour a day of knitting releases endorphins into your brain," Suzy said, taking a seat next to Lavina. "Endorphins not only reduce stress, but are anti-aging."

"Woot!" Janice yelled. "I'm knitting more!"

"Me too. I'll knit or crochet more. I've aged since I moved up here." Marge sighed.

"I don't know if crocheting releases endorphins," Suzy said wryly, and then winked and grinned at Marge. "I feel so much better being here. Janice dragged me out the door, and I'm glad she did."

Granny heard Tillie and Millie giggle as they swung on their tire swing. How free they were. But her heart felt as heavy as stone. Miriam was the name of Colleen's aunt? Could it all be true? What she suspected all along? And her son was encouraging Nathan to consider Sarah? She looked past the women and over to the vast fields. Hundreds of lightning bugs flickered, even though twilight hadn't set in. How bright they were when night fell. When she said her casting off prayers later tonight, she knew her Lord would cut through this darkness that threatened her soul.

~*~

Granny said her prayers and sunk into bed, weary from the day. She took in the scent of peonies that wafted from the window. Taking a deep breath, she slowly let it out, hoping her body would relax. She turned on her side and closed her eyes, but soon jumped when Jeb bellowed a snore. Granny rolled her eyes and wanted to nudge him, tell him to turn on his side. But she knew he was exhausted, so she simply closed her eyes again, hoping for silence. She felt sleep quickly come on when Jeb started to snore even louder.

Granny clenched her teeth, and got up. Taking the pillow, she was tempted to wake him with it, but as she looked at her dear husband, flat on his back, snoring louder than she could recall, she took her pillow and made her way out to the living room. She lay on the couch and tried to find sleep. Granny listened to the constant ticking of the pendulum clock, and hoped it would rock her to sleep. She heard a cow in a distant field and the barn owls started to hoot.

Why was she so distracted? She was used to these sounds, but they annoyed her tonight. She was always able to sleep after her prayer time. Did she cast everything on God? Granny knew she hadn't, so she closed her eyes:

Dear Lord,

I fear I'm angry with my son. How could he ask Nathan to come to Smicksburg to find a bride, then spin him around when Sarah decided she wants to be Amish again? Lord, the girl is like the pendulum clock I'm listening to. But now, I also have to admit I see something I've never seen before. Lavina is not fickle. She has steadfastness of heart. She would be a better match for Nathan. Lord, I fear for my grandson. Keep his heart from wayward women...from Sarah. I'm not judging her, Lord, just saying what's in my heart, which you already know.

I give this whole situation to you,

In Jesus name,

Amen

Dear Readers,

Thank you for following *Amish Friends Knitting Circle*. We're half-way through the series, since this will be in eight parts. Granny served Peach Spoon Cake. It's a pudding-like cake made for large groups. Here's a family size recipe, but you can expand it to feed a circle of friends.

Peach Spoon Cake

1 c. flour

2/3 c. brown sugar

1 t. cinnamon

½ t. salt

½ t. soda

½ c. sour cream

1 t. vanilla

1 egg

1 ½ c. sliced peaches

Beat all ingredients together, except peaches, for one minute. Pour batter into a greased 8x8 pan. Arrange peaches over batter. Bake at 375 for 35 minutes. Serve warm with whipped topping or ice cream.

EPISODE 5

The Bridge

This story is dedicated to Cindy…may your faith be strengthened to cross troubled waters.

~*~

The robin sang her many songs and Granny supposed the creature was trying to cheer her up. *Wake her up.* It might be the best thing, since her dreams were full of horror, seeing Roman fall over and over again from the roof. His arm broken in three places? Granny locked her eyes, trying to make the images disappear, but they only intensified. Jonas sobbing, saying it was all his fault. He should have let Roman build the new structure where he thought best. Lizzie and the girls sobbing as Roman lay unconscious for a spell, wondering if he'd passed on.

She turned to take Jeb's arm to put around her middle. "Jeb, are you up?"

"Don't think I slept at all, Deborah." He pulled her close. "After the medics left, I sat on the porch for the longest time."

"When our *kinner* hurt, we hurt, even if they're grown, *jah*?"

"*Jah*, for sure. But I'm puzzled. I've seen Roman build barns, walking on the high beams without falling. How'd he lose his footing?"

Granny took a deep breath and drew closer to Jeb. "He couldn't have slipped. No rain…"

"Heat exhaustion, maybe? It is the end of August."

Granny groaned. "Corn picking time at that." She covered her face and let the tears flow. "What are we going to do?"

"Aw, Love, about our boy's pain?"

"*Nee*. Nathan left, leaving all the work to Clark, who's new to rocker making. And the harvest? How will we –"

"God will provide," Jeb hushed her in a whisper, stroking her long gray hair. "He always has. And we have the People."

"It's scary to be old sometimes," she gasped. "So dependent on others."

"Our *bopplis* were mighty dependent on us, *jah*? They know the circle of life. 'Tis natural."

Granny buried her head in his chest. "I'm so afraid."

"*Jah*, I am too. For Roman. Could be months before he regains the use of his right arm." He cradled her head against his chest. "*Faith is a bridge over which we can cross all the unknown waters of tomorrow…*"

"*Ach*, I don't need to hear that."

"Why?"

"Because I'm tired. Don't have the strength to cross that bridge." Granny couldn't remember the last time she'd cried in Jeb's arms so. Most likely Abigail's death… What was wrong with her? Did she need to knit so her endorphins increased, since Suzy said they were anti-aging? Was she to knit to relieve stress? Right now, being cocooned in Jeb's arms was where she wanted to stay all day.

"We'll cross it together…"

"Cross what together?"

"The bridge, Deborah. We may be two old folks, but we're still *goot* for leaning posts, *jah*?"

Granny looked up, tears brimming her eyes. "And when my leaning post is gone?"

"Deborah, why such talk? You're being too gloomy. Need to send up some casting off prayers before your feet hit the ground?"

Granny knew he was right. She needed to sit in silence, feel the sense that her Creator was in control, and submit. Plain and simple.

Jeb withdrew his arm and sat up. "How about I make you breakfast in bed?"

Granny beamed. "I'd like that. Need to seek Him with all my heart, since it's all wound-up. *Danki*, Love."

~*~

Lavina stacked pancakes on a platter. "Jenny, can you take these over to your *oma* and *opa*?"

Jenny nodded. "When's *daed* coming home? *Mamm*, too?"

"As soon as the doctor lets them."

"But *Mamm* didn't break her arm," Millie chirped. "Why's she in the hospital?"

Lavina handed the jug of maple syrup to Millie. "She wouldn't leave your *daed*. Slept in the recliner by his bed."

"*Mamm* sure does love *Daed*," Jenny said. "Come on, Millie. Let's take this over to *Oma*'s."

Lavina turned to watch the two girls leave the kitchen. Tillie sat at the table, sullen. "Your *daed* will be just fine."

"I miss him. Couldn't sleep without him in the house."

"I was here."

"But I feel safe when my *daed*'s here."

Lavina's heart tightened, pushing the air out of her lungs. She'd always felt safe when her *daed* was gone. The house was peaceful when he fell into a drunken slumber somewhere in the woods. Sometimes she had to admit she envied Roman's *kinner*; he was a stable man with a *goot* wife now, and the girls had grandparents right next door.

Her mind turned to the book Suzy gave her, The Secret Garden. She felt like Mary Lennox in the book, never really loved by her parents. Always in the way. She missed her *mamm* at times, but lately was fighting anger toward the woman who should have kept her safe.

Lavina, don't be so contrary, her *mamm* would say. Just follow the rules. Basically, her *mamm* told her not to think for herself, which led her down the muddy road of sin, giving birth to twins out of wedlock.

Well, she was not going to let another man spin her emotions out of control. Yes, she missed Nathan, but he too proved to be untrustworthy. To not tell her about Sarah, the reason he left Montana to begin again, made her believe a lie. She wasn't the apple of his eye. She was more like a safe place, shelter from a storm, until Sarah came with an umbrella to take him home. To the one he really loved.

She put a plate of little pancake bears before Tillie. "Will these cheer you up?"

Tillie let a smile slide across her face. "*Danki*, Lavina."

"You're welcome, honey." She brushed flour from her apron and sat at the table to read the Bible verse she was meditating on. The family Bible always sat on the table, another nice touch to Roman's family. A constant reminder that Christ was a guest at every meal and the center of the home. She fingered the pages until she got to Proverbs 4:23-26.

Keep thy heart with all diligence; for out of it are the issues of life. Put away from thee a froward mouth, and perverse lips put far from thee.

Let thine eyes look right on, and let thine eyelids look straight before thee. Ponder the path of thy feet, and let all thy ways be established.

Jeb had warned her to guard her heart concerning Nathan. She understood that part. But what did *froward* mean? Forward? Nathan was mighty forward when they first met, saying he loved her a little too soon. She sighed. And what did it mean to ponder your path when there wasn't any other choice? Life without Nathan, she supposed. So, she wouldn't write back, for sure. He flip-flopped like the laundry outside, and if she needed to keep a straight path, she couldn't get dizzy watching him move about so.

She thought of Hezekiah. He was stable man who knew what he wanted. Set his hand to the plow, literally, and was making his path straight, row after row. Now he had enough to buy Ella's farm, get married and raise a family. Since she'd been over at the farm, along with Colleen to help weed the pumpkins, gourds, and squash that Ella would be selling at her roadside stand, she'd taken quite a liking to Hezekiah. But why did her mind still turn to Nathan?

Lavina looked down at the verse again, and stared at: *Let thine eyes look right on, and let thine eyelids look straight before thee.* Yes, it was clear what she needed to do….or was it?

~*~

Granny saw a car pull down her driveway as she swept the front porch. Colleen waved, as did Clark. She was accustomed to Janice driving Colleen over for their Wednesday pie-making frolics, and then Janice would come back to pick up the pies for Forget-Me-Not Manor.

Clark stopped the car by Granny's porch steps. To Granny's surprise, he came around the front and opened the door, helping Colleen out.

"Don't tell me you're hurt, too," Granny gasped.

Clark burst into laughter, the edges of his black eyes crinkling. "Janice and Jerry want to teach me 'Southern' manners. A man opens the door for a woman where they came from."

"Even in the summer, when there's no ice on the ground?"

Colleen joined in with Clark's mirth. "The Southern Baptists are really big on manners."

Granny cringed. "Colleen. You're to be respectful of the Baptists."

Clark put up a hand to defend Colleen. "She's not being rude. It's just that Jerry's lessons are… intense."

"Intense? How?"

Colleen tried not to laugh again, but did. "Clark's been taking landscape classes at the community college and Jerry makes him pick flowers to fill Forget-Me-Not. To remind us we're princesses, daughters of the King, like the sign in front says. He does look ridiculous carrying bouquets around."

Clark took Colleen's hand, bowed and kissed it. "The coach awaits when you want to depart, fair maiden."

"We need the church van to lay the pies in," Granny said. "Where's the van?"

"Church is using it today. Clark can make two trips if we don't have room. Only three miles away."

Clark bowed again to Colleen, and they both laughed. Colleen playfully hit his shoulder. "Go make yourself useful. This fair maiden's making pies that most likely you and Jerry will devour."

Granny watched as they bantered back and forth. It reminded her of her courting days with Jeb. He was shy to let his feelings be known, so became quite the tease. Still was one. Did Clark want to court Colleen? Did Janice know? Well, she had more things on her mind than a romance going on between the Baptists. Her morning quiet time and the breakfast Lavina made gave her strength to do today what she'd planned, even though her mind often crossed over to seeing Roman groan in pain.

Colleen walked up the stairs and embraced Granny. "So sorry about Roman. And sorry for acting so silly when I know you're upset."

"Well, I can't deny that when a *kinner* hurts, even if he's thirty-four now, a *mamm's* heart aches, too."

Colleen bit her lower lip. "I feel that way about Aurora. Sometimes it just stings that my own parents were never concerned about me. It's not natural."

Granny couldn't help but touch Colleen's sweet face. Her amber eyes glowed a rare light. "I worry about you, do you know that?"

Colleen looked down. "Really? Why?"

"There's just something about you, that's special-like. Feel like I've known you more than a few months."

Granny heard Lavina call across the yard. "Granny, I can't come over to make pies. Need to watch the girls."

"Have them come over to help peel apples. Got a bushel." She turned to Colleen. "Got one of those apple peelers and the girls love to turn the crank, watching the ribbon of red skins spiral into the bucket."

Colleen smiled, but Granny could tell something was on her mind. "What is it, Colleen?"

She walked over to a cedar chair and plopped down. "You'll think I'm crazy."

Granny walked over and pat Colleen on the hand. "What's crazy?" She took a seat in the chair next to her. A flock of Canada Geese honked loudly overhead, making it hard to hear much else. "They're practicing," Granny said loudly.

"For what?"

"Migrating. Need to get ready for their long flight."

Jeb came out on the porch, his hair all disheveled. He nodded and forced a smile to Colleen. "Making more pies, *jah*?"

"Yes. I always look forward to Wednesday mornings."

Jeb put a hand on Granny's shoulder. "I'm heading down to the hospital. Going to take the buggy over to Joe's and see if he can give me a lift."

"What if Clark needs help making a rocker? He's not fully trained."

"He's trained, Deborah. He fulfilled the last shipment."

Granny pat his hand. "If you think it's alright, you go on ahead."

Jeb spryly made his way to the buggy and hopped in. Granny chided herself for her behavior this morning, clinging to Jeb, fearful he might die, and now fretting about the business. No, she had faith, and would cross over all unknown waters on this earth until she stepped into heaven.

"*Opa, Opa*, can I go with you?" Jenny hollered as she ran across the yard. "I want to see *daed*."

"I don't think it's wise, Jenny," Granny warned. "And we need help with peeling apples."

Jeb put a hand up. "She'll be fine. Almost eight years old, remember?"

She huffed and turned to Colleen again. "We best be washing those apples." The fear on Colleen's face confounded Granny. "What's wrong?"

"Nothing..."

"Spill the beans," Granny said, trying to lighten the conversation.

Colleen leaned her head against the back of the rocker and looked up. "What does it take to become Amish?"

Granny leaned forward. "Well, most everyone's born into it. I think it's too hard to adapt if you're older..."

"I could. I love it here. I love the Amish. And I don't want to leave."

"Who said you have to leave? Janice and Jerry?"

"I can't live here forever. Need to pick a school and get some training to support myself." She forced a smile. "Maybe I'll become a pastry chef. I do love to bake."

Granny had asked the Good Lord to order her steps this day, and was hoping not to be burdened by others' problems. But here was Colleen, someone in need, and surely God had planned this meeting. "I think you'd make a *goot* chef."

"But I don't want to leave Smicksburg."

"There's a pastry school in Punxsutawney. Why not look into it?"

"Because I want to be Amish..."

Granny sighed. "You'd need to live like Marge, and from what I can see, I just don't know if she'll make it. Living off the grid is losing its luster, at least in Marge's eyes."

"But I know I'd be different," Colleen pressed. "I feel somehow like it's in my blood."

Granny saw the girls running across the yard, braids flying. "I think you need to talk to Marge, and get a clear picture of what Amish life would be like. And she doesn't go without a car. That's what I understand is the hardest part when someone converts."

"So people do convert?"

"*Jah*, but it's rare. Very rare. Mostly done for love..."

~*~

Joe put the book in the top corner of the outhouse and exited the little shelter. If someone had told him a few months ago he'd be living without indoor plumbing, he would have laughed them to scorn. Now, here he was, living close to nature, loving it, but concerned that Marge wanted to leave. Cancel the land contract with Jacob, and go back to their rented-out house.

He never thought he'd love the quiet like he did. Yes, he and Marge started to go to restaurants to watch the Steelers, but the commercials bothered him. *Buy this, and then you'll be happy, happy, happy. Never a care again in the world.* What a lie!

Since they've downsized, he never felt better. Less to think and care about.

No, he liked feeding his turkeys, but knew he needed to stop naming them. Well, his favorites were now like pets. And the rabbits? They were pets. Marge's Flopsy, Mopsy, and Cottontail. His heart felt full when Marge cared for them as her children. She wanted a child, he knew, and the more they lived among the Amish, they realized the world wasn't such a bad place to bring a baby into. But he and Marge were bickering something fierce lately, and he knew why. *Religion*. Always made people sour.

He heard the crunching of gravel and saw a buggy pull back to their little *dawdyhaus*. Again, Joe wondered what to do with the big farmhouse Marge didn't want to live in. No, she wanted to be all snug and cozy in the little house in the back. His stomach tightened. His attitude toward his wife wasn't improving…

"Morning Joe," Jeb said as he got out of the buggy.

"Hi Joe! Can I see the rabbits?" Jenny squealed.

Jeb put his hand on Jenny's shoulder. "Hold on now. We need to go visit your *daed*."

"Need a ride?" Joe asked, hesitantly, hoping Jeb would say no. With Marge gone, he had lots of peace and quiet.

"*Jah*, we do need a ride. Payment as usual?"

Joe looked back to the fencing he needed to put up. He promised Marge she could raise two alpacas of all things. Another lure to get her to stop talking about moving. She could learn to spin from Granny and the wool was warm....biting off more than she could chew again. He'd have to rethink this whole alpaca thing. "No problem, Jeb." Joe walked over to the white metal hand pump and yanked it a few times until water came flowing out. He slashed his face and rubbed his hands together. "Sure is hot."

"It's good for my butterflies," Jenny chirped.

"I'm sure it's good for all the bugs," Joe said with a wink.

Jenny looked up at Jeb. "Are my butterflies bugs yet?"

Jeb rubbed the top of Jenny's head. "Don't make it harder than it is. When they come out of their chrysalis, then they'll be bugs, having six legs."

Jenny jumped up and down. "Maybe they'll come out today, since it's so hot!"

"What are *yinz* talking about?" Joe asked. "Butterflies come out of where?" He motioned for them to get in the car. "I see lots of orange butterflies. Some yellow ones, too. Do you collect them, Jenny?"

"I raise them. The orange ones are called Monarchs and the yellow ones are Swallowtails."

Joe snickered. "Oh, I see. And how do you raise butterflies? Poke holes in a jar lid and feed them?"

Jeb burst out laughing. "Go ahead, Jenny. Tell him how many you have."

"What a chrysa…whatever you just said?"

Jenny giggled. "Joe, you're so funny. Everybody knows what they are."

"He's not Amish." Jeb nudged Jenny playfully. "May need to tell him."

Joe knew how educated the Amish were concerning birds, but bugs? Were they that bored? "Okay, educate me, Kiddo."

"I have at least a hundred hanging in my aquarium. And some of them are ready to hatch."

"Back up. What's a crystal?"

"Not a crystal. A chrysalis. It's like an egg shell. Joe, you do know inside chicken eggs is a baby chicken, right? The yoke is really a baby chicken not grown."

Joe had to admit to himself, he never really looked at it that way. "Sure, I know that. So, inside a crystal is a butterfly yoke?"

Jenny eyes grew round. "Joe, not a crystal, a chrysalis. And it's not a yoke, but a caterpillar inside. Actually it's really larvae…"

Joe turned the car on the main highway to head south. He wished Jenny would stop chattering on about her bugs, but she was awfully cute. "Go on…"

"Well, I collect the caterpillars and put them in my aquarium. I feed them milkweed all summer and watch them spin a little house to live in while they change into a butterfly. Now they're ready to come out and show me their new wings."

Joe grimaced. Marge gave him a religious tract with a butterfly on it. *Born Again* was on the cover. He read it in the outhouse, only taking a few minutes to read. Did Marge set Jenny up to explain to him about metamorphisms? He knew what that meant. Something changed completely into something else. And, according to the tract, we're all worms that can be born again into butterflies...He thought it corny, but it did make him think.

"You can get wings, too, Joe." Jenny leaned her head on his shoulder. "You seem like you need some wings."

"What do you mean?"

"You seem sad."

Jeb put his hand on Jenny's shoulder. "Best not to pry too much."

"Marge wants to move back home. Keeps saying she's dog tired. Can't say just 'tired', but has to be dramatic and say 'dog tired'. My nerves are getting mighty frayed."

"What does she do just for herself?" Jeb asked.

Joe wanted to scream, *This whole homesteading thing! He did it for her! What was Jeb getting at?* "She's the one who wanted to move here."

"And now that she's here, how does she unwind?"

"She knits."

"And do you encourage it?"

"Don't object to her going to the circle."

Jeb tapped his fingers on his trousers nervously. "I have a plan."

~*~

Granny smeared chicken salad on her homemade bread. Then she opened a jar of chow-chow and placed it on the table. "Now, all you girls eat up. We did a day's work in a morning's time."

"Can we eat in our tree house?" Tillie asked.

Granny knew Tillie, her timid girl, rarely spoke up and asked for anything. It was apparent she loved the new tree house Jonas had built. But it was up too high for her liking. What if Tillie fell? Millie fell? *Ach*, Deborah Weaver, have faith. "Let *Oma* put your sandwich in a paper bag first."

"I'll do it," Lavina said, getting up before Granny could stop her.

"*Danki*, Lavina." Granny was happy Lavina was taking Nathan's departure so well. With such an unknown future, her faith was inspiring. When Tillie and Millie skipped out of the little house, Granny took a deep breath. "Lavina, I was thinking of asking Nathan to come back to help."

Lavina sat down slowly, beside Colleen, and looked warily across the table at Granny. "There are plenty of men here willing to help. Do you have to?"

"Well, he's an expert rocker maker. Clark's still learning."

"But most Amish men can make a hickory rocker. Why not ask someone local?" Lavina asked, emotionless.

"Well, I miss Nathan, truth be told. And that Sarah. *Ach,* she's not the one for him."

"Who's Sarah?" Colleen asked.

"The girl I told you about, Nathan's old fiancé," Lavina snapped.

Not liking the tone in Lavina's voice, Granny put a hand up. "He wasn't engaged when he came here. It was in the past."

Colleen put a hand on Lavina's shoulder. "We're like Mary Lennox, aren't we?"

"*Jah,* we sure are…"

"Who's Mary Lennox?" Granny asked.

The two girls across from her gave supportive glances to each other. Colleen got up and pulled a book from her huge paisley print purse. "She's a character in this book, *The Secret Garden.* Neither of her parents wanted her, and Suzy thought it would be a good book for Lavina and me to read."

"Suzy? Did she order it for you?"

"No, went over to Serenity Book Nook and got it. Oh, and I almost forgot, the man who works there said your new book should be in by Friday."

"Jane Austen." Granny put her hand on her heart. "She touches me in here."

"That's how we feel about *The Secret Garden*," Lavina said. "It's nice to know that there are other people who know how we feel, even if they're not real."

Granny nodded in agreement.

"Suzy has a good idea. She wants to start a knitting and reading circle. She calls it a Knit Lit Group."

Granny had to admit it was appealing. But summer and fall were so busy, she hadn't picked up a book, except her Bible. "How about we do that in the winter?"

"Why not now?" Colleen asked.

"The Amish are busy morning 'til sunset in the summer," Lavina said.

"And Roman's help will be sorely missed. That's why Nathan needs to come back." Granny felt tears well in her eyes, but blinked, forbidding them to show. "I'm making the call."

Granny jumped when Jack barked ferociously. What on earth? She sprang up and ran out onto the porch. The Baptist church van was coming mighty fast down the dirt road, leaving a cloud of dirt behind. *I tell the Baptist not to drive so fast.* When

221

the van jerked back to a stop, right in front of her, she wanted to scold, but was too stunned to move. The entire van was full of Amish men, some she hadn't seen in a long while.

Jonas got out of the passenger seat. "Where do we start?"

"What?" Granny covered her cheeks. "Start what?"

"Well, some are here to make rockers, and some to build the *dawdyhaus*. Where's Jeb?"

"Gone," she found herself saying. "But you can all decide who does what."

Granny turned and ran back into the house. She headed toward her China closet drawer and pulled out a handkerchief. The one her *mamm* made her long ago, red roses embroidered on the corners. She let the tears flow freely.

Colleen encircled her in her arms. "It's good to cry, right?"

Granny laid her head on Colleen's shoulder. "*Jah,*" Granny sobbed. "*Jah.*"

~*~

Roman gazed up at Lizzie, her eyes mirroring the fear in his own. He heard the doctor speak the same words, but didn't look his way.

Lizzie took Roman's left hand. "Doctor, it sounds serious."

"Well, it could be the reason your husband fell. We'll need to do further tests to see if he needs medicine prescribed."

222

"Medicine?" Roman blurted. "I'll only take what's natural: herbs." Lizzie tried to hush him, but to no avail. "So no further tests."

Lizzie stomped her foot, to Roman's shock. "Roman Weaver. You are one stubborn man. You will take more tests, like the *goot* doctor said, and stop being so rude."

The doctor stifled a snicker. "Are other Amish women as straight-forward as you?"

"*Jah*, my *mamm*," Roman snapped.

Lizzie put her hands on her hips. "Doctor, Roman will do the twenty-four hour test. It's battery operated, *jah*?"

"Yes. Right now, the EKG only gives us snapshots of his heartbeat pattern."

"It's my arm that needs help, not my heart." Roman jutted his chin up, eyes on the ceiling.

"And it's set in a cast for a while." Lizzie bent down and kissed his forehead. "And I'll be taking care of you."

Jeb slowly walked into the room, pulling his gray beard. He nodded to the doctor. "Have to confess. I heard what you said from the hallway. Is my son sick?"

"I can't disclose private information without the patient's consent."

Jeb tapped one foot on the floor nervously. "He's my son."

Roman was glad there were privacy rules. He didn't want his *daed* to know.

"Go ahead, Doctor," Lizzie said. "You can tell him."

The doctor looked over at Roman in a questioning way, and he sighed. "*Daed*, you can't tell *Mamm*."

"I'll be the judge of that…" Jeb and the doctor walked out into the hall.

Jenny came in, holding Joe's hand. "*Daed*. Why's *Opa* upset?"

Roman forced a smile. "He doesn't like hospitals."

"But he just told me how important it is to visit sick people. Said he liked coming here to visit." Jenny let go of Joe's hand. "I want to tell you a secret. *Opa*'s going to surprise *Oma*."

"Most likely he will…" Roman laid his head back on the pillow and moaned.

~*~

Suzy stepped on the pedal of her spinning wheel, evenly feeding it alpaca. "See, it's easy."

Lavina stared in amazement. "You make it look easy."

"It is. And once you get the hang of it, then you'll be spinning, too. Like I said, a decent spinning wheel for two-hundred is for sale…and you can sell yarn."

"And I can buy an alpaca for five-hundred. But it's an impossible amount of money to get."

"Not if you keep coming to knitting classes. You're a quick learner."

"*Danki.*"

"And, I have some simple patterns." Suzy pointed to a cream vest on a hanger in the shop. "That's called an 'Instant Vest'. You can make it in one night. If you make ten, I can sell them, and you'll have your spinning wheel."

"Knitting and gardening, both *goot* for the nerves, *jah?*"

"Yes. And how is your secret garden coming along?"

Lavina only told Suzy about the 'healing garden'. She and Colleen picked a spot in the woods, in a place they could both easily walk to. "We planted late pansies in a circle. Then we go into the center and talk. I feel like a *kinner.*"

"And how are your nerves?"

"Much better."

"I'm glad. Have you written back to Nathan?"

"*Nee.* Jeb told me to guard my heart." Lavina shifted in her chair. "Suzy, do you have a Bible like Janice's?"

"Electronic? No. I like the feel of books, although I'm tempted at times to buy one. So many versions of the Bible, literally at her fingertips."

"Do you have the version that talks like people do today?"

Suzy stopped her spinning wheel. "I think the Amish only use the *King James Version*, right?"

"Well, Jeb reads books that have other versions in them…."

Suzy got up and stretched. "What version do you want? I have several."

"*The Message Bible.*"

Suzy walked up the steps and out of sight. Lavina admired how the woman lived so frugally, living on top of her shop. She looked over at Suzy's beloved dog, Mollie. The poor thing just laid in her little bed, motionless. Lavina leaned forward and stared, and when she saw movement, she put her hand on her chest, relieved. Suzy soon appeared with a paperback Bible. "Let me look up the verse. This version's a little different."

"It's Proverbs 4:23-26. Jeb said to memorize it, but I'm not sure of the meaning."

Suzy licked her fingers and flipped through the Bible. "Okay…here it is:

"Keep vigilant watch over your heart; that's where life starts. Don't talk out of both sides of your mouth; avoid careless banter, white lies, and gossip. Keep your eyes straight ahead; ignore all sideshow distractions. Watch your step, and the road will stretch out smooth before you."

Lavina soaked it all in, but *white lies* threatened to drown her. "So, avoid anyone who tells white lies?"

Suzy looked down at the Bible again, her mouth silently moving rapidly. "'Avoid careless banter, white lies, and gossip.'

Wow, need to stop talking to some people I know," she chuckled.

Lavina thought of Nathan not telling him about Sarah. It was a white lie that there was no one in Montana. He was careless in his speech. Forward, or froward, like her version of the Bible called it. Lavina got up and started to finger the alpaca Suzy was spinning.

"Lavina, what is it?"

"I know why Jeb wanted me to memorize that passage. I'm to forget about Nathan. Guard my heart."

Suzy put the Bible on her kitchen table. "Jeb's a smart man."

Lavina thought of Nathan's kind, tender ways. She'd miss him, but she wouldn't write back. Lavina jumped when she heard Suzy scream. The dog appeared to be motionless, and Suzy hovered over her, calling her name, *Mollie, Mollie, Mollie....* Soon Suzy was crying hysterically, bent over her little dog. Lavina lifted her dear knitting teacher up in prayer to God.

~*~

Joe rolled his eyes. "I said, I want to go to church with you."

Marge stood motionless, not knowing if she should laugh or cry. Had Joe gone mad? Or had little Jenny finally gotten to him? *Little female Amish preacher*, Marge mused. "Okay. But tell me, was it Jenny or Jeb who convinced you to go?"

"No one, really. Although Jenny sure tried to tell me about her butterflies. You put her up to that?"

"Up to what?"

"Oh, Marge, you know. The cheesy tract you gave me about being changed from a worm into a butterfly?"

"The cheesy tract you keep by your C.S. Lewis book in the outhouse?" Marge scrunched her lips to one side, trying to stifle a laugh.

"I keep books in there just in case…"

"Of what? Run out of toilet paper? I keep it stocked, and yes, I do clean cobwebs and see your books. Looks like you gave Oswald Chambers back to Jonas. Does he charge late fees?" Marge couldn't hold it in any longer, but let out a howl. "Joe, I know you. Why not admit you're sorry for being a prodigal?"

Joe gripped the side of the table. "I don't want anything to do with that poor excuse for a father!"

She felt her heart start to melt. "Oh, Honey, I'm not talking about your dad. I'm talking about God. You know about the wayward son who came home. God's arms are open wide…"

Joe put a hand up in protest. "Don't preach to me. I said I'd go to church, and let's just leave it at that."

~*~

Colleen walked down the path to the garden. "What do you think?"

Hezekiah's eyes twinkled. "Looks *goot*. But only pansies?"

"Well, we don't know what else will grow in these woods."

"Bleeding hearts, clematis, hosta…But bleeding hearts cost a lot."

His eyes penetrated hers, and shame filled her soul. "Who told you?"

"About shade plants?"

"No, about me. And my problem."

Hezekiah took off his straw hat and fidgeted with the edges. "Colleen, we all have problems."

"So you know?"

He sat down on a large rock. "We were having a nice walk, *jah*? But when I told you about shade plants you got upset. Why?"

Colleen felt her chest beating in her ears. "*Bleeding hearts.* So you know."

Hezekiah looked down. "I know it's wrong…"

"Me too. I never meant to…"

He looked up, hopeful. "What?"

"You know…my problem."

Hezekiah got up and took Colleen's hands. "Looks like our problem now."

She pulled back. "You cut yourself, too? And you're Amish?"

Hezekiah shook his head. "Colleen, you're not making any sense."

Colleen wanted to run. She tried to pull her hands away, but Hezekiah held them fondly, as if he cared for her. How had this conversation gotten so mixed up? She thought back to what upset her. Bleeding heart. She felt heat threaten to choke her as blushed. "I'm so sorry. I misunderstood."

"What?"

"When you said the flower, Bleeding heart, I assumed something about cutting."

He took her hands again. "All I know is that you cut me to my heart. No other girl has before."

Again, Colleen pulled back. "I don't mean to cut your heart. I'm not Amish."

"But I think you care for me, a little, *jah*?"

She recalled all their berry picking at Ella's, when she first met this kind man. So handsome, she was afraid at first, since good-looking men thought women were easy to get. But over their many walks, she knew he was a gentleman and a good friend. Someone she could talk freely to. And here he was, asking if she cared? Of course she did, but he was Amish, and she wasn't. And she had to leave Smicksburg at some point.

Colleen turned to him. "We better get back to Forget-Me-Not."

~*~

Joe clucked his tongue audibly and Janice turned around, eyebrows high. Marge elbowed him, and he turned to her. "How many people are in on this?"

"What?"

"My conversion."

"What?"

Joe winced as the children standing in front of the church sang *Bullfrogs and Butterflies have both been born again over and over again.* Then the lady, who was up there with them pointing to the overhead projector, asked them to sing along. He soon heard Marge sing and clap her hands:

Joe was so outraged; he just stared at the words. He sighed in relief when the song was over. Everyone clapped for the kids, but Joe clenched his fists. A little boy came forward. "Next week, we'll sing another song from Agapeland, called, *Diamond In the Rough.*" The lady with the children thanked the congregation for giving to the children's ministry, and talked about Agapeland again. She seemed to be staring at Joe.

He turned to Marge again. "What in the world is she talking about?"

"Agapeland. It's music the kids love."

He felt sweat forming on his upper lip. It was August, but at seven o'clock, it cooled down a bit. *Or was his blood boiling!* He always thought Marge should have chosen a military career. She could muster up an attack from several fronts. When she wanted to move up to Smicksburg, how many people "just happened" to bring up how exciting it would be to live off-the-grid? Yes, he was sure Jenny's butterfly story, Jeb's talk, and now this whole church was in on her mission. How many had contributed to the *Save Joe Smith Campaign?*

The spirited woman told the children to take their seats, and then smiled at the audience, a little too happy. "I told *yinz* I had a surprise, and here he is. My dear friends from Pittsburgh, Mike and Cheri Lee. And Mike is going to sing an original song for us. Come on up, Mike!"

The middle-aged Chinese man seemed dwarfed in comparison to the size of his large acoustic guitar. When he turned to talk to the lady, Joe saw that his guitar strap read *Jesus Saves* across the back, and moaned.

"What's wrong, Honey?" Marge asked sweetly.

"Oh, nothing," he said evenly. "But I'm on to you, Marge. I'm not the village idiot. One more thing, and I'm out of here."

He looked ahead, but could feel Marge's eye bore into his head. But he was not as easily brainwashed as she was, and still had his full senses.

Mike Lee tapped the microphone. "Can you hear me?"

"Yes," everyone chanted back.

"Okay. It is so good to be here with you fine people. I wrote this song for prisoners in maximum security in Pittsburgh. But you don't have to be in a physical jail to be a prisoner. Maybe some of you are in a jail of your own making, trapped and can't get out. Unforgiveness, being judgmental, and so many other things can forge bars much stronger than any jail. So, examine your hearts as I sing, *When Your Heart is Far Away...*

Joe believed right then, if his head was not attached to his body, it would have blown off. "Get your purse. We're leaving!"

Marge head spun toward him, her eyes ablaze. "No," she snapped. "Janice said this guy's a real talent. I'm staying."

"You going to walk home?"

"No, Janice will take me."

Joe felt numb. It was as if Marge couldn't hear him, so transfixed on the man as he began to play the guitar. Brainwashed. He whirled around and stomped out of the church. But his anger turned to concern for his wife. He stood outside the porch long enough to listen to the song...

People crying in the night
'Cause their hearts are far away
People runnin' for their lives
'Cause their hearts are far away

Chasing after thing they do not know
That the things of earth can't feed their soul
Who will open up their eyes to show
That their hearts are far away

Jesus wants to be the light
To the heart so far away
Wants to be the morning light
Cast your sin so far away
Laying all your cares before the throne
Putting all your trust in God alone
Turning hearts of flesh to hearts of stone
Jesus is the only way…

Joe blinked his eyes rapidly to force back tears. Jonas had asked him *What you are going to do about Jesus. Is He a liar, lunatic or Lord?* After reading *Mere Christianity* in the outhouse, and seeing genuine faith in the Amish and Baptists, he knew what he was going to do about Jesus…his hypocrite of a father was a different issue…He walked back into the church…

~*~

Granny sat on the porch knitting. She put the soft alpaca yarn to her cheek. *Some little baby will have warm feet this winter.* As she continued to knit, her concern for Lavina didn't go away. Where was she? No one had seen her since three o'clock.

When Maryann stopped by looking for the girl, it was apparent that Lavina had become like a daughter to her. Such fear in her eyes as she confessed she'd been having nightmares that Lavina's *daed* or boyfriend would come down from Troutville again and try to get Lavina to go back.

Granny rocked as the anxiety in her rose. *Lord, keep Lavina safe.* She continued to knit, wondering if this bootie would turn out as badly as her last attempt, but she was determined. She heard the squeaky hinge on the screen door, and soon saw Jeb sit in the chair next to her. Granny knew he'd been avoiding her since he came back from the hospital. "What is it, Love?"

Jeb rocked, not saying a word.

"Something in the *Gmay* you're not willing to talk about?"

"*Nee*, someone else…"

As Jeb's voice quivered, a shiver shot down Granny's back. "What is it? Tell me. Roman's still not home."

Jeb licked his lips, but still said nothing.

"Old Man! Is Roman alright?"

"*Jah*, he'll be fine. Just running more tests."

"For what? He broke his arm…"

"He got dizzy. That's why he fell."

"What caused the dizziness?"

Jeb didn't speak. Crows cawed from the cornfield. Granny knew this morning she just had to take the next step in faith, every hour. *Faith is a bridge over which we can cross all the unknown waters of tomorrow…* "Tell me everything," she said steadily.

"Roman has an irregular heartbeat."

Granny dropped her needles. Her *daed* had heart troubles…

"He'll need to be monitored for twenty-four hours. It'll show the doctor what kind of arrhythmia he has. There's medicine for it now, Deborah."

Granny picked up her needles. "Medicine can fix it?"

"Won't know until he does the test. And he's staying longer because the doc thinks he's allergic to morphine."

"No he isn't."

"Well, he's acting so agitated, the doc said he's sure it's a reaction to the medicine. I told him he doesn't know my son, but he dismissed what I said."

~*~

"Daed, I'll get the doctor!"

"Get…your mamm…"

Deborah ran through the cornfield, but soon got lost in the maze. Which way was home? Then she realized she left her boppli, Roman, by the creek. What if he drowned? She spun around the cornfield, its long stalks falling in on her.

Then loud banging could be heard. Was it someone already making her daed's pine casket? Or was it for Roman?

I need to get my daed help! I need to get to Roman!

More pounding....

Deborah sat up with a start. Her nightgown clung to her body as sweat streamed down her face. She forced herself to breathe deeply, letting air out slowly. *Ach, a nightmare!*

She turned to Jeb, but he was gone. What time was it? Granny turned around to see her alarm clock on her nightstand. Nine o'clock. What kind of bishop's wife slept in so late?

She heard talking in her kitchen, and shame filled her. Why didn't Jeb wake her up? Granny slid out of bed, and took the pitcher of water she always had filled on her dresser, and quickly took a sponge bath and dressed. But as she did this daily routine, she realized her hands were still shaking. Well, she'd have to take her calming herbs she grew, for good reason.

When Granny entered the kitchen, she was doubly embarrassed to see Ella, Zach, Ruth, and Luke. She had slept in the last time they came over. The blush rising on her cheeks would be undeniable. *How embarrassing.*

Ella and Ruth got up from the table and embraced her.

"I haven't slept in like this since the last time you came."

"*Ach*, Granny. We understand. So much going on with the workers here," Ruth said as she rubbed Granny's back. "But take a look."

They led her to the front porch and her eyes widened. "Workers here today, too? No wonder I heard pounding in my dream." She looked around the yard. "I don't see many buggies."

"Joe made two trips, picking them all up." Ella shielded her eyes from the morning sun. "We counted twenty workers at least. The Baptist church van holds a lot of people."

The heat on Granny's face now seeped into her heart. How she loved being Amish. Such generosity. Such community. She noticed there were workers from their old *Gmay*, along with their new. Melvin was up on top of the roof, and Granny thought of how much she missed Fannie, now that she was in a different church district. And now Ella and Ruth were here, most likely to tell her they're moving to New York.

"So, how was New York?" she asked as she walked over to the coffeepot. "Will you be making your new home there?"

Ruth gasped. "We can't leave with Roman laid up."

Jeb ran his fingers through his gray hair. "It's what we've been talking about. These young folk feel they need to take care of us. Forgo moving to New York for a while and stay here and make rockers."

Granny felt tears sting her eyes. "That's so sweet. But we have other workers. We'll be fine."

"What other workers?" Luke asked. "Not for the rocker shop."

"Clark makes fine rockers, and yesterday a crew fulfilled all the orders for the week." Granny put the coffee to her lips and took a sip. "And I wrote to Nathan."

Jeb tapped his fingers on the table. "Was that necessary?"

"*Jah*," Granny said. "He was Roman's partner, and said he might come back…" She looked across the table at Ella and Ruth, who were both grinning. "What's wrong?"

Ella chuckled. "*Ach*, you don't fool us. You're the matchmaker, like Emma. Ruth and I read your Jane Austen book in New York. You're so much like her."

"Jane Austen?" Granny asked.

"*Nee*, Emma!" Ruth said, joining in on the laughter that spread around the table.

Granny sat up as straight as a board. "We need a skilled rocker maker. It's our livelihood."

"Calm down, Deborah. Don't get your dander up." Jeb put a hand on her shoulder. "Luke's a skilled carpenter, having been trained by his father-in-law. He's offered to help run the place until Roman's back to work."

Granny's eyes narrowed. "Ruth, you didn't like New York?"

"I did, but with a *boppli* coming, we decided to wait." She turned to Ella and Zach. "We're so sorry. Hope you find someone else to split the land."

Zach took Ella's hand. "The settlement in East Otto is real friendly. They know of other Amish families moving in over from Cherry Creek. Said we could buy half the land."

Granny noticed that Ella didn't waver on moving to New York. "Must be a nice place."

Ella nodded. "So much farmland. It makes me sad for everyone here in Smicksburg."

"Why?" Jeb asked.

"Because most Amish families in New York farm. So few in Smicksburg do now."

Jeb exhaled loudly. "It's why our boys moved. Land out west." He stroked Granny's hand. "But Smicksburg's our home…"

Granny feared at times that they'd have to move to Ohio or Montana if Roman ever decided to join his brothers. But here was Jeb, knowing her heart and calming her. How blessed she was to have a husband to walk by her side as a leaning post. A loud knock on the door jolted Granny.

Joe looked through the screen. "Jeb, I need to make that trip now, so I'll be back to drive the men home." He shifted. "Deborah, Marge wanted me to tell you she'll be coming tonight, just in case."

"In case of what?"

"Suzy's dog dies. Real nice of that Amish girl to stay with her…"

"Which Amish girl?" Granny asked.

"Oh, what's her name? Latvia?"

Granny's brows furrowed. "Lavina. She's been at Suzy's?"

"*Jah*, I mean, yes. She stayed overnight. Like I said, real nice of her to do that."

Granny put her head down, and clasped her hand.

"What's wrong, Granny?" Ella asked.

"Don't you see? Lavina's the one for Nathan." Granny ignored Jeb groaning next to her, and the girls laughing, calling her Emma again.

~*~

Colleen sat next to Emma Miller, ripping one-inch strips of material for a rag rug. The comfort this dear woman gave only made her draw towards being Amish stronger. But would it be wise to raise Aurora Amish? Only have her go to eighth grade?

"Emma, if you're Amish, can you do distance education?"

Emma pursed her lips. "I don't know what that is, really."

"Well, I know you don't use the Internet, but there are courses to take when you're older. Everything's done by mail. Is it allowed?"

"Well, we're always learning. Books teach us a lot. I learned to crochet from a book. Is that what you mean?"

Colleen didn't want to be rude, but how could she ask an Amish person if they felt an eighth grade education was enough? "What if an Amish person wanted to learn how to be a chef? Could they go to school?"

Emma snickered. "Why would you do that? An Amish *mamm* teaches her *dochder* how to cook and bake." Emma smiled warmly. "Colleen, we get all the education we really need in eight years. If someone has a hobby, like birding, we can take a course to learn more about birds. Iva likes to learn about herbs, and is taking special classes from our local herbalist. And here you are, learning to make rugs from me. No, the Amish aren't against learning."

Colleen grinned. "Thank you. It's been on my mind…" She avoided Emma's warm brown eyes and stared at the baby quilt hanging on the wall. But the same feeling of déjà vu swept over her. She was in a crib with a quilt with red kittens embroidered on each square, and the walls were blue. Her eyes darted through the window into the main house. *Blue and plain like Emma's house.*

"What is it?" Emma put her hand on Colleen's knee

Colleen shook her head. "I don't know. Sometimes I think I'm going crazy."

"Why would you think that?"

"I told Granny and Janice. I keep having memories or it's my imagination. I don't know, but since I've moved near the Amish, I feel like I've lived here before."

"Beside memories, is anything else peculiar?"

"Well, I can understand Pennsylvania Dutch more and more. Maybe it's a gift or something, but I never had a lesson. It's almost like it's a second language." She took in a deep breath. "My mom's crazy. Maybe it's hereditary."

Emma reached for both of Colleen's hands. "And what else do you remember?"

A car horn honked outside. "Clark is here. I need to go. Will we meet next Thursday?"

Emma squeezed her hands. "I'm taking a train trip to New York to help watch my *kinner.* They get an earlier frost, so their harvest time's upon them soon. But I'll be back down here mid-September. Iva and Marie will run the store." She got up and went to the other end of the store. "Here's the iron-on pattern for the kittens on the quilt. Do you embroider?"

"I can do a straight stitch and satin. French knots confuse me still."

"Well, just read the directions on the back. Iron the pattern on and it'll show up on the squares." She hit her forehead. "Almost forgot." Emma ran through the door, into her living room.

Colleen followed, knowing Clark was patiently waiting. Emma had a pile of white material stacked on the side of her sewing machine. A trestle sewing machine...Colleen was sure she'd seen it before...maybe at an antique shop.

"You'll need quilt squares. Here, take ten. Straight stitch goes fast and you'll have those kittens done when I get back. Then I can help you make a quilt."

Colleen stared into Emma's beautiful Amber-brown eyes, and for a split second, thought she saw someone else...

~*~

Fannie let Melvin help her out of the buggy. "I won't break. Only pregnant."

Melvin's green eyes went through her. "*Jah*, and it's my *boppli* you're carrying." He took off his straw hat to fan his face. "I'll be in the rocker shop if you need anything."

Fannie chewed on her bottom lip. She was proving to be a disappointment to Melvin, and the weight he carried on his shoulders since marrying her was obvious. How she wanted a marriage like Granny's, so she relished this day together with her. The wisdom found from this other *mamm* of hers had helped in the past.

The squeaking of the screen door was soon heard and Granny stood on the porch. "*Ach*, we have time together, just the two of us."

Fannie ran up the steps into Granny's arm. "I'm so glad."

After a warm embrace, Granny took her by the shoulders. "What's wrong? You don't seem glad…"

"I, ah…had a fight with Melvin."

Granny led her over to her porch swing on the far-side of the porch. Two stainless steel bowls filled with peas sat on the floor. "Can you help me with my peas while we talk?"

Fannie nodded. "Sure."

"With Lizzie tied up with Roman, we're mighty busy bringing the harvest in. But so blessed to have our *Gmay*'s support. Almost every ear of corn is picked and put in the corncrib."

"Your sheep will eat *goot, jah*?" Fannie asked.

"*Jah*, because they'll birth in spring and nature tells them they need to eat…"

Fannie took a few peas from the bowl, opened the pod and let the peas fall back into the bowl. She threw the pod into a bucket Granny had in front of them so she could feed them to her pig later. "I know what you're thinking. Melvin, too. But I just don't have much of an appetite."

Granny threw pods into the bucket. "Fannie, we've been through a lot together. I deserve a better answer than that."

"What?"

"You can be honest with a true friend."

Fannie remembered Granny catching her at Punxsy-Mart looking at glamour magazines, comparing herself to their perfect bodies. Then Suzy showed them on the computer how their bodies were changed to look perfect. It was a long road they traveled together, but she seemed to have gone in a circle, being right back where she started. "Okay, sometimes I still battle in my mind, as my middle starts to grow, that I'm fat. Then I tell myself it's my *boppli* growing in there. But I look at my knees and ankles and I see my *mamm's* legs…fat."

"It's water retention," Granny chided. "And I told you that."

"But what if it doesn't go away? This has been my latest fear. Why do so many women get fat after having a *boppli*, and say they can never take the weight off?"

"Fear. There's that word again. Fannie, God has not given you a spirit to fear, but a sound mind. Are you looking back into the scriptures we went over this past winter?"

"*Jah*, I am. But…" Fannie was too embarrassed to tell Granny…

"Tell me."

"Melvin. He's handsome and thin. I still can't believe he married me. What if I'm not attractive if I can't get rid of this '*boppli* fat'? I got pregnant on our wedding night, so I'm bound to be pregnant again soon after I deliver. Supposing I'm always pregnant and Melvin gets tired of looking at a cow?"

Granny tapped her foot against the floor to move the swing. "You need to give Melvin more credit."

"What do you mean?"

"Melvin isn't a vain man, only caring about temporal things. He looks at you and sees *kinner* that will bring joy."

Fannie slid her finger down the side of a peapod. Where each pea grew was a bump. She was carrying Melvin's seed…and had a bump now. It was natural. "It's natural to gain weight while pregnant, but is it natural for a man to love a fat woman?"

Granny sighed. "You're having irrational fears again. No amount of talking will make these fears go away. You need faith."

"Faith?"

"*Jah*. Jeb's helping me with my fear of aging. I imagine him dead and not being able to go on. Feelings of loss overtake me. He reminded me of the proverb, *Faith is a bridge over which we can cross all the unknown waters of tomorrow…* You need to just keep walking over these troubled waters, knowing the Lord is with you, holding your hand."

Fannie leaned her head on Granny's. "And you'll be with me too, *jah?*"

"As long as the Lord gives me breath."

~*~

The Baptist church van pulled up to Granny's porch, and she looked again at the pendulum clock. Seven o'clock, and Jeb still wasn't home. He never missed dinner, especially when they had guests. Fannie and Melvin sat patiently chit-chatting but in the end, they had to eat without Jeb. Was he hurt?

She forced a smile at Fannie and soon the girl's arms were around her. "Jeb's the bishop now. Most likely he's visiting someone in need of counsel."

Granny put her hand on her chest, indigestion creeping up. "I'm sure you're right." She turned to point at the bowls of sherbet. "Can you take the tray out? I'll grab the iced tea."

Fannie nodded, and then kissed Granny on the cheek. "Remember, don't fear. Like you told me…"

"Faith…I know. I need to live out what I'm always telling you." She grabbed the cups and pitcher and met the women out on the porch. "So nice of you to pick everyone up, Janice."

"Half of us were over at Suzy's anyhow. So we left from there."

Suzy was bent over her little dog, stroking her black-and-white-furred head. "Almost lost her last night, but I sure do know who my friends are." Through tears that pooled in her eyes, Suzy looked around at each member of the circle. "What would I do without *yinz*?"

"We're knit-picks," Janice beamed. "We knit and pick each other up."

"Well, let's get to knitting then," Suzy quipped. "How many know a purl from a knit for sure now?"

All heads nodded.

"Good!" Suzy clasped her hands in front of her. "You don't know how knowing that lifts my spirits."

"Why?" Marge asked. "Is knitting that important?"

Suzy's eyes grew round. "Absolutely. It's my gift, and I like to pass it along."

Janice chuckled. "Jerry says I have the gift of gab. I could just kill him sometimes…"

Granny put her hand over the ever increasing heartburn making its way up her throat. "Janice, you shouldn't talk like that."

"I'm just kidding," Janice said. She turned to Suzy. "Can you show me how to cast off? I made a scarf, but can't get it off the needle."

Granny leaned toward Janice. "You shouldn't kid like that, then."

Janice's head spun around. "Deborah, what's wrong with you? It was a joke, like I said. No one's going to find Jerry murdered in his bed…at least not this week." She looked up and laughed.

Granny took a deep breath. "I think all us women need to say encouraging things to our husbands. Be happy they're here for us. Words can tear us down."

Janice put down her knitting needles. "You think I tear Jerry down?"

Granny looked evenly at Janice. "Being a *goot* preacher is hard work."

Janice slouched back in her chair. "Whatever…"

Fannie looked up from her knitting. "Jeb didn't come home for dinner. Granny's upset."

"Has nothing to do with it," Granny said steadily. "Since Jeb's been made a bishop, the weight around his neck has pulled him low. Jerry's a preacher and must feel the same way."

Janice's eyes softened. "I'm sure you're right. I do tease Jerry a lot. But I am frustrated. He's never home. I call the church his wife."

Granny gawked. "Out loud? In front of Jerry?"

"Yes…"

"I say the same to Joe about his stupid turkeys," Marge blurted. "I named the bunnies, because that's normal, but he's got names for those turkeys and it's driving me nuts."

Colleen let out a chuckle. "So funny the differences between us. We English say things fast, don't we, Granny?"

"I'd say so…"

Suzy stood in the middle of the circle. "I made this pattern for mittens. I'll pass it around and if anyone thinks they can do it, let me know."

Ruth took the pattern and stared at it. "So many abbreviations I don't understand."

She passed it to Lavina. "Me neither, but if you can give us a sheet, telling us what the letters mean, I'm sure it can't be that hard." She narrowed her eyes. "Some I can guess at, but what's BO?"

Colleen, Janice, and Marge snickered.

Suzy cleared her throat. "Bind Off, what else could it mean?"

"What's DC?" Lavina asked.

Marge jumped out of her seat. "Double crochet! Ha, I beat you Suzy, since I crochet."

Suzy rolled her eyes. "DK is what you'll need to know. It means double knit."

Marge sat down and turned to Lavina.. "If you ever want to crochet, I'll teach."

Janice glared at Marge, and quickly nodded toward Mollie lying on her bed. "We all want to knit though, Marge. It's good for the nerves, like Suzy said."

"You right," Marge admitted. "And no one teaches better than Suzy."

Suzy put both hands up. "Don't pacify me. I have lots of students." She looked at Janice fondly. "But thanks for caring. The whole church has been so supportive. Did you know Jerry called me this morning, wondering how Mollie was fairing?"

Janice looked up from her knitting. "No, I didn't. He makes lots of calls in the morning…"

"And he counseled me this morning, too, before we went to Emma's," Colleen said. "He really listens…"

Janice bit her lower lip. "Then why doesn't he listen to me? It always seems like his mind is elsewhere."

"Jeb gets like that when he's real tired. Can you lighten his load?" Granny glanced at the paper Fannie passed to her. "*Ach*, we can learn this easily."

"Lighten Jerry's load? Can't see how. He spends so much time studying for his doctorate."

"Well, then learn to live in the season. It won't last forever, him studying all the time," Granny said.

"But I feel, I don't know. Rejected somehow. Seems like he enjoys studying more than being with me."

Ruth knit slower. "God sees the broken heart of a woman and fills the cracks with his love."

"Is that an Amish proverb?" Marge asked. "I like that."

Ruth smiled at Granny. "*Nee*, it's something Granny made up."

Granny swatted at the air. "Not me. My *mamm* told me that long ago." She slowly stood up when she saw Joe's truck coming down the driveway. When she saw Jeb inside, she exclaimed, "Praise be!"

Fannie stood by Granny. "Fear never did any *goot, jah*?"

Granny saw Jeb wave at her with a huge grin as the car drove past the porch, down to the barn past Roman's house. "*What on earth?*"

Marge stood up, grinning. "Okay, Deborah. This is where I come in. I need to blindfold you."

"What?"

"Jeb has a surprise. Joe told me all about it."

"I'll just close my eyes."

"Promise not to peek?" Marge asked. "Jeb went to a lot of trouble."

"I promise."

The circle of women put down their yarn and led Granny down to the barn. So touched that Jeb went to so much trouble, and it wasn't even her birthday, made her want to cry. The girls told her to take tiny steps so she wouldn't fall, so she leaned on the arms around her. Leaning posts, she mused. And *I have so many*. As they led her along, she was tempted to peek, but locked her eyes tighter.

Granny felt Jeb's hand on hers. "I'll take her from here. It's private-like. But *yinz* can come in in a few minutes."

"How romantic," Janice said, putting her hand on her heart.

Colleen leaned toward Lavina. "I want a man like Jeb."

"Me too…if there are any." Lavina shielded her eyes from the setting sun.

Granny let Jeb lead her into the barn and she soon saw two sheep, both black and white, like the ones she saw in Troutville. Overwhelmed, she let the tears flow. "Jeb, *danki.*"

Jeb cradled her head against his chest. "I know you've been having lots of fear lately, about the future. *Faith is a bridge over which we can cross all the unknown waters of tomorrow…* but sometimes we need our animal friends to cross that bridge with us, *jah?*"

Granny looked up at her beloved husband, went on her tiptoes and kissed him tenderly. "What did I do to deserve such a man?"

"Now, I just don't know," Jeb said, with a wink. He bent down to kiss her. "I'm never going to even hint at any displeasure concerning your spinning and knitting. I know you need it."

Granny grabbed his middle and felt she could live in his arms. "*Danki*, so much."

As Jeb rubbed her back, she heard sobbing. Granny turned toward the barn door but didn't see anyone. Then she looked out the window and saw the faces of her friends, all crying. "What on earth?"

She motioned for them to come in and they did. "What's wrong?"

"It's so romantic," Lavina said, wiping at her tears. "And at your ages."

Jeb chuckled. "We're not old in here." He pointed to his heart. "And I'm not the only romantic."

He looked over at Joe, whose face was increasingly becoming the color of beets. "Marge, honey. This one's for you." He pointed to one of the sheep. "Jeb and I bought a pair. Can't afford an alpaca but…"

Marge rushed at Joe and kissed him on the lips. "Oh, Pooh Bear. I love you so much."

"Pooh Bear?" Jeb asked. "What's that?"

Joe eyed Marge. "Tell them why you just called me that…"

Marge hugged Joe again. "Winnie the Pooh's full of honey. He's sweet. So is Joe, when he shows it. So I call Joe my 'Pooh Bear'."

"What's a Winnie?" Granny asked.

"I'll bring the book over," Marge said. "When you read it, you'll be calling Jeb your Pooh Bear, too."

I doubt it, Granny thought with a chuckle.

"And what else do you have to tell Marge?" Jeb urged.

"Now, that's something I want to tell her in private…"

~*~

That night Granny sat on an old chair in the barn, stroking her new lamb. How blessed she was to have a husband who cared about her fears of the future. Having animals around her was one thing she did have control over, and maybe they would be good company to cross all the bridges in the future…uncertain bridges. Along with a lot of faith in God, she'll make it through. The Lord was ever at her side; the one she really needed. But like Jeb said, animals are mighty comforting.

She looked around the barn. Roman's absence was too apparent. Did he have the same heart condition that took her *daed*? She hugged the lamb around the neck. And she tried to think of others to pray for, but being a *mamm*, it kept going back to Roman. So she closed her eyes and prayed:

Lord,

You know I have a mamm's heart. And a mamm's heart can be troubled, even when they're grown. When I think of Roman falling because of a dizzy spell, I think of my own daed, and fear just consumes me. I'm sorry I don't trust you like I should, and I'm thankful you know I'm made from the dust.

Lord, I cast Roman on you. He is yours, not mine. You created him, and have had your eye on him over his thirty-four years. You see a sparrow fall, and you saw Roman fall. I give him to you, but need your grace to not keep taking him back.

And Lord, danki *for Jeb. Bless him for being so thoughtful, giving me this here sheep.*

In Jesus' name,

Amen

Dear Readers,

Thank you for following Amish Friends Knitting Circle. In this episode a song was sung by Mike Lee (Mike Yee in real life) Mike wrote *When Your Heart if Far Away* and sung it for prisoners in a maximum security prison, receiving a standing ovation. Remember, you're never too far gone to have a relationship with Jesus.

Granny served sherbet, and I leave her recipe with you. Enjoy!

Homemade Sherbet

2 c. boiling water
¾ c. sugar
1 small package Jell-O, any flavor
5 c. milk

Mix sugar and boiling water. Pour over Jell-O and let it cool slightly. Add milk and put in cake pan to freeze. Thaw until it can be beaten. Beat until smooth, and then return to freezer. Freeze again. Enjoy!

EPISODE 6

Putting Up

Granny wiped the sweat beads above her lip. A sudden urge to take the buggy to Suzy's yarn shop overcame her. Air conditioning… her egg timer let her know it was time to take the green beans out of the boiling water. Quickly lifting the metal strainer full of beans from the steaming stock pot, she plunged them into the bowl of ice water.

"*Mamm*, you need to sit down. Have some ice water," Lizzie insisted. "Lavina and I can blanch the next few batches. Still don't know why you just don't can all the beans. Why dry them?"

"Don't lose as many nutrients, and takes less space to store." Granny sat at the table and reached for her Back to Eden book. "I've been reading this book and planning all summer." She turned to Jenny, Millie and Tillie, who were all breaking beans into halves. "Can you girls go and pick *Oma* all the dill and sage in my herb garden?"

Millie clapped her hands. "I love hanging the herbs in the attic. It's my favorite part of putting up."

Granny remembered helping her own *oma* tend her herb garden at Millie's age, the smell of sage being her favorite. Fond memories of her *mamm* and *oma* tying strings around herb stems to hang upside down to dry overwhelmed her. Long term memory increased with aging, she mused.

Jeb came in the side door, exhaustion etched on his face. "Lots of wild leeks this year, that's for sure. How about you girls help *Opa* pick more?" Jeb put the basket of leeks on the counter.

Jenny's shoulders slumped. "*Oma* wants us to pick herbs."

"You girls go along and help pick leeks," Granny said. "Says here in this book they're part of the garlic family. Wouldn't you rather drink leek tea than garlic tea, come winter?"

Tillie wrinkled her nose. "Garlic tea's awful."

"*Jah*, it sure is," Jeb said. "I say if *Oma* will let us drink leek tea when sick, we best be finding a lot more." He put his hand on Jenny's shoulders. "Can you spare them, Deborah?"

"*Jah*, sure. But the beans need tended to when you get back. Will you help the girls put them on the drying racks?"

Jeb nodded. "Where's Colleen? She's here on Wednesday to learn Amish ways."

"Has a cold. Most likely allergies. I'm taking her over some leek tea tonight."

"You'll be too tired," Lizzie protested. "I'm sure the English have their own remedies."

"I have to leave at noon and help Maryann," Lavina said. "Could drop it over on my way."

"*Danki*," Granny said. "Could you take some iced tea out to the men in the rocker shop?"

Lavina's eyes narrowed and she put her hands on her hips. "You mean take Nathan some iced tea?"

Granny rolled her eyes. "You can't ignore him forever."

"Jeb said to guard my heart. Doesn't want to see me hurt."

Granny couldn't figure out why on earth Nathan had chosen Sarah, who was such a fickle Amish girl. What if Sarah left the faith again, after her sudden baptism? She'd be shunned, and Nathan would still be bound to her. No, Lavina had shown she was Amish in her heart of hearts, and she was surely the one for her grandson. "I'll take them the iced tea..."

"*Ach*, Granny, now I feel awful. Didn't mean to snap, either." She took a paper towel and wiped her brow. "I just don't want to talk to Nathan."

Lizzie put up a hand. "I need to check on Roman. See how his corn grinding's coming along. It was so clever of Jeb to make a foot pedaled grinder."

Granny grinned. "When he brought home that English exercise bike from a garage sale, I just shook my head, but it really works."

"Well, it makes Roman feel useful. Sure do wish he could make something for my *daed* to use...to feel useful..."

~*~

Lizzie tried not to laugh when she saw Roman pedaling, his face contorted as if in pain. She knew his arm wasn't in pain as much as his pride. "So, looks like it's working fine."

Roman looked over at her as she entered the barn. "*Goot* to see you. Gets lonesome in here."

She looked at the belt that Jeb attached to the bike's wheel that worked as a pulley to turn the grain grinder. The feed sack was on a table higher than the funnel of the grinder. All Roman had to do was push dried corn into the funnel with his left arm, sit on the bike, and pedal. The coarsely ground corn would provide cornmeal for bread all winter.

"Just think of how much cornbread I can make this winter. Fried mush, too."

Roman moaned. "I should be out there with the horses, bringing in the wheat."

"Well, Nathan's here now, and we have help from the *Gmay*. How many times have you helped others?" Lizzie dug her toes into the dirt floor of the barn. "Did you take your medicine?"

"*Nee*. Took herbs."

Lizzie felt light-headed, and had to remind herself to breath evenly. "Roman, you promised me you'd take the medicine for your heart. You could have another spell, or worse."

Roman stopped pedaling and soon the only thing heard in the barn was the clucking of chickens and the baaing of sheep. "It's too expensive."

"We have the money. We paid for my *daed's* medicine…" As soon as Lizzie said this, she realized what Roman was saying. He'd been pouring over the checkbook all morning, and chose to put her *daed's* MS medicine before his own needs. She ran over and hugged Roman around the neck. "I can make a quilt in my spare time."

"What spare time?"

She kissed his cheek and cradled his head against her chest. "Roman, we make time for what's important. There isn't anything more important to me than you." Lizzie leaned her head on his, and to her surprise, he pulled away from her. Now all she could see was the back of his head. "Roman, I know you're a proud man, but there's lots of ways to make money. Are you forgetting how my *daed* is getting paid for Amish Camp?"

Roman was still silent.

"Janice is bringing a group of children from the city to see Amish folk, and *daed's* going to tell them stories. The Baptists insist on paying him, and it covers your medicine."

Roman looked down and Lizzie heard a sob. She slowly put her hands on his shoulders. "Roman, it's alright, really."

He turned to her, eyes fixed on hers. "I can beat this on my own."

Lizzie put her hands on her hips and groaned. "So you can make your heart beat regularly? Sounds like something only God can do."

"I don't like medicine. You know I only take herbs."

Lizzie pounded her foot a little too hard on the ground, and pain shot up her leg. "Roman Weaver. You're as stubborn as a mule. We went over this, and you promised to take medicine. I'm holding you to your word, understand?"

~*~

Lavina plopped herself on Granny's porch swing, on the far side of the wraparound porch, and opened Mansfield Park to the dog-eared page. Going into the world of Fannie Price, a girl so poor she had to live with rich relatives, helped her feel more at home living with Maryann and her family. But she missed her *mamm* and sisters, just like Fannie Price, too. As she read this new Jane Austen novel Granny lent her, she let the emotions surface and cast them on God, and was finding healing, along with the "Secret Garden" she and Colleen made in the woods. Warmth filled her heart. Colleen was becoming like a sister as they sat in the garden and shared their hearts. But she'd seen a man's footprints around the garden, and maybe she needed to tell Colleen why they should go there together. Knowing what happened to Lizzie, she knew the woods weren't always safe, even in the country.

Lavina looked down at the page she was on, and her eyes fell on, I hope... I hope you know how much... how much I shall... write to you. Lavina wanted to shout at Fannie, Tell Edmund how you feel! I want you to know how much I love you! The suspense of not knowing if Fannie would end up with the one she truly loved made her read this book more than she should, it being putting up time. Granny assured her it had a happy ending.

She heard footsteps and soon Nathan appeared around the side of the house. Had he followed her? This side of the porch she savored as no one could see it from the ever growing population on the farm. She looked evenly at Nathan. "Do you need anything? I'm busy."

Nathan sat in a rocker near the swing. "Miss our talks….Miss you."

Lavina thought of the flirty Henry Crawford in Mansfield Park. Was Nathan really like him? Jeb told her to guard her heart… "Nathan, I don't mean to be blunt, but I guess I have to be. There's someone else in my heart. He's all I need right now."

She noticed Nathan's forehead redden and his jaw shifted to one side. "Who is he?"

"Never you mind. You have Sarah, and I chose to lean on someone else."

"It's Hezekiah, isn't it? All the single women folk love him. And now that he's buying a farm he –"

"It's none of your business, Nathan. But it's not Hezekiah. He has his attentions elsewhere."

Nathan leaned back on the rocker with a humph. "He's Amish, *jah*? I see you talking to Clark a lot."

"Clark works here, remember? And I'm here a lot helping Granny. She's like a real *oma* to me, so let's just look at each other as cousins, okay?"

He looked at her in the most unusual way, a mixture of regret, admiration, and sorrow. She looked down at her book. "I need a break before I go in and help again. If you don't mind, I'd like to read."

~*~

Nathan got up and slowly walked away, but Lavina's eyes haunted him every time he looked into them. A rare color, sometimes hazel, sometimes green or brown. But it seemed when she was saddest, they appeared green. Or was it the blue dress she wore that made her eyes look green? When she wore a brown dress, her eyes looked darker. Why did he care? He'd already given his heart to Sarah…

Lavina had someone else in her heart already? How was that possible if she really cared for him? Selfishness overcame him. He so quickly forgot Lavina when around Sarah. Could he blame her if she cared for someone else too? And why did he feel like his heart sunk into his feet when she told him of this other one who filled his heart?

Because he still cared for Lavina. But he'd have to get over her, since he couldn't go into a marriage with a divided heart. Nathan felt like turning around and going right back to talk to Lavina. He missed their heart-to-heart talks. She was one of the few people he could really talk to. Maybe they could act like cousins.

Nathan turned to visit Lavina again on the far side of the porch. Her nose was in a book, and her face was twisted. "Come across a sad part?"

Lavina's eyes darted at him. They were green, definitely green, and she was definitely sad.

"Can we talk…like cousins?"

Her mouth gaped open, but said nothing. Nathan walked closer, since she didn't protest, and took a seat again in the rocker. As Lavina stared at him in disbelief, he looked beyond her to the see the purple martin gourd house high on its pole. So many birds shared the same gourd feeder. Could he share grandparents with Lavina? "So, what are you reading?"

"Mansfield Park," Lavina said, evenly.

"What's it about?"

"A poor woman who really has no family, so she's easy prey for men to play with her heart." Lavina put the book on the swing. "I won't be a Fannie Price, Nathan. Understand?"

The icy cold look she gave him made him shiver, even though it was a hot September day, and at high noon. He'd never seen Sarah look at him so unkindly. Was this the real Lavina? He thought of Sarah, got up, and walked away.

~*~

Marge chugged down a whole glass of ice water without coming up for air. She collapsed on the kitchen chair. "I don't see how you Amish can handle living without air conditioning."

Ruth continued to put hot green beans into canning jars. "We don't know what we're missing, *jah?*"

"*Jah*, I mean, yes. To be honest, I'm at the end of my rope with this whole homesteading, off-the-grid thing. The magazines don't tell you that you have no spare time to relax…"

"But Joe bought you a sheep and even a spinning wheel. Isn't that relaxing?"

Marge was touched that Joe encouraged her knitting, but when she did sit down to knit, a billion chores crowded her mind and it stressed her out. "Knitting isn't relaxing when you're too tired and worried about too many things that need down now. Seems like the cow's the one running our lives. She needs milked twice a day…"

"How come you didn't get a Jersey cow? They only need milked once a day."

Marge groaned. "Are you serious? Joe just plunged ahead and bought a Holstein at the auction, never asking anyone for advice."

"But he sure did take advice from Jerry and Janice, didn't he?"

"About cows?" Marge cocked her head toward. "What do they know about cows?"

"Not cows," Ruth said, laughing. "About God, and his conversion…"

Marge knew everyone at the church and even the knitting circle was happy about Joe admitting he needed God in his life. That his view of God had been tainted by his hypocritical father, but she had little time to enjoy the fact that the prodigal had come home, because they were too busy. What appeared to be a life of rest and relaxation, living like Laura Ingalls Wilder, had turned into one long nightmare.

Marge leaned an elbow on the table. "I can't take it anymore."

"You don't mean that," Ruth said sweetly. "You have a fine turkey farm. Wait until Thanksgiving when you'll be busy selling all those turkeys for a *goot* profit."

Marge put her head down. "You're right! I'll be busy around the holidays, too! I'm so near-sighted."

"Your break will come in the winter, just like the earth. You'll both rest."

"But I hate winter. Why should I only get out in winter, of all things? No, Joe said if I couldn't handle it, we'd find someone else to take over our land contract."

Ruth spun around. "Really?"

"Why, you interested?"

"Well, it might get Luke to stop dreaming about New York if we had more land and he could farm."

Marge slowly sat up. "Hallelujah. He came to set the captives free! We didn't know who to ask. Ruth, you've given me great hope."

Ruth sat at the table across from her. "I'd hate to see you lose this place after only four months. Why not get electricity? Your life would be so much easier."

"It's being connected to the grid. May as well move back to Indiana."

"Did you have land in Indiana? Amish friends? A knitting circle?" Ruth asked questions with deep concern etched on her face.

"No, I didn't...And I do love the country and my new church. Can't spin and raise sheep, and hopefully alpaca someday, in the city." Marge pursed her lips. "I have a lot to think about...*jah*?"

"*Jah*," Ruth grinned. "And don't make a hasty decision. Look at all your options, like indoor plumbing and electricity. I know right now, Suzy's putting up with a vacuum sealer. All she does is slice things up, throws them in a bag to vacuum seal and then she simply stores everything in a freezer."

Marge had to admit, if she could do all this putting up by pressing a button, it would be more her speed.

~*~

Suzy put one of her favorite knit shawls over her shoulders and plopped in a chair. Having put up a bushel of beans in her vacuum sealer was easy, but after spinning all morning, the last thing she wanted was to preserve. But as usual, Amish friends brought over produce and she welcomed it.

How she missed the sweet country air, but customers who came into her shop needed their air conditioning. What did people do without it? She sighed. And it wasn't free, either. The little gold bell on the door jangled and she soon saw an Amish woman, shoulders hunched, dark lines under her eyes.

"How can I help you?" Suzy asked.

The woman held on to the side of a table display, but soon collapsed on the ground. Suzy ran to get a glass of water and quickly lifted the woman's head. "Here, drink this. You must be dehydrated."

The woman pushed the glass away. "*Nee. Danki.*"

Suzy looked out the front window, but didn't see any buggy, only a white car. "You're not from around here, are you?"

"*Nee.* But I saved every penny to get here."

Suzy helped the woman up, and led her to a chair, confused as to why the woman would save to come to her shop. "Did you want to buy some yarn?"

The woman shook her head. "I only have a few minutes. Do you know a girl by the name of Lavina? She's Amish and from Troutville."

Suzy didn't know what to say. Was the man inside the car her husband? Was he looking to make Lavina's life miserable again? "Lots of Amish women named Lavina. What do you want her for?"

Tears filled the woman's eyes and she let out a cry that Suzy recognized. The cry of a mother. "Lavina's a relative?"

"My *dochder.* I mean, daughter." She pulled a letter from her apron pocket. "Can you give this to her? I can't stay any longer…"

Suzy took her hand. "What are you so afraid of?"

Another sob and gasp. "Being caught. My husband doesn't know I've come here."

Suzy clenched her jaw. She wished her husband would show his face so she could give him a piece of her mind. Obviously, this woman was being abused to have such fear. "But why come here to my yarn shop?"

"Word has it Lavina came up to Troutville to see some sheep. Sheep for spinning wool. So I thought I'd start here. Avoiding any Amish…"

"Why?"

"Like I said, the Amish grapevine. My husband can't find out I'm here."

"Why do you stay?" Suzy blurted.

"What?"

"How can you stay with such a…m-man?" She wanted to say monster, but caught herself in time.

"I'm Amish. There are no divorces." She bowed her head. "And I have little ones who need a *mamm*."

Suzy looked down at the letter in her hand. To my dearest Lavina, was written in beautiful script. "Lavina's only eighteen and needs a *mamm*, too."

"She's old enough to get married, and I pray she finds a *goot* man." She quickly got up and headed toward the door. She looked back. "Will you give her the letter?"

Suzy nodded. "There's no return address. Where can she reach you?"

The woman started to speak, but put an index finger to her lips as if stuffing the words in, spun around, and ran out of the store.

~*~

Fannie shoved sliced cucumbers into the hot jar, poured the pickling solution over them, wiped the brim and attached the lid. A dozen put, Fannie thought, but when she turned to the other bushels of cucumbers near the back door, she feared her anger would overwhelm her. Why couldn't she have a normal *mamm* like Granny? Her *mamm*'s depression always made her bedridden, especially during putting up time.

She looked around the empty kitchen. Her sister, Eliza, was sorely missed. Having had a *boppli* last month, Eliza's postpartum depression was like a handicap, not able to do her normal routine.

Would she be like that too? Depression was hereditary, she'd read. Fannie immediately thought of knitting. Why on earth hadn't she asked her *mamm* to knitting circle before? If it increased endorphins, maybe it could help her.

Well, it never hurt to try. She sprung to her feet a little too fast, and the vertigo that came with being pregnant kicked in. The room spun around as she gripped the table. Taking deep breaths, she got her bearings, and headed toward the stairs.

When she reached the top, a sense of triumph filled her heart, quite unexpectedly. How many times had she run up these stairs to a lonely bedroom to sob or obsess over her weight? Looking in the tiny mirror at her face she thought so fat, sucking in her cheeks to see what she'd look like thin. Praise God for Granny and my knit-pick friends! They helped her overcome her self-hatred, which made her more attractive to Melvin, her beloved husband. Now, daily, Melvin was at her side when she slid into old thinking patterns. And Granny always had the time to talk.

If her *mamm* hadn't always had a problem with depression, would she have even had such a distorted body-image? Lord, forgive me for resenting my *mamm* at times, but I needed a listening ear growing up. Her *daed* thought his wife was a hypochondriac and never got her help. But Luke got help and was a changed man. Would her *mamm* go to the doctors? Most likely not. Could Granny talk her into it if she knew the whole situation? Most certainly. Granny would go with her.

Fannie opened the door to her *mamm*'s room. All the shades were pulled down, making the afternoon appear like night. "*Mamm*, are you up?"

"I am now…"

"I was thinking…would you like to go to knitting circle tomorrow night?"

~*~

Colleen wondered if she should have stayed home to nurse her cold, but when Janice agreed to watching Aurora, she decided to take a walk to The Secret Garden. When she arrived, she was glad to see Hezekiah there, getting out of the afternoon sun, and most likely wanting to see her too. Not being Amish, she had to end their friendship that was quickly crossing over to a romance. Only one kiss, but she'd learned every time she kissed a man, she felt a part of her heart was given away. After reading a book on courting, Colleen was determined to never kiss again, until it was her wedding day.

But she felt so flushed, and wondered about her temperature. She asked Hezekiah to feel her forehead, and to her shock, he kissed it. "No, Hezekiah. Just feel it with your hand."

He grinned, and then flashed his perfectly white teeth, accenting his chiseled jawline. "You can only tell if someone has a temperature by putting your lips on their forehead."

"Oh," Colleen said, head down. "Well, do I?"

"*Nee*. No fever. But I could check again, just in case." He winked and took her hand. "Why are you so uptight? I thought you cared for me."

She withdrew her hand. "It's not possible. I won't be here much longer, you know. I'll be hearing any day if it's not too late to start college. Planning on being a pastry chef, remember?"

"But you'll only be in Punxsutawney, right?"

"Yes, but –"

"And you'll still live at Forget-Me-Not, so what are you worried about?"

Colleen didn't look into Hezekiah's enchanting blue eyes, fearful she'd be mesmerized. He was the most attractive man she'd met in years...and the kindest. But if he wasn't drop-dead gorgeous, would she still be attracted to him? She'd only cared for Aurora's dad because of his looks.

He took her chin and tilted it toward his face. "Colleen, I really care about you. Don't you feel the same?"

She turned her head and looked at all the Bleeding Heart plants she and Hezekiah planted last week. It was a memorial of sorts. She was done with cutting, and as they dug holes, they imagined her past being buried. Tears stung her eyes. She could share the most shameful things, like being an unwed mother and cutting, and he unflinchingly looked at her the same way...with love. "Why do you care for me? Is it pity?"

He took her hand and she let him stroke it. "It's not pity at all. When I see you, I see a strong woman, and I find that attractive."

"Strong? Me? I'm not strong at all. I'm a charity case..."

"You left parents that were drug addicts and lived alone with a little girl. And you went without eating so you could feed her, *jah*? Then came here. I say that's being strong. You could have taken the easy road...gotten into drugs..."

"But I'm not pure. I have a child in a moment of weakness. Great weakness. So don't call me strong."

He continued to stroke her hand. "You're human. We all need love and you just found yours in the wrong place. I don't judge."

Colleen slowly turned to him. He didn't judge. That's what attracted her to this dear man. "Thank you for saying that. But, Hezekiah, I'm not Amish."

"But you could be…" He tilted her head towards his, and their lips almost met, but she turned away.

~*~

Janice couldn't believe she'd let another one of her snide remarks escape her mouth, right before Jerry had to go up to the pulpit to teach Bible study. Deborah has told her to build Jerry up, but it just flew out of her mouth. The Amish are busy putting up, and I put up with *yinz* the time. Although a joke, the defeat in Jerry's eyes floored her.

She'd tried to compliment Jerry over the past few weeks. Encourage him, but he didn't seem to listen. The truth was, she needed encouragement, too, and didn't get any because Jerry's nose was in a book if he wasn't out ministering to church members. She crossed her arms, bowed her head to say a "casting off prayer," but to her shock, emotions surfaced and although she tried to swallow them down, tears gushed out.

Embarrassed, Janice put a Kleenex to her nose, and walked quickly to the back of the church. Opening the door to the smell of pine trees only made her cry harder. Jerry used to have time to plant trees, and they'd planted the pine windbreak years ago, when they first came to Smicksburg.

She saw a car pull in. Another person late for church, as usual. When she saw it was Marge and Joe, she cringed. Joe had admitted to not being an atheist, and was taking a baby step in his newfound faith. What would he think of Christians...their church...if he saw her crying on the doorstep? She needed to look strong, filled with the Fruits of the Spirit: love, joy, peace, patience, kindness, goodness, faithfulness, gentleness and self-control.

When the dust settled after Joe parked, always too fast, she saw Marge's piercing glare. It's obvious I'm a mess, Janice sighed. To her horror, Marge ran to her, arms open wide. "What's wrong?"

Janice put her trembling lips together, trying to compose herself. "I'm having an off day. Think I'll go home and knit. "

"But Jerry's such a good Bible teacher. This is the first church I've come to with my journal. Can't take notes fast enough." Marge hugged her Vera Bradley journal. "Come on into church."

Joe walked up the steps and nodded. "Hello Janice. Are you a smoker?"

"What?"

Joe grinned. "When I used to go to church, there was a man who used to leave the service to take a smoke outside. I always thought he was going to go straight to hell." He looked fondly at Marge. "Don't think that anymore."

Janice didn't know what to say or do, tears still welling up inside her. She didn't want to gush in front of this new church attender. "I just needed some air..."

"So you're staying?" Marge chirped. "I'm glad. Want to talk to you afterwards about something."

Janice curled her toes inside her penny loafers. Lord, help me not to cry. "You go on in. I'll be just a m-m-minute..." She buried her head in her hands and sobbed. Soon, she was escorted by Joe and Marge to the side of the church where they had their bonfires and picnics. Janice plopped down on one of the benches and Joe and Marge sat across from her. "I'm so sorry..."

Marge leaned forward. "Cleansing tears. That's what Granny calls them."

Janice tried to smile, but only managed a slight grin. "I did it again."

Marge shook her head. "Spent too much money on yarn? It's addicting, isn't it? Joe and I just made a budget I plan to stick to. But with no electricity, what else am I supposed to do at night?"

Janice looked at Marge, not sure what she'd just rattled off. "I don't overspend. If anything, I need to go out and do something for myself." Janice looked over at Joe. "I'm sorry you have to see me like this, being the pastor's wife. You're new here."

Joe's eyes mellowed. "To be honest, this is a relief."

"A relief? Me being a mess?"

"Yah. People are real, and it's helped me see God is real. When I see folks working through their problems, like Jonas and his handicap, Luke and Ruth on their marriage, I see God helps them." He motioned to the bonfire pit and benches that surrounded it. "It's laid-back here. I've sat at this bonfire over the past few weeks, and people share all kinds of things. And they pray for each other. I see God working...that He's real."

Janice wiped away a stray tear. "This was Jerry's idea. Likes to have people in the church get together, real casual-like."

"Then why is he never here?" Marge probed.

"He's always working on his dissertation. Almost done, but needs to defend it to get his Ph.D." She looked up at the sky, past the towering pines. "I pray he finishes soon. I miss him. I feel like a widow."

Joe got up and pulled Janice to her feet. "I'm going to pray for you."

Marge beamed at Joe, as she took Janice's free hand. "You go ahead, Honey. Lead us in prayer."

~*~

Jonas took a deep breath, trying to compose himself on the porch of his new *dawdyhaus*, attached to the main farmhouse. When the families from the Baptist church came for Amish Day Camp at ten o'clock this morning, what if his MS kicked in and his speech became slurred? MS had never affected his speech, but with such an unpredictable disease, what if it happened today?

He looked down into the devotional Jeb lent him, Grace for the Moment, by Max Lucado. He shook his head in amazement. Jeb was a *wunderbar goot* bishop, and knew what he needed.

Even though it was August, he started at the beginning, January 1. His eyes landed on the title, God Listens, and quickly read the Bible verse at the top of the page:

I cry out to the Lord; I pray to the Lord for mercy. Psalm 142:1

He went on to read how God listens to the cry of everyone: elderly in resting homes, prisoners on death-row, alcoholics, businessmen...everyone. Jonas bowed his head, asking for grace to be able to talk coherently to the families that would arrive soon.

Jenny, Millie and Tillie ran up the steps. Jenny, as usual, took the lead. "*Opa* Jonas, we were watching you. Are you okay?"

Since Jonas had the tree house built on their favorite tree, the girls had been calling him *opa*. Only having one child, he'd never been a grandparent. And now he had three beautiful little granddaughters. "*Ach*, I'm fine. Just a little nervous to speak in front of the English."

"But you talked to the English in your store," Millie quipped.

Jonas pulled at his beard. "You're right, but it wasn't about anything personal. These folks want to know about Amish life."

"We can help answer questions," Jenny said.

Tillie went to Jonas and put a hand on his shoulder. "*Jah, Opa* Jonas. We can stay here the whole time."

Joy filled Jonas' heart, and spread across his face. "I'd like that. But these folk are paying money and are told they'd be talking to an Amish man." He winked. "I guess you girls will be a surprise bonus."

Before the bus turned onto the driveway, its sound could be heard. "Can't believe they had enough signed up to hire a bus driver."

"No wonder you're nervous," Jenny said, taking a seat next to him on the bench. "We're here to help if you need us."

Jack barked at the gray bus, darting in front of it, as if to warn it to come no closer. The girls screamed, thinking he'd get hit. But Jack turned when he heard them, thinking they were in need of protection, and ran towards the porch. Jenny made him sit at her feet, and he plunked down obediently.

As the bus neared, Jonas could tell the Englishers were taking pictures from inside the bus, and he lowered his head. He'd told Janice no cameras, but the English couldn't seem to resist. The bus door opened and families came out, each parent responsible to watch their own *kinner*, like Janice explained. Jonas counted thirty people and realized his mouth was dry. Could he speak at all?

Janice had everyone sit on the benches the Amish church wagon had provided in the yard, and Jonas made his way to the front of the benches. The girls followed and sat on the bench facing the audience, lending Jonas their support.

Janice introduced him and told people to raise their hands if they had a question. Soon several hands were up, and Jonas looked at a teenager in the front row, and nodded.

"How can you live without television? I'd die." He had a pierced nose, jet black hair to match his black clothes.

Jones wasn't sure if he was seeing things clearly, as it appeared the boy had a dog collar around his neck. He cleared his throat. "Well, television hasn't always been around, you know. It's kind of a new thing, when you think of all the centuries people lived without it."

The teen rolled his eyes. "But now that we have it, you can, too. Why don't you?"

Jonas noticed the boys' need for attention and knew if he told them they didn't want to be connected to the "grid", he'd have a slew of other questions. He looked down at the grass, then evenly at the teen. "How can you live with television? Don't you feel like you're wasting your time watching how others live, and not living yourself?"

The boy glared at Jonas, but his parents grinned. The mom spoke up. "That's why we're here. To see how to make a stronger family."

The teenaged boy shot a look of distain toward his mom, making Jonas cluck his tongue. "When I was a teenager, I spend lots of time coon hunting. My *daed* and I would be out all night, tracking down coons. Have you ever done anything like that?" he asked the boy.

"You hunt?"

"*Jah*, we sure do. And the price of hides used to bring in lots of money, but not now. I'd get up before milking, around three, to check my traps. I was like Daniel Boone." He chuckled. "Wanted to wear a coon-skinned hat but the bishop wouldn't let me."

The teen gawked. "So you know who Daniel Boone is?"

"Doesn't everybody?"

The crowd laughed, but Jonas, being serious, was confused. "Tell me, what do you folks do besides watch television? Do you have hobbies?"

A hand went up, and a little girl stood to her feet. "Well, sometimes we put a puzzle all together, if it's a holiday…"

Her father reddened and shifted. "Yes, we need to do things more often."

The girl stared at her dad. "Mom and I play cards when you watch the Steelers, twenty-four-seven."

A nervous laugh came from the burly dad. "They're not playing twenty-four-seven, like you call it."

"But some other team is, and every season it's a different sport and –"

"We'll work on that, honey," her mom said gently, looking up at her husband sympathetically.

Jonas looked at the girls and Jenny shrugged her shoulders. "How about a different question?" Jonas asked.

A woman stood up. "What's your definition of marriage?"

Jonas froze. Didn't everybody know that? He looked at Janice, who buried her face in her hands. Confused, he looked at the girls, and Jenny stood up. "My *daed* just go married, so I know the answer. It's when two people really love each other and live in the same house."

"And want to have *bopplis*," Millie added. "We're praying our new *mamm* has a *boppli* soon."

"What's a *boppli*?" the woman asked.

"*Ach*, a baby," Jonas said. "We talk German in the home and sometimes a few words slip."

The woman put her hands on her hips. "So you think marriage is between one man and one woman?"

Jonas clearly didn't understand the question. "Well, we're not polygamist, if that's what you mean. In the Old Testament the men had more than one wife, but when Jesus came, he set the record straight: one man to one woman."

The woman sat down, scowling. Jonas looked at Janice again, but she only looked at the ground. Did he say something wrong? Maybe he just wasn't cut out for this. "Any other questions?"

A man stood up. "I like the Amish. They have a moral compass, having a clear line between what's right and wrong." He shifted his baseball hat. "But I'm a military man. Why are you pacifists?"

"Thou shalt not kill is one of the Ten Commandments," Jonas said, relieved to have a question he understood.

"But what if someone came into your house with a gun, and started to threaten your family. You said you hunt, so you have guns. Wouldn't you shoot someone who was trying to hurt your family?"

"We don't even lock our doors. We believe the Lord will protect. And I could never kill another human being."

The man crossed his arms. "So, do you think I'm a sinner for being in the military?"

Jonas put up a hand. "I don't judge. That's God's job."

The man huffed and sat down. Jonas wished he hadn't signed up for this. He didn't think the English would be so confrontational. He imagined easy questions, like how to milk a cow.

A man raised his hand, and Jonas nodded. "We homeschool our eight kids. We think the public school is corrupting young minds. Is that why the Amish still have one-room schoolhouses?"

"Well, I went to public school, back in the day. Had to, until the law changed, allowing us to have our own schools. We do like having a say-so in what the *kinner* are learning. And all the kids can walk to school, too. We have schools all over the place as needed."

The mom put her hand over her heart. "So, it's like Little House on the Prairie. Laura with her braids flying in the air, following her sister Mary to school…"

"Well, the girls can wear braids in their hair, if that's what you mean." Jonas felt fatigue wash over him. "Would *yinz* like to see a cow being milked, and Amish rockers being made?"

Jonas looked over at Janice, hoping she'd understand his meaning.

Janice stood up. "Any more questions?"

The teen in the front, dressed in black from head to toe, raised his hand. Jonas grimaced. "*Jah?*"

"How come you need crutches? Don't the Amish believe in medicine?"

Jonas searched the youth's eyes. Was he making fun of his handicap, or was he concerned? After a few seconds, his heart warmed. He was concerned.

"I have MS. I'm on an experimental drug that stopped most of the damage. Wish I'd had it when my symptoms started. But no real side effects yet. My brain hasn't turned to cheese…"

The teen's brows furrowed. "Can that happen?"

The audience laughed, and the youth put his head down.

"You're exactly right," Jonas blurted. "One side effect is that the drug can make holes in my brain, much like Swiss cheese. I joke about it, but I was awfully fearful. I figured if this here drug worked, it could spare lots of people being bound to a wheelchairs or worse."

The teen looked up, and to Jonas' shock, his eyes were misted. "Thanks a lot, then. My grandma's in a wheelchair. I was just wondering…"

Jonas motioned for the teen to come forward, and he did. "How about we become pen pals?" Jonas asked softly. "You seem like a nice man."

He rolled his eyes. "Try telling my parents that."

"I can if you bring them over."

He laughed. "It's just an expression." He looked down and fiddled with a stone on the ground. "Can you give me your address?"

"*Jah*, if you'll give me yours. What's your name?"

"Charles."

Jonas grinned. "Nice to meet you Charles."

~*~

Colleen traced the red kittens she embroidered on the white quilt square, wondering why Iva and Marie had to leave the quilt shop so suddenly. She'd just gotten there, and was hoping they'd talk over some homemade sticky buns again, like last week. Well, maybe it was because their *mamm*, Emma, was home from New York and they weren't needed. They bid her good-bye and out the door they went…in a hurry. Amish were never in a hurry.

Emma appeared from her house, but looked pale. "How are you, Colleen?"

"Fine, and how was your trip to New York?"

Tears formed in Emma's honey-hazel eyes. She took out a handkerchief from her apron pocket and dabbed her eyes. "*Ach*, I miss the *kinner* so. New York is so far away."

"I can drive you up anytime," Colleen offered. "But I know what you mean. It's not like Marie and Iva, huh? Living so close."

"*Jah*," Emma agreed. "Did you finish the squares?"

Colleen held up the pile of quilt squares, and Emma flipped through them, taking her glasses off first, her nose almost on the material. "I'm real near-sighted, seeing things up close that others can't see. Your stitching is perfect, similar to my daughter…Mad."

Colleen was stunned Emma started to cry again, and then took her hand, asking her to come into the house. Emma sat sticky buns on the long oak table. "Would you like iced-coffee?"

"No thank you," Colleen managed. "Emma, please tell me what's wrong."

Emma took a well-worn letter from her pocket, fidgeting with it as her hands shook. "I have a letter here I'd like for you to see. Only the signature…"

Emma smoothed out the letter, covering up the content only to reveal the bottom. "It's from my daughter, years ago."

Colleen stared at the signature. Mad. Who would sign a letter 'Mad'?

"Does this handwriting look familiar?"

"Well, lots of people write that way...."

Emma's shoulders hunched in defeat. "*Ach*, Marie and Iva told me about your conversations while I was away. And we're awfully suspicious..."

Colleen stared at the signature more. "I know you're suspicious of us Englishers. Did I say something wrong?"

Again, Emma burst into tears, and motioned for Colleen to get up. Emma took her hand and kissed it, and they ascended the creaky wooden steps to the second floor. Was Emma alright? Was the trip to New York too much on her? When they reached the top, she was led into a bedroom. Colleen stared at the log-cabin-style blue quilt on the bed, and déjà vu overwhelmed her. "I've seen this quilt. This room." She turned to Emma. "I don't understand why this keeps happening to me. I'm going crazy!"

Emma led her to the hickory rocker and asked her to sit down, as she took her place on the nearby bed. "Colleen, I'd like to read part of this letter to you. Just to confirm."

Confirm? Confirm I'm crazy? "Go ahead."

Emma trembled as she read:

Dear Mamm,

This is the last letter I'll be sending for a while. I've made a decision to stay with Jared, and Colleen's little visits, he's forbidden. She's three now and...

Emma could read no more. She buried her face in the letter, sobbing. Colleen tried to soak in what she just heard. Her father's name was Jared. Could it be?

As Emma sobbed, Colleen looked around the room. The cuckoo clock had squirrels carved on it. Deja vu again! Colleen felt Emma's hand on hers, and through pools of tears in her eyes, she said... "I've missed you so...and Maddie."

Colleen felt the room blur and spin. Her mother's name was Madeline, but Maddie on rare occasions...when her Aunt Miriam visited. "Emma, you don't have a daughter named Miriam, do you?"

Emma nodded and rocked at the same time, not even attempting to hide her tears. "*Jah.* Two *dochders* left..."

Colleen cupped her mouth with her hands and gasped. When Emma looked up, she was drawn in...eyes that held warmth...like a distant memory. "Grandma?" Colleen whispered...

~*~

Granny plopped a heaping spoonful of bean casserole on Jeb's plate, and then Nathan's.

"Beans?" Jeb groaned. "We've been pickin' them all day. Do we have to eat them too?"

Granny cocked her head back in disbelief. "Jebediah Weaver. Be happy you have something to eat."

Jeb winked. "Just joking, Love. It looks *goot.*"

Granny took her seat to the right of Jeb and they bowed their heads in silent prayer. Granny was truly thankful this year for the rain. A dry August had shot fear throughout the community. Corn wasn't as big as last year, but most families had enough to feed livestock.

Jeb said amen, and then Granny passed the basket of homemade bread to Nathan. "The drought in Montana affect anyone you know?"

"It was further south, but, *jah*, some had few crops."

"And your parents? Do they have enough to put up?"

"It looked mighty *goot* when I came down." He shoveled a spoonful of casserole into his mouth, and Granny resisted the urge to tell him to not eat like one of the farm animals, but knew he was mighty busy helping bring in the harvest and make rockers.

"So, will you be heading home?" Jeb asked. "You've done a *goot* job here, but shouldn't you be getting home to –"

"I think you should stay longer," Granny blurted. "Roman's arm's still in the cast and –"

Jeb cleared his throat loudly. "I think he should go home to Sarah…"

Granny knew Jeb was protective of Lavina, and as much as he loved having Nathan around, was fearful for this girl who was like a *dochder*. He noticed how Lavina ignored Nathan, following his instruction to guard her heart.

"Sarah's fine with me being here," Nathan said. "I can stay."

Granny tapped the table with the handle of her spoon. "Nathan. Are you sure about Sarah? She did leave the People once, and it concerns me."

"She's a baptized member of the church now. Sarah told me why she left, and it satisfied me."

Jeb put his hand on Granny's shoulder. "And she took the baptismal classes and had her trying period. She's Amish now."

"It's just peculiar that –"

"It's not our place to pry." Jeb turned to her, mouth scrunched up to one side.

Granny knew he wanted her to drop it. To not say what she was about to say…That it's mighty peculiar for an Amish woman to be so fickle. She'd said it before, and she'd say it again, but knew Jeb rarely hushed her. Why did he treat Lavina like one of her China cups? She'd shown such strength lately. Had Lavina told Jeb something? Did she still love Nathan?

Jack's bark made Granny jump. What on earth? From outside the window, she saw Janice's van come to a screeching halt in front of her porch. The banging of car doors and running up the porch…An emergency? A loud pounding on the door made Nathan bolt up to let her enter. Colleen followed Janice into the house.

Colleen was radiant, glowing from inside out. Granny put a hand on her heart, feeling its pounding.

"So sorry to intrude," Janice blurted, "but Deborah, we have news!"

"I'm Amish!" Colleen squealed with delight, twirling around.

"Huh?" Jeb asked.

Granny patted the table, asking them to sit down.

Colleen quickly nestled in next to Granny. "Emma's my grandma. Can you believe it? Maybe you can since you and Janice had suspicions and made me work there so we'd figure it out, but now I know I'm not crazy."

Nathan leaned forward, gawking, and Granny pursed her lips so she wouldn't laugh. She embraced Colleen. "You discovered the reason we wanted you to help Emma, *jah*?"

"Janice told me all about it. I can't believe I'm Amish!"

Colleen's honey eyes sparkled like Granny had never seen. This girl, who came to Smicksburg homeless with a child, found her roots...her family. "We can trust God to make things right. *Ach*, I'm ever so happy for you, and Emma."

"And I'm Amish!" Colleen said. "I. Am. Amish!"

Jeb put a hand up. "Well, you come from Amish roots, but you can't be saying you're Amish..."

Granny shot a glare at Jeb. "She's just excited. Using the word loosely."

"No I'm not," Colleen quipped. "I'm going to be Amish. Live with my grandma and everything."

Granny slowly looked at Janice. "Really?"

"Well, we're going down to Pittsburgh to confirm everything. She has an aunt who was Amish, too."

"Miriam," Granny added.

"Yes. And we'll find her mother."

Colleen leaned her head on Granny's shoulder. "I don't want to see her, but I need to know beyond a shadow of a doubt."

"But she'll know where you'll be living," Jeb groaned. "And she pestered her *mamm* for ages, asking for money. Will she leave you alone? And Aurora?"

Everyone was silent. The pendulum clock ticked and Canada Geese honked overhead.

"We need a better plan," Janice said, taking Colleen's hand from across the table. "We can't put Forget-Me-Not in danger."

Jeb pulled on his beard. "Let me think about this…I may have an idea…."

~*~

Granny placed the sticky buns Emma sent over with Colleen on the table, and lifted her face upward. Thank you, Lord. I've had no time to bake. She handed the tray to Colleen, who was now forlorn after her talk with Jeb about all that was entailed about being Amish: baptismal classes, a proving time, the *Gmay* voting her in. She smiled at Colleen. "Faith is the bridge to carry us across all the troubled waters of tomorrow, *jah?*"

Colleen took the tray and froze. "I'm an unwed mother. The Amish will never let me in."

"We don't judge, and you'll have time to explain what led you astray. We all can be lost lambs at times."

"But six months? It's so long."

"Not for a decision that will affect decades. No, time is needed." Granny cocked an eyebrow. "Why the hurry? Do you need to leave Forget-Me-Not for higher education?"

"Well, I hope to live with my grandma. Janice still wants me to look into being a pastry chef. And that means college."

Granny saw Janice come in the side door, and needing some privacy, asked her to take the tray of sticky buns and paper plates from Colleen and greet the women. She'd be out shortly. Janice gave her a cynical look. Didn't she want Colleen to be Amish? And why not?

Granny asked Colleen to sit down at the kitchen table. "You're not baptized into the church so we won't be faulting you for going to college. Some Amish don't convert until they get that out of their system…"

"Out of their system? So learning isn't encouraged?"

"As long as you're breathing, you're learning something. Look at me, learning to knit. *Nee*, we believe you learn everything you need in eight grades. And all Amish are literate, not letting children graduate without knowing how to read…"

"Some kids who graduate from high school can barely read," Colleen said.

"I know. I read the paper. It's sad. Our *kinner* don't have fancy calculators but can make change in their heads. They learn mental math since wee ones." She pat Colleen's hand. "Like I said, you'll have six months to ask questions…and be questioned. What's the rush?"

Colleen was silent, but her neck and cheeks grew red. Not looking at Granny, but staring at the bowl of fruit on the table, she said, "Someone wants to know."

"Hezekiah?"

Colleen slowly met Granny's stunned gaze. "*Jah*, I mean, yes. We've formed an 'attachment', as Jane Austen would call it."

"Is there an 'understanding' as Jane would call it?"

"No. No engagement, if that's what she means." Colleen smiled. "Lavina and I are reading Mansfield Park. We can both identify with Fannie Price."

Granny grinned. "And as time passed, Edmund realized he loved Fannie. Fannie was patient. Love is –"

"So he dumps that awful Crawford lady? We're not done with the book."

Granny put her hand on her heart. "I'm sorry. But look for the theme of patience and 'your sin will find you out' throughout the book. Yes, our Jane was a believer."

"Can't wait to have our Knit Lit circle come fall."

Granny winked. "Me too."

~*~

Granny entered the circle, greeting everyone with an embrace. After taking a second look, she asked, "Where's Lavina?"

Suzy stood in the center of the circle to take her place as teacher. "I gave her a letter that her mother brought to the store."

"What?" Colleen asked. "Will she go back and live with her family? Her *daed*?"

"No. She spun into the store as quickly as she spun out…"

Janice smirked. "Suzy, you and your knitting talk. 'Spun in', 'I'm unraveled'. You crack me up."

"Well this won't. Lavina's mom won't leave her husband, thinks Lavina's old enough to not need a mother. It was heartbreaking."

"All the more reasons for us to make her feel like we're her family," Colleen sighed. "I know this circle makes me feel at home."

Lizzie leaned toward Colleen who she shared a bench with. "We're so glad you're here. Maybe you can help my *daed* with the English…"

"Didn't go well, did it?" Fannie asked. "I just visited before I came over. He's mighty down."

"Well, they asked him the oddest questions. Some he didn't even understand, so he felt like a fool. Don't think he'll do it again."

Janice grimaced. "I have another bus full coming up. And the money helps the church's children's program…and Jonas."

"I can help," Colleen offered. "Since I might be Amish in six months."

Silence. Even the needles the women started to click fell dumb. Granny noticed the women all looked at each other for an explanation, and when none was given, she asked Colleen to explain.

"*Ach*, I mean, Oh," she giggled. "Emma is my grandma."

Silence. A barn swallow swooped in and out of the porch and no one jumped, thinking it was a bat. But slowly, a smile slid across Fannie's face, and then Ruth's.

"Are you sure?" Fannie asked.

"Yes. I was the little girl who Emma secretly watched. I came for long vacations. Sometimes a week or two. So when I was having flashbacks when seeing Ella's root cellar, and believing I was here before, well, it wasn't my imagination. It was Emma's root cellar…"

Suzy spun around to look at Granny. "Didn't you know Emma did this?"

"*Nee*. But I knew about her *dochders* leaving for the English world. When Colleen said she has an Aunt Miriam, Janice and I thought it best if Colleen volunteer at Emma's shop. If my instincts about Colleen were correct, they'd be brought to light." She sat her needles down and glowed across the circle at Colleen. "When I first saw Colleen, there was something about her. It was as if she didn't belong in the English world."

Janice cleared her throat loudly. "But she's not Amish…."

"Not yet," Colleen said evenly. "Jeb and I are talking about baptism classes. And I hope to live with Emma, but it's all such a shock, Granny just advised me to be patient and be like nature…move slowly."

Janice flashed a smile at Granny. "I'm glad. This is such a big step."

"And living off the grid is a pain," Marge uttered. "Joe and I think we've had our fill." She nudged Ruth next to her. "Hoping Ruth and Luke can take over the land contract."

Granny felt tears sting her eyes. "Marge, are you sure? I mean, Joe just got you a black and white sheep. And you were going to learn how to spin after harvest."

Marge stared at her yarn as she knit vigorously. "Indiana's only fifteen miles away. I can visit, but I'm losing it. And Joe and I found the peace we were looking for…"

"Why are you leaving?" Granny probed further. "If you found peace?"

"We were looking for peace outside ourselves, but found it in here." Marge stopped knitting long enough to point to her heart. "Joe found peace in Christ, and I found peace in being involved in a church again."

Granny leaned forward. "Look at me, Marge."

"No!"

"Why not?"

"Because I might cry. I'll miss everyone here."

"I give knitting classes to lots of women from Indiana. Why not enroll in one and visit? And you're still a home healthcare nurse. Try to get patients in Smicksburg."

Marge slowly looked up, tears streaming down her pudgy cheeks. "It won't be the same."

Ruth rubbed Marge's back. "When Ella moves to New York, we have a plan to stay in touch. You need a plan or time slips by. And we don't have car. It's so easy for you to come up and visit."

Marge swiped at a runaway tear. "You're right. I need to take a class at your place, Suzy."

"Or teach a crocheting class!" Suzy squealed. "I've had a few knitters who've inquired about that 'other way of knitting…'"

Marge laughed. "The better way, huh?"

Both women laughed, and then the circle all joined in...except Fannie.

"What's wrong, Fannie?"

She shifted in her rocker. "My *mamm* almost came to the circle. But of course, didn't feel *goot* enough."

Granny knew Fannie had a heavy burden to bear, having a *mamm* who was depressed. All Fannie's life, she'd had no one to really nurture her, her *mamm* not having much emotional energy.

"Why won't she come?" Ruth asked. "Is she tired putting up?"

Fannie filled her cheeks with air and then blew it out. "I do it all for her. Poor Melvin. Hasn't seen his wife in weeks."

"But why?" Colleen asked.

"My *mamm* gets depressed. A lot. So I've always put up food for her. But even though I'm married now, she still asked me to do it, pregnant and all."

"Why can't Eliza help?" Ruth probed further. "You shouldn't be lifting heavy pots."

"*Ach*, she's depressed, too. Ever since she had her *boppli*."

"Postpartum Depression," Janice quipped. "It passes in time."

"My *mamm*'s didn't." Fannie knit slowly but with determination. She held up her pink scarf. "Suzy, can you check this? Looks like I purled too many. Pattern looks funny."

Suzy held up the scarf and examined it closely. "Right here. You purled two. It's knit one, purl one. I can fix it." She took the scarf and quickly started to knit.

"What are you doing?" Fannie asked.

"Knitting backwards to fix your mistake."

All the women groaned.

"We're trying to simply knit, and you can knit backwards?" Lizzie asked, defeated. "I don't think I have this gift of knitting. Jenny does though."

"It takes practice," Suzy said. "Where is our little student?"

Lizzie broke into matronly smile. "Reading with my *daed*. Those two have quite the bond."

"Does Jonas have her reading Oswald Chambers or C.S. Lewis?" Marge asked, grinning. "Joe calls her 'The Female Amish Preacher'. Her innocent little spirit helped him see his bitterness."

"His bitterness?" Granny asked.

"Yes. His dad's real religious, you know, like in a bad way. Legalistic. But he saw in Jenny her ability to accept a new mom, Jonas living with them. Well, her loving little heart, and it only made him see his need to change. Forgive his dad."

Granny felt pride swell in her heart. Jenny had been a light to Joe? And she was only seven… "The girls all have their birthdays soon. Can't believe the twins will be six and Jenny eight."

Marge squeezed her yarn. "Oh, let's have a party for them!"

All the women in the circle nodded enthusiastically and started to plan a party.

~*~

Lavina felt the moisture of the moss on the log seeping through to her dress. But she was too glued to the letter to notice. She read it again, mulling over each word:

Dear Lavina,

I've missed you so, having fond memories of us putting up the garden this time of year. I hired a driver to get this note to you. Your daed doesn't know about it.

I just can't go on anymore, with you thinking I don't love and miss you. But my place is with my husband. I live outside Troutville in a house I'm not too happy with, it being run-down, but it seems like your daed is listening to our new bishop. Pray for him.

You may recall me mention relatives out in Ohio. They know of my situation, and I've asked Claire to send you letters from me. Enclosed is her address. Can you write to her and give her your address? I'll write again, but there won't be any return address. Write to me and Claire will enclose it in hers. Your dad has forbidden me to write, but I have a mamm's heart and I love you, Lavina.

Mamm

Lavina kissed the letter and put it to her heart. Her *mamm* never told her she loved her; it was assumed, but it was nice to hear. And she would pray for her *daed*. Anyone could change, although it would take time to mend her feelings toward the man.

Lavina jumped up when she heard, "Kissing a letter from your new boyfriend?"

She turned to see Nathan, standing near a tree, several yards behind her. "Are you spying on me?"

"*Nee*, just saw you walk this way, and thought I'd join you. Beautiful night."

Lavina felt like crinkling up the letter in a ball and throwing it at him, but it was too precious.

"How could you find someone else so soon?" Nathan took his straw hat off and tossed it on the grass, and sat next to it.

"*Ach*, I'm free. And you're engaged."

Nathan fidgeted nervously with the brim of his hat. "Can we talk?"

"*Nee*, we can't."

"So you're engaged, too?"

Lavina thought of Henry Crawford in Mansfield Park. Nathan was the same, a flirt. Beware of swoons, Fannie Price had to keep reminding herself of the villainous Henry. How could she not see this in Nathan before?

"I miss you," Nathan said. "And since I got back, you're different."

Lavina just told him she didn't want to talk. She took a deep breath and slowly let it out. "How am I different?"

"You're more confident and steady. Like you have someone else in your life."

Lavina sat back on the log, even though it was moist. What else could she do? "Nathan, when I said I have someone else in my heart, I can't be deceptive. It's not a man, but God. And He makes me steady. And I'm finding that He's enough."

Nathan looked up, eyes wide, but brimmed with tears. "I still love you…"

"You said you loved Sarah."

"I do when around her, but when I come here to Smicksburg, I love you."

Lavina stiffened. Do not faint, Fannie had admonished herself. Beware of swoons.

Nathan sprang up and took a seat next to her, taking her hands. "Can you forgive me?"

"For what? Being a flirt with me right now?" She pulled away and stood up, poker straight.

Nathan stood next to her, taking her by the arms. "Lavina, what's wrong with you? You've understood my predicament...until now."

"I'm guarding my heart, like your *opa* told me to do."

He pulled her close, trying to steal a kiss, but she recoiled. "What are you doing?"

"Trying to show...I love you."

The temptation to hold Nathan started to overwhelm her, but she resisted. "Go back to Montana."

"What?"

"Go back to Montana, and be around Sarah. You'll fall for her again. You love the woman you're with." She looked down, away from the hurt in his eyes. "Forget about me."

~*~

The roses on Granny's porch let out a sweet aroma, and anticipation filled her. The yearly tradition of making rose jam with Abigail had continued even after she passed. But this year, the girl's new *mamm*, Lizzie, would be there to help make the luscious jam.

She closed her eyes as she continued enjoying the scent. You give us beauty for ashes, Lord. When the only daughter I would have had died, and Jeb planted these roses, to give me hope. And now I have four girls around me at all times: the *kinner* and Lizzie.

She thought of Lavina, coming back to the knitting circle, eyes red with crying. How she wanted this girl to marry her Nathan. She'd warned Nathan that Sarah was fickle. But he didn't seem to care.

She thought of Colleen. Could she be Amish? Should she be Amish? Granny hoped the girl knew she'd have an *oma* with Emma even if she didn't convert. But was she really taken with Hezekiah? Was that the pull to be Amish?

Granny closed her eyes:

Lord,

Danki for a wunderbar goot harvest, and food to put up. May the food we donated to the Baptist to take to Pittsburgh bless the homeless. I'm ever so thankful to have a home, family...love.

Lord, I don't understand Nathan's behavior, and don't know why Lavina came back to the knitting circle crying. But you do. You saw Hagar in the wilderness, and she called you, The God who Sees. You see Lavina's heart: her love for her mamm. Danki that she got word from her. Lord, help Lavina's daed change, like Joe did. Bring a little girl like Jenny to him to help him see how hard his heart is.

And Lord, help Colleen during this testing time. Lord, I'm so shocked she really wants to be Amish. Marge couldn't handle living off the grid. Will Colleen? Oh Lord, give Jeb the wisdom he needs to guide that dear girl.

I give all my knitting circle friends to you...my 'Little Women' as Jeb calls them.

In Jesus name,

Amen

~*~

Thank you following Granny and her knitting circle in *Amish Friends Knitting Circle.*, an eight part series.

Emma's Sticky Buns

1 c. Biscuit Mix (recipe below)

1/3 c. milk

2 Tbsp. melted butter

½ c. white sugar

1 tsp. cinnamon

2 Tbs. butter

2 Tbs. firmly pressed brown sugar

¼ c. pecans, walnuts, or nut of your choice.

Combine biscuit mix and milk. Knead several times and roll into an 8 inch square.

Brush the pastry with melted butter.

Mix the sugar and cinnamon together and sprinkle over the dough.

Roll the dough up and cut into 1 inch slices.

Place slices into greased 8 inch square pan.

Brush with melted butter combined with brown sugar

Sprinkle nuts evenly on top.

Bake at 375 **degrees** for 20-25 minutes.

Biscuit Mix

(Most Amish families keep this on hand, kept in an airtight container)

8 c. flour

8 tsp. white sugar

2 tsp. salt

1 ¾ shortening

1/3 c. baking powder

1 c. powdered milk

2 tbs. cream of tartar

Sift all dry ingredients thoroughly. Cut in shortening, and store. To make biscuits, use 1 c. mix to 1/3 c. water. Bake at 450 degrees for 10 minutes.

Episode 7

The Pumpkin Patch

Granny gripped her middle as Jeb put a cold washcloth on her forehead. "I need to take your temperature again, Love."

Nathan fidgeted with the edge of the bed sheet as he sat in a chair next to his *oma*. His gaze fell on the embroidered pillowcase edged with red roses, her favorite. The image of his *opa* as a much younger man, separating a rose bush and planting them along the edge of his *dawdyhaus*, flashed before him. His pa had told him that a rosebush was planted after his *oma* gave birth to a still-born daughter, and Jeb planted a rosebush in her memory. When the *dawdyhaus* was built, he'd separated the bush into two and continued each year to do so until roses climbed the wraparound porch. Now they were so heavy on the trellis on the far side of the porch, they needed pruning.

Another groan from Granny stabbed at his heart. How he loved this woman, and how she loved him. Their talk a few weeks back made him realize he'd stay in Smicksburg, and try to win back Lavina's heart. But was it too late?

He heard a sob, and looked up to see his *opa* in tears, gripping Granny's hand. "Her fever broke." He bent down to kiss her cheek. "Love, we need to keep giving you liquids."

She shook her head vehemently and pointed to her stomach. Jeb stroked her hand, insisting, she might end up in the hospital for dehydration, but she only pushed back the glass of water when Nathan put it to her lips.

"*Nee.* Nothing…" She gripped her middle again and cried out in pain. Then she turned away from them, saying she needed to sleep.

Nathan looked at his *opa*, concern and love etched on his face. Jeb hadn't left her side in the past three days, even rocking her like a child, stroking her long gray hair. How Nathan longed to have a marriage like this. His eyes met Jeb's, then darted toward the door. Nathan supposed he wanted time alone with Granny, but Jeb followed him out into the main part of the house.

Jeb headed toward the kitchen, straight for the coffee pot, and poured two mugs full. "Nathan, what's ailing you?"

Nathan leaned up against the kitchen counter, the scent of roses wafting in. "Me? Nothing."

He handed him black coffee. "Tell me."

"What?"

Jeb rubbed his forehead. "What's wrong? You're so forlorn. Why aren't you out working in the rocker shop?"

"Concerned for *Oma*. She's really sick…"

"Look at me. It's something else, and I know it. Tell me."

Nathan took a sip of coffee. "I've been watching you and *oma*. I want a marriage like yours."

"Then go back to Montana, marry that Sarah, and work on it. Marriage is being a servant, so serve Sarah."

Nathan eyes widened. "You know I broke it off with Sarah."

"*Jah*, but you're not going to play with Lavina's heart like a harmonica. She's been through a lot."

"But I love her, *Opa*. Why don't you believe me?"

Jeb swatted at the air. "You broke her heart. That's not something you do to someone you love."

Nathan rolled his eyes. "I'm not a *kinner*, but I sure felt that way back home. *Mamm* thought Sarah would stay true to the faith if she married me. I was supposed to keep her on the straight and narrow."

"But you wrote to Lavina telling her you were in love with Sarah."

"Honor your parents is one of the Ten Commandments. I figured that love would come in time."

Jeb plunked down at his place at the kitchen table. "Do you know how your words hurt Lavina?" he boomed. "I am her bishop, and counseled her to guard her heart against you. And I'm sticking to it until your words are straight. You're

Amish. Our word should be *goot* to sell a farm, how much more a marriage? You broke your word to Sarah."

Nathan didn't know why, but sorrow shadowed his heart, and to his shame, tears rolled onto his cheek. He angrily brushed them away. "*Oma* doesn't agree with you. I love Lavina, and *Oma* can see that. She always sees things right!" Immediately regretting this outburst, he felt the need to run. And so he did, out the door and around the house towards the back fields.

~*~

Lavina stopped the swing when she heard voices in the kitchen. The squeaking of the chain drowned out Nathan's voice. How she longed to just hear him talk. How she missed him, but she trusted Jeb's judgment, although Granny gave the opposite advice. Forgive and move forward, she'd said.

Her mind turned to Granny, as did fear. Would she be alright? Was it something serious? Being seventy with a fever of one-hundred-four, she agreed with Marge that she should be taken to the emergency room last night. But Jeb stayed up all night, the ever-caring husband.

Lavina looked down at the pink trim she was embroidering at the top of the black socks she'd made. One her wedding night, she'd wear these socks, the only time she'd be able to dress fancy. Only her husband would see them as he took them off her feet…

Was it her imagination, or was the conversation in the kitchen becoming an argument? Then go back to Montana, marry that Sarah. Lavina froze, needle suspended in mid-air. She was working on forgiving Nathan, but now he'd be leaving? Nathan's voice was too low to make out, but then Jeb started talking about a harmonica? She shook her head. What?

Lavina had always been taught not to eavesdrop, so she set to work on the socks to be put in her hope chest. Maryann's idea of filling a hope chest was a *goot* idea. It helped her look down the road to the day when she'd wed.

Do you know how your words hurt Lavina? She couldn't help but overhear Jeb's loud voice. If only she could hear Nathan's. The memory of their first kiss, in the buggy along the dirt road, intruded her thoughts. She was afraid Nathan would be like her old boyfriend, and how fearful she was. But Nathan was so tender. His kiss full of love, not lust.

Oma doesn't agree with you. I love Lavina… Lavina dropped the socks. Had she heard Nathan right? He loved her? She heard the screen door slam, and heavy pounding on the porch steps. Getting up and running to the front of the wraparound porch, she saw Nathan, hands raking his light brown, shaggy hair as he disappeared around the side of the house.

I love Lavina played over and over in her mind. She wanted to run after him, but then thought of Jeb's advice. Lavina looked down at the socks clenched in her hands, and soon tears fell on them. She jumped when Jeb came out on the porch and stared at her, mouth gaping.

~*~

Ella poured lemonade into paper cups, placed them on a tray and headed toward the back porch where parched workers patiently waited. But she stopped and stared at the picture window. Zach had put it in for her, since winters were gloomy and she yearned for sunshine. This was the home that they built. The mint green walls throughout the house…they picked the color together at Lowes. Images of family and friends filled the room, carrying paintbrushes and rollers. It was a cool autumn day, apple cider was plentiful, along with apple crisps, apple dumplings…any dessert which included apples.

She clenched the tray tight. Why had she agreed to move away? How would she ever feel at home in New York?

The side door opened, and Colleen appeared, eyes wide. "Ella. Are you okay?"

Ella shook her head, biting her lower lip to will back tears. "I'll miss it here."

"Change. I don't like it either."

Ella slowly looked into Colleen's honey-hazel eyes. She knew this girl looked to her as a role model in being Amish.

How Colleen complimented her until she blushed. "Want to talk?"

Colleen nodded. "Let me take the lemonade outside first, though."

She took the tray and headed out the side door. The screen door. Their late Collie, Tess, had lain in front of that door, and Zach always joked that she knew what they were talking about. Tears stung at Ella's eyes, but soon Colleen would be in, and needed a listening ear. What a decision she had to make. Why Janice needed an answer soon was understandable, to a degree. But the English moved too fast for Ella's liking.

Colleen appeared at the door, and Ella noticed she was wearing a jean skirt. She'd always worn those short pants that hung right below her knees. Was she trying to see if she could bear to wear a dress every day? Ella patted the oak table. "Come sit down."

Colleen lowered her gaze as she took a seat on the bench across from Ella. "I think he's worth it…"

"But being 'in love' isn't the best reason to be Amish."

Colleen cocked her head. "I was talking about Zach. If I had a husband like him, I'd follow him anywhere." Ella raised both eyebrows, and Colleen laughed. "I don't mean it like that. I'm not attracted to your husband. Just saying that you have a nice family…"

Ella composed herself. "I should be more thankful. I know how you're struggling."

"I'll miss you something awful. You promise to write?"

Ella nodded. "Of course. And who knows, maybe it won't work out in New York and we'll move back..."

Colleen traced the wide oak grain on the table with a finger. "At least you can change your mind. If I live with my grandma, move out of Forget-Me-Not, I lose my spot. And if I'm not cut out to be Amish, I'll be homeless again...and I have Aurora to think about..."

Ella reached for Colleen's hand. "Emma would never let you be without a roof over your head. If you decide not to be Amish, you'll still be her *kinner*. And you'll still have the knitting circle friends..."

"Emma, I mean, *Oma*, or whatever I should call her, assured me of that. So did Granny."

Ella squeezed her hand tight. "Live each short hour with God and the long years will take care of themselves."

"An Amish proverb?" Colleen asked.

"*Jah*, and one I find hard to do. Give each moment to God, trusting Him for my future." A tear slid down her cheek. "I'm sorry. I guess I'm not trusting..."

"You're human, Ella. That's one thing I just love about Hezekiah. Not that I'm totally in love yet, I don't think." She smirked. "When I talk about the past, especially about cutting myself, he just says, 'We're all human, made from the dust.' Somehow, that makes me stand taller.'"

Hezekiah had confided in her that he wanted to make Colleen his bride, trusting she'll turn Amish. *Ach*, her problems were nothing compared to this young couple. Ella tilted her head, realizing for the first time that Colleen and Hezekiah would be living in her house if they wed. It was time for her to move on, making room for someone else in this home she loved so much; it was the love in the house she cherished, and it was portable. The thought warmed her heart, and she told Colleen it was time they get back to the road side stand, and sell more pumpkins.

~*~

Granny stretched her toes as she lay in bed, trying to rest as Jeb demanded, but the laughter, blowing like an October wind, wafted through the open window. She swallowed the lump forming in her throat, knowing that self-pity never had good results, only a spiral down into gloom, so she quickly started to count her blessings.

She thanked God Lizzie was now the girls' *mamm* and had made a special birthday celebration prepared for them. She could also have knitting circle tomorrow night, since her flu-bug wouldn't be contagious, being on antibiotics for twenty-four hours by then.

The sound of gravel flying broke into her thoughts. When would Joe and Marge ever learn to drive slower? Goodness. They were always in a rush. Maybe they did need to live in a more fast-paced world. But who would take over the payments on their farm? The Amish wouldn't take anyone to court, so she hoped Marge and Joe would keep up their agreement. Granny quickly dismissed such a notion, not borrowing trouble. That Jenny insisted on inviting Joe and Marge to her party made her grin. A little child shall lead them. Joe had always called Jenny a "Little Female Amish Preacher"; somehow she got through to him in her child-like faith.

Little footsteps patted across her living room floor that sounded like Tillie's. The door slowly opened, and in popped her little head. "I'm six now, *Oma*."

A front tooth was missing, and Granny wished she could take a picture, like the English, to treasure this memory always. "Happy Birthday, Honey. But *Oma* is sick. You best stay away."

Tillie tried not to frown and put on a forced smile. "Can we do something tomorrow, when you're not conta...con...I don't remember the word."

"Contagious. When you can't catch what I have. *Jah*, I'd like that." Tillie, her timid one with a sensitive heart, hovered over her like Jeb. It was love, and Granny relished in it. "You go on out and have a *goot* time, Tillie."

She broke out into a heartfelt smile, said good-bye and shut the door. Granny looked up at the white ceiling, her joints aching so, but she counted another blessing: Tillie. A grandchild who lived right next door, not thousands of miles away, like some of her others.

Granny looked over at the socks she was making, but even the joints in her hands hurt too much to knit. So she just took the black alpaca yarn and curled her finger in and out of the soft ball. Lavina was also making black socks, and trimming them with flowers at the top. Was something going on, a secret romance, she wasn't telling anyone about? Such socks were for a wedding night. Lavina and Jeb spoke in hushed tones over the noon meal, but she thought she heard Lavina crying. Was it cleansing tears, tears of joy...or sorrow? Had Jeb counseled her, once again, to stay away from Nathan?

How she loved Lavina and Colleen, and missed their usual Wednesday morning pie making for Forget-Me-Not Manor. Colleen, realizing she had Amish kin, and now knew her *oma*, was a blessing but she was moving too fast. Wanting to be baptized into the church in a few months? *Nee*. Too soon. But what hopes and dreams filled Hezekiah's heart toward her? If he loved her, would he try to use his impeccable Amish character to persuade Jeb to let her be in baptismal classes?

Knowing she needed to cast her concerns on God, Granny closed her eyes, and prayed:

Lord,

I love these girls, but You love them more. You have a plan that's for their good, so I'm going to stop trying to figure everything out, and trust that You will direct their paths.

~*~

Lizzie told the girls to open their eyes, and their squeals flooded her soul with joy. The toy wheelbarrow she got at Punxsy-Mart was filled with chocolate pudding, and candy worms were crawling throughout. It was something Marge saw in a magazine, and showed it to her. But she wasn't going to let the girls dive into the chocolate and get the 'dirt' on them, like the article suggested. The English indulged their *kinner* a little too much, she'd observed.

Marge passed out bowls to Roman, Jonas, Jeb, Lavina, Nathan, Clark, Joe, and the girls, who sat around the long oak table. Lizzie handed her metal soup ladle to Jenny and told her to take all the 'dirt' from the wheelbarrow that she wanted, including worms. A round of laughter filled the room.

Marge pouted as she took Lizzie by the elbow. "Would have been more fun to do this outside, let the girls dive in," she whispered in her ear.

Lizzie clenched the handle of the pitcher full of cold milk. "You wash clothes on a scrub board, *jah?*"

"No, I go to the Laundromat..." She lowered her eyes. "But it's their birthday..."

"And your craft idea with the pumpkins is *wunderbar*. I couldn't have planned this party without your help."

"I'll miss your family when we move..." Tears pooled in Marge's eyes. "But it's for the best..."

"Honey, come here." Joe patted the bench next to him. "Have some dirt."

Marge forced a smile and sat next to her husband. "Do you girls like eating dirt?" Marge asked.

Three heads nodded but no one spoke, too busy eating, and another round of laughter filled the room. But it didn't have the volume loud enough for several people, and Lizzie wondered why Lavina and Nathan only smiled politely. She hoped the girls didn't notice the tension between them.

When everyone had their fill of dessert, presents were put on the table. The girls opened paper dolls from Lavina, a set of Dutch Blitz cards from Nathan, coloring books and crayons from Clark, and Jeb presented them with new lunch pails, pink with purple flowers on them.

"*Opa, danki*," Jenny said, one eyebrow cocked. "Are they for school?"

Jeb waved his hand. "*Nee*, you can't fit all your food in those little things. It's for having picnics with *Oma* and me. "

The girls clapped their hands, and Millie stood up. "When can we go?"

"Today," Roman said, with a grin. "We're all going for a picnic to your favorite spot."

"The pumpkin patch!" the girls shouted in unison.

Joe put a hand up. "Marge and I can't go, but we brought a surprise." He looked sheepishly at Roman. "Sorry, I just can't wait any longer."

Roman laughed and told him to go ahead and bring his present in the house. The girls looked at each other, confused. "Why couldn't he wrap it and put it on the table?" Jenny asked.

"You can't wrap it," Marge blurted, eyes wide with anticipation. She winked at Tillie. "You'll love her." She clasped her mouth with both hands. "Oops".

"Her? So it's alive?" Jenny asked slowly, deep in thought.

Marge let out nervous laughter. "Oh, you know me. I named my car! Her name is Red. It's a lame name, but it's what I call my girl." Marge shot up when Joe entered the room with something large and square with a white cloth covering it.

"Can you guess what it is?" Joe asked, as he placed it on the floor.

Jenny sprung up and went over to Joe. "I think I know."

"Now how can you know?" he said, jabbing Jenny in the side. "It's covered."

"I can smell it."

"You're bluffing," Joe said. "Now guess."

Jenny put a finger to her cheek. "Well, I smell woodchips. Wet woodchips. But they're clean, and don't smell funny. So it just tipped its' water, or something."

"A guinea pig!" Millie put her hands on her heart. "I've always wanted a guinea pig."

Joe beamed. "Something better."

"We have three," Marge hinted. "Can you guess now?"

Jenny leaned forward and hugged Joe around the neck, and then ran to Marge. "A rabbit."

"You're right, Preacher Girl," Joe teased. "When I first met you, you ran away to our place to find the rabbits, remember? Trying to find the dwarfs?"

Marge chuckled. "After you read Snow White?"

Jenny pursed her lips to compose herself. "I remember, but I'm eight now, and don't believe that story anymore."

Tillie and Millie ran over to see the rabbit. "She's so small. Is she a *boppli*?" Tillie asked.

"She's a dwarf rabbit," Joe said, laughing. "They don't get big. Your *mamm* insisted."

Lizzie nodded. "*Jah*, that's for sure. Some rabbits are too big to keep in the house."

"In the house?" Jeb asked. "Keep a rabbit in the house? Why not the barn where animals belong?"

Jonas cleared his throat. "Lizzie had a little rabbit when she was a *kinner*. She didn't pay for hers, though, but found it, abandoned, so she raised it."

Roman looked at Lizzie with star-struck eyes. "I remember that rabbit. And our girls will be just like their *mamm*, and have a big heart to care for not only all of us, but animals too."

The girls ran to embrace Lizzie. "*Danki, Mamm*," they all said.

Lizzie kissed the tops of their heads. How she loved these girls. Though she wasn't the natural *mamm*, she had a heart like one, she supposed. Fearing she may cry tears of joy, Lizzie quickly told everyone to go out on the porch and she'd soon have everything ready for their picnic.

They all obeyed, except Roman, still staring at her. He drew her close with his good arm, the other still in a cast, and leaned down to kiss her. Not a short peck, but a sweet kiss that lingered. "*Danki*, my love."

Breathless, Lizzie didn't hurry to get all the cold-cuts out of the refrigerator to make sandwiches. No, she soon found herself lost in another kiss and didn't care if anyone walked into the room. When she leaned back for air, her eyes met Roman's. She knew he had something to say. "What is it?"

He leaned his forehead against hers. "I'll take my medicine. I want to be here to see many more birthdays…and grow old with you…"

Lizzie closed her eyes and thanked God. She hadn't nagged, only prayed, and it worked. Yes, she'd spoken her mind, and then cast her care on God, not nagging. Tension left the home and peace filled it once again. *Danki*, God.

~*~

Tillie slipped her hand into Lavina's, and the sweetness of this girl helped the sour feeling in her heart. She was to ignore Nathan, as Jeb had instructed, but she had overheard their conversation. He said he loved her, but she didn't dare tell Jeb when they had another long talk at the noon meal.

Lavina took in the scent of dried cornstalks as they approached them, halfway down to the pumpkin patch. How she loved autumn and the scooping out of pumpkins seeds and roasting them, as Lizzie had planned, carving stenciled designs on the skin, and using them as lanterns. She'd try the flower stencil, since it looked simple. The girls would be delighted at yet another surprise. What a *goot mamm* Lizzie was to the girls, and seeing Ella with her twins, gave her a deep joy.

She felt a tap on her shoulder and turned to see Nathan, eyes sheepish. "Lavina, want to take a walk through the corn maze?"

She stopped so abruptly that is jerked Tillie back. "Sorry, Tillie."

Tillie looked at her, then Nathan, and then smiled and skipped ahead to meet the others. As Lavina faced Nathan's anxious eyes, she saw Jeb out of her peripheral vision. She needed to listen to her bishop, but to her shock, Jeb came closer, a grin on his face.

"Why don't *yinz* young'uns go take a walk in the corn maze?" He winked at Lavina.

"But you said that I should..." She looked at Jeb, shaking her head. "We talked at the noon meal, *jah*?"

"*Jah*, we did. Never said you young'uns couldn't play in the cornfield."

Lavina reached her hand out to Jeb and grabbed him. "Jeb, what's wrong? You've never called us 'young'uns' before. We're not *kinner*. Are you alright?"

"Right as rain. You forget about me, and go have some fun for a change. Us old folk can get awfully cantankerous."

Lavina gasped. "What?"

"Cantankerous. Crabby. Well, at least me. Deborah's still like a young lamb, skipping along life's roads. She sees things I just can't."

Nathan took her hand and pulled her toward one of the entrances to the maze of corn. What was going on? Only an hour ago, Jeb had forbidden her to be alone with Nathan!

Digging in her barefooted heels to stop, Lavina's foot caught a jagged rock and she cried out in pain. Reaching for her foot, she sat down, right there in the dirt.

"Are you alright? Lavina, I'm sorry."

Lavina, realizing the stone hadn't even broke the skin, felt heat rise, making her ruddy skin much redder. She didn't look up for a few seconds, hoping to compose herself. "I'm fine."

Nathan helped pull her up, but withdrew his hand quickly as soon as she was on her feet. Was he listening to Jeb? Going back to Sarah? Is that why Jeb was so happy? Lavina set her face like flint, looking ahead as they walked through the tall, stiff cornstalks. The path getting narrow at times, Nathan always let her go through first, holding back any stalks in her way.

Nathan was the first to attempt to break the tall wall between them. "How are Maryann and Michael?"

"Busy, as usual. Maryann likes my help with the *kinner*."

"So, you'll be staying with them for *goot*?"

Lavina paused. "I found a relative in Ohio. One I never knew of. We write…I want to visit."

"Only visit, right?"

"Don't know."

"Won't you miss Smicksburg?" he prodded. "You couldn't leave permanently."

"I can always visit. And you have two uncles out there, *jah?* People move all the time." She heard a loud rustling sound not far off. A grunt. Lavina spun around. "Nathan, the pig's in these cornstalks."

"*Jah*, I know. He won't go far. Only digging up roots, having a *goot* meal."

Lavina clenched her fists. "But I'm afraid of pigs because…" before she could finish, a black pig headed toward them. Lavina screamed and clung on to Nathan. "Pick me up!"

Nathan scooped her into his arms, but let out laughter so loud, the crows on the stalks all took flight. "Never known an Amish girl to be afraid of pigs."

As the pig circled them, more excited now than ever, Nathan called to the pig. "Christmas, get out of here." He ripped off a piece of stalk with one hand, and smacked the pig's behind. "Now shoo. Away with you." Soon, the pig darted off down the path.

Lavina wiggled out of his arms. "He could hurt someone. One of the girls."

Nathan adjusted his straw hat, and more laughter followed. "A pig won't hurt you. And he's not a seven-hundred pound sow, but, well, Christmas."

Lavina tried to calm down and count to ten slowly to herself. Colleen had taught her this. She let out a deep breath. "What is Christmas?"

"What we call the pig. That or Thanksgiving or Wedding…"

"My *daed* named the animals we had."

"But you get too attached if you name them, and then it's like losing a pet."

Lavina's mouth grew dry when Nathan looked up, sensitivity in his eyes. He'd just said…losing…was she losing him forever? He'd laughed up to this point, but now, the more she searched his eyes, she saw fear. "So, Nathan, when are you leaving for Montana?" she forced herself to ask.

"Do you still want me to go?"

Why were his blue eyes darkening? And when his shaggy brown hair tried to cover them, he didn't brush it away as usual. He was hiding something. But he asked her if she wanted him to go, like she'd said before, when angry. You love the girl you're with Nathan. Go back to Montana. She'd spit out these words like venom, feeling ashamed afterwards. But trying to guard her heart, she got defensive, and shot quite an arrow into his heart. *Ach*, the painful look he'd given her.

"Nathan, I've been so mean to you. I'm sorry."

He rushed to her and took her hand. "No, I should be apologizing. I hurt you. Can you forgive me?"

The image of another woman in Montana, waiting for him, overpowered her, and she pulled her hands away. "What about Sarah?"

He readjusted his straw hat. "Can we talk about that?"

"*Jah*. I think I can. Jeb seemed to encourage it."

Nathan took her hand, and she didn't pull away for some reason. It almost seemed like Nathan needed her support, to be able to share what weighed on his heart.

"My *mamm* and Sarah's *mamm* are best friends. They've been upset about Sarah since she was a *kinner*, her being mighty head-strong. When we were in our teens, looking back, they encouraged me to court Sarah a little too much. They'd always say she'd stray from the Amish, and I was the strong one who could keep her in the fold. So we planned to wed when we were eighteen, but she disappeared."

"Disappeared?"

"*Jah*, she ran off with some English friends. My *mamm* and Sarah's have been sick with worry for over two years, until she came back a few months ago. That's why the sudden call to go back home. They figured the sooner the two of us go hitched, their problem with Sarah would be solved." He squeezed her hand tighter. "I felt forced, Lavina, understand? And I didn't want to see my *mamm* and her friend, the whole extended family, hurt again."

"But, didn't you love Sarah?" Lavina asked slowly, preparing herself for the blow.

"I thought I did…until I met you."

Lavina felt her heart leap like a deer. The tone in Nathan's voice was sincere, she was sure. She looked up through the cornstalks to a blue sky. "*Danki.*"

"What?"

"I said '*danki*.'"

"For what?"

"I was talking to God, not you." She squeezed his hand. "Nathan, I feel like you're my equal for the first time."

Nathan rubbed the back of her hand with his thumb. "Go on. I want to hear it."

"I was young, only fourteen when I felt forced into a relationship, and gave in. I just wanted to make my *mamm* not worry so and feared my *daed*. And you did the same thing. You were being forced into marrying Sarah."

"Forced is too strong a word. My parents weren't abusive like yours."

"But you were manipulated, *jah*? Like I was, and you gave in?"

Canada Geese flew overhead, and the sound was deafening. Nathan took her by the chin and said something, but she couldn't hear. She shrugged her shoulders and pointed to the birds ahead. He pulled her close, and she heard, *I love you, Lavina. Will you be my bride?*

Tears sprung from her eyes as she nodded yes, and Nathan threw his hat up and yelled a *yippy*! But no one heard, only Lavina's heart.

~*~

Fannie balanced the pumpkin on the top of her ever-expanding stomach. "*Mamm*, I'll be having a little pumpkin come winter. And you'll have two *grandkinner*." Trying to make her *mamm* smile was a task. The woman had a permanent frown, like the scarecrows the English had in their fields. "Aren't you excited?"

She slowly bent down to pick up the baskets of miniature gourds at her feet. "*Jah*, I suppose so."

Suppose so? Didn't she want the precious life inside of her daughter? Old feelings, buried deep, that she was never wanted threatened to surface. But Granny had taught her well. Self-pity was the first step she always took in her spiral down into her inferiority complex. Fannie gave thanks to God for Granny and her knitting friends....and the circle tomorrow night. "*Mamm*, are you still going to knitting circle tomorrow?"

"I suppose so."

I suppose so. She was like one of Melvin's clocks that chimed, always the same song. I supposed so, usually meant, if I'm not sleeping, sick again without any medical explanation. But some of the women at the circle said they thought she was depressed. Could depression make a soul so lifeless, tired…uncaring? Surely God would give her strength if she tried harder.

Resentment tried to grip her, but Fannie quickly thought of one of her Bible verses on forgiveness: Let he who is without sin, cast the first stone. But it seemed like her whole life her *mamm* had been throwing mental stones at her, and she never flung any back. She didn't cast stones, so why was she feeling guilty of unforgiveness? Fannie found herself counting the minutes until knitting circle so she could chat with Granny. And thankful she had her to really be there for her. Granny had her struggles, too, but fought the good fight of faith, as the Bible instructed. Her *mamm* cowered under every dark cloud that blew her way. Why?

~*~

Ruth placed pumpkin pie on two plates, and set them before Luke and little Micah. How her boy was growing, almost three, and would soon want more. She stared down at the pie as she cut herself a slice. She was eating for two, so she cut a quarter of the pie, and slid it on a plate.

When she met her family at the table, Luke stared at her growing middle. "You sure you're carrying one *bopph*?"

"I don't know. Ravished all the time." She met Luke's merry blue eyes, and they savored this moment. The first pumpkin pie from their patch. They'd planted this pumpkin patch together, for the first time, and she couldn't help but keep her eyes locked on Luke's. What a *wunderbar* husband he had become. So good that she didn't fear moving away from her parents…

"Luke, have you thought more on Marge and Joe's place? Still want to buy it?"

He nodded. "I'd like to. No land here."

Ruth felt debt was a noose around the neck, and just talking about it made her throat constrict. "I don't like debt."

"Me neither. And I like working with your *daed*. Never thought I'd take to woodworking, but I'm keen on it." He sighed, and put another piece of pie in his mouth.

"How much does farming mean to you?"

Luke pulled at his blond beard. "I think it's the animals I like best. They calm me."

"Me too. I'd love to have alpacas and learn to spin their fur. Sheep too." Ruth blurted this out without thinking. She really didn't want the debt, and knew Luke weighed what she said very seriously.

"Is there money in raising alpacas?" he asked.

"I don't know. I was just thinking out loud."

Luke reached across the table for her hand. "I think I'm leaning toward buying it…and some sheep. I think knitting has been *goot* for you. Remember how I called your knitting circle a bunch of knit-picks, always picking out faults in others? I was so wrong."

"*Jah*, you were. We pick each other up." The thoughts of having sheep made her heart skip. And all the land for birding. The idea of this farm took root in her mind's eye, as she imagined sheering sheep, carding the wool and going to Granny's and spinning together. Was it worth it to be in debt, though? And the shell for the addition was already attached to the house. Were they being foolish?

"What's wrong? Luke asked. "You're miles away."

"Like I said. I don't like debt…and moving. We've only been here for nine months."

A glow washed over Luke's face. "It takes nine months for God to create a new life, *jah?*"

She knew what he meant. God had given them a whole new marriage in nine months. Neither of them were the same people. Her knit-pickin' friends had been a part of this, and so was the *Gmay* leadership. How Ruth treasured her Amish life. And that life could be lived where they were, or where they moved to. She smiled at Luke and prayed that the Lord would direct their path. Surely the unity they now shared would lead them down the same path.

~*~

That night, Joe thought of the events of the day. The birthday party for the girls would have been a disappointment to most other kids, but Amish children weren't spoiled, he'd come to see. Although, they made a fuss about the rabbit, which cost a pretty penny compared to the other gifts, they didn't show any contempt for Clark's meager present: crayons and a cheap coloring book.

He looked across the little living room to watch Marge knit in her rocker. How soothing the constant rhythm of the needles, and contentment on her face. "You're just glowing tonight."

"Keep thinking about Jerry's sermon. Those Beatitudes are taken very seriously by the Amish, but I didn't understand them, really, until Jerry read the verses out of the Message Bible."

"Ya, I want one. Always thought I was dumb, not understanding the version we had in church, back in the day."

"I have a paperback," Marge quipped, springing out of the chair before he could stop her. "I'll just run upstairs and get it."

Joe stifled a laugh. Marge wanted to make sure they were on the same page spiritually, so she was feeding him a repertoire of books. He wished she'd just relax and trust him; he believed in God, and was now a Christian, but he had spiritual baggage. His whole view of Christianity had been skewed by his dad, the one who deserved a gold medal for being a hypocrite. It was like he had to unlearn the concept of God all over, take the 'lighting and thunder, hell and damnation' God out of his head. How blessed the girls were to see God at a young age as a loving God. One who disciplined, but did it out of love. Love...he'd always missed that part.

When he looked up, Marge was standing over him, eyes wide. "Honey, what's wrong? You in some kind of trance? Deep prayer?"

"Deep thinking, is all."

She gently passed the Message Bible to him. "You read the Beatitudes out loud."

"Why?"

The glow had returned to her face. "It's romantic."

"Romantic? Reading the Bible is romantic?"

She picked up her yarn again to knit. "It is. I feel more connected with you. It's like God's the glue in our marriage, drawing us closer together. Worked for Ruth and Luke."

"We aren't having problems anymore. I mean, we spat at times, but I think we're okay."

She looked up, eyes twinkling. "We're fine. Can you read the Beatitudes? It's where I put the bookmarker."

He shrugged his shoulders. Happy wife, happy life, he'd heard. Clearing his throat, he started:

"You're blessed when you're at the end of your rope. With less of you there is more of God and his rule.

"You're blessed when you feel you've lost what is most dear to you. Only then can you be embraced by the One most dear to you.

"You're blessed when you're content with just who you are—no more, no less. That's the moment you find yourselves proud owners of everything that can't be bought.

Joe stopped and slowly reread, you find yourselves proud owners of everything that can't be bought. Then he read it again, ignoring Marge who asked him to read on. "Marge, we've always been chasing something, don't you think? New boat, the next vacation. But I've noticed the Amish don't do that, most likely because they can't. "

"They're allowed to have boats for fishing, I know that."

"But they don't live for the next 'big thing' to happen. They're content no matter what happens."

"They keep their minds on things that are really important…spiritual stuff," Marge added. "

Joe leaned his head back on his chair. "We came here to live off-the-grid, but it didn't make things simple. You think we're trying to buy peace?"

"If we are, it didn't work!" Marge blurted, a little too loudly. "Sorry. I miss my conveniences too much." She looked over at Joe sheepishly. "It's hard raising a baby off-the-grid. I'm not doing cloth diapers…

Joe shot up so fast he lost his balance and tipped his rocker over.

Marge let out a howl. "That news knocked you off your rocker, literally."

He raced over to her and scooped her out of her chair. "How long have you known?"

"As long as I can keep a secret from you, so under twenty-four hours. Took the test this morning, but we haven't been alone all day."

Joe cupped her cheeks and kissed her. "I'm going to be a daddy? And you a mommy?"

Marge laughed. "I need to confirm with a doctor, since it was a home pregnancy test, but I believe we are and am so glad, still in my thirties and all."

"Almost forty," Joe teased.

"In two years," Marge said in an even tone, and then broke out into laughter. "Isn't it funny?"

"What?"

"We both said we didn't want kids, just pets. Granny said that was 'plain foolishness' and she was sure we'd have *kinner*, I mean children. *Ach*, the Amish have rubbed off on us in a *wunderbar goot* way, *jah*?

Joe chuckled. "*Jah*."

~*~

Colleen grabbed Hezekiah's hand and put it to her heart. The cool morning dew and the scent of the mossy woods around them, in her secret garden, her secret place to meet with God...was he answering a prayer? "Are you sure? I have a child. Are you ready to be a dad?"

He leaned down and kissed her. "Aurora's a princess, *jah*? How could I not love a princess?"

Tears filled Colleen's eyes; tears of joy for sure. But a restlessness frightened her. So many obstacles and she hadn't known Hezekiah that long. Only since the spring, six months. But she'd finally felt at home, especially when she was in his arms.

"So, will you marry me? After you're baptized?"

Baptized. To get to that point, she knew there was a narrow path in between, and like a tightrope walker, if she fell off, it could be hazardous to not only her, but to Aurora. Even though Ella had assured her that her grandma, Emma, would not let her be homeless again, no one really knew what living on the streets was like, so they couldn't empathize with her fears.

The advice from Jerry and Janice was to go to school; an education was something that no one could take from her. And she'd had skills to live independently. But the Amish women were homemakers, something she'd always yearned to be. Was it her Amish heritage, or a lack of parenting in her own life that made her long for a permanent nest?

She looked up into Hezekiah's pensive blue-green eyes. "I can't believe you want to marry me. Are you really sure?"

"Well, this is a secret, *jah*? An Amish man can only propose to a baptized Amish girl. What I'm saying is, I want you to promise to be my wife after your baptized." He ran his fingers through her honey-colored hair, and cradled her head against his chest. "Do you love me?"

"I do."

"Then I'll wait, even if it takes years."

Colleen pulled away and searched his eyes. "Years? It can take years?"

"*Jah*, it can. It's a serious vow, to live within the Amish community. It's like a marriage vow. That's why people who leave after baptism are shunned; they broke a vow to God and their community."

Years! How could she put Aurora through a long limbo? Put her in Amish school? Hold off on an education, paid for by the Baptists and financial aid? Was she just so star-struck with Hezekiah she couldn't see? And what if… "Hezekiah, what if I'm never allowed to be baptized? Then where will you be? Still single? Be a bachelor for life?"

He lowered his gaze. "I know a few English who converted, and it took a year, from the time they met us to when baptized. They all said they needed to take the step, knew they were Amish deep down."

"I need to talk to Emma," Colleen blurted. "I mean Grandma."

"What's the hurry?"

"We need to prepare." She pulled his face close to hers. "It's the first step in being your wife. But I'm so afraid, and Emma helps me."

Hezekiah cupped her cheeks in his hands. "I promise to wait for you, until I'm an old man, if you promise to be my wife."

He'd wait for her forever? "How can you promise that?"

"Because I see you're Amish in your heart, already, and it won't be too long."

Colleen bit her lower lip, trying not to smile. "I'll say yes to marrying you, if we wed within two years. If I'm not accepted into the Amish church by then, you're free."

Hezekiah picked her up and twirled her around. Their laughter echoed through the woods as the morning sun kissed the blue sky.

~*~

Granny rubbed her knees. This flu was harder to get through than she imagined. And Tillie was in the living room waiting to go on a birthday picnic. She felt her heart swell with love as she looked over at the canning jar filled with flowers set on her dresser, all picked by Tillie. Such a tenderhearted girl, similar to Nathan in many ways.

The news Jeb brought yesterday made her want to get up and jump for joy, if she had the strength. Nathan, always wanting to please, finally stood up to his *mamm*! As soon as she thought this, she quickly asked God to forgive her of any ill-will toward her daughter-in-law. But her own son had married a woman who didn't let him rule the roost. Granny clenched her hands as memories of her urging him to move so far away threatened resentment to grow afresh. *Nee*, I will not. I will think the best, not holding a grudge, like the Good Book says.

She laid her head back on the pillow, fatigue overtaking her. What was wrong with her? Was she really sick or was this old-age? Her bedroom door opened, and she covered her mouth with the corner of her lap quilt, fearing it was Tillie and she'd catch the flu-bug. But she soon saw Jeb, and Fannie? Granny motioned for her to leave, being pregnant.

"I came by to help. Wanted to say hello," Fannie said in the doorway. "Anything I can do?"

"Take Tillie on a picnic."

Jeb held up a hand in protest. "She means help around the house. Lots of work needs to be done, and I can't do it all."

"But I promised Tillie."

"Tillie can wait, *jah*? She's not a spoiled Englisher."

Fannie gasped. "Jeb, we have English friends in our knitting circle. They're not all spoiled...or too pampered, like you think."

Jeb groaned. "I'm sorry. We have Amish camp here again. And I'm praying my hardest Jonas makes it through."

"He feels needed," Granny said with a groan, holding her middle again. "Need to lie down. Fannie, can you wash trousers and dresses in your condition?"

"*Jah*, I'm feeling mighty fine."

"*Danki*, I'll return the favor."

"You can do it today. Pray my *mamm* comes to circle tonight."

"There won't be one," Jeb said, evenly. "She's sick."

"I'm well enough to sit and knit," Granny said, almost in a whisper. "But I need rest right now."

Jeb went over to feel her forehead again. "No fever. *Goot*." He took her hand. "I'll take Tillie on a little picnic for you, since you gave your word about it. Now, just rest."

"*Danki*, Love."

~*~

Jonas bowed his head as a bus full of Englishers unloaded. Jenny was by his side again, so eager to help. He was glad they moved Amish Camp to the afternoon, since he was much too stiff in the mornings.

Jenny leaned her head on his shoulder. "*Opa* Jonas, don't be nervous. Just answer their questions."

"Wish they'd just ask how a cow's milked. Seems like folks ask about controversial issues."

Jenny leaned back. "What's that mean?"

Jonas groaned. "Things people disagree on, and I don't like it."

As the benches filled, Jonas said another silent prayer, and faced them with a smile. Janice got up and introduced him, and asked that hands be raised if you have a question.

An elderly man raised a hand and Jonas nodded. "Do the Amish here milk their cows using machines? I've been to Amish farms where they use diesel power to milk cows."

Jonas thanked God for this question, and then shook his head. "*Nee*, we milk by hand."

"So are you of a stricter Amish branch?"

"We're Old Order Amish, not New Order, if that's what your mean."

The man readjusted his glasses. "This Amish farm I went to was Old Order, though. They said so."

Jonas, again, was thankful, since he had a ready answer. "We're broken down into *Gmays*, or church districts. There's over twenty-some here in the Smicksburg Area. Each one has about two-hundred people in it, and they vote on a thing called the *Ordnung*, the English word for ordinance. In German it's *Verordnung*, but we say *Ordnung* for short."

"So each 'little church' has its own rules? How come?"

"Because we have to abide by them. We come together in the spring, when everything is new, and make new changes to our *Ordnung*, if needed. This past spring, I was dogged determined to have glass-enclosed buggies, since the bone cold winters are hard on my arthritis."

Everyone leaned forward, eyes full of anticipation.

"But it was voted down…"

"That's not very nice," an elderly woman snapped. "I have arthritis and it's painful. Don't the Amish respect their elderly?"

Jonas's jaw gaped open, stunned. Why so much confrontation all the time? He took a deep breath. "Well, if I got a glass-enclosed buggy, everyone would have to get one, and the expense was too much. So the bishop agreed that the *Gmay* would hire an English driver for me in the winter months. I was touched deeply, that the People cared so much to agree on that. English drivers are expensive."

The audience's tone soon cheered up. "That's a wonderful story," Janice said. "I didn't know that. So, everyone votes, even the women?"

"Of course," Jonas chuckled. "Why wouldn't they?"

A lady with black hair streaked with chunks of blonde stood up. "Because most churches are run by men. Gets on my last nerve."

"Well, all the ministers and bishops are male, but the women-folk feed us, and we want to eat," Jonas said with grin.

But this made the lady sneer at him. "My husband helps cook at our church. Are you saying women are only good for cooking, cleaning…having babies? Barefoot and pregnant all the time?"

He felt his heart sink. "I lost my wife years ago. I think she did many *goot* things, not just cook. She was a *wunderbar mamm*, friend to many, helped me run our dry-goods store. We were what some folk call 'two peas in a pod.' And I miss her."

The woman with blond streaked hair put her hand to her heart. "I'm so sorry for saying such a thing. Being so rude."

"Well, you got one thing right; she ran around barefoot all the time."

The crowd roared with laughter, and Jonas looked at Jenny, who just shrugged her shoulders.

"Another question?" Jonas asked.

A middle-aged woman sitting in between her two young children raised a hand. "I see carved pumpkins on the porches here. Why?"

Jonas didn't know what a carved pumpkin had to do with anything. He looked at Jenny who just looked at the woman, baffled. "Well, it's fun, for one thing. And we roast the seeds to eat. We don't put faces or anything on them, if that's what you're wondering. The English do, but we make no image of man on anything."

The lady outstretched her arms around her children, as if to protect them from something. "Do you celebrate Halloween, or think it's the devil's day?"

Jonas cocked his head back as if hit in the face. "Halloween? The devil's day? *Nee*. I won't give one day to that old serpent. My Bible says, 'This is the day the Lord has made; I will rejoice and be glad in it.'" Jonas lifted his hand crutch up toward the sky. "All days are God's, at least in my book."

The woman's eyes narrowed. "But my question was, 'Do the Amish celebrate Halloween?'"

Jonas felt dizzy with emotion. "*Nee*, we celebrate very few holidays, only Christmas, Second Christmas, Ascension Day, Easter and Pentecost. Although Thanksgiving is celebrated by many since they work for the English and have the day off." He sighed. "Any more questions?" he asked, wearily.

An African American man put his hand up. "Are all Amish white?"

"We're all German or Swiss, so our ancestors were Caucasian."

"If someone of color wanted to be Amish, would you allow it?"

Of color? Everyone had a different color. He must mean the color black. "*Jah*, it's a sin to show favoritism. Some Amish have adopted children of other races. The *kinner* are raised Amish, but they have to decide to be Amish in their own mind. It's a serious vow, but if they decide they want to live plain, they're baptized into the church."

The man's brilliant white teeth made his smile seem all the bigger against his black skin. "Thank you."

The air was crisp and windy, and soon orange, yellow, and red leaves danced over the people. The mood was a little lighter than the last few Amish camps. Was it that he was less nervous, or was he getting more acquainted with the English? He looked over at Jenny and nodded.

Jenny took the cue. "There's apple cider on the porch if you want some. That's free, but my *mamm* has pumpkin pies for sale, too."

Janice stood up. "Thank you Jonas, Jenny. Anyone needing a drink or want to buy pies that are out of this world...I mean heavenly....please go over to the porch."

Jonas leaned down and whispered in Jenny's ear. "How'd I do?"

"You're getting much better, *Opa* Jonas. And I like doing this with you."

Jonas leaned his head on hers. "Me too, Jenny. Me too."

~*~

Granny stared at the black alpaca, feeling too tired to wonder if she needed to decrease or not. She laid the half knit socks in her lap, and put her head against the back of her rocker. She looked over at Jeb, stirring the chicken soup, hunched over the large blue speckle ware pot. Jonas had shared that during Amish Camp a woman seemed to think Amish men didn't cook or clean. Well, her Jeb did, and the aroma of sage, parsley and chicken broth made her mouth water. "Love, you didn't have to make soup, but I'm thankful."

"Not a problem at all. Chicken soup is still the best remedy for the flu."

"And antibiotics, *jah*? It's *goot* that Roman's got it through his head he needs to take his heart medicine," Jeb said with relief. "Don't need a repeat of your *daed*."

"*Jah*, taken too soon with his heart condition." Granny looked down at the socks and rubbed the soft alpaca with her fingers. Sometimes it seemed like yesterday that her dear *mamm* and *daed* were alive. Gone home to glory. The sound of buggy wheels on gravel jarred her into reality, and she looked out the window. Hezekiah and Colleen in a buggy? What on earth?

When the buggy came to a halt, the horse neighed and tossed his sleek black mane to and fro. Hezekiah quickly got out of the buggy and took the reins, nuzzling the horse's nose against his cheek. Such a caring, fine man; no wonder Colleen is so taken with him. But she's not Amish...yet. As they ascended the porch steps, Granny sent up a prayer, knowing they didn't come over to borrow sugar.

Jeb met them at the door, one eyebrow cocked. "What brings *yinz* around? And Colleen, you in a buggy? Why not a car?"

Colleen looked up at Hezekiah and beamed. "I'm practicing."

Jeb spun around and looked at Granny, as if needing help. No words came out of his mouth, but she knew that look. He needed her gentle ways to break the tension. "Come on in and have some soup. Jeb made enough for the whole settlement."

Hezekiah took off his straw hat and hung it on a peg on the wall. "*Danki*. But we just got done eating over at Emma's."

Jeb motioned to the long oak table. "Then just have a seat while we eat. Deborah's almost over the flu, but she's still weak." His eyes met hers. "You sit in your rocker, Love. No need to get up."

Granny nodded, thankful for the rocker in the kitchen. Always near the woodstove, nice and warm for winter. She just couldn't peel her eyes off of Colleen's glowing face. This girl, once so sad she couldn't cry and cut herself instead, was having no problems showing her emotions now. She was as bright as a firefly at night. Hezekiah sat almost too close to her on the bench, as if they were a married couple.

Jeb cleared his throat, twiddled his thumbs nervously on the table, and then met Hezekiah with a stern look. "What's all this about? You're Amish."

"And Colleen will be, too. It's what we've come to discuss," he said, unflinching. "Emma's moving into the dawdyhaus, and is mighty lonely, being a widow and all. She's real excited to have Colleen for company."

"And Iva and her *kinner* will be moving into the big farmhouse," Colleen added. "She offered me a job, too, at the quilt shop and I'll be doing farm chores and whatnot."

"Whatnot?" Granny asked. "You sound Amish, but do you know what 'whatnot' means?"

"Yes, whatever needs to be done, I suppose."

"So cleaning a pig pen wouldn't bother you?" Jeb asked with a snap. "How about shoveling horse manure from the horse stalls? Or –"

"She understands, Jeb," Hezekiah interrupted. "We've been working together over at Ella and Zach's place. I can vouch that she actually likes farm chores." He looked over at her fondly. "It's the Amish in her."

Jeb quickly got up, mumbled something under his breath, and ladled soup into a bowl. He took the tray over to Granny. "Here now. You enjoy this."

Granny remembered the last time she was served on a tray. Ella had stayed with her while she was sick. How she'd miss that dear, sweet girl. "*Danki*, Jeb. But I can come to the table."

"*Nee*, sit tight. Garlic tea is coming up next."

She groaned. "Can't you just make it all honey, with no garlic? It's awful."

"Are you feeling any better, Granny?" Colleen asked. "We can come back. It's not that important."

"I think it is," Granny corrected. "If you move in with your *oma*, you'll be out of the program at Forget-Me-Not."

"I know, and I'm thankful for all the Baptists have done, but I want an Amish life."

"And Aurora? Have you settled that part in your heart, too? Only going to eighth grade?"

Colleen nodded enthusiastically. "Emma told me kids learn all there is to learn in eight grades, and she can be a life-long learner. Guess we'll be like homeschoolers, once she's out, always reading something, and learning from life experiences." She put her hands on her heart. "I can't say how much I feel Amish in here. Always have…"

Jeb's eyes softened. "Your actions tell me you're sincere. Giving up the Baptist program and further education is admirable, from an Amish perspective. No disrespect for the Baptist and all, but being Amish is very different. "

Silence filled the kitchen. The wind rustled outside, shaking the windows. Granny glanced out the window, seeing autumn leaves cascade from the heavens. Leaves that were once green, now yellow, crimson, and russet; nothing ever stayed the same, but it was God's handiwork, so change was part of his plan as well.

Granny looked over at Jeb, praying God would help him change with the times. More English than ever wanted to be Amish, and Jeb was always more guarded as to their motives. Being Amish meant faith in Jesus Christ, not just living without conveniences. But Colleen was a believer, and Granny felt deep in her heart she would make an outstanding Amish woman. That Hezekiah seemed to be choosing her above all others, was a testament to her character; many hoped Hezekiah would draw the lot, being a minister, admiring his devotion.

Colleen broke the silence. "Don't you want me in your church? Me having a child out of wedlock and all?"

Jeb cocked his head forward. "Of course I do. I don't judge the past if there's repentance, and you've talked to Deborah enough for me to know your story. *Nee*, it's just that being baptized is a life-long vow, to God and the community, much like a wedding vow. It can't be broken, understand?"

"I think of all people I would understand, since my own mother was shunned. I see the wisdom of living in community. Being out on your own, well, it's like those nature shows: once an animal wonders from the pack, it gets picked off…eaten."

Jeb's smiled softly. "I remember your *mamm*. It's a pity what happened, and I have been praying for years that God would somehow redeem the situation for Emma."

Granny leaned forward. "Maybe this is an answer to prayer. Maybe Colleen will be to Emma what Maddie couldn't be…a faithful Amish daughter."

Jeb looked evenly at Colleen. "You could be an answer to prayer, but you must take the baptismal classes very serious-like."

Colleen clasped her hands. "Then you'll let me take the classes?"

"*Jah*, after you've lived with Emma for a spell and with no car. And I promise to be extra hard on you, since all other baptismal candidates have been raised Amish, and know what they're getting into. But you really don't." Jeb forced a wink. "I'll give you an education."

"*Danki*, Jeb. I knew you'd be fair," Hezekiah said. He looked over at Colleen, smiling his brilliant white smile.

"Now, Hezekiah, you have no right courting a woman not Amish."

"Can't court without kissing. Colleen said she won't kiss me until we're married."

Jeb's jaw gaped. "Is that true, Colleen?"

She nodded and poked Hezekiah in the side. "You're going to have to keep an eye on him, more than me. He steals, and calls himself Amish."

Hezekiah laughed. "Only tried to steal a peck on the cheek."

Jeb's eye met Granny's. As he grinned, she knew what he was thinking. *Young love. It's so beautiful.*

~*~

Jeb slid the pumpkin whoopie pies out of the oven, and nailed his fists to his hips. "They're burnt. *Ach*, how'd I do that?"

Granny opened her eyes, having fallen asleep in her rocker. "What?"

Jeb took the tray over to her and leaning down, displayed the now black pies. "How can you cook with wood? Too hard to know what temperature it is."

"Lots of practice...Old Man. Lots of practice." She yawned and rubbed her eyes. "I dosed off and should have helped you more. I have lots of cookies to serve."

"Are you sure you're up to having the circle? Why not cancel?"

"Because people are living on the streets, and we made a commitment to the Baptists to help." She held up the black socks in her lap. "They need warm feet."

Jeb bent down and kissed her cheek. "You're an angel of mercy."

"I'm an agent of mercy."

"What?"

"We're God's hands to a needy world, *jah*? His agents?"

Jeb put his hand on her cheek. "I do worry about you. We're no spring chickens."

Granny knew Jeb meant well, but did he have to remind her of her age almost daily? "Well, speak for yourself...Old Man." She looked up with a wry smile. "Now, the cookies are in a metal container under the bed. Can you fetch it?"

Jeb shook his head as he headed toward their bedroom. "Under the bed. No wonder I can't find any sweets..." he mumbled.

Granny heard rumbling and Jack barking as she saw from the window a few buggies pulling up to the hitching posts. A van followed, and since it was coming at a slow pace, Granny knew Janice was driving, not Marge. She watched as Colleen ran from the van to Lavina, take her hand and whisper something in her ear, and then Lavina embraced her. Granny prayed Colleen didn't get her hopes up too high. So few English who wanted to become Amish could handle it, but then again, Colleen had lived Amish while a *kinner* from time to time, when her *mamm* dropped her off at Emma's.

She noticed Suzy carrying Molly's bed from the van. Poor little dog. Granny gasped when she saw Mona get out of a buggy with Fannie. Praise be. Knitting was sure to cure Mona's ailing heart. As the girls came into the house, Granny couldn't help but sorely miss Ella. She was probably selling pumpkins and gourds at her stand, putting every penny away for their trip to New York.

"Hello, Deborah," Janice said as she walked over to Granny. "You sure you're up to this?"

"*Jah*, and we'll have it in the living room. Getting nippy outside."

"Let me help you up then."

Granny grimaced. She wasn't an invalid, but let Janice take her by the elbow to the other room, while Lavina followed with her rocker. "*Danki*, but I'm much better." She took her place in the rocker, and Lavina grabbed a lap quilt from the long bench. "Here, you need to keep warm."

Granny had to admit, she was touched by all the pampering. As they all took their seats, knitting in hand, everyone looked at Suzy.

"Well, I see we have a new member. Fannie, do you want to introduce your mother?"

Fannie furrowed her eyebrows. "Everyone knows her, *jah*? Janice and Colleen, you met my *mamm* outside."

Suzy snickered. "I'm sorry. I've taught so many classes, when I see a new face, I always want to introduce. Anyhow, welcome to our knitting circle, Mona. Some call us 'Knit Pickers' because we knit and pick each other up."

Mona's expression was lifeless. Granny couldn't tell if she was sad or glad. She quickly said a silent prayer for Mona and

Fannie. What Fannie must deal with, being pregnant, newly married, and having no real support from her *mamm*. She also prayed that Fannie's sister, Eliza, would get medical help for her post-partum depression. There was always too much put on Fannie.

Suzy's voice cut into her thoughts. She was instructing them again on how to decrease, and many had made mistakes in their socks. Suzy walked around the circle, fixing or instructing, while the others knit.

Jeb appeared out of the kitchen. "I whipped up these cookies in my spare time." He laughed. "If you want one, come and get it. I'm putting them on the kitchen table."

A round of thank you mixed with *danki* filled the room, and the women looked at each other and laughed. Granny heard Colleen say '*danki*' and noticed Janice glare at her. Did Janice know Colleen planned to drop out of the program at Forget-Me-Not?

Granny looked over at Lizzie who was knitting quickly, almost as fast as Suzy. "How was Amish Camp today?"

Lizzie slowed her knitting pace. "It's getting better, but *Daed* thinks the English ask such odd questions. And he so tired after they leave."

"What odd questions?" Janice asked. "I find them all educational."

"Well, they seem to stare at everything around them, and then ask about carved pumpkins. He just never knows what to expect."

"He's doing fine," Janice said, picking up the ball of yarn that fell from her lap. "I do know there are plenty of differences between the English and Amish, though." She looked evenly at Colleen, and stared.

A hush fell over the women, as Janice's tone wasn't too pleasant. Colleen looked around the circle. "Janice is upset that I'm moving in with Emma. I dropped out of the program."

Suzy sat down in an empty spot. "Colleen. How could you? You were making such progress."

All eyes ascended on Suzy. She cupped her mouth. "I'm sorry. Not that being Amish is...not progressing." She shook her head. "I'm just shocked, I guess."

The door flew open and Marge appeared. "So sorry I'm late! But I'm tired a lot lately." She beamed at all the women in the circle. "Can anyone guess why?"

"Living off-the-grid is harder than you thought," Ruth offered.

"I'm pregnant!" Marge twirled around and clapped her hands. "Can you believe it?"

Granny relished the scene. Marge and Joe had changed so much since living among the Amish. First, Joe's faith in God, and then him warming up to children. She wondered if it all started with Jenny. And a little child shall lead them.

Lizzie quickly congratulated Marge, and then got up, saying she needed to check something at home. What on earth could be wrong? Did she see tears in Lizzie's eyes? How she longed to get pregnant, and this must have upset her.

Marge took Lizzie's spot, and quickly took out her knitting. "I'll be making booties now. Crocheting them, since it looks lacier."

Suzy turned, and gasped. "You can make knitting look lacey, too."

Marge chuckled. "I just wanted to get a reaction out of you. Crocheting and knitting are both *wunderbar*, I mean, wonderful."

All the women laughed, except Mona. Fannie's shoulders seemed to sink lower and lower. Suzy went over to Mona, telling her she cast on beautifully and showed her a knit stitch. Again, there was no emotion on Mona's pale face. The mousy brown hair that peaked out from her *kapp* only added to her lifeless face, making her green eyes seem out of place. Granny's met Fannie's gaze and she tried to give her an encouraging look.

Lavina whispered something to Colleen, and she gasped. "Really?"

Janice shook her head. "It's not polite to tell secrets while in a group."

Lavina had light shining from her eyes ever since she'd walked in. "Lavina, do you have *goot* news? Making plans to visit Ohio? Ruth asked."

Lavina lowered her eyes to knit. "I can't say."

Colleen giggled, and Fannie and Ruth's heads shot up. "A secret? We know what that means," Fannie blurted. "Who is it? Hezekiah?" I've seen *yinz* working over at Ella's."

"*Nee*, it's not Hezekiah."

Fannie wrinkled her nose up, deep in thought. Ruth clucked her tongue. "It must be the new family in our *Gmay*. Their son is your age, *jah*?"

Lavina put a hand up. "I said it's a secret, so let's keep it that way." She looked over at Granny who knew full-well it was Nathan. He'd told her this morning, and Granny was just thrilled at the news. But being sick and so fatigued took some of the joy out of the news. And now as she sat, trying to just keep her attention on the conversations going around the circle, she felt her headache coming back. Was it the flu or concern over Lizzie…or Janice's coolness toward Colleen? All she knew was she needed to lay down.

She motioned for Fannie to come over. "Can you help me over to my bedroom? I'm worn out."

Granny heard the concerned voices from the circle, but took hold of Fannie's arm as she led her toward her bedroom. How she loved this circle of friends, but just couldn't stay awake. She bid them all goodbye, apologizing for not being a good hostess. The women one by one got up to kiss her cheek or embrace her. She hoped the doctor was right: not contagious after being on antibiotics for twenty-four hours. She had three pregnant women in her house.

~*~

That night, Granny tossed and turned. Jeb put his hand on her forehead to check for a fever, but she didn't have one. Though weak, she made her way to her rocker by the window. Jeb would be up half the night if she kept disturbing him. She never got tired of looking up at the moon. Tonight it was a half-moon. How appropriate, she pondered. The knitting circle was half Amish, half English, and they were as different as night and day at times. Why was Janice so angry? Was it so awful that Colleen wanted to be Amish? Did Janice think deep down that their way of living was odd? Why not be happy for Colleen? She was. And Marge was moving for sure. Didn't she want her *boppli* living off-the-grid? Joe said the English spoiled their *kinner* too much. Would they do that, too, always following English ways when they knew it wasn't right?

Her mind turned to Lizzie. She'd seen through her bedroom window Roman walking with her, hand-in-hand, down to the pumpkin patch while the other women were knitting. Or was she dreaming? She was awfully tired. Had she dozed off in this rocker? Or did Marge's announcement affect Lizzie that much?

Granny closed her eyes and prayed.

Lord,

I love my Amish life. Always have and always will. Danki for it. Long ago, when people thought us odd, I cherished it. Now, we're such a curiosity, outsiders pay to learn our ways. But why is Janice upset? And why isn't Marge raising her boppli on the best spot on earth? Ach, Jenny could be a wunderbar influence on the child, and could even be of help to Marge. She and Joe didn't seem to have much family. And…neither did Janice. Is that why she's so upset? Is her church, and the girls at Forget-Me-Not, like her own kin? If so, that would make the English more similar to the Amish than I thought. Fannie is like my own…

Fannie…Lord, help her. Help Mona and bring healing to their relationship. I know Fannie feels cheated in life, having no mamm really there for her. And then there's Lizzie, who longs so much to be a mamm, not only to the girls, but her own boppli. Having so many women pregnant at the circle upset her so. Touch her heart.

I cast all these women I dearly love on you.

In Jesus name,

Amen.

~*~

Thank you following Granny and her knitting circle. In the last episode, we'll see many changes come to the women in the group:

I leave my dear reader with a recipe for Pumpkin Whoopee Pies. Enjoy!

Pumpkin Whoopie Pie

1 c. Crisco or oil
1 c. pumpkin
1 tsp. cinnamon
1 tsp. baking powder
1 tsp. baking soda
½ tsp. salt
1 egg
1 c. brown sugar
2 c. flour

Mix together Crisco, pumpkin, sugar and egg. Beat well. Sift dry ingredients and fold in. Beat and drop by teaspoon full on greased cookie sheet. Bake at 350 degrees. Take two cookies and spread with filling, holding them together.

Whoopie Pie Filling
2 egg whites
2 t vanilla
4 T flour
4 T milk
4 c. powdered sugar
1 c. Crisco

Beat egg whites until stiff. Add other ingredients. Spread between cookies and enjoy.

If you'd like to have a simple pumpkin cookie, don't sandwich together with filling. You may add nuts or raisin to the cookie recipe for a more filling cookie.

Episode 8

Autumn Changes

Granny ran to the window and pulled it shut. The late autumn winds had blown over the chicory wildflower bouquet the girls had placed on her table. Colleen and Lavina quickly got paper towels to wipe up the water that poured from the canning jar used for a vase. "*Danki,* my girls," Granny said. As she watched Colleen collect water off the floor, she was seeing something from the past; Madeline, Colleen's *mamm,* in Amish clothes. She observed that Colleen look pretty in her new mauve dress and black apron. *But Colleen could stray from the Amish, too.* Was Hezekiah setting his cap on a woman he may be unequally yoked with? Surely not, Granny hoped, since Hezekiah had waited for so long to find the one he loved.

"I can see why the Amish always wear aprons," Colleen said, beaming. "Always work to do*, jah?*"

"How do you like wearing Amish clothes?" Lavina asked. "You used to wear such bright colors. Do you miss it?"

Colleen shook her head. "No, it's actually easier. I have five dresses and aprons. Not much to pick from, so I can get ready in no time." She went back over to the counter to roll out more pie crusts. "I do miss the girls at Forget-Me-Not, though. So does Aurora…she starts Amish school next week."

Granny sensed concern in Colleen's tone. "And is Aurora looking forward to going to school? Dressed plain and all?"

"She misses her pants, and does complain a bit too much. But Emma, I mean, Grandma, is so good with her and gets her smiling again." Colleen peeled the waxed paper from the top of the dough and flipped it into the pie plate. "I don't see how my mother could ever leave the Amish…"

"She fell for your dad, an *Englisher*. And in a way, you're following in her footsteps," Granny said, measuring flour to make more dough.

Colleen spun around. "I am nothing like my mother," she snapped.

Lavina went over to put a hand on Colleen's shoulder. "Granny just means you both fell for someone outside your…people. Your *mamm* and an *Englisher*, and you an Amish fella."

"*Ach*, I'm sorry Colleen, if you misunderstood. Having both parents on drugs, being neglected as you've been, well, we all know you're a fine *mamm*." Though Colleen turned to her, nodded to accept her apology, Granny noticed something she didn't like: bitterness and unforgiveness. That may be harder for Colleen to conquer than living plain. Surely Jeb would address the issue while she went through baptismal classes.

Nathan came in the side door, and locked his eyes on Lavina. She turned and gave him a knowing look. He wanted to take a walk…*again*. Granny cleared her throat. "Nathan, it's not time for the noon meal yet."

"I know. Just taking a break. Looks like *yinz* need one, too."

Granny plopped white flour into the large stainless steel bowl. "Nathan, we're having fun making pies. And we won't be taking a break until the pies are done, *jah*?"

Defeat registered in Nathan's forlorn eyes. Granny had to stifle a laugh. He was like her dog, Jack, always wanting to be next to her when she was outside. But being the bishop's wife, she knew more than she wanted. Jeb wanted Nathan and Lavina to wait until February so they'd know each other for a full year, before being married. Granny remembered how they met on her seventieth birthday party, Nathan coming down from Montana to surprise her. When introduced to Lavina, he was taken with her immediately. How things had changed. Granny was appalled that Nathan would want to court a girl who had *kinner* out of wedlock. *How judgmental she'd been.* Now she knew Lavina's story. Now she knew the real Lavina, and she was her choice for her beloved grandson.

Granny heard Nathan make his exit out the side door and she went back to making dough. Another strong wind rattled the house, and Granny looked out the window. Red, yellow, and orange leaves cascaded from the trees in the back woods, leaving bare branches once again. How she loved autumn, but she couldn't preserve it in a canning jar; no, winter was coming and she'd try to see the good in it. *The treasures of the snow*, as was written in the Book of Job.

"We'll talk at dinner about our situation, *jah?*" Lavina asked. "Nathan's determined to have a wedding next month."

Granny closed her eyes as she kneaded the dough. *Lord, your will be done. And if Jeb's being stubborn, show him.*

~*~

Suzy sat spinning yarn, and wished she could do it all day, non-stop. How she loved to see the fluffy wool spin together making strong yarn. She thought of the knitting circle, and warmth filled her heart. Women *were* stronger when spun together, like Granny always said. Teaching the Wednesday night class spun them all closer, but it was getting too large.

Fannie's mom had been coming again last week, and she saw her smile for the first time. Maryann and her daughter, Becca, came to the last circle, too. It was heartwarming to see a mother and daughter doing something together, as much as they'd resisted knitting with needles and not looms. And Maryann looked the picture of health, and the women at the circle were confident she'd beaten breast cancer, for sure. But still, the five year wait to be considered cancer-free must have been unnerving to Maryann. The knitting circle encouraged her to come, since the craft was good for the nerves. And to think that Maryann wanted to make prayer shawls for cancer patients would help her as much as the recipient.

This was Suzy's ministry the Lord gave her. The gift of art and knitting. Seeing people learn this craft and share it with others. Everyone had their place in the world, and Suzy knew her knitting shop was where she was to be. She glanced over at Mollie, lying on her little brown cushion. As usual, she needed to stare with her hand on her heart. *Was she breathing?* After a few seconds, she called the dog's name. No response. Deep down, she knew. Her little Mollie was gone. Suzy's body shook from deep within, no matter how much she didn't want to believe what she was seeing. She called to her dog again, but the little thing didn't move.

"Dave!" She cried out for her husband, but then realized her was at work. She needed someone to be with her. Suzy ran to the phone and called Janice. When she picked up, Suzy couldn't even talk, just sob. Janice said she'd be right over.

~*~

Granny shielded her eyes from the sun that peaked through the clouds. When the Baptist church van came to a stop in her driveway, Janice's face told her something tragic had happened. She ran down off the porch and met Janice as she made her way to her. "What happened?"

Janice swiped a runaway tear, then pulled out her handkerchief, and wiped her eyes. "Mollie's gone."

Granny embraced Janice, wondering how Suzy was doing if the death of the little dog affected Janice so much. She didn't understand the bond the English had with animals. It was as if they were real people. Jack slept in the barn and ate regular dog food bought at the feed store in bulk, not fancy little containers she'd seen at Punxsy-Mart. The food looked good enough for humans to eat.

Janice pulled away and stood tall. "I know she wasn't mine, but that little dog was by Suzy's side during hard times. My side, too. And how she helped Ginny Rowland after her mother passed away. It was like she was a human trapped in a dog body."

"Now, now," Granny said as she rubbed the side of Janice's arm. "Let's just get her another dog."

"Too soon," Janice said in a hollow, monotone voice. "She needs to grieve Mollie's loss."

"*Ach*, Janice. We need to move forward. I saw a little dog at the pet store in Punxsy. I wonder if it's still there."

Janice scratched the side of her cheek. "I don't think Suzy's up to it."

Colleen talked and giggled with Lavina as they brought pies wrapped in aluminum foil out to the van. But when they saw Janice, they froze. "Janice, what's wrong? Are you still upset with me?" Colleen asked. "I thought we'd talked and there was —"

"Mollie died, and my dear Suzy is a wreck. Can't even spin her wool." Fresh tears sprang from Janice's eyes, and once again, she raised her handkerchief to blot her tears.

"It hurts to see a friend in pain, *jah*?" Lavina asked. "And the closer we get the more pain...."

Janice peeked up at Lavina. "Exactly. I've never seen Suzy cry so. It ripped my heart out."

Granny looked at Lavina in admiration. What a sensitive girl. Janice was hurting because her friend was hurting, and she wondered why Lavina picked up on Janice's feelings so easily. Was it that Lavina had seen more heartache than was normal for her eighteen years? She hoped the dinner with Lavina and Nathan tonight didn't cause more pain in her life...

~*~

Granny urged her horse forward, eager to catch Marge at home. The woman worked so much on their little farm along with being a nurse to homebound patients; no wonder she was burnt out. The wind beat her face, along with a few stray leaves. Jenny, the little scientist, had told her that all the splendors of fall, all the reds, yellows, and oranges in the leaves, were their true colors, after the green chlorophyll drained out. She thought people were like that; when drained, their true colors came out. Drained of themselves and putting others first; what a beautiful sight. Her knitting girls were all an array of colors, she mused, all looking to one another's needs.

She spied Marge's red car and Joe fixing wire fencing so none of their prized turkeys could escape. Granny waved, and with shoulders hunched, Joe waved back. "Marge's in the big house," he yelled. "We're getting it ready for the buyers." Granny nodded and wondered who these new buyers were. Ruth and Luke had decided to stay at their place so their little Micah and new *boppli* on the way would live by their grandparents. To think that Luke only wanted to do it for Ruth made Granny's heart glad, once again. It was a sure sign of a healed and happy marriage: trying to bless your spouse more than being blessed.

Soon Marge appeared, a red bandana hiding her red hair. "Hi Granny. Still painting. Come on in."

Granny shook her head. "You're pregnant and do too much. Why are you painting?"

Marge went into the small living room and dipped a paintbrush into a bucket of white paint. "The Amish need white walls, right?"

"*Nee*, just earth toned, according to our *Ordnung.* You've seen blue or green walls in Amish homes, *jah*?"

"Well, I think white walls look clean."

Granny never thought of fall colors being used in their homes. She was instantly drawn to the crimson-colored walls in the new doctor in town's office. *Ach*, she'd been Amish all her life, yet never questioned such things. The white paint

Marge put on the walls hid every blemish, and she agreed, white looked clean. "Marge, can you drive me up to Punxsy?"

"What for? We were up there a few days ago."

"*Jah*, when we took those poor kittens up to the shelter. And remember that little black dog?"

"The Pomeranian? Most likely it's gone. They're an expensive dog."

"Suzy's dog died," Granny said.

Marge spun around, cupped her hands over her cheeks, not thinking that a loaded paintbrush was now leaning on her red bandana. "Oh, that's horrible news."

"It's natural. Mollie *was* fifteen years old, and I think it's time for a new dog. That little black one we saw…"

Marge's eyes softened. "Granny, you are so sweet." She made her way to Granny with open arms. "I just want to squeeze the goodness out of you."

Granny put a hand up. "Not covered in paint."

Marge pursed her lips, and to Granny's shock, they began to quiver. "Wish I *was* as good as you, for real. Joe doesn't really want to leave this place, and I feel I've let him down."

Granny stepped onto clear plastic drop cloth, dodging pools of white paint, taking a seat in a rocker. "Marge, when I first met you, I told you it was hard to live off the grind, remember?"

Marge grinned. "I remember you saying that. 'Off-the-grind'. In a way, you sure were right. It is more than drudgery than I ever thought."

"Drudgery? Such a strong word."

"I know. Joe says I can be a drama queen. Let's just say it's too hard for me."

"Your expectations were too high. How could they ever be met?"

"What do you mean?"

Granny leaned her head back on the rocker. "*'Say not thou, What is the cause that the former days were better than these? For thou dost not enquire wisely concerning this.'*"

Marge cocked her head back as if hit in the face. "What? You lost me on this one."

"It's in the Bible. Ecclesiastes 7:10. It warns to not look back to those old-fashioned days you talk about. All generations have their problems."

Marge arched an eyebrow, and then rushed into her kitchen, bringing back a book. "I need to look that up in *The Message*. Can't understand the KJV for the life of me." She flipped through the Bible as fervently as the sale items at Punxsy-Mart, looking for a 'find' and then sighed. "Where is Ecclesiastes?"

"It's right after Proverbs."

Marge looked up, cheeks turning pink. "Thanks." She skimmed through the book a few seconds, and then held it close to her face. "Don't have my reading glasses, but here goes. *'Don't always be asking, 'Where are the good old days?' Wise folks don't ask questions like that.'"* Marge slowly turned and looked out the window. "*Little House on the Prairie*...the good old pioneer days." She struck her forehead with the palm of her hand, leaving a white blotch of paint. "Oh, I've been such a fool."

Granny leaned forward. "Don't be so hard on yourself. Lots of English think we live trouble free, like Laura Ingalls. I read the book, and it's *wunderbar*. We need stories that make us really think about what's important. Laura found out it was family and community, *jah*? And you did, too?"

Marge went to Granny and collapsed at her feet, now getting paint on her jeans. "Am I being hasty?"

"Hasty? I don't know. You've worked hard to raise all those turkeys. Aren't you going to sell them next month to the English for Thanksgiving?"

"Joe teased me for naming rabbits and getting too attached. Guess who named some of those turkeys? Now, Joe's stomach turns when he thinks of people coming to pick one to slaughter. We're such failures at farming; it's almost comical."

Granny knew she needed to get some fresh air, since the paint fumes were giving her a headache. "How about you clean up and we talk on the way to Punxsy. I'll treat you to a pumpkin ice-cream shake."

Marge licked her lips. "Yum. Hey, that's not fair, bribing me with ice cream." She shifted. "Don't you think it's too soon for Suzy to have a new dog?"

Granny swatted at the air. "It's a dog who died, not a person. Suzy will love having a new pet." As Marge stood there contemplating what to do, Granny sighed. "Okay, a pumpkin ice cream shake *and* pumpkin pie."

Marge cupped her mouth. "And you're a respectable Amish woman! Bribing me with pie, too?"

"*Ach*, Marge, you have a white mustache now. Paint all over you."

Marge gasped. "Really? I best get washed up so we can go. But I'm telling your bishop on you." She winked. "You're not supposed to prey on people's weaknesses or bribe. I can taste the pumpkin now."

"I'm not bribing," Granny offered, but Marge had run out of earshot already, lunging up the stairs, climbing two steps at a time. *Preying on another's weakness? Surely not!*

~*~

Ella swallowed hard, forcing herself not to cry. Seeing Ruth and Fannie packing her dishes into boxes, wrapping each one in newspaper for padding, made fear run through her. What if she was lonely in New York? What if she didn't make *goot* friends? Ella continued to fold the cloth diapers, when another fear invaded her mind. What if she never got over being homesick? She'd known many an Amish woman who had to move and always missed Smicksburg, never adapting to their new home. *If I had a car, it wouldn't be so bad.* As this thought rushed at her, Ella felt overwhelmed. She'd never once in her whole life felt deprived with a horse and buggy. What was wrong with her?

"What's wrong, Ella?" Fannie asked. "You look pale."

Ella sat in the rocker near her. "My mind isn't at peace. Are we doing the right thing?"

Ruth picked up a petit China cup. "Need some tea? Chamomile for the nerves?"

She shook her head. "The oddest thing happened this morning. The smell of tea made me sick. My nerves are completely unraveled."

Fannie nudged Ruth. "Morning sickness?"

"What?" Ella blurted. "I'm barren. It's my stomach doing flip-flops at the thought of leaving Smicksburg...and my *Gmay*...and my knitting circle friends."

Fannie stood up and pat her ever growing stomach. "Have you been snippy?"

Ella closed her eyes. Fannie got such notions. "The twins can be a handful, but I try to keep an even temper."

"Do you snap at Zach?" Fannie probed.

Ella thought of Zach's reaction to her last night. *I don't know who you are anymore.* She'd deserved it, having yelled at him like never before. She didn't actually *know* herself anymore. Maybe this move was too much. God didn't give his children more than they could handle, so maybe this move wasn't God's will.

Fannie continued, hands on her hips. "Do you have swollen ankles?"

"Swollen ankles? Of course. I've been moving and lifting boxes. Anyone's ankles would be sore and swollen."

Ruth placed another wrapped dish in a box. "Fannie, Ella has enough to think about right. Let her be."

"*Nee.* Ruth, you know the signs. I'm getting my five month check-up later today, and Ella, you're coming."

"I am not. I have too much to do and I was told I couldn't have children by a doctor." Ella hoped this would put the issue to rest, so she closed her eyes and rocked, trying to shut out the world.

"Sarah. She was barren too and had a *kinner* in her old age. Elizabeth, John the Baptist's *mamm* was barren, too. And

Rachael in the Old Testament." Fannie paused to breathe. "And how about Hannah, my favorite Bible character?"

Ella put a hand up. "I'll go with you if you need the company…"

~*~

Janice sat in the overstuffed chair, in her bedroom on the first floor of Forget-Me-Not Manor. The blue alpaca scarf was bound to make some homeless boy or girl warm in a few months. She knit one, purled one, seeing the pattern clear enough to not have to wonder what she needed to stitch next.

Knitting was her solace behind the closed door that shut out the problems and worries of the girls, the princesses that came to live at the refuge to get off the streets. But she knew today, when she broke down sobbing about Mollie, she was going over the brink, into a valley. A cavern of despair. One tear could unleash a whole dam of welled up tears, and that's what she did at Granny's. How embarrassing. Even though Joe said he came to faith by seeing the folks at the Baptist church, along with the Amish, be real and, and through that, saw a real God at work in their lives…she scared herself at the lack of self-control.

She'd have to go to counseling; it was obvious. Maybe some childhood pain was buried deep and she just hadn't dealt with it yet. Maybe some degrading thing said about her African American heritage in elementary school. All she knew was that she felt hollow one minute, then sad, then grouchy, and happy. Was she manic depressive? Or was it menopause?

A heavy knock on the door made her jump. "Who is it?"

"Guess who, sugar." The door opened and a hand clenching a bouquet of red roses appeared. "Can I come in?"

Janice stared at the red flowers wrapped in green tissue paper. "Jerry, did I forget something? What day is it? What month, for that matter?"

He stepped inside the room, a smile extending from ear to ear, accenting his sparkling white teeth. "I'm done."

"What?" Janice clenched the yarn in her hands. "You're done with what?"

He came over, pulled her out of her chair, and started to waltz around the room. "I just got word from the school that I am finished." He twirled her around. "Every bit of paperwork for my dissertation is in and I am now Doctor Jerry Jackson. Woo Hoo!"

Janice tried to shake off the confusion running through her mind. "How come I never knew you were so close to graduating?"

Jerry pulled her close. "Because you kept saying to stop talking so much about school."

Janice searched Jerry's eyes to see if he was serious. He was. "Oh, honey. No wonder I've been feeling so left out in the cold. You needed my support."

He stole a kiss. "And you've needed mine the whole time I was in school. Now sit down again. I have a surprise." He put the flowers on their dresser as Janice sat back down in her chair. Jerry knelt down before her. "Honey. We can move...back home."

Janice's eyebrows furrowed into one straight line. "Say what?"

"I can get a job at a college now. At a Bible college down south, in the Bible Belt."

"Do you want to? I mean, leave Smicksburg?"

Jerry eyes grew as round as buttons. "You do, right? You're always talking about the South, and how much you miss it."

Janice covered her eyes and let the tears flow. "I've missed *you*."

"And I've missed you, too." He leaned on her knees. "But I'm done with school for good, and we have more options. So, what do you want to do?"

Janice clasped her hands over her heart. "I don't want to move. I just want us to work together in the ministry like we used to."

"But I can make more money as a college professor. You'd have a nice house, drive a nice car and not the church van..."

Having Jerry next to her, talking heart to heart like they used to, his mind completely calm and not unnerved by school was such a delight. Janice leaned forward and locked her hands around Jerry's neck. "Honey, I see those signs in the Amish stores in town that read, 'The best things in life aren't things', and I can say right now, I totally agree."

Jerry comically scratched his chin. "Translate that."

She laughed. "I'm saying I don't care about things. Things aren't the best things in life, but people are. And the ones I love most live in this tiny little town, where you get paid as much as a church mouse."

Jerry got up and swung both arms in the air. "Touchdown!" He ran over to his side of the bedroom and got his Steeler's Terrible Towel and swung it in a circle over his head. "Woo Hoo!" He ran back to her side. "I thought you deserved better, Janice. Are you sure?"

"I'm positive. But, you went to school to better equip yourself too, right?"

"I went for that too. And I do feel more able to deal with counseling issues. Getting tougher ones all the time."

Janice sighed. "You think it's the signs of the times?"

"I don't know, but there's a lot of work to do…right here in Smicksburg." He pulled her close and kissed her until she was out of breath.

~*~

Colleen pulled a red maple leaf from Hezekiah's blond hair, and then turned to run further down the path. "I'll beat you."

"I'll let you," Hezekiah called out.

She turned and scooped up an armful of leaves and threw them at him, and his laughter echoed around the forest. Colleen dashed ahead, making it to the log seat in the Secret Garden and plopped herself on it. "There. I told you so."

Hezekiah's eyes twinkled. "You're too English, being so competitive…"

Colleen grinned, knowing he was kidding. "If God can change a leaf from green to red, he can change me, *jah*?" He sat next to her, leaning close, and she felt the warmth of his breath against the crisp autumn day. As they drew closer, she turned and stared at her black apron. "I'm more Amish than you, listening to my bishop."

Hezekiah took her hand. "I'm sorry. But this is harder than I thought. No kissing…"

"I know. It's hard for me, too."

A red squirrel skittered across a trail of leaves, then down a hole. "He's preparing for winter. Wonder how many holes he has nuts stored in?" Hezekiah attempted to direct their minds in another direction.

Colleen wished that she and Hezekiah could just run off and be married. *Your mamm never considered long-term consequences,* her grandma, Emma, had confided in her. What started as a mere flirtation with Colleen's dad soon absorbed her mother and she landed in a world filled with darkness. Colleen thought of her parents, the unstable home, having to steal at a young age for drug money. Drug money for her parents. *Her own parents,* a missing ring from her friend's house in fourth grade, a necklace from another girl. No wonder she fell for the first man who came into her life; it was her ticket out, so she thought. But when he heard she was pregnant, he was gone.

"Are you upset with me?" Hezekiah asked.

His question brought her from her daze, and she squeezed his hand. "No, not at all. I was just thinking…"

"About what?"

"What is real love? I mean, I see it in Granny and Jeb's marriage, but is it real or a show?"

Hezekiah looked ahead as another squirrel scurried up a nearby tree. "*Nee,* it's real. Love is a sacrifice."

Colleen nudged him. "That's not very romantic."

"*Nee,* it is. When we say our vows in the Amish church, we will promise to be loyal and care for each other during adversity, affliction, sickness, and weakness."

She leaned her head on his shoulder. "Sounds like you've memorized that."

"I've been to plenty of weddings, and every time I've heard those vows spoken, I've asked the *goot* Lord to give me someone I can sincerely promise that to." He put his hand on her new prayer *kapp*. "But I don't have to pray that anymore, since He brought me you."

Colleen felt like she'd melt into a puddle. This was the most romantic thing she'd ever heard, even in a movie. Too afraid to look up over at him, knowing that if there was ever a time she wanted to kiss him, it was now, she simply whispered, "I love you so much…"

Hezekiah leaned his head on hers and they simply sat in silence, enjoying a moment that seemed sacred.

Colleen fidgeted with the hem of her new mauve dress. "It's daylight savings time next week. We'll need to turn back the clocks and it'll be dark at five."

"See, you're so *English* still. I can see why Jeb says we need to wait for six months…"

"What?"

"We Amish don't ever change our clocks. Only the *English*."

She turned toward him, eyes wide. "Seriously? Why not?"

"I don't know. Just never have, but if you work for the *English,* you need two clocks, so you're not late for work."

His blue eyes were drawing her in. She knew it wasn't intentional luring, but they just radiated love, something she'd been starved of for so long. When their eyes continued to lock, the image of her mother, a foolish, headstrong woman who never abided by any rules, flashed before her, and she got up. "Best be getting home…"

"*Jah*," Hezekiah said. "And maybe we shouldn't be coming here alone anymore. We could sit on Emma's porch…"

Colleen couldn't believe the integrity this man before her possessed, and right then, she knew good marriages like Granny and Jeb's must be true. Not something without problems, like a fairytale, but one that sacrificed fleeting pleasure for long-term happiness. How sad it was that her mother grew up in Smicksburg, having a nice family, and gave it all up due to a lack of self-control.

Hezekiah led the way back to the path, and Colleen for the first time felt sorry for her mother…or was it forgiveness? She didn't know, but she knew she'd be praying for her parents on a regular basis, since she now knew what happiness was…

~*~

Granny nuzzled the little black Pomeranian up against her cheek. "Such a pretty little thing. I'm sure Suzy will like her."

"Beatrix," Marge said. "We need to call her by her name so she doesn't forget." She rubbed her hand on the little dog's head. "You are so cute with those brown eyebrows."

"And she has an Amish beard," Granny mused. "All under her chin."

Marge let out a howl, as she opened the door to Suzy's shop, but soon stifled it. Suzy was in the store, to their shock, standing on a ladder, placing yarn on the top shelves. "Suzy, we're so sorry about Mollie."

"*Jah*, we are very sorry," Granny added. "But look at this little black dog we got you."

Suzy stared at the dog, not flinching. Granny couldn't tell if she was happy about seeing Beatrix or not.

"Do you want to hold her?" Granny asked.

Suzy, still speechless, made her way down the ladder and took a seat at her desk. After fiddling with some papers, she looked at Beatrix. "I'm sorry. I can't take her."

Granny made her way towards Suzy, the dog held out to her. "Here, just hold her and see how sweet she is."

Marge cleared her throat. "Suzy, I tried to tell Granny, but she insisted."

Suzy's eyes welled up with tears. "It was a really nice thought, but it's too soon. I need to grieve the loss of my old friend…" She pursed her lips as tears rolled down her cheeks. She took a Kleenex and wiped her face, and took up her knitting. "Maybe in a few months or so, but not today."

Granny didn't want to admit it, but this little dog had grown on her the whole way back from the shelter. Her huge brown eyes were filled with hope. "I'll keep her until you're ready."

Suzy reached out and took Granny's hand. "Deborah, you are one beautiful woman. I appreciate your concern, but I think I'm going to get another toy fox terrier like Mollie…when I'm ready."

Granny thought of Jack, and wondered if she'd feel the same about Black Labs. Would she want another dog just like him? She didn't think so, since she liked all types of dogs. Jack was a stray in need of food and shelter. She nodded to Suzy and looked at Marge. "Well, maybe you can take her."

Marge rolled her eyes. "No way. I'm moving and don't want the bother."

"The bother?" Granny asked. She looked at Beatrix. "She's not a bother; she's adorable."

To Granny's shock, Suzy laughed. "You're taken."

"Come again?"

"You're attached already to that little dog," Suzy said. "Little dogs are nice to cuddle."

"Cuddle? Dogs are used for a purpose. What would I do with Beatrix?"

Suzy looked at Marge for help. Marge hit her knee and howled. "You can spin her fur."

Granny tried not to laugh, but she couldn't help it, and joined in, noticing Suzy was laughing, too. "That's *lecherlich*."

"What?" Marge asked.

"*Ach*, sorry. I meant to say ridiculous."

Suzy opened her desk drawer and pulled out a book on how to spin pet hair. "Lots of people do it..."

Granny felt the little dog's heart beat rapidly as the noise got louder in the room. "It's okay, Bea. No one's going to hurt you." She nuzzled her nose into the dog's deep, shiny black fur. "Granny's here." She looked up and saw Suzy and Marge staring at her, as if in shock. "We Amish like dogs too, but we find a purpose for them, and it won't be for spinning fur."

Suzy got up and pet the little dog's head. "You go on home now and meet your dad. Jeb will be a good daddy."

The English, no matter how long you've known them, never ceased to surprise Granny. *Jeb, a daed to a dog? Lecherlich.*

~*~

Joe held Marge's hand as Jerry made his way to the podium to teach Bible study. They'd be living fifteen miles away, and it would be hard to come consistently to Wednesday night church, and they both knew it. Living down the road again from his father would be a challenge, but somehow he felt sorry for the old man. Did faith do that? Soften a heart, as Marge put it.

Jerry asked Janice to put the words of the chosen scripture up on the overhead projector, as usual, but he had a twinkle in his eyes. And he didn't look tired. Why?

"Please open your Bibles to Ecclesiastes 3. I'm going to read this familiar scripture from the Contemporary English Version. Sometimes we're so familiar with a scripture, it loses its impact.

"Everything on earth has its own time and its own season.
There is a time for birth and death, planting and reaping, for
killing and healing, destroying and building,
For crying and laughing, weeping and dancing,
For throwing stones and gathering stones, embracing and parting.
There is a time for finding and losing, keeping and giving,
For tearing and sewing, listening and speaking.
There is also a time for love and hate, for war and peace."

Joe reread, *embracing and parting…*Somehow, he'd felt like such a failure, not being able to live off the grid. And friends from Indiana always teased them about their harebrained schemes, along with his father. But he knew that in a short time, he'd learned more about himself and Marge than in years of marriage. And being in the quiet so much, without distractions, made time slow down enough for him to notice God…and children. Amish kids playing happily with a jump rope, or pulling a homemade wagon, gave him great hope that they wouldn't be bringing a child into a hostile world.

Marge felt the move was worth it. Her *Little House on the Prairie* fantasy was over, but she'd gleaned a lot from the Amish lifestyle. The television wasted too much time, and she only wanted to have one to watch Steeler games.

A peace he could not describe settled in Joe's heart. They were moving, and it was the right thing to do. Some seasons were short, but their impact lasted forever.

~*~

Suzy had to concentrate on breathing, let alone understanding the Bible tonight. But she knew she needed the support of her church. Every hug and kind word helped lift her burden. She knew Jerry had picked the text for tonight, just for her, knowing she needed the comfort of knowing, *"There is a time for birth and death, planting and reaping."* Granny was right; it was natural that someday Mollie would pass on, as sure as the dying leaves outside fell from the trees. But the dead leaves nourished the ground, and the memory of Mollie would feed her soul forever.

Janice slid in and sat next to her. "Are you alright?" she whispered in her ear.

Suzy nodded. Being in this special church always brought rest. The large wooden cross hung on the wall, plain and simple; the church had been a place where she'd laid many a burden down.

"Are you sure you're okay?" Janice said, squeezing her hand. "You look pale. Really pale."

She slowly turned toward Janice. "I'm drained, not a tear left to shed."

Janice bowed her head, sandwiching Suzy's hand in hers, and Suzy knew that her dear sister was lifting her up in prayer, right then and there. That's what a true church was for, carrying one another's burdens, and joy filled her heart. She was a blessed woman to have so much: faith, family, community. And to think, God had enabled her to bring women together in community through the art of knitting.

A new sense of purpose bubbled in her, quite by surprise, and she knew, that she was going to be alright. Yes, there would be days ahead filled with sadness and loss, but she'd only dive further into her God-given gift: knitting.

~*~

Granny felt warmth nuzzle up against her back, and she was thankful for the cold nights. Jeb snuggled up against her and it was her favorite spot on earth: to be in Jeb's arms. Then a bark pierced into her head, and she whipped around to see the little black dog, right next to her on the bed. "*Ach*, Jeb, you held her all night? On the bed?"

Jeb scooped the dog up in one arm. "She was crying in the middle of the night. Didn't you hear?"

"*Nee*. And I don't want a dog on the bed, of all things." She picked up some stray fur that lay on her white sheets. "Fur, everywhere."

"You can spin it, *jah*? A reason to keep her?"

Granny tried to look at Jeb sternly, but couldn't, and let out a laugh. "It's you who wants to keep her, Old Man."

Jeb snickered. "That I am. A very old man who wants to see his old woman have a companion."

She shook her head. "You think I'm lonely?"

"I think you like to hold something soft, like yarn. It's *goot* for your nerves. And when your nerves are *goot*, my nerves are *goot*."

Granny squinted. "What? Jebediah Weaver, what's come over you?"

He chuckled. "Maybe Bea is *goot* for my nerves. My bones don't seem to ache this morning."

"Bea? Good for your arthritis? So cuddling with a dog at night is better than snuggling with me?"

Jeb kissed Bea on the head. "I think she's come between us, Deborah. But look at those big, brown eyes. She needs love."

Granny got out of bed, slid her slippers on and took her robe off the pegboard, and wrapped it around her. "I'm going to the phone shanty and calling the doctor. You need to get your head examined."

"*Ach,* Love, why don't you admit you're happy. Glad that I want to keep her? Like Lizzie's keeping that rabbit of hers?"

She looped her long gray hair around the back of her head and started to pin it up. "She's sleeping on the floor, though. Don't want Little Bea coming between us, *jah*?"

Granny gave Jeb a knowing look, and he put the dog on the floor, and stretched his arms out to her. "Come, Deborah. It's too early to get up."

She could never resist being held by Jeb, so she was immediately drawn into his arms. She could hear his heart beating, and he started to unpin her hair. Granny closed her eyes, taking in the rich, deep love they shared, but soon a sharp bark broke the dreamlike moment. Bea was back on the bed, again, trying to squeeze in-between them, and to her surprise, she felt Jeb's body start to jiggle; he was laughing...and soon she was too.

~*~

Lizzie cuddled the rabbit, glad to have something warm to hold on this cold autumn morning. The pitter-patter of feet coming down the steps, mixed with the scent of coffee, pancakes and sticky buns made her realize something. *She was blessed.* Even though she wasn't pregnant, and was sometimes hopeless about the prospect, she had Roman and the girls. And her *daed* was happily adjusted in the little *dawdyhaus* attached to the house....

"*Guder mariyer, Mamm*," Tillie said as she hugged Lizzie's middle.

"*Guder mariyer*, honey." She looked over at Jenny and Millie, already sitting at the oak table. "Are you girls hungry?"

"*Jah*, I am," Millie said. "And I can't wait to play with *Oma's* new dog, so I'll eat fast."

Lizzie put the rabbit down, and put the breakfast, along with a pitcher full of apple cider, on the table. "What about Petunia? Have you forgotten your rabbit so quickly? She still needs help being litter trained."

Tillie pet Petunia's head. "I'll help her."

"*Opa* says that keeping a rabbit in the house is silly," Jenny said before taking a bite of her pancake. "But now *he's* keeping a dog in the house."

Lizzie heard Jack bark outside, announcing that a visitor had arrived. She pulled back the white curtain to see Ella get out of her buggy. *She must need help packing.* Knowing that Granny and Jeb were always overdoing it for their ages, she took her shawl off the peg, and ran out on the porch. "Ella, come in and have breakfast with us."

A smile slid across Ella's face as she made her way over to embrace Lizzie. "I came to talk to Granny."

"I can help. The knitting circle should have had a work frolic, let the English know how they're done."

Ella stood up on her tip-toes and cupped her hands over her cheeks. "I could just burst from happiness, and I wanted to tell Granny before tonight at circle. She's going to cry; I know it."

Lizzie tilted her head to the side. "She knows you're moving, and has shed her tears. She's happy for you now. Why would she cry?"

"I'm pregnant!" Ella blurted.

"What? How?"

Ella swiped some stray red and yellow leaves off a rocker, and took a seat. "The doctor in town said it happens sometimes. When a couple adopts, the woman finds she can bear *kinner*. I don't know why, but, Lizzie, I'm ever so happy."

"I'm so surprised. So happy for you." She bent down to embrace Ella, and then took a seat in the other rocker.

Ella took her hand. "It will happen for you, too, Lizzie. I'm sure of it."

Lizzie had shared with Ella her struggle with feeling barren, since she could relate. And here was Ella pregnant and she felt no envy or sadness. She had *kinner*. She was a *mamm*, and who knew, maybe the girls would make her be able to get pregnant. Lizzie squeezed Ella's hand, not wanting her friend to move more than ever. "It's all in God's hands, but how will we see your *boppli* grow up? No pictures and all…."

Ella sighed. "I know. There are things I'd like to change, pictures being one. But it's not worth it to lose what we have in being Amish, *jah*?"

"*Jah*, for sure. How does Zach feel about the news? Moving and having a *boppli* with no relations around."

Ella looked off into the distant field. "Zach's mighty happy. And I keep thinking about the saying, 'bloom where you're planted'. I think there's lots of truth in that."

"*Jah*, me too," Lizzie agreed. "It may take time to bloom, though. Remember the problems I had with Jenny. Sometimes I wanted to give up, but when we dig in the Bible, being rooted in Christ, like it says, we....eventually bloom."

Ella slowly turned towards Lizzie. "*Danki*, for that. I am afraid, truth be told. I fear a long winter season is coming."

"Well, you're moving to the heart of the Snowbelt, *jah*?"

Ella smiled. "*Jah*, and I was thinking, as part of adapting and 'blooming" in the land of snow, I'd make the most of the long winters, and start a knitting circle, or join one."

Lizzie admired Ella's optimism. "That's a *wunderbar goot* idea. And maybe we can share patterns, back and forth with your circle. *Ach*, Ella, I think East Otto needs a sunny person like you."

They both stood up and embraced. "I love you, Ella. Write often."

Ella clung to Lizzie like never before. "You have my word."

They soon heard Granny call from her porch. She wanted Ella to come over for a visit, and Ella ran like a deer over to her, embracing her, and telling her the good news. Lizzie was still amazed that she felt not one ounce of envy, or the need to run and cry, like when she heard that Fannie and Ruth were pregnant. No, she had all she wanted with a loving husband and her three girls. She was content.

~*~

Jonas looked up at the swiftly moving clouds, a sure sign that autumn had come, and he said a prayer of thanks. This was his last Amish camp, and he didn't reckon he'd do it again. Too many spats between the English; he wondered if it was a hobby of sorts. To agree and make peace, like he'd done in the spring concerning glass enclosed buggies, was a distant memory. Why did the English not talk things out? Although sparks flew at some of the Amish meetings, in the end, they agreed and walked in unity as best they could.

Jack barked, signaling the bus was ready to pull into the driveway. How that dog could hear things from afar was a wonder. So was Deborah and Jeb's new fascination with the little black dog. Sleeping on their bed? *Lecherlich*. At least his Lizzie had the sense God gave geese, insisting the rabbit not sleep with Tillie.

The bus came to a stop, and Jonas immediately missed Jenny sitting by his side. *Kinner* had a way of seeing things from a purer angle, and broke any tension. But the girls were busy enjoying the apple butter frolic. Jonas noticed that some of the people filling the benches were wearing red, white, and blue, some wearing pins with elephants and donkeys, and it dawned on him, the presidential election was next week. His stomach flipped; he hoped they didn't ask him political questions.

Janice and Jerry sat in the front row. Janice was radiant again, and Jonas couldn't help but smile. How nice to have the company of a companion; he'd cherished his wife's memory always.

Jerry got up and introduced Jonas, and then asked that hands be raised for questions. A girl with blond hair and *blue* streaks raised her hand first, and Jonas nodded. "How do the Amish take a bath, with no bathroom?"

He tried to stifle nervous laughter. *What an odd question.* "Well, we have a large round tub we fill up with water. Makes you clean as a whistle."

The girl's mouth gaped open. "You don't have a shower?"

"A shower? What do you mean?"

"It's like....a.....place to stand and water falls on you."

Jonas had always used the washtub, but Lizzie did use a shower of sorts. "My daughter has a bucket with little holes on the bottom. She fills it with water and works similar to a sprinkling can."

"A sprinkling can?"

Jerry ran up on the porch where a watering can sat. "Here's one."

"*Jah, danki*, Jerry. The water comes and sprinkles a body."

The girl's mouth hung open again. "Do all Amish live like this?"

Jonas hadn't known any other way of bathing, so he looked to Janice for help. She stood up. "Jerry and I have been to other Amish settlements. Some have bathrooms, just like we do. Every group of around two-hundred is a church district and they have their own rules."

An elderly woman raised her hand. "But if they don't have electricity, how do they get their water?"

"Gravity-fed," Jerry said. "Some Amish around here have gravity-fed water to their sinks."

Jonas felt humiliated to be asked how he bathed, and hoped the next question would soon come, but the elderly woman continued. Her eyes misted over, and she seemed to hover in a dream-like state. "I'm almost ninety, and lived through a time when there were no modern conveniences. We all shared the same wash tub. No electricity during the Great Depression and sometimes, I wish it was never invented."

The crowd murmured to a din. Jerry stood up and asked that the lady be able to talk. She thanked him, and continued. "We lived like the Amish really, and folks had time for each other, since there was little to do. We made up our own fun. Cutting paper dolls, playing board games, reading a book out loud around the woodstove; we were poor, but when I look back, we were mighty rich."

The crowd was silent. Only the rustling of leaves falling off the trees could be heard or laundry flapping in the wind.

A middle-aged woman raised her hand. "I agree that we have too much today; we barely know each other. Can anyone be Amish?"

Jonas cleared his throat. "You mean live off-the-grid?"

"Yes…"

"Well, some people try, but it's mighty hard once you're used to living with all the fancy gadgets. Why not just cut back a little at a time? Read by candle-light. There's something soothing in the glow of a candle."

The woman grinned. "Thank you. I think I'll do that. Maybe have one day a week for no television."

"Sounds like a *goot* plan," Jonas said with a smile. He could tell the woman was struggling, wanting a peaceful home. It appeared her *kinner* were sitting next to her and they were now scowling and rolling their eyes.

A man with a little flag in his hat raised his hand. "Do the Amish vote? And if they do, are they Republican or Democrat?"

Jonas took in a deep breath, getting ready for a confrontation. "We vote if we feel the need."

"Feel the need? What do you mean?"

"Well, the politicians come around and tell us the issues. If it's something that we know will affect us, we vote. But other than that, we're not political."

"You know the Bush Tax cuts will be dropped soon. How do you feel about that? No more stimulus checks."

"We don't cash them."

"What?" the whole crowd said in a rumble.

"We have separation of church and state, *jah*? So it goes both ways. They keep out of our business and we don't profit from them."

A lady shot up. "Don't you pay taxes?"

Jonas nodded. "*Jah*, and it's a lot of money. We pay local school taxes, even though our *kinner* go to Amish schools that we pay for, too. Then we have property tax."

The lady was still standing, wanting to challenge. "Well, I'd just put the money from the stimulus check towards my taxes if I were you…"

"If you were me, you'd have to follow what the church decides. We move as one."

"Are you serious?" she gasped. "You're not free to choose?"

"I have the freedom to not have to make big decisions by myself. I have the counsel of many, and there's safety in it."

Her eyes softened. "Aw. It's like the Waltons. They'd disagree on things, but always came into family harmony…"

"Well," Jonas said. "I don't know the Waltons, but they sound like sensible people."

A roar echoed through the crowd that made Jonas cringe. Were they laughing at him?

He looked at Janice, who could read his mind. She shot up. "Now, now. Jonas doesn't watch television, so he doesn't know who the Waltons are. Like people in many countries, there is no television in the Amish home." She walked over to Jonas. "You look tired. How about we see the apple butter demonstration now."

"*Danki*, Janice. Lizzie and the others are down by Jeb's fishing hole. The copper kettle is hot, so don't let people get too close, and only one jar per family." He winked. "I need my own apple butter on warm toast in the winter."

Janice flashed a smile, and directed the crowd away. Jonas looked back up into the clouds. *Danki, Lord. It's over!*

~*~

Granny stirred the large copper pot with the wooden paddle, worn out to the bone by hard work and the questions the English asked. But she felt a pride, in a good way, for knowing the art of canning, and kept thinking of her *mamm*. She was ever so patient with her, showing her how to wipe the rim of the jar until dry, so the rubber ring would seal properly.

She looked over at Fannie, shoulders down, as usual when around her *mamm*. Mona's negative comments had made Granny want to speak-up, right in front of everyone at the frolic, but she held her tongue. But she did add a word of praise towards something Fannie did right, for every harmful word Mona spoke. Why did she always compare Fannie to Eliza? No wonder Fannie still struggled with comparing herself. Granny thought of the familiar proverb, *'The kind of ancestors you have is not as important as the ones your children have.'* She decided right there and then that she'd be the loving *oma* the little *boppli* Fannie carried would most likely not get in Mona.

She walked over to Fannie and put her arm around her. "*Danki* for the help. How many jars of apple butter do we have?"

Fannie wiped her forehead. "I'd say over two-hundred."

Granny steered her away from Mona, who was helping clean the copper pot. "Fannie, you are fearfully and wonderfully made, *jah*?"

Fannie looked at her, puzzled. "What?"

"I just wanted to remind you of that. Seems to me like you needed to hear it."

"Why?"

"Because, well, your *mamm* seemed to be making comments to the contrary."

Fannie stopped in mid-stride. "I didn't notice…"

Granny pat her on the back. "Maybe I'm a little protective of you. Wasn't my place to say anything."

Fannie gripped her middle. "I felt the baby again." She turned to Granny and smiled, but then her face contorted. "Is it normal to have so much movement at five months?"

"*Jah*, better than no movement." Granny thought of her still-born daughter, and quickly shot a prayer of thanks that the little one was in the arms of Jesus.

"What if I have twins?" Fannie's voice was low and even.

"Well, you'd be blessed indeed."

"What if I loved one over the other? Is there enough love in a *mamm's* heart to love two *kinner*…at the same time?"

Granny knew where the question was coming from: hurt. Fannie would wonder such a thing, since her own *mamm* didn't seem to have love for anyone, even her long-suffering husband, but Eliza. How she praised that girl to a fault. "Fannie, every *mamm* has faults and makes mistakes. But just remember, what the Bible says love is…patient, kind, not rude, hoping the best…you know 1 Corinthians 13, *jah*?"

"But what if I can't?"

"Love comes from God first. When He fills us with love, we can overflow with it on to others. If we don't know love, we're like a dry plant, sucking the water, or life, out of others. Understand?"

Fannie narrowed her gaze at Granny. "*Nee*, not the part about the dried up plant."

"Well, you've seen some plants grow well in a garden, but it seems like the one next to it is sometimes dying. The growing plant is stealing water from the little one that's not making it."

"*Ach*, Granny. I'm so tired I don't understand."

Granny didn't know if she should say anything derogatory about Fannie's own *mamm*, but her heart ached for this girl who was like her own. "Fannie, your *mamm* doesn't seem to have enough water, or love. So she can't love like she should."

Tears pooled in Fannie's eyes. "You see it too? I always dismissed it." She blinked her eyes rapidly, as if to keep the tears at bay. "She seems to have enough love for Eliza, though."

"*Jah*," Granny blurted. "But I love you like my own *dochder*." She cupped her hand over her mouth, in horror over her lack of self-control coupled with anger toward Mona's comments all day. "I'm sorry."

Fannie embraced her. "I'm not. It's nice to know that. To be loved like a *dochder*."

Granny wrapper her arms around Fannie's growing middle. "And between the two of us, we'll have enough love for these twins…if my intuition is right…"

Fannie pulled back and searched Granny eyes. "You think it's twins then?"

"Or one mighty big boy," Granny said. "Only the *goot* Lord knows…"

Mona came near and startled them both. "We'll hardly have time to get home *and* come back for knitting. Best not come tonight."

"You can stay here for dinner. I have apple butter chicken in the oven." Granny forced a smile at Mona.

Mona nodded in agreement, and they walked around the side of the house, towards the front porch. Jeb was sitting on a rocker, petting Little Bea. The gentle way he stroked the poor little dog, starved for attention, touched Granny's heart, she had to admit. Jeb had enough love to meet the needs of man and beast. *Danki for Jeb, Lord. He's wunderbar.*

~*~

Granny watched Fannie and Mona put plates filled with Apple Dapple Cake on the table. *Couldn't Fannie even cut cake the right size in Mona's eyes? You're making them too large,* Mona had harped. Granny walked over to her China closet and took out her favorite teacup. When her nerves were raw, the little blue and white cup calmed her for some reason; being handed down in the family for ages, it evoked happy memories. She went over to the stove and put a ladle full of hot apple cider into it, and then took a sip, and rubbed the knot in her neck. *Help me be kind to Mona tonight, Lord.*

One by one, the girls arrived, and to Granny's surprise, Suzy came. She'd told her to stay home and rest, being so fatigued due to crying. She went over to her old friend and knitting teacher and welcomed her. "Suzy, so *goot* of you to come."

"It's my gift to teach. And I can do it, although I might sniffle at times," she said, her voice a little too measured.

"Have some apple cider and some cake. We won't be needing too much help tonight, seeing that we're surprising Ella. Did you bring it?"

Suzy nodded with a glint in her eyes. "It turned out better than I thought."

"You're a *goot* teacher." Granny said, leading her over to the apple cider in the kitchen. She spun around in shock when she heard Maryann's voice...and then her daughter Becca's. *Ach, they're back!* The cold weather had come again, and everyone from the original circle would be here tonight; the last night Ella would be with them. *How Ella's sunny disposition would be needed with Mona attending.*

When the women all had their fill of refreshments, they sat in a circle on the many benches and rockers Granny had in her living room.

Granny nodded to Ella, who then stood up. "I have *wunderbar* news." She put her hands to her cheeks. "I'm pregnant."

If *Englishers* thought there was always a peace and calm in Amish homes, they were mistaken, Granny mused. The shouting and laughter that echoed around the room could most likely be heard in downtown Smicksburg, three miles away. All the girls took turns embracing Ella, asking her how it was all possible. Ella said repeatedly, "I'm like Sarah in the Bible. A Miracle." When Mona embraced her, it appeared painful, but nevertheless she made the effort.

Suzy sat by Granny. "Why didn't you tell me? I could have brought a matching one."

"It was a secret. Ella told me this morning."

"Well, should I give it to her now?" Suzy asked.

Granny nodded, knowing that Suzy wasn't her independent self. She always took charge, but tonight, she needed rest from making even the smallest decisions. After two days, Granny loved her Little Bea to a fault, and she wasn't afraid to admit it. Lap dogs were the next best thing to knitting, and especially a poor creature that hadn't been loved or even fed enough.

Lavina took a seat by Granny. "Are you going to bring it up, or should I?"

"*Ach*, I don't care. It's your news, *jah*?"

Lavina beamed. "*Jah*." She stood up as the women all took seats. "Since the weather is cold again, and putting up time is over, it's time to read again, *jah*?"

"Yes" and "*Jah*," filled the air.

"Well," Lavina continued, "what if we knit and read books, like a book club and knitting circle combined?"

"Long books?" Maryann asked. "Those thousand- page books I see in the library?"

"*Nee*, ones that we all agree on." She looked over at Granny. "I think we can all agree on Jane Austen, for Granny's sake."

Granny put a hand up. "Pick what you want to read. We don't have to choose my favorite author."

"Isn't the Bible your favorite book?" Mona asked, her tone cool.

Granny bit her lower lip, and looked down. The urge to tap her foot nervously washed over her, but she planted her foot down. She slowly looked over at Mona. "I'm talking about human authors…"

Mona rolled her eyes. "I see no reason to read something that isn't true."

"The Prodigal Son in the Bible wasn't a real boy," Granny said in a very measured tone. "Jesus told stories to teach a lesson."

Mona looked perplexed. "Well, I won't be coming then."

Fannie, who sat next to her mother, seemed to be begging Granny to say something. Something to make her *mamm* come, but she only looked over at Colleen. "Will you share how the book, *The Secret Garden*, helped you?"

Colleen put down the knitting she just took up. "Well, I didn't feel loved, like the main character, Mary Lennox. Her parents really didn't love or care for her, but she found love in another place. She found family somewhere else." Colleen looked around the room at everyone fondly. "Before I read that book, I felt alone, and *yinz* know I couldn't cry, so I cut myself. But as I kept reading, Mary became me, and when Mary expressed hurt, my own hurt came to the surface, and I cried. Cast it on God. And I found a family here, with Emma, and with *yinz*."

Fannie's eyes were round as buttons. "Sounds like a *goot* book."

"It is," Lavina interjected. "Colleen and I read it together. I felt like Mary Lennox, too, and it's nice to know you're not alone...even though Mary's not real."

Mona's stone-cold face seemed to soften. "Well, maybe I'll come just to knit. Can I do that?"

Suzy stood behind Granny with a large box at her feet. "If you're willing to learn, I'm willing to teach, even though my Mollie is gone..."

Ella got up to give Suzy a hug. "I'm so sorry about your dog. Are you alright?"

Suzy pursed her lips and nodded quickly, as if she needed to change the subject. "Ella, we all chipped in to give you this surprise." She pointed to the box. "I couldn't find a gift bag big enough, and I didn't have time to run out and get wrapping paper. So excuse the plain, brown box."

Ella stared at the box hesitantly. "It's not alive, right? I mean, I'm not one to have a little dog in my house, like....you...and Granny."

Suzy smiled. "The love for little pooches is contagious, as you can all see. Jeb and Bea are quite the pair."

The women chuckled, but Marge almost screamed in laughter. "Jeb made fun of the girls getting a bunny, and here he is, out on the porch...in love with a dog!"

"*Jah,*" Ruth added. "I've never seen a grown man cuddle a dog so. What does Jack think?"

Granny put up both hands to hush everyone. "Jeb cares, plain and simple. He cares about the birds outside in winter, stringing up all kinds of goodies for them. And I have to say, I believe it says a lot about his good character to be so tender with a dog that's been abused."

"Abused?" Fannie asked. "How?"

"Well, we don't know all the particulars, but the shelter up in Punxsy has others, like Bea, who aren't fed at all. Some are half-starved."

Suzy clasped both hands to her chest. "Deborah, I am so amazed. I thought the Amish didn't care for animals…"

"…Like the *English*?" Granny said. "*Nee*, we do. Some of our horses are like family. We just don't grieve the loss like the English, seeing it as the cycle of life." She grinned. "But I don't know of any other Amish person who lets a dog sleep on its bed."

More laughter filled the small room, and Granny joined it. "*Jah*, Jeb knows Bea is afraid, and she slept in between us."

"Then she came between you and your man," Marge quipped, and more mirth broke out.

Soon all eyes were on Ella, and she bent down to open the box. She slowly pulled out a striped afghan of many colors and held it to her cheek. "It's beautiful. So soft. *Danki.*"

"It's alpaca," Suzy said, "and each woman here is a different color. Pink is what Granny knit, Fannie knit the green, Janice the blue, Ruth the yellow –"

"*Danki*," Ella gasped, now hugging the large blanket. "I'll miss *yinz* so much." Tears sprang to her eyes. "This circle has changed my life in many ways. I don't have words to express what I feel."

Granny got up and put an arm around Ella's back. "And you've helped us, too. Remember last winter, when I got the flu? Who nursed me back to health?"

Tears slid down Ella's cheeks. "But I won't be here this winter if you take ill."

"You'll visit, *jah?*" Granny said in a soothing voice. "It's not so far away."

Ella shook her head, not able to talk. Several women got up, making a circle around Ella, patting her back, or saying a kind word. Granny hoped to say good-bye without shedding a tear, but now knew it just wasn't going to happen. How she loved this dear girl...She overheard Suzy say something that sounded familiar. *To everything there is a season...a time for every purpose under heaven.*

~*~

The sound of a child crying...whimpering....broke Granny's sound sleep. With a start, she sat up in bed, looking around. *Tillie? Millie? Jenny?* A little black ball darted across the bedroom floor: Beatrix. She poked Jeb to get up and let the little thing relieve herself, but he only turned over and snored louder.

Feeling the work frolic still in her shoulders, she rubbed them, and then slowly got up. Making her way to the leash that hung from the peg by the door, she attached it to the little red collar and went out on the porch. Little Bea made a beeline down the stairs and onto the grass.

Granny sat in a rocker, getting a chill in her bones. How she loved autumn, but the cool, damp weather, her body did not. *Old age*, she reckoned. Mona came to her mind...she'd just been dreaming of the woman, and even in her sleep, she was serving her a mouthful of advice. *Ach, Lord, she's so mean to my Fannie, and Eliza can do no wrong.*

She bowed her head right then, learning over the past year that fretting didn't change anything. And harboring unforgiveness and anger towards someone never made the situation better.

Lord,

I'm sorry, but I see Mona's tongue doing harm. Like your Word says, the tongue is a little thing, like a spark, but can burn down a whole forest. Lord, minister to Fannie how fearfully and wonderfully she is made. Close her ears to her mamm's criticism somehow, and let her see all the love that I and the girls at the knitting circle have for her.

The girls at the knitting circle...Lord, I'll miss Ella sorely, and you know that. What a fine young woman, Amish to her core. Christian to her core, I mean. Guide her steps and give us all the grace we need to bear her absence.

And Lord, bless our new circle, the 'Knit-Lit' circle, as Colleen wants to call it. Danki for the women so eager to knit for charity. So many homeless will have wool or alpaca socks, scarves, and mittens this winter, all due to our summer to autumn circle. And the women are stronger when together, being spun together like a three-strand cord. We are not so easily broken when in fellowship with others. Show our new circle who we should knit for…so many needs in the world.

In Jesus name,

Amen

~*~

The smell of fresh brewed coffee roused Granny from her slumber. By the slant of the sunshine that poured into her bedroom, she knew it was nigh eight o'clock. *Ach, I slept in and Jeb made breakfast.* She blinked her eyes a few times, and then remembered why she was so tired; up half the night with the little dog. Well, it was an hour, but it seemed like all night.

She heard Nathan's voice, loud and…happy. Jeb's voice got louder, saying he didn't feel up to a ride. It was cold. *What on earth?*

Granny quickly got up, scooped her long gray hair up in the back, pinned it, and shoved a *kapp* on. Feeling like it would be a dreary day, she picked her black dress with blue apron to quickly put on, and then made her way into the kitchen. Lavina was there?

"*Guder mariye,*" Granny said, searching Jeb's eyes. He looked besides himself. "What's wrong?"

Jeb tapped the table with his fingers. "I told Nathan they had to wait. Now he says he's sure I'll change my mind. But I said, just like the Bible says, '*Let your yeah be yeah, and your nee, nee*', and I said *NEE!*"

Nathan's eyes danced merrily, as if he had a secret. "Nathan, is there something you want to tell us?" Granny asked.

"*Nee*, there's something I want to *show* you, but *Opa* said he won't take a buggy ride."

"Why not? Jeb, why not go out and have a talk."

"About what?" Jeb snapped. "I've heard it all before, and I said *nee*. They have to wait until February."

She noticed that Lavina looked confused as well. "You don't know what this is about?" Granny asked.

"*Nee*. Nathan just told me we were meeting here at eight to see something."

All eyes turned to Nathan, who was totally unshaken by Jeb's poor disposition. Granny went to get coffee and sat by her husband. "Jeb, what is it?"

He hesitated, and then said, "Now, Deborah, I like that little dog and don't want to get rid of her. Understand? But I took Bea out several times last night, and I'm worn out."

"*You* were dreaming. That was *me* who took her out...." Granny looked at Bea, sound asleep on the blue braided rug by the woodstove, her long bushy tail wrapped around her like a blanket.

Jeb sighed. "*Nee*, I'm not daft. *I* took her out. Got sick of it, and tried to wake *you* up to help."

Granny stared into her black coffee, and then scrunched her lips to one side, trying to hold it in, but to no avail. She burst into laughter, which turned into a good belly laugh. "Jeb. We both...got up?"

Jeb slowly looked up. "Huh?"

Nathan intervened. "*Opa*, seems like the dog had you both awake half the night, and you're tired, *jah*?"

Jeb glanced over at Granny. "You took her outside, too?"

"*Jah*, and then she wanted cuddled. Starved for affection she is. So I rocked her."

Now Jeb let out a hoot. "You rocked her like a *boppli*? Deborah...I did too." He slapped his knee, and then got up and picked up the little dog. "Wake up. You wake up. You're not sleeping all day and then keeping us up all night." He went over to the door and grabbed her leash. "Nathan, we're all going on that buggy ride, Bea included."

The little dog licked his face, and then nuzzled up against his gray beard, and closed her eyes.

~*~

They put the black flaps down on the buggy as the wind kicked the leaves into their faces. Granny turned to Lavina. "Want to collect leaves and press them?"

"Whatever for?"

"Craft projects of all kinds. Didn't you ever dip them in wax? They keep their color and form to enjoy all winter. The girls put leaves under paper and rub a crayon over it, and the veins and outline of the leaf appear. It's fun, and educational. The girls know almost every tree by its leaf."

Lavina seemed to not be interested, her mind on what was ahead. She leaned toward Granny. "Nathan said it was a surprise. Is it a surprise for Joe and Marge, too? Why are we stopping here?"

"I don't know. Maybe to check on them to see if they need more help packing."

As they approached the little *dawdyhaus* behind the large farmhouse, where Joe and Marge decided to live, the smile on Nathan's face seemed to grow. Joe came out on the porch, giving something to Nathan, and then Nathan climbed back into the buggy. He turned it around, and headed towards to road again, but stopped in front of the large farmhouse.

"I want to show you something." He jumped out of the wagon and swiftly took Lavina's hand. He pulled her along, until they were running on the side walk that led to the house.

Jeb stared at Granny, shrugged, and made his way out of the buggy, meeting her on the other side. "Want to hold Bea?"

"Okay. She keeps me warm."

They made their way to the house. Crimson and yellow hardy mums had been planted in the once deserted flower bed out front. When Granny entered the house, all the walls Marge had painted white did make it look crisp and clean.

Nathan took Lavina's hand, and it appeared he was going to burst from too much joy. "I bought it!" he blurted.

Lavina stared at him, her mouth hanging open. "Nathan, we talked about debt, *jah*?"

"Well, we don't have much. Only forty-thousand left on the land contract."

Jeb held on the banister leading upstairs. "What? Did Jacob come down that much on the land contract?"

"*Nee*, just a little. It's a miracle of sorts. Sit down on the benches."

Granny looked over and for the first time noticed the new hickory bent benches. "Did you make those?"

"*Jah*, with Roman's help."

Nathan took Lavina's hand and sat on the bench that faced the other, and Granny and Jeb followed suit. Nathan's eyes misted. "We had a bumper crop of corn and soybeans in Montana, and with the drought, the price of both went up. Wheat, too. So, my parents sent me a rather large check, along with their blessing for me to marry Lavina and settle here in Smicksburg."

Granny sprang up, and Bea flew off her lap. "Nathan, praise be. We'll be neighbors!"

"*Jah*, come February for sure. But I was hoping that once you saw that I bought a farm, then you'd know I was serious about Lavina." He slowly looked Jeb in the eyes. "The Bible says to plant a garden, buy a home, and then take a wife. Or something like that." He gripped Lavina's hand. "And we'd like to wed next month."

Granny wanted to clap, not being able to contain her excitement. She looked over at Jeb, whose countenance had changed considerably. He looked wide awake, and filled with joy.

He got up and kissed Nathan on the cheek. "This is *goot* news. *Jah*, you can wed next month. You've shown your commitment to stay here, and I trust your heart is with this *wunderbar* girl who's like a *dochder* to me."

They embraced and slapped each others' backs. "*Danki, Opa.*"

Granny went to embrace Lavina and then Nathan. Her grandson, who was her shadow growing up, was living right down the road for *goot*. Warmth filled her heart, and she turned to hug Lavina again, the girl she'd come to love like a *dochder,* too.

The door front door opened, and Marge poked her head in. "What's the verdict?"

"Verdict?"

"We're getting married next month." Lavina flashed the happiest smile Granny had ever seen.

"Did you tell them the rest?"

Nathan put a hand up. "I was getting to it." He faced his grandparents, standing mighty tall. "I'm not only going to be a farmer, but a landlord, too."

Granny sat back down on the bench. "How? Are you renting out the *dawdyhaus*?"

"*Jah*, I am."

Granny spun around and looked at Marge. "We'll miss you."

Marge did a jig. "No you won't. We're the renters."

"What?"

"We're going to come up here for our camp. Of course, Nathan will own it, but we can rent out our little house for weekend retreats or for weeks at a time. I can't live off the grid all the time, but some of the time. Make sense?"

Marge's animated ways always made Granny chuckle. "It makes perfect sense. *Goot* idea."

"Well," Nathan said, "you won't be the only renters, Marge. Folks who came up for Amish camp want to try out the

Amish way of living, even if only for a weekend." He grinned. "Marge, you better book a weekend before it gets filled up."

"Thanksgiving. I want Thanksgiving. And Christmas week." Marge said, concern etched on her face.

"*Okey Dokey*," Nathan said, his eyes never dimming, only beaming with joy.

Granny thought she would burst from happiness, but having to say good-bye to Marge bothered her more than she was willing to let on. She was getting more attached to the *English* from the Baptist Church, and was realizing that they were bound together by God, all a part of His Body, the Church. God had knit them together in love. And she could hardly wait for her third circle to begin…combining good literature and knitting.

~*~

Dear readers,

Another knitting circle has concluded, but rest assured, Granny and the girls will continue to knit for charity at their new Knit-Lit Circle. Thank you from the bottom of my heart to all my faithful readers. I couldn't write these continuing shorts without your encouragement. *Danke!* To stay in touch, please visit me at www.karenannavogel.com, on my author page on Facebook, or at my blog, *Amish Crossings*.

I leave you all with this recipe for Apple Dapple Cake that wash down *goot* with apple cider. Enjoy!

Apple Dapple Cake

2 eggs

2 c. white sugar

1 c. vegetable oil

3 c. flour

½ tsp. salt

1 tsp. baking soda

3 c. chopped apples

2 tsp. vanilla

Nuts

Mix eggs, white sugar and oil. Sift flour, salt and baking soda. Add sifted ingredients to beaten egg mixture. Add apples, vanilla and nuts. Mix well. Pour into greased cake pan. Bake at 350 for 45 minutes or until done.

Icing

1 c. brown sugar

¼ c. milk

¼ c. butter

Mix ingredients and cook 2 ½ minutes. Stir a little after removing from stove, but do not beat. Drizzle over the cake while the cake is still hot. A few nuts can be sprinkled on top.

CONTACT THE AUTHOR

Best-selling author Karen Anna Vogel is a trusted *English* friend among Amish in Western PA and NY. She strives to realistically portray these wonderful people she admires, most stories being based on true events. Karen writes full-length novels, novellas and short story serials. She hopes readers will learn more about Amish culture and traditions, and realize you don't have to be Amish to live a simple life. Visit her popular blog, *Amish Crossings* at www.karenannavogel.blogspot.com

 She would love to get to know you better on her author page on Facebook, where all things Amish, knitting, gardening, simple living, recipes…..all things downhome goodness are shared amongst Karen's readers.
https://www.facebook.com/VogelReaders

Recipe Index

How to Know God

God so loved the world, that He gave His only Son, that whoever believes in Him should not perish but have eternal life. John 3:16

God so loved the world

God loves you!

"I have loved you with an everlasting love." — Jeremiah 31:3

"Indeed the very hairs of your head are numbered." — Luke 12:7

That He gave His only Son

Who is God's son?

"Jesus answered, 'I am the way and the truth and the life. No one comes to the Father except through me.'" — John 14:6

That whoever believes in Him

Whosoever? Even me?

No matter what you've done, God will receive you into His family. He will change you, so come as you are.

"I am the Lord, the God of all mankind. Is anything too hard for me?"

— Jeremiah 32:27

"The Spirit of the Lord will come upon you in power, … and you will be changed into a different person." — 1 Samuel 10:6

Should not perish but have eternal life

Can I have that "blessed hope" of spending eternity with God?

"I write these things to you who believe in the name of Son of God so that you may know that you have eternal life." - 1 John 5:13

To know Jesus, come as you are and humbly admit you're a sinner. A sinner is someone who has missed the target of God's perfect holiness. I think we all qualify to be sinners. Open the door of your heart and let Christ in. He'll cleanse you from all sins. He says he stands at the door of your heart and knocks. Let Him in. Talk to Jesus like a friend...because when you open the door of your heart, you have a friend eager to come inside.

Bless you!

Karen Anna Vogel

If you have any questions, visit me at www.karenannavogel.com and leave a message in the contact form. I'd be happy to help you.